FLAWED • FLAWED
FLAWED • FLAWED • FLAWED
FLAWED • FLAWED • FLAWED
WED • FLAWED • FLAWED
WED • FLAWED • FLAWED
LAWED • FLAWED • FLAWED
AWED • FLAWED • FLAWED
AWED • FLAWED • FLAWED • FLAWED
AWED • FLAWED • FLAWED • FLAWED
LAWED • FLAWED • FLAWED • FLAWED
FLAWED • FLAWED • FLAWED • FLAW
FLAWED • FLAWED • FLAWED • FLAW
VED • FLAWED • FLAWED • FLAW
• FLAWED • FLAWED • FLAW
D • FLAWED • FLAW
• FLAWED

Spencer Hill Press



Contact: Spencer Hill Press, PO Box 247, Contoocook, NH 03229, USA

Please visit our website at www.spencerhillpress.com

First Edition: August 2014

J.L. Spelbring
Flawed : a novel / by J.L. Spelbring – 1st ed.
p. cm.
Summary:
Just when Ellyssa thought her father's ideas died with him, she learns her siblings live, and they are determined to finish his work.



Cover design by Trista Semmel
Interior layout and chapter artwork by Marie Romero

ISBN 978-1-939392-18-3 (paperback)
ISBN 978-1-937053-67-3 (e-book)

Printed in the United States of America

# FLAWED

J.L. SPELBRING

*To Trista, whose talent and creativity are just awe-inspiring.*
*Thank you for helping me through the rough patches.*

# 1

The cold slicing through Ellyssa's flesh and burrowing into the marrow of her bones had nothing to do with the frigid temperatures of the Missouri winter. Rocks that had at one time hidden the entrance to the abandoned coalmine from prying eyes of rangers and search parties now lay scattered across the ground. As soon as she'd stepped over the rocks and through the entrance, she felt the eerie quiet. Death thickened the air.

None of it was a good sign.

Ellyssa pulled down the hood of her parka, freeing her blonde strands, then slipped her hand back into Rein's. Closing her eyes, she released her mind to search for any signature of life, even though she knew the attempt was futile. She'd seen her father's mind before she'd killed him. The Renegades' hideout had been discovered, which meant her newfound family and friends were either imprisoned or dead, and fault lay with her.

"Anyone?" asked Rein, his hand squeezing hers in desperation… in hope.

Ellyssa glanced at Rein. Dying light, filtering through the entrance, reflected off jade-colored eyes and cut across his face, casting shadows under his angular cheekbones. His dark hair was disheveled from the hood and lay flat against his head. His lower lip trembled.

Ellyssa's heart wrenched at the sorrow on his face. At one time, the emotion would've been lost on her, a lesson of her dead father's upbringing. Now she could barely contain the tears wanting to break free.

Up until a few weeks ago, Ellyssa had been nothing more than a hollow shell of a human, created for the sole purpose of destroying anyone who went against the ideology of Aryan perfection. Thanks to her father, Dr. Hirch, the only emotions she'd been allowed were anger and hate.

Rein had changed all that. Through him she'd learned to love.

He meant everything to her.

"I can't feel anyone," she replied.

"Maybe when we move closer?" said Woody.

With his back to the entrance, the falling sun peeked between Woody's ash-blond strands and darkened his features. Ellyssa didn't need to see his face or his grey eyes to know his worry; his voice was steeped in apprehension. She owed Woody everything; he'd been there to pull her together when she'd crumpled into a weeping emotional wreck after Jordan had passed, and again, to help her rescue Rein.

And all she'd done was cause sorrow to both; Woody *and* Rein.

"Maybe," Ellyssa agreed, but she didn't believe it.

Taking the lead, she walked into the blackness of the cave, into the emptiness. She moved easily through the unlit passageways of her adopted home, as did Rein and Woody. They reached the opening leading into the hospital where years of training had been stripped away from Ellyssa, leaving a hole to fill with the true meaning of friendship, of family…of love.

Memories of Mathew and Trista, along with the others—the chubby toddler holding the handful of flowers—washed over her. The tendrils of Ellyssa's mind snapped back with the flood of emotions. She hesitated, afraid of other memories the hospital setting would invite.

"It's okay," Rein whispered in her ear, his breath warm and soft against her skin.

Although he couldn't see her in the dark passageway, Ellyssa nodded. *Control.* She adopted her soldiering façade and redoubled her efforts. All sensations were erased. Once again, her mind expanded, searching.

As Woody switched on the high-powered flashlight, Ellyssa stepped into the room that had served as the Renegades' hospital. Light pushed away the edges of the black, but it did nothing to push away the building dread and tension in the air. The hospital was as lifeless as the nonexistent signals she searched for.

Rein looked at Ellyssa, jade eyes questioning and scared. Clouds of unease darkened his features.

She shook her head. "I cannot get any reads. Just... blank." Her voice had returned to the robotic tone with ease. Ellyssa hated that part of herself, but once in a while, especially in times like this, she had to rely on the emotionless response of her old self.

Rein pulled his hand through his dark hair as he looked away, chin quivering. "So," he paused while he sucked in a breath of air, "I guess we should still check out the rest of the cave."

"Yeah, maybe someone is hurt and unconscious or something," said Woody, his voice desperate. "It's harder for you to get a read when they are like that...right?"

"Yes," Ellyssa replied, although she knew unconsciousness had nothing to do with the blankness. The glimmer of life was absent.

Rein moved forward and she followed. The beam of light swiveled back and forth as Woody walked, casting undulating shadows in front of them.

Just down the tunnel, they reached the tunneled-out room where Jason had died after he'd tried to assault Ellyssa. Generated light bounced off the low ceiling and caressed the contours of the walls, casting dancing shadows. All that was left was a crumpled blanket tossed to the side. Rein had told Ellyssa how Detective Petersen had tossed the dead man's remains at his feet when he'd been held captive, in an attempt to sway him.

No surprise that it hadn't worked. The Renegades were known for their closed-mouthed loyalty.

Try as she might, Ellyssa couldn't imagine the emotional turmoil Rein had endured. All she knew now was that he would never be subjected to such violence again. He'd promised her they would never be separated again, and she intended to make sure he kept that vow.

Grasping Ellyssa's hand, Rein pulled away from the room. Tension shot through his fingers and into hers. She might've forgiven Jason his atrocities before he'd passed, but Rein had not. Two different sides of a coin, the victim and the loved one who had been victimized.

Without a word, they reached the room where the walls overlapped, creating an illusion of a dead-end. Without faltering, Rein slipped between the two walls and disappeared.

Before Ellyssa could join him, Woody placed his hand on her shoulder. "Anything?" he asked.

"I am sorry."

Woody's face crumpled, like the dim light of hope had gone out. Wishing she could change the inevitable, Ellyssa brushed her fingers against Woody's cheek. He responded with a smile meant to be courageous, but it lacked conviction.

Unable to say anything comforting, Ellyssa moved between the two walls and stepped to the edge of the opening that dropped off into the cavern below the Renegades' evacuation point. The beam of light stopped by her feet, and a veil of darkness hung between the two levels.

"Rein?" she said.

"I'm here," he answered, his voice shaky.

Ellyssa closed her eyes. *No.* She crouched and dropped through the hole into the inky blackness. Rein was waiting for her, and as soon as her feet touched the ground, his arms wrapped around her and pulled her close. He hid his face in her hair.

Even with coming to terms with feelings and emotions and responses, all the things she'd been conditioned to suppress and control all her life, Ellyssa still felt uncomfortable at times like this. She awkwardly held him, wishing she could change everything for him. Wishing she never had followed Jeremy's siren call.

"They're gone. I know they're gone," Rein said.

"We can hope they escaped," Ellyssa said. Deep down, she knew that wasn't the case.

Woody landed next to them and the small tunnel washed with bright light. He looked at Rein, then at her, his eyes glistening.

Ellyssa swallowed hard and breathed in deeply. She shoved the emotional whirlwind that threatened what little strength she still had into a small box, and locking it away. They had to investigate the cavern before anything could be decided.

Rein released her. "Let's go," he said, his words sounding more determined than his voice. He turned and walked to the first intersection. "Which way?"

"Go right," answered Woody. "That's most likely where they would've gathered."

The evacuation cavern was smaller than the connecting tunnels above, where the Renegades had resided and flourished for decades. At least, until Ellyssa came and shattered their haven, like Kali, the Hindu goddess of destruction.

A few meters in, they entered a small room where stalactites met their counterparts in conical pillars. To the left was the community room where they would've all slept together. Unlike the cavern above, with personal rooms, which they'd called *holeys*, privacy here was nonexistent.

Ellyssa stilled as soon as she entered the room. Although subtle, the sickeningly sweet smell of decaying flesh underlay the heavy mineral scent, and by the looks on Rein's and Woody's faces, they detected the odor, too.

Rein glanced at Ellyssa, dread weighting the contours of his face. Then, without warning, Rein broke into a run toward the sleeping quarters, zigzagging between the natural formations with Woody close behind. Bounding light reflected off the surfaces of the moist deposits.

Ellyssa rushed after them, the odor of minerals and death strengthening with each step.

"Rein," Ellyssa called. Her voice, reverberating off the walls, sounded hollow.

Ellyssa slowed when she saw their backs. Both had stopped just inside the entrance, and then Ellyssa heard the worst sound she'd ever imagined—Rein howling with agony and horror.

"No!" he screamed, his hands gripping his hair. "No! No! No!"

Every piece of Ellyssa's heart shattered. Rein's cry sounded worse than when her sister, Aalexis, had tortured him with the mental equivalent of setting him on fire. Ellyssa would've done anything to save him from this. She reached out to touch him, to comfort him; instead, she let her hand drop uselessly.

Woody said nothing, just stared straight ahead as if he didn't trust his eyes. His flashlight dangled in his hand, then clattered to the floor, creating distorted silhouettes across the brown and grey stone to reveal a grisly tomb.

Ellyssa's thought process jammed. Her control shattered, opening Pandora's box and flinging out all the repressed emotions at once. She couldn't even begin to name everything she felt, one feeling slipping into another into another too fast to fully comprehend.

Greeting them at the mouth of the entrance lay Candy. The back of her head was gone, flaming red hair matted and stuck in a dried dark puddle, face frozen in a wide-eyed state of shock.

As much as Ellyssa wanted to, she couldn't look away. Her eyes slid from Candy across the other crumpled bodies of the Renegades. Old, congealed blood surrounded meaty flesh and tainted the rocky floor in rust-colored macabre death.

Ellyssa's eyes locked on to a chubby hand, the fingers curled around something dark. The rest of the body lay hidden behind a stalagmite.

Ellyssa's mind screamed "no" but her feet ignored the message. As if a magnet drew her, she stepped toward the hand, knowing full well who she would discover.

Heart pounding, mouth dry, she looked behind the formation. Dilated, cloudy eyes set into a cherubic face stared up at her. In the center of the forehead was a small hole. A dried, thin stream of crimson trailed from the point of entry and disappeared into the brown hairline.

Grief and guilt won out over the whirling feelings and slapped cuffs on Ellyssa, dragging her down. She collapsed onto her knees and covered her face with her hands. Tear after tear fell. She tried again and again to draw from her training, to lock the emotions away, but agony wedged the box open and refused to let the lid slam shut. Images of the little toddler holding a handful of wildflowers ran rampant, stuck in a perpetual loop.

Ellyssa knew about the brutality of the police and the *Gestapo*. She knew, but never had witnessed the destruction they were capable of leaving behind. What was worse was the knowledge that *she* was capable of more. Her genetically enhanced soldiering skills surpassed those of ordinary citizens.

Ellyssa was the monster straight from Mary Shelly's nightmare.

If Ellyssa hadn't changed...evolved...this type of destruction could've been left in her wake.

Ellyssa had no idea how long she'd stayed crushed into a defeated ball. She had no idea how long she'd cried. She vaguely remembered hearing Rein's and Woody's deep sobs from different points of the room as they moved from one dead person to another.

After some time, though, Ellyssa felt a hand on her shoulder, gentle and comforting. Careful to avoid the murderous scene, she looked up. Woody gazed down at her, his stormy grey eyes drowning in sorrow.

"We need to go," Woody said.

"We can't leave them like this," said Rein.

Culpability consumed Ellyssa. She hated the emotion even more than incapacitating fear. It ate at her with razor-sharp teeth. She gulped down a sob and bowed her head. "This is my fault," she choked out.

Rein dropped next to her and brushed her hair away from her eyes. "Don't ever say that. You didn't do this. *They* did this."

"If I had never come, you all would still be alive. Thriving."

Sliding his hand under Ellyssa's chin, Rein made her look at him. She couldn't meet his eyes, though; she stared at his mouth. She couldn't stand to see the storm of pain she'd caused him.

"Please look at me," Rein pleaded.

Afraid, Ellyssa closed her eyes. "I can't."

"Please, Ellyssa."

She nodded once and opened her eyelids. Grief hovered within the depths, just as she'd feared, but so did love. She chewed on her bottom lip. "I'm so sorry."

"You're not responsible for the actions of others. Do you understand?"

"Ellyssa, listen to Rein," said Woody. "You became part of our family for a reason. Fault lies with those who pulled the triggers. Fault lies with your father."

Caressing her cheek, Rein said, "If it wasn't for you, how many people would have died when Dr. Hirch's plan came to fruition? How long would we have stayed alive then? You saved us."

Inhaling, Ellyssa broke eye contact. The true credit belonged to Jeremy, the Renegade who'd led her to the discovery of her father's plans to splice together her and her siblings' genes into a creation of true "perfection," capable of destroying all of what Dr. Hirch had considered inferior humans.

Of course, her whole pseudo-family was dead now. She'd killed them and destroyed The Center in the process. Ellyssa was the last of The Center's children.

Rein gestured to Woody to help. "Come on."

"Wait," she said as she glanced down at the toddler's hand. Wrapped tight within the little fingers was a shiny, round black rock, a cave pearl. Ellyssa worked it free and slipped it into her pocket.

With their help, Ellyssa found her feet and stood. Rein pulled her close and, needing his support, she leaned into him. Warmth spread through her and helped her to find strength.

Together, they walked through the tomb of their fallen friends. Most of the people she'd barely known. A few, she was acquainted with. There was Bertha, who'd cooked for the Renegade population, and Brenda, the only other female council member, lay twisted around a speleothem pillar. Then she came across Summer, the teenager whom Ellyssa had taught to find wild carrots. Anguish clawed in her midsection again. She choked back a sob.

"How could they do this?" asked Rein.

A chill passed through Ellyssa. "This is what I would have done."

"No." Rein shook his head.

"It was the reason I was bred."

"That's not true. Something inside of you was different than the others. Do you believe just because Jeremy sent you thoughts was all it took to bring about such a change?"

Ellyssa thought for a moment. How she wanted to believe she was different. That she would've broken free anyway, but the fact was she didn't know. What happened was what happened. For whatever reason, Jeremy had awakened her and led her to the truth.

Casting her eyes down, she shrugged, a natural go-to response.

Once again, Rein placed a finger under Ellyssa's chin. She looked into his eyes and drowned in the love she found there. "If it wasn't already alive in you, it wouldn't have mattered what Jeremy did. I know you, Ellyssa. I know who you are in here." He gently tapped the place over her heart.

Woody patted her shoulder. "Rein's right."

Even if what they said was true, the tinge of guilt still sickened Ellyssa.

Woody turned in a circle. "What are we going to do?" he said, his voice despondent. "We can't give everyone a proper burial."

"I don't know," answered Rein.

Unlike The Center, the Renegades did not just toss the dead into an incinerator like yesterday's garbage. Ellyssa straightened her spine and pulled her shoulders back. She needed to be strong for Woody and Rein. They needed her strength to draw upon just like she needed theirs. "We will say goodbye to them here," she said.

Stepping around a woman with hair the color of ebony and a large hole in her chest—Ellyssa thought her name was Melissa—to a man with greying hair nicknamed Pops, Ellyssa looked around. She'd been so consumed with her emotional rollercoaster, with her guilt, she hadn't even realized *who wasn't* there. "This is not everyone," she said. "Have you seen Mathew? Trista?"

Rein pushed hair back off his forehead. "No."

Hope bloomed, but before Ellyssa set herself up to be crushed by a more likely reality, she held the emotion at bay. "This could mean…"

"That they are somewhere else in the cavern," Woody said, his words full of dread, "dead."

# 2

Ellyssa skated along the edges of sleep, but every time she came close to falling into the blissful abyss, the image of the cherub-faced toddler snapped her wide awake. That image would fade to Candy's frozen eyes, Brenda's cold waxen skin, Bertha lying face-down. One image flipping after another, like the frames of a movie. Her fingers clasped around the toddler's pearl within her pocket. Her thumb ran across the smooth surface, soothingly.

Ellyssa rolled to her back and inhaled the mineral scent of the abandoned coal mine. The inky blackness matched the feeling inside her.

Guilt gnawed her insides raw. The feeling of being the catalyst that had started the violent reaction was hard to shake, the aftereffect lying a level below them in pools of dried blood. Brutality and complete disregard of human life delivered from the *perfect* society.

Staying in the cavern wasn't the smartest thing to do. Even with *The Center of Genetic Research and Eugenics* destroyed, her father and siblings dead amongst the twisted metal, safety was something they couldn't enjoy. Not only had the *Gestapo* and *Kripolizei* been alerted of their transgressions at The Center, but the area had to be crawling with police searching for Renegade strays. They should've left after they'd said their goodbyes and found shelter in the safety of the woods, but the promise of warmth and familiarity lay within the holeys for Rein and Woody. She couldn't deny them that. She felt the same way. The dark caverns, and now an earthy tomb, were her first true *home.*

Besides, not everyone was accounted for. A thorough search of both levels of the cavern hadn't produced any other corpses. Out of one hundred forty-seven, they'd only found ninety-six bodies. That left the possibility of fifty-one survivors.

*Survivors.*

The thought of any of her newfound family and friends being alive was what kept Ellyssa from crumbling into a useless lump of overly emotional flesh. Trista, Mathew, Eric and the others might still be *alive.*

Maybe at a concentration camp.

Maybe being tortured.

Ellyssa's fault.

Swallowing the lump that'd formed in her throat, Ellyssa took the guilt and locked it away. If anyone survived, she had to find them. She couldn't think clearly if she was busy bearing the onus of her father...of society.

Ellyssa rolled back onto her side and snuggled against Rein's back. In need of a trimming, his dark hair tickled her face. His scent filled her nose.

"I love you," he mumbled in sleep talk.

Warmth traveled with Rein's words. Ellyssa kissed the back of his neck. "I love you, too."

Rein breathed in deeply, then the rise and fall of his chest settled into a slow, even pattern. Woody's soft snores came from the holey next to theirs, rhythmic and soothing. Ellyssa concentrated on the sounds of their sleep.

"Wake up."

Frantic words knocked against her slumber. Ellyssa fought against the heavy blanket of sleep that had pulled her under. She tried to force her eyes open, but tiredness kept them sealed.

Rein shook her. "Someone's coming."

Ellyssa's eyes popped open. Disorienting webs of sleep clung to her brain, and black swirled in front of her. She shook her head to dislodge the numbness and clear her head. She couldn't see Rein, but felt him crouched to the side of the holey's entrance, his breathing shallow and light. No sound came from Woody at all.

Ellyssa tensed; her ear cocked to the side.

After a moment, she heard the muffled scraping of leather soles across a rocky surface, echoing lightly down the passage. The *ping* of a small pebble bouncing was followed by a soft, irritated voice.

Definitely female.

The tiredness evaporated in a surge of an adrenaline-soaked, blood-pumping rush. Ellyssa sprang onto her haunches, muscles tensed.

The scraping moved closer, turning to hurried padding. Whoever was rushing through the network of passages was alone…at least in the section Ellyssa, Rein, and Woody occupied.

Woody remained silent. Rein shuffled as if preparing to leap into danger. As if she'd let that happen after just getting him back. Ellyssa blindly reached out into the dark and grasped his arm. She shook her head, even though he couldn't see her.

Suddenly, light washed through the passageway, filtering through the flimsy curtain, and bounced down the stony enclosure. Grey shadows lengthened through the cover hanging over the entrance.

Muscles coiled, waiting to strike, Ellyssa projected her mind and latched onto the signature. Surprised relief filled her.

"Trista?" Ellyssa said, disbelief soaking her words.

"What?" Woody whispered from the holey next to them.

"Trista!" Ellyssa scrambled through the opening.

A gasp of surprise, and the footfalls stopped. A beam of light from Trista's flashlight blinded Ellyssa, tipped down, then blinded her again.

"Ellyssa?"

Holding her hand in front of her face, Ellyssa stood. Rein and Woody fell in behind.

"Rein? Woody?" Trista hesitated as if she couldn't believe her eyes. "I knew it."

Hard leather soles thundered down the passage as Trista's silhouette bounded toward them; the sound of a coat flapped behind. The light alternated between blinding and reflecting off the grey walls.

"I can't believe it." Trista engulfed Ellyssa in her arms.

Ellyssa hesitated for a moment, the touching still feeling a little alien, but then she returned the embrace as joy released within her. Heart swelling, Ellyssa tightened her arms around her friend. Trista's exuberance brought warm feelings and fed Ellyssa's hope. If Trista was alive, then there was a possibility that the others were, too.

"I knew I was right. They tried to tell me differently. But I knew."

*They?* She exhaled a sigh of relief. "Mathew? Is he with you?"

Trista didn't answer; she rattled off a whole series of questions. "What happened? How'd you get back? Did you run into any trouble?" She paused for a moment as she stepped back, her blue eyes sparkling with excitement. "Oh, Woody! Rein!" she squealed.

Trista flung herself into Rein's arms, then into Woody's. Utter shock froze their faces into wide-eyed, slacked-jawed expressions. Finally, Woody snapped his mouth closed and ran his hand over his face.

"I knew you were alive. I had to come just one more time before we left."

"Leave?"

"To find the others." Trista reached up and touched Ellyssa's face as if she feared she'd disappear. "Explanations later." Spinning around toward Rein and Woody, Trista asked the males the same series of questions and added in a few more. *When did you get back? You destroyed The Center?*

Suddenly, Trista's display of happiness and excitement slid away. The smile fell from her face as a solemn expression took dominance. The ease with which Trista transferred from one emotion to another still amazed Ellyssa.

Trista looked down at her wrist and pushed a button on the side of her watch. Red light glowed, showing digital numbers. "We have to go. They will patrol the area soon."

"Who?" Rein asked.

Trista shrugged. "The *Gestapo*, the *Schutzpolizei*, area police and rangers. The groups rotate, but they do keep up the patrols. It seems we have created quite the stir."

With all the excitement and the bouncing light, Ellyssa didn't notice the type of coat Trista wore at first. She yanked the light out of Trista's hand and shone it on her friend. Her eyes widened in disbelief. Even with the minor changes that had been made throughout history, there was no mistaking the uniform of the *Gestapo*.

Black.

Ellyssa's blonde friend, acceptable to live within society, with blue eyes and trim physique, wore a woolen black overcoat. A red arm band with black trim and a swastika adorned her left upper arm, on the right collar was a red SS rune insignia and, on the left, two gold bars—a section inspector.

Ellyssa pulled back the flaps of the jacket. Beneath the coat was the uniform of betrayal—an ironed black tunic with red piping, the collar mimicking the same adornments as the overcoat; black breeches; a black tie hung from the collar of a brown shirt; black-laced boots; and, hanging from the black belt, a holstered P229. The flashlight beam reflected from brass buttons. Trista's blonde hair was pulled back into a tight bun of authority.

Smooth forehead crumbling into little lines, Trista pulled away. "What's the matter with you?"

Ellyssa's lids narrowed as she processed the information her eyes fed her brain. She could feel herself slipping into her soldiering ways. Anger and suspicion swirled inside her, like another entity. "Why are you wearing this?" Ellyssa asked, her voice dead.

Trista looked down, her hands running over her tunic as if to smooth out nonexistent wrinkles. She smiled grimly. "It's a long story. So much has happened."

The instinct to survive, to protect, brewed in the pit of Ellyssa's stomach, traveling to her heart, and pumped adrenaline throughout her body. Her fingers curling tight around the flashlight, she clenched her jaw and swallowed, holding back the instinctive urge to slam the blunt object against Trista's head.

*Trust.*

Deep down, she knew Trista would not betray her family. Trista was incapable of such an act. But after discovering the tomb below them, the sight of the *Gestapo* garb stabbed a painful reminder and left a bad taste in Ellyssa's mouth. "How did you acquire the uniform of the *Gestapo*?"

Apparently sensing tension, Rein draped his arm over Ellyssa's shoulder and pulled her toward him. Ellyssa went reluctantly. Her muscles still twitched stubbornly.

Trista stared at her, vertical lines carved between her eyebrows. She blinked, looked away, and then met Ellyssa's eyes, again, and understanding dawned on her face. "I would never," she said, insulted. "I know what it looks like. There is much to explain. But we have to go…now." She gazed down the dark hallway, then turned to Rein. "Right now. A lot has happened. I know what it looks like, and I'll explain everything. We have to go now." She touched Ellyssa's arm. "Please."

Although Ellyssa had promised not to invade her friends' thoughts, she couldn't help but brush Trista's mind. Instantly, shame coursed through Ellyssa. After all that'd transpired, being accepted by her newfound family, working with the Renegades, and disposing of her father, her soldiering instincts still surfaced on cue, her innate need to survive and, now, to protect.

"I am sorry," Ellyssa said. The words didn't feel right on her tongue, unable to convey how awful she felt for not fully trusting, for not being able to control instinctual responses that'd been hammered into her since childhood. She shed her old skin, wishing she could stop depending on it during times of uncertainty, that she could just handle situations as a normal person would.

The corner of Trista's lips pulled into a tight grin. "I know it's hard. I do understand," she said, her voice soft.

Ellyssa offered a little smile. "A section inspector?"

"First thing we grabbed." Trista took the flashlight. "We have to go. I took a chance coming here, but I had to. I had to check one more time. And I was right." She flipped around and headed down the passageway. "Come on," she said, gesturing for them to follow.

"One second," Rein called after her. He disappeared into the holey, then reappeared with the gear and coats in hand.

Woody emerged with the flashlight and his bag. He flipped the switch, and between Trista's light and his, day visited the tunnel.

After slipping into their coats and backpacks, the three followed Trista into the unknown.

As soon as Ellyssa stepped from the cover of the cave, icy wind whipped through her coat, making her breath catch in her chest. The temperature must've dropped at least twenty degrees since they had first entered the caves. Off on the horizon, dark grey clouds churned as they moved in their quest to block the sun from view.

Ellyssa pulled the hood of her parka over her head. Rein came up behind her and slipped his hand into Ellyssa's. Tingles caressed her skin.

"Wherever we're going, we need to get there. I don't like the looks of the clouds." Rein's gaze moved from the sky to Trista. "By the way, where *are* we going?" he asked.

"To the road," Trista replied as she climbed down the hillock and skirted along the edge of the field.

Ellyssa looked into the tree line. Long bare branches struggled against the wind, bending at nature's will. Movement flashed in the corner of her eye, and she turned her head. A small brown rabbit hopped out from a bush, only a meter away from where the small innocent child had toddled into the clearing a few weeks ago when green still dominated the landscape and early fall warmth still moved on the breeze.

Ellyssa's eyes stung from the memory. She stored it away. She stored them all away—waking to Mathew in the hospital for the first time, the look of Rein's green eyes glaring down at her, the friendships that'd formed, Woody as the pillar of strength she'd clung to after Jordan passed, the butterflies fluttering around her as she laughed, the electricity of her lips brushing against Rein's.

*Goodbye*, Ellyssa thought to her first true home as Rein tugged her hand.

# 3

aloo
re branches and
fested ground.
reezing temper
npending promis
Ellyssa's sweater
r back. Smokey puffs
breath escaped her mo
gged behind Trista, ea
up with her. Rei
crunched thro

Grey clouds caught the sun; the fading light haloed through the bare branches and splotched the leaf-strewn ground. Even with the freezing temperatures and the impending promise of snow, Ellyssa's sweater stuck to her back. Smokey puffs of warm breath escaped her mouth. She jogged behind Trista, easily keeping up with her. Rein and Woody crunched through the brush behind.

When they reached the tree line, Trista faced them; a light sheen glistened across her forehead. Placing her finger to her lips, she peered around a fir's trunk. She looked left, right, and then she waved her hand frantically behind her back in a downward motion. Ellyssa froze, as did Rein and Woody, at the whine of an approaching motor whirling with the wind. All three of them ducked low.

Trista stepped onto the road and waved to the newcomers. Two males, dressed in black snowsuits and helmets, pulled over four-wheelers. Green swastikas decorated each helmet and right breast, marking them as area police.

They climbed off their quads, then saluted. Trista returned the gesture.

The officer in front pulled off his helmet, revealing blond hair, cut high and tight, and a young face. The other was older, grey tingeing the sides of his hair, his eyes scrutinized the tree line just to the left of where Ellyssa, Rein and Woody hid. She hoped the camouflage of their coats was enough to keep them hidden in the sparse winter vegetation.

Reaching with her ability, Ellyssa gated off Trista's surging anxiety and slipped into the unwelcome newcomers' minds. Suspicion dominated the older male's thoughts, especially since there wasn't a patrol scheduled for another hour. High and Tight thought Trista would look great on his bed.

"May I ask what you're doing?" High and Tight asked.

Trista pulled her shoulders back and faced the younger male. "You do realize who you are talking to?"

"I'm sorry, Inspector, but we were given strict orders to check everyone," he said, no-nonsense, gloved hand held out. "Papers?"

"In my car," Trista answered. She led the males to the SUV parked ten meters down the road.

Ellyssa released pent-up air, the sound of her heart rushing into her ears. Trista had performed splendidly. The ease which with her friend had slipped on an air of authority was amazing, especially after being raised within the confines of the old abandoned coalmine where such stringent convention was not the norm.

As Trista disappeared into the cab, Rein's hand slipped into Ellyssa's. The tension firing through his fingertips matched her own. She looked over her shoulder to two sets of wide eyes, a green pair and a grey pair, and paper-white faces. Rein leaned toward her, and his lips brushed her cheek.

For a brief moment, Ellyssa relished the sense of love. If anything ever happened to her, at least she wouldn't perish like her siblings, devoid of emotions.

A throaty chuckle caught her attention. Ellyssa peeked between the green needles. Trista, now wearing her visor cap with a silver death-head pinned in the middle, and High and Tight walked toward the four-wheelers, with the older male on their heels.

"As I said, Inspector Klein, I'm sorry for the interruption, but orders are orders."

"No problem, Officer Livingston. I understand. These days, extra precautions are needed." Trista stood at-ease. "Have any other Renegades been captured?"

"Since the last report, no."

"Well, maybe the area is clean of the scum."

The older male glanced back over at the tree line. "Pardon me, Inspector," he said, pointing, "but may I ask what you were doing over there?"

Trista turned slightly, looking toward them. She lifted her chin and faced the older officer. "I'm performing my assignment, Officer Frey. Unlike you, I'm in a vehicle where it's hard to examine the road thoroughly. Every one hundred meters or so, I exit the vehicle to walk along the tree line. It has thrown me way behind schedule.

"Now, if you will excuse me, I have to finish my patrol," she continued, dismissing the officers with a curt nod.

Both officers extended their right arms, eye level, and said, "Heil."

After returning the Nazi salute, Trista stood in the middle of the road as the two males slipped on their helmets and mounted the quads. As soon as the rumble of the engines disappeared, she waved for Ellyssa, Rein and Woody to come, then ran to the SUV.

"Hurry," Trista said when they reached her. "We need to go before something else happens. Take off your parkas."

"It's freezing," Woody protested.

"It won't be for long," Trista said, pulling the back seat's cushion up and revealing a small metal box. "It'll get warm, I promise. Besides, do you want to lie on the metal?"

Looking into the space, Woody shook his head. "I guess not."

"Then take off your parkas."

Ellyssa shrugged out of her coat and handed it to Trista. Icy cold sank razor-sharp claws into her skin. Shivering, she hugged herself, rubbing her hands up and down her arms. Teeth chattering, Rein and Woody huddled close to her.

Trista took the parkas and lined the bottom of the space. "Hop in."

Ellyssa eyed the cramped compartment. Her mouth pulled to the side. "I do not think we will fit."

"You really don't have a choice. Now, hop in. I don't like the way Officer Frey questioned me."

"I'll take the back," Rein said, sliding his arm around her shoulder. Warmth escaped his body and grazed her skin. "You in the middle. Woody up front."

"Is there a way out?"

"Yeah, when I let you out." Trista gestured with her hand. "Climb in already."

"Where are we going?"

"To a safe place." Trista frowned. "What's up with you?"

Ellyssa blanched, and Rein kissed her temple. "I promise nothing is going to happen to you. Trust me," he said through chattering teeth.

Ellyssa swallowed the lump that had formed in her throat. Trust, so foreign still, yet so much part of who she was, too. "Okay. But I don't like this." She faced Trista. "As soon as you let me out, I have questions for you."

"And I'll have some answers." She looked from one to the others. "As a matter of fact, our little group is a lot bigger than we'd ever imagined." She smiled. "Now climb in and let's go."

Ellyssa could have easily gleaned the information; Trista's mind was an open book, but she refrained. It was part of the whole "trust" thing.

Rein settled into the cramped space, lying on his side. With reservation, Ellyssa slid in next to him, her back against his stomach. He wrapped his arm around her waist, pulling her closer. Woody followed, facing away from them.

The last thing Ellyssa saw was Trista's face as she replaced the cushion. Darkness enveloped them in a tight cocoon. Movement was impossible. Oxygen seemed depleted.

"Relax," Rein breathed in her ear, apparently sensing the rolling tension. His lips grazed her earlobe.

Struggling, Woody managed to slip his hand behind him and, awkwardly, patted Ellyssa on the thigh. "It's going to be fine. Just like when we went to Chicago."

Closing her eyes, Ellyssa inhaled deeply and exhaled slowly. She concentrated on Rein's touch, the warmth he radiated, the electricity that pulsed where their skin touched, his breath grazing her ear. She concentrated on Woody, the feel of his back against her stomach, the way his chest rose and fell.

By the time the engine purred to life, calm had settled into Ellyssa, her heartbeat slow, soothing. She kept her eyes closed as she listened to the hum of tires and felt the vibrations of the SUV moving down the road.

After a few minutes, though, she began to realize what Trista had been talking about. Beads of sweat formed along her hairline.

"God, it's hot in here," Woody said, voicing what Ellyssa had just thought.

The faint sound of a giggle reached Ellyssa's ears. "I told you," Trista said.

# 4

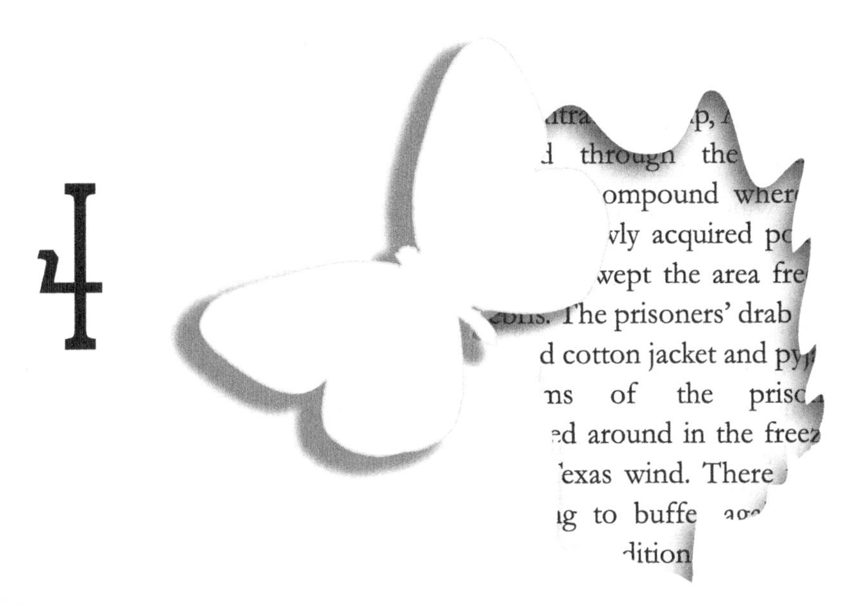

Commadant Hans Baer, commander of the concentration camp, Amarufoss, looked through the window into the compound where the line of newly acquired political enemies swept the area free of debris. The prisoners' drab grey-striped cotton jackets and pyjama bottoms whipped around in the freezing West Texas wind. There wasn't anything to buffer them against the extreme conditions, just flat land stretched across the expanse formerly known as the Panhandle. The commander knew they were freezing; they had to be, but such treatment might persuade them to be a bit more cooperative during interrogations.

The Resistance had proven to be much more complex than any of the State had ever dreamed, a labyrinth of secrecy that wound deeply into dead-end trails. It was their own fault for thinking the small bands of Renegades they had raided and caught showed the decline in the old belief system. The Nazis had become complacent, sure of their control, while the strength of the Resistance had grown.

This last batch of prisoners, hiding in a cave in Missouri, had proven the military's arrogance. That a band that large had survived and held the type of technology the *Gestapo* had found confirmed the Resistance was much more resourceful and ingenious than previously believed. Also, it confirmed they were receiving outside help.

Fifty-one prisoners had been brought in. Fifty-one. Many he watched now, working detail in the windy cold with their flimsy uniforms. The number was astounding. And that didn't include the ones who had perished during the raid.

The Commandant glanced at the clock, then resumed his at-ease stance, calm and cool, completely opposite of how he felt, and stared out the window. A bead of sweat formed at his hairline. He quickly wiped it away.

The young girl in faux-cherubic disguise was to pay him another visit, and he didn't have any new information. Even after torturing the prisoners, he had been unable to force confessions from any of them, just like all the other enemies of the state who had visited his camp before. Their loyalty still proved unbreakable. One day, though, he was going to find a chink in their armor.

Worrying about the report, Hans watched the camera feed as a silver Audi Q7 with tinted windows rolled to a stop outside the gates. Two of Commandant Baer's men, dressed in olive-green tunics and field-grey breeches, stepped out of the checkpoint with their rifles. They fought for purchase against the wind as they made their way to the automobile.

Commandant Baer turned around and walked away from the window, annoyed at how the two strange teens affected him.

Pale, blond hair, flawless skin, full lips, perfect-lined facial features. They looked like angels. Beautiful. The epitome of perfection.

But hidden within the depths of sky-blue eyes, danger lurked—intelligent, cold and calculating, especially the little girl. Her stare sliced right through his aplomb and burrowed into his flesh, leaving him unsure and unsteady, something he was not accustomed to.

Hans still remembered the way Aalexis had walked into his office with her brother, Xaver, at her side. The boy couldn't have been older than fourteen, fifteen tops, the girl maybe thirteen.

Contrary to their youthful appearance, though, they were both tall, very tall. The boy already was close to Hans' height, and the young girl reached just below his chin. Their demeanor had been mature and rigid, and their speech was thick with a German accent, as if they'd been born in the Fatherland, and devoid of emotion, robot-like.

Plus, the way Aalexis had gazed at him, as if he was as lowly and detestable as a Renegade.

The memory unsettled him.

At the time, Hans would had sent her packing if it wasn't for his commanding officer, Colonel Fiedler. Apparently, the little girl had some sort of influence over the military and *Gestapo,* probably the State, too, which was even more unsettling. The Colonel had ordered his complete cooperation without the courtesy of explanation. The only thing Hans' commanding officer had divulged was that both children were from The Center that had been destroyed, special, and an important link.

A link to what, Hans hadn't a clue. The Center had been a lab for genetic research; some children of a purer descent were born there, and the Center developed had specialized training. He held no doubt Aalexis and Xaver were byproducts of one or the other, probably both. But there was nothing extraordinary or new that he was aware of. The Colonel had refused to elaborate when Hans had asked.

Commandant Baer stared at the wall-length mirror. Besides a slight flush in his cheeks, his external physique hid the twitching nerves inside; his blue eyes revealed nothing. His silver hair was parted down the right side and combed back, and his mouth was a thin, carved line.

He straightened his black tie, brushed imaginary lint off of his dark blue *Waffenrock,* then pulled the seams down so the red piping lay straight along the hems. A sharp crease ran down the legs of his slate-grey breeches.

Frowning, the Commandant leaned closer. A fingerprint marred the silver eagle above his right breast pocket.

*That will never do.*

He grabbed a tissue from the dispenser on his desk and buffed until the silver gleamed. Then he polished the four diamond insignia and the SS rune.

*Better.*

Straightening the silver braided belt, he turned just as the door swung open.

Corporal Niklas Kraus, his senior clerk, stepped through. "*Heil Hitler,*" he said, arm extended at eye level.

The Commandant returned the salute, and Niklas stood at attention. Hans inspected the enlisted man; he looked sharp in his dark-blue tunic and grey breeches. The brassy buttons were polished to perfection. His honey-blond hair, trimmed and neat, looked very professional.

"At ease."

Relaxing, Niklas placed his hands behind his back "*Fräulein* Aalexis and *Herr* Xaver have arrived, sir."

"Yes. Yes. I know. Are they through the gate yet?" he said, taking a seat in his leather chair.

"The front-gate just called to verify the papers, sir."

"Very good," Hans said, with confidence he didn't possess. "Escort them in when they arrive."

"Yes, sir." Niklas closed the door behind him, leaving the commandant alone with his thoughts.

Aalexis turned in her seat and watched the two inferiors who had greeted her and Xaver at the gate rush back inside the checkpoint. The guards watched the SUV, their lips moving with unheard words, as the metal gate slid across the road and clanged shut. She turned back around, listening to the tires grate across the pebbles and dirt, while Xaver navigated toward a long rectangular building with stairs. He pulled right in front of the door and pushed the ignition button that turned off the engine. Without speaking, he turned toward her, his blue eyes iridescent under the glow of the interior lights. She ignored him and looked out the window.

Amarufoss Concentration Camp was as flat and boring as rest of the area she'd seen thus far. Four-meter-high walls made of thick concrete blocks encircled the camp with rolls of razor wire crowning the tops, the sharpened edges glinting in the sun. On the other side of the barrier, unseen from the inside, lay more rows of the razor wire and, surrounding the perimeter, a chain-link fence. Off to the right, another block wall separated the camp into two. The female barracks lay on the other side, but Aalexis wasn't interested in them. All the names Rein had called during interrogation were male. All except for her sister's.

Xaver opened the passenger door.

Reminiscent of cold gusts off Lake Michigan, the wind blowing across the plains held the same icy feel that cut right through any clothing and bit tender skin. The only difference was that the plains' wind held the odor of dust and the stench of filthy Renegades, instead of a wintery clean scent blowing off the water.

Aalexis didn't like it.

Grabbing Xaver's extended hand, Aalexis scooted free from the passenger seat. She released him as soon as she was upright, then closed her fist tight, wishing away the tingling and the sense of comfort he provided for her. She couldn't understand the feeling his touch elicited.

She didn't like that either.

Until her father had died by Ellyssa's hand, any physical contact had been forbidden. Since his death, however, Xaver had touched her freely. Helping her out of cars, placing a hand on her back as they walked.

It was confusing. Physical contact led to emotions. Emotions led to weakness. Aaelexis was not weak. As a matter of fact, she was the strongest, bestowed with a unique power.

Aalexis was omnipotent.

With just a twinge of thought, she could reduce any full-grown man to a sniveling dog, and never lay a finger on him. That had been the reason why Dr. Hirch had left instructions to Xaver to protect her at all costs.

But Ellyssa had changed the rules when she'd destroyed her father and The Center. Aalexis loathed her sister.

Hatred was an emotion Aalexis could understand. She, as all her siblings, had thrived on the emotion. It wove through her being, making her strong and sure...and vengeful.

Ellyssa would pay for her indiscretions, for reducing the goals her father had worked toward in the name of *der Führer* to a pile of ash. Now, her father's unfinished work fell on Aalexis' and Xaver's shoulders. A task she would see through.

"Are you ready?" asked Xaver, his hand centimeters from hers.

Aalexis could feel his warmth through the biting temperature. She moved her hand away. "Yes. Let us proceed."

Turning around, Xaver led the way up the stairs and through the door. He stepped aside so that she could cross the threshold. Warm air greeted her as soon as she entered, as did the sterile environment she'd encountered during her previous visit. The walls were made of cement blocks, painted white, with no décor to cheer the room. Grey metal filing cabinets lined the wall next to the entrance and matched the grey of the desk where the corporal stood. Off to the right, a door marked *STORAGE* was closed.

"*Heil*," said the corporal in his pristine, freshly ironed uniform.

"*Heil*," Xaver returned.

"May I take your coat, *Fräulein* Aalexis?" The corporal started to walk toward them with his hand extended. He stopped when Xaver stepped in front of him.

"Do *not* touch her," Xaver said, his voice flat and emotionless. Aalexis could hear the implication behind the monotonous tone, though. Her brother was to protect her at all cost, and he took the task seriously.

Halting, the corporal blinked, surprised at the confrontation. He looked lost for a moment, unsure how to proceed as he watched Xaver help her out of her coat. Finally, the corporal stepped back and waved his arm toward the Commandant's door. Xaver handed him both of their coats.

"Commandant Baer is expecting you," he said, draping the outerwear over his arm. He opened the door, then stepped as far off to the side as possible, granting room for Aalexis and Xaver to enter. "*Fräulein* Aalexis and *Herr* Xaver, Sir," he presented.

Aalexis entered first. As she stepped past the corporal, she glanced at him. His anxious eyes remained straight ahead.

No wonder the Resistance still existed when such inferior humans were still allowed to walk. The civilians and military should have been subjected to the intense programming she and her siblings had endured. Not that it mattered. Even with such training, they'd still be substandard. They lacked the genetic makeup and the intelligence of superior beings such as herself and her brother. Ordinary people still possessed useless emotions.

Her father had been right; they were weak, low-grade beings.

Aalexis' meeting with Colonel Fiedler had further confirmed her father's teaching. The Colonel had been impressed when she'd demonstrated her ability—very impressed, indeed. Yet he hadn't understood. He had tried to hide his awe behind a cool countenance, but he'd failed. She didn't need Ellyssa's power to read the greed and hunger for power lurking behind the Colonel's gaze.

Power without the work.

Aalexis had thought a military education would've taught that borrowed technology without the effort only led to downfall. It seemed history was doomed to repeat itself amongst the flawed.

*Narren nicht erkennen,* as her father had said time and time again. *Fools do not recognize.*

She disregarded the male officer and turned her attention to the office where the more sterile environment of the clerk's office met warmth and color, the Commandant's tastes reflected in the decor. Dark paneling and green curtains. Pictures of landscapes and, she assumed, family hung from the walls. Books and bric-a-brac littered the shelves behind the large mahogany desk.

Aalexis knew the desk was meant to intimidate people by making the commander seem large and important. Such psychological games were lost on her and Xaver, though.

"*Fräulein* Aalexis and *Herr* Xaver."

The Commandant indicated with a wave of his hand for them to make themselves at home in the green-upholstered chairs. "Did you have an enjoyable flight?" he asked.

One of the lessons she and her siblings had been taught was to appear polite before the bite. The bite was coming soon enough, and she saw no reason to engage in such petty subhuman niceties.

"Yes. Thank you."

He looked at Xaver. "And the car was to your liking?"

Xaver acknowledged his question with a curt nod.

Alexis studied the commander. His height was within the acceptable parameters of the average male, a hard face with wrinkles engraved on his forehead and around his mouth. His file indicated fifty-six, but he looked older than her father had at seventy. His silver hair was neat and parted to the right, and the uniform he wore was ironed and sharp, polished medals of honor hanging from his chest. Hard, steely blue eyes tried to hide uncertainty as he stood behind the desk. Anxiety radiated from the commander of the camp. He feared her, as well he should.

Nervousness was a sign of hesitation. Hesitation meant avoidance. Apparently, the commander didn't have the information she sought.

"Hans," Aalexis paused as the commander's eyebrows shot up. Apparently, he was unused to being addressed by his first name and appeared to be contemplating a reprimand, but when her eyes narrowed, his courage seemed to dwindle. Better for her to establish her position over him.

"Let us put formalities aside for the time being," she continued. "You know the reason why I am here."

Surprised the girl had the gall to address him so informally, Hans' gaze swept from Aalexis to Xaver. Void of any emotion, both sat in the green chairs, still as statues, backs rigidly straight, hands resting on knees, like a perfect young lady and gentleman. Aalexis' full lips curled into a chilling smile after she addressed him, her German accent strong. Xaver's lips mimicked the falsity.

They might look like regular teens in civilian clothing—him in a bright-colored sweater and jeans, she in a blue-and-white knit dress, his hair short, hers tied into a braid. Both were beautiful with flawless skin, his features chiseled and hers deceptively cherubic.

Danger lurked behind the façade. Knowledge and secrecy lay hidden within the depths of their appearance. Their eyes were as cold and hard as the last time they had visited.

Lifting his chin, Hans leaned back in his chair, his fingers folding across his chest. "I'm sorry to inform you, but as I stated during our last communication, there's nothing new to report." He was relieved the words sounded more confident than he felt.

For a brief second, the fire of anger flickered behind Aalexis' blue eyes, then extinguished into smoldering ashes of disgust. "I see," she responded. "It is unfortunate. I was under the impression your camp was efficient."

Lifting his chin, Hans proudly stated, "My camp is the most feared."

"Yet you have no information about where the Renegade, Ellyssa, is hiding."

"It's unfortunate, but I'm not surprised. It's not unusual for the information to be kept secret. Many prisoners have died while under my command for their refusal to cooperate. Their loyalty to each other is unwavering."

Aalexis stared at him, her gaze steady, as if trying to pry the information from his mind. Her blue eyes amazingly cooled even more, although her face showed no change in emotion.

A chill crept up Hans' spine. His forehead pricked with perspiration, and he looked away, afraid she could see how much she unsettled him. Her eyes never left him, though. He could feel them on him. The same lump climbed back up his throat.

Hans couldn't stand the effect the little girl and her brother had on him. He was a Commandant after all, efficient at his job, awarded medals for his loyalty and accomplishments. He'd be damned if a little girl and her lackey brother would make him feel as lowly as a roach in his camp, all while seated in his office. Somewhere, Hans mustered his fleeting courage and met Aalexis' eyes again.

The young girl's composure hadn't changed at all. She still stared with the same cold in her eyes. Having had enough, he stood. The next thing he knew, Xaver towered over him—the boy had to be close to two hundred centimeters. Danger crept behind the anger in Xaver's gaze, and a grim line tightened his lips.

Surprised at the speed with which the teen moved, Hans' mouth dropped as he stepped back, his daring fleeing. In all his years as a soldier and as an officer, he'd never witnessed someone move so fast. The boy was nothing but a blur.

"I suggest you sit down," Aalexis said, emotionlessly. "My brother is well trained in all disciplines of combat arts." She dipped her chin and her eyes became snake-like slits. "As am I."

Hans held no doubt she was telling the truth. The quickness with which her brother moved had completely caught him off-guard. For a fleeting moment, he thought about the gun in his top drawer, but quickly dismissed the idea. Based on the movement of the boy, he wouldn't stand a chance.

He understood, now, what the Colonel had meant by the "next link." Earlier, he had thought them the epitome of perfection. They were much more. It seemed The Center had achieved a training program beyond the information allotted to him. Without a word, Hans slowly sank back into his chair.

"I do understand," Aalexis said in the same monotonous voice, as if nothing had transpired, "the Renegades' ability to withstand much in order to protect their society. Perhaps I might have a word with them." It wasn't a question.

"The barracks are off-limits to..." He waivered, forcing composure. He had to maintain control. "...civilians. I don't think that would be appropriate for you."

Aalexis looked at Xaver, who was still standing. They exchanged words in German, most of which Hans was unable to hear; they spoke low and quick, but he was able to pull a few words out of context—*dispose, camp, Father.*

Finally, the young girl faced him. "Let me reiterate. I am *not* requesting."

Suddenly, the commandant felt like chum in shark-infested waters.

As soon as the door opened, the stench of the male barracks wafted up Aalexis' nose. Sweat, filth, too many un-bathed people living in close proximity.

Aalexis curled her nose at the creatures; their malnourished frames swallowed by striped pyjamas. They were disgusting and pitiful. Different shades of dark hair, red hair, improper blond, with faces marred with freckles and scars and eyes differing in color and shape. She'd never seen such a large conglomeration of imperfections. How could they stand themselves, knowing they could never measure up to society's standards?

She glanced up at her brother. Xaver, too, stared at the subhumans. Although his face held no indication, she knew his revulsion matched her own.

The prisoners looked up in surprise as early-evening cold air whipped around the small fire in the one potbellied stove, threatening to extinguish the low flames. Then, like the little rats they were, they scurried away from their source of heat and formed a line in front of the bunks. They pulled their shoulders back and looked straight ahead.

With his chin held high and crop in hand, Commandant Baer strode in front of the rank of pathetic creatures. Except for the occasional cringe when the crop cracked against his gloved hand, the political criminals didn't move.

"You have a visitor this evening."

As Aalexis studied the prisoners standing at attention between their bunks, their gazes sliced toward Aalexis and Xaver with confusion. None looked for long.

She remembered the names Rein had called when he'd writhed on the floor from the furnace she'd created in his mind, but was unsure if any had survived the raid or what they looked like. Their emotions would give them away, though. Their inability to hide their weaknesses.

Pathetic creatures.

Stepping forward, Aalexis examined one prisoner, then the next. Each time one dared to meet her eyes, he'd quickly look away, like a submissive dog.

Her eyes stopped at one male with unkempt dark hair peppered with grey. He didn't look away like the rest, but stared at her with fascination, as if he recognized her. His sand-brown eyes were wide, and his lips pursed together. When he noticed Aalexis watching him, he quickly averted his gaze.

Trying to ignore the odor, Aalexis went and stood directly in front of him. "Woody?"

Although he stared straight ahead, his mouth twinged, subtly, right around the corners.

"Jordan?"

A shadow crossed his face and a line formed over his nose.

There was only one name left. "Doc."

His eyes flicked down and back up, and she watched his Adam's apple move as he swallowed. He didn't acknowledge her, though.

Within the next moment, the prisoner hung from Xaver's grasp. The others next to the male flinched away.

"My sister requires an answer," Xaver said with no nuance in his voice or face, as if a person wasn't dangling from his fingertips at all.

Eyes bulging, he clutched pathetically at Xaver's hands. "Yes," he croaked.

"You know Ellyssa?" she asked, although she knew the answer.

As expected, the male named Doc attempted a nod.

Xaver released him.

"You will come with me," she said, and walked away.

# 5

By the time the SUV slowed and turned, Ellyssa's clothing stuck to her skin, her hair damp. Being stuck between Woody and Rein was unbearable; their bodies were like radiators. If Trista didn't pull over soon, she was going to melt.

A few uncomfortable bounces down the road later, she received her wish. Muffled voices shouted.

Rein and Woody stiffened; their tension rolled into Ellyssa. Knowing she was at the mercy of strangers, she fought the instinct to kick out the cushion and escape.

The window hummed as it rolled down. Trista said, "Open up, would you?"

Rein relaxed, pulling her closer."It's someone she knows," he whispered, his breath brushing against her ear. His words didn't calm her instincts.

Indecipherable words were spoken. The SUV edged forward, then came to a stop. Heart thundering in Ellyssa's ears, Trista opened the driver's side door.

"Where have you been?" a muffled male, the tone familiar.

Trista didn't answer. Instead, she grunted as she wiggled the cushion free.

Light spilled through, blurring Ellyssa's sight. She flinched, blinked a few times and opened her eyes to Trista's triumphant smile.

"I told you I'd find them," she said, stepping back.

Two familiar faces poked their heads inside the car. Wearing overalls over a thick, blue sweater, Tim's eyebrow-less eyes were the size of saucers, and Sarah, dressed in a long coat as yellow as the sunflowers Ellyssa remembered in her kitchen, nodded. Her youthful eyes sparkled, defying the wrinkles embedded around her mouth and eyes.

"Oh, my lord," the older female said. "I can't believe it. You were right, Trista. Here, you three, get out, get out." She playfully hit Tim on the shoulder, waking him from his stupor. "Would you move?"

Tim blinked and shook his head, casting light reflections across his bald head. "Yeah, sure." He stepped back. "I can't believe it. You really did find them."

"I told you."

Grunting, Woody pulled himself over the side, landed on the floorboard and eased himself through the door, where he was instantly engulfed in Sarah's thin arms. Laughing, Woody returned her embrace. Tim patted a greeting on his back.

As soon as Woody had moved, relief from the insufferable heat poured into the little compartment in the form of freezing temperatures. Ellyssa took in a deep, cool breath. She climbed out and stepped into the chilly air of the garage where Sarah and Tim had hidden them in coffin-like boxes. So much had happened since then; it seemed like ages ago. The garage was the same—boxes and containers stacked against the walls to transport goods and people, the same type that had transported her and Woody. The smoothness with which the Resistance operated still astounded Ellyssa, right under the nose of society.

The cold penetrated her clothes and inched over her skin, raising goose bumps. After sweating for the last few hours, she didn't mind. She smiled and was about to greet her hosts, but before she had a chance to say anything, she found herself in the same predicament as Woody had. For someone as small and frail as Sarah, she was incredibly strong. Her arms wrapped around Ellyssa in a vise-like hug.

Surprised, Ellyssa stood still for a moment, arms dangling uselessly. But Sarah's warmth and spirit fed Ellyssa with a sense of familiarity she was growing accustomed to. Finally, she hugged the older female.

Sarah didn't seem to notice Ellyssa's hesitation at all. She pulled Ellyssa in for one last squeeze, then stepped away, wiping her hands on her yellow coat. "My, you are all just soaking wet."

"Yes," she said, feeling the warmth seep away. She wrapped her arms around herself. "It is cold." She turned and grabbed her parka from the sweat box she'd just escaped. It was damp.

"Tim, we need to go inside," Sarah said, pulling blankets free from a box. "Here, dear." She unfolded the blanket, then pulled it around Ellyssa's shoulders. "This will help until we get you inside the house." As she spoke, her eyes suddenly lit up, erasing away another ten years. "Rein."

Rein held his arms open. "It's been a while."

"At least a year," Sarah said, muffled in his chest.

As Rein and Sarah greeted each other, Ellyssa noticed Trista walking toward Tim. The older male looked at her, his brow bunched in questioning wrinkles. Trista gave him a subtle shake of the head.

Ellyssa wondered what secret message the two exchanged. Going by their worried expressions, whatever it was, it wasn't going to be good. Narrowing her eyes, Ellyssa asked, "What's wrong?"

Tim nervously fingered his beard. "Let's get in the house first."

Ellyssa felt a hand on her shoulder and turned to see Sarah smiling sadly. The older female dropped her hand and reached for Rein and Woody.

"I'm so sorry for the loss you've endured. It was terrible when news reached us, then Trista," her head lowered, "filled us in on the rest of the gruesome details."

"I haven't had time to tell them everything," Trista piped up.

Sarah nodded. "I see. Well, there will be plenty of time for all that. I'm sure you must be starving."

Tim approached Rein and gripped his shoulder. "We're truly sorry, son."

"Thank you," Rein replied, looking away and blinking.

Tim fidgeted for a moment. "Well, then, I guess we should go in the house."

Sarah opened the door. Snow swirled in and freezing wind snuck under the folds of her blanket. Shivering, Ellyssa filed out after the others into the backyard that had been green at her last visit. Browns and gold, with a light powdering of snow, dominated the landscape. The fruit-bearing trees' bare limbs stretched into a cloudy sky.

Tim took the lead as they neared the back door. With his hand on the doorknob, he hesitated, then turned around. He rubbed his bearded chin. "Do you remember what makes up the Resistance?"

Both frowning, Rein and Woody nodded.

"Remember that." He turned and opened the door to the sunny kitchen.

As Ellyssa walked inside, a remembrance of hominess and warmth enveloped her. She'd never lived in a real home, and the love and comfort flowed as if alive. Yellow lit the room like sunshine, from the walls to the sunflower tablecloth. Knickknacks littered every open space, and French doors opened into the living room.

Rein walked in behind and slipped his arm around her shoulder. He looked around, apparently expecting to find something, but the kitchen was empty. "What's all this about?" he asked Tim.

"There's someone you need to meet," Sarah said, walking toward the living room.

Rein exchanged a curious look with Woody. "Okay. Someone who defected?"

Chewing on her bottom lip, Trista's eyebrows drew together. "You could say that."

*Someone new?* Ellyssa visibly tensed, her soldiering instincts uncoiling. With everything that'd happened, she couldn't believe everyone else was so calm.

Rein's fingers trailed down Ellyssa's arm, leaving behind tingles, and slipped into her hand. "This is how our society is made. We accept people for who they are, not what they did in the past."

"I understand...trust. But with everything that has happened, how can you be certain they are not a spy...or worse?" she questioned.

"I don't." Rein shrugged. "We've never known for certain."

Woody leaned toward her ear. "You can, though."

Ellyssa gave a short nod, but before she had a chance to expand her mind, Trista brushed by, grabbing Woody's hand.

"I promise you that he is not some sort of spy," she interjected.

With a slight shrug of his shoulders and a reassuring smile, Rein released Ellyssa's hand and followed.

As soon as Rein and Woody crossed the threshold, they stopped. A tsunami of angry tension crashed.

Something was wrong. Very wrong. Whoever was in the other room, Rein and Woody definitely recognized him.

"What is this?" Rein asked through clenched teeth.

He didn't wait for an answer as he flew into the room. A crash sounded, followed by a bang.

Fear squeezed Ellyssa's heart. "Rein!" She bolted forward, passing Woody and Trista, where she skidded to a stop.

Rein's fingers were locked around a male Ellyssa recognized from Detective Petersen's mind. Muscles bulging beneath his shirt, Rein knocked the captain's head against the wall. "What the hell," Rein yelled. *Thump.* "What. The. Hell." *Thump.*

Captain Dyllon Jones was up on his toes, head bouncing off the wall, sea-blue eyes swollen. The dark-green uniform of the area police he wore was crumpled, the swastika armband ripped. An electroshock weapon hung from his belt, but the captain made no move toward it. Instead, the captain's hands fluttered around Rein's wrists, trying to free himself. Red splotched his face as he gasped for air.

"Rein," Trista squealed, horrified. She pushed around Ellyssa.

Woody reached out to stop her, but the blonde ducked under his outstretched hand. She darted to Rein and hit him on the back. "Let him go! Damnit, Rein. Let him go!"

Rein didn't even seem to notice Trista. He kept knocking Captain Jones' head into the wall.

*Thump.*

Woody grabbed hold of Trista and yanked her away.

"You don't understand," she said, her voice high with anger as she tried to pull free. "God damn it, Rein! Stop it!"

Ellyssa stood mesmerized, unsure. Confused. Surely, Trista hadn't betrayed them, but there was the male who had accompanied Detective Petersen.

"Please, Ellyssa, make him stop," Trista begged from behind her. "I promise, he's done nothing but help."

Certainly Trista wouldn't lie. It definitely wouldn't hurt to look since Rein had him under control.

*Thump.*

Ellyssa opened the door to the captain's thoughts. Fear and confusion circled in his head, vying for dominance. He remembered Rein, remembered Woody, but that was all Ellyssa could read. The emotions were too loud to get a clear scan of his true intentions. She released his thoughts and went to Rein.

"Let him go," Ellyssa said.

Rein glanced at her, his eyes circles; wildness raged within the green. Red splotched his face as well. A slew of cussing saturated the room.

"Let him go, Rein. If he is a spy, *I* can get information from him."

Rein stopped knocking the captain's head but didn't let go of his neck. His knuckles were bleached white from the death grip he held. "It—It's him," he stuttered, his words pained and angry. "He helped her."

The *her* Rein referred to was the now-deceased Detective Angela Petersen, The Center's *Schutzpolizei.* Ellyssa's father, Dr. Hirch, had sent Angela to find Ellyssa when she'd escaped from under his control. It was the detective who'd delivered Rein to Dr. Hirch, and ultimately into the hands of Ellyssa's sister, Aalexis.

Rein's lips curled into a snarl as he turned back toward the captain, their noses almost touching.

*Thump.*

Plaster dust fell. A bluish grey tinted the captain's face.

"Stop it!" Trista screamed, still trying to break free from Woody.

Ellyssa didn't need to read Rein's mind to know what he was thinking. The pain and suffering he'd experienced under Aalexis' influence had been torturous. She herself had felt the faux fire lick through her veins as her sister manipulated his pain receptors. Even with Ellyssa's genetically enhanced capabilities and high threshold for pain, the intensity had crumpled her to the ground like a ragdoll. Frankly, it surprised her that Rein, a normal human, had been able to withstand such agony.

"I know. I understand," Ellyssa said. Calmly, she reached up and stroked Rein's face. "I can get to the root of this if you let him go. If you give me the chance."

For a moment, Rein acted like he wasn't going to listen to her, the tips of his fingers hidden in the flesh of Dyllon's neck. Then, he let out a breath and, slowly, he nodded. One by one, Rein's fingers relaxed. Blood rushed back into his knuckles, turning them pink.

Hacking, Captain Jones slid down the wall to his knees. "I..." he croaked.

Ellyssa knelt before him, her face clear of emotion. "I know who you are," she stated.

The captain looked at her, understanding filtering into his eyes.

"I need you to calm down."

He acknowledged her words, but his expression, and the way his eyes darted around, showed lack of ability.

Ellyssa looked up at Rein, whose face was still flushed in fury, then at Woody. He held Trista by her upper arm; she no longer struggled, her blue eyes locked on Ellyssa. Back by the French doors, holding hands, Tim and Sarah stood.

They were all watching her.

"I want you to understand," she said, facing Dyllon, "as of right now, no one will hurt you. But you must relax."

Hand around his neck, breath ragged, Dyllon stared at her, apparently confused. He glanced at Trista, pleadingly, as if he expected her to save him.

Ellyssa shook her head. "Do you understand?"

He nodded and exhaled a raspy breath.

She looked into his eyes, the bluish-green peeking around the edges of dilated pupils. "Calm," Ellyssa said in a soothing voice.

Surprisingly, the captain did. His pupils constricted slightly, and the anxiety on his face dimmed. As Dyllon sucked in a ragged breath, Ellyssa swung her mental door open. Images and emotions filed in, one fading into another, a blend of past and present.

First, instant recognition of Rein when he'd barreled in the room. Rein grabbing him off the chair and slamming him repeatedly against the wall. Fear, confusion and betrayal. Trista had assured him he'd be accepted.

The captain was infatuated with Trista. Blonde hair and blue eyes, Trista could blend so easily into society. Yet, Trista was part of the Renegade camp. If Dyllon hadn't helped her, Trista would've been amongst the exterminated, captured or lying dead in a pool of blood back at the cavern, like so many of the Renegades.

The picture shifted.

Males and females dressed in black riot gear, armed. Darkness, then flashes of light. Shots fired, screams of terror. A river of crimson, thick and flowing. Men, women, and children falling to the ground, eyes glazed over in permanent accusing stares.

Guilt saturated Dyllon, wiping free the fear and confusion. He hadn't pulled a trigger; his eyes stayed glued to the macabre, unable to step forward and stop the madness.

Through the captain's mind, Ellyssa lived the horror, feeling Dyllon's repulsion. Her friends and family gunned down without mercy. Bile bubbled in her midsection. She wanted to stop looking but couldn't, just like when she'd been drawn to the toddler down in the cavern that was now a tomb.

Finally, the captain's gaze shifted to Trista. Like a tether broke, Ellyssa slammed the mental door, cutting off his thoughts. Trying to blink away the nightmare she'd just seen, Ellyssa shook her head. She looked up.

Rein stood over her, his eyebrows pinched together over the bridge of his nose and arms crossed over his chest. Woody was behind him with the same expression, his hand locked around Trista's arm; her blue eyes had narrowed to angry slits.

Standing, Ellyssa nodded once. Rein's and Woody's postures relaxed a little, but not completely.

Hesitantly stepping forward, Tim said, "Why don't we all go into the kitchen?"

Ripping away from Woody's grip, Trista ran to Dyllon and helped him to his feet. She faced Rein, her eyes like icy shards. "If you guys would've listened..."

Rein didn't reply, his face set hard and angry.

"Are you okay?" Trista asked Dyllon.

Massaging the tender flesh where Rein's fingers had dug in, Dyllon nodded. Trista helped him into the kitchen.

Sour moods cast an ugly grey over the yellow, covering the sunshiny ambience of the kitchen. Woody stood behind Captain Jones. Tim took the seat at the head of the table while Sarah went to Trista, who leaned against the counter. She patted the younger girl's shoulder consolingly. Looking apologetically at Trista, whose eyes flashed dangerously, Ellyssa sat across from the captain.

"Start talking," Rein said, plopping into the seat next to Ellyssa.

"I can't believe how you're treating him," Trista mumbled.

Rein and Woody both glanced at her, but neither commented. The tension in the kitchen thickened, almost suffocating.

For a moment, Dyllon didn't say anything. He just massaged the sides of his neck as he stared at Ellyssa, then Rein. Finally, he set his hand on the table and cleared his throat. With him calmer, Ellyssa locked onto his mind. If he told one lie, she would finish Rein's job.

"There's a lot to tell you," he said, grimacing with each word. Finger-shaped marks shaded his neck.

Leaning back in his chair, Rein crossed his arms over his chest. His jaw worked nonstop. A vein pulsed in his temple.

"It was awful." The captain closed his eyes and swallowed, loudly. He massaged his neck. "I'd never witnessed anything like it," he said. "Before, we captured Renegades and sent them to concentration camps. I had never been on the front lines." He opened his eyes, his expression apologetic. "Children, women..."

"Shut up," Rein said, looking away. "Just shut up."

"I'm so sorry."

Slamming his fists on the table, Rein popped out of the chair. "Sorry!" he yelled, his body rigid, like he was ready to climb over the table to finish what he had started.

As soon as Rein jumped out of his seat, Dyllon's thought process jammed, and images looped around—back at the cave, the murderous scene, Trista—making it hard to get a read on him.

Trista brushed by Woody, pushing him out of the way. "Stop it," she said between clenched teeth. "I want you to stop it, right now." She jabbed her finger in the air at Rein. "That's enough."

Ellyssa grabbed Rein's hand. The gesture seemed to calm him a little. He fell back into his chair and covered his face.

"We have always accepted people. Always. Including her," Trista said, nodding toward Ellyssa. "No offense."

Ellyssa waved her off in understanding.

"Did you think for a moment, that everyone we ever accepted was innocent? I'm sure plenty of them had marks against them before they had enough...saw the light...Whatever, and defected from society."

"Maybe not," Rein said, lip quivering, "but that was our family."

"Don't you think I know that? I was there." Her voice broke, tears forming in her eyes. "Dyllon might not have been able to save everyone, but he saved me." She swallowed. "*Me.*"

Rein glanced around the room. Besides Woody, who looked at the back door, everyone else warily stared at him. Exhaling, his body deflated as the anger left. He slumped forward. "Thank you," he mumbled under his breath.

"Don't thank me," Dyllon said. "It was terrible, and I'm sorry I..." He stopped. Trista held out her hand, and he wrapped his fingers around hers, pulling strength from her. "It was a madhouse. An utter madhouse. Gunfire ricocheted. The screaming. The cries for help."

"That's enough," Woody said, pinching the bridge of his nose. "We saw what you left behind."

"There was nothing I could do. Nothing." His voice was desperate, as if needing them to understand and forgive. "What could I do?"

What seemed like an eon ago, Ellyssa had said the same exact thing to Rein back in the cavern. She felt his eyes on her, and turned to look. Remembrance of that time reflected within his green eyes as well.

Putting her hands on Dyllon's shoulders, Trista said, "You didn't see it...didn't hear it. There was nothing anyone could do. Don't you think I would have? I was armed, too, and just as helpless. If either one of us tried, we would have just been added to the body count."

Woody cringed at Trista's words.

"Any courage I had died the moment gunfire flashed from the barrels," Dyllon started, his head lowered. Shame accompanied the memory Ellyssa had witnessed. "Like a coward, I backed out of the cavern and ran. The barrage and screams chased me down the passageways. In my confusion, I went right past the opening to the upper level."

"It was lucky for me he did," Trista continued, her blue eyes swimming in grief and unshed tears. "He ducked behind the rock formation I had been hiding behind."

"The coward I am," he mumbled.

Trista lowered her head to his ear. "If not for you, I'd be dead," she whispered before straightening back up. "I dropped my gun in surprise, and I thought that was going to be it. I closed my eyes, waiting for the sound of gunfire, waiting to feel the impact of a bullet. Instead, I felt his hand over my mouth as he slipped in behind me, pulling me back further into the darkness. *Shh,* he whispered to me, *I'm not going to hurt you.* And I believed him. For some reason, I believed him.

"We stayed hidden, listening to the sound of footsteps of the police patrolling the areas. I remember being shocked that I could hear them at all with my heart pounding in my ears." She paused for a moment. "It's funny where your mind travels under times of stress.

"As time passed, the frequency of the patrols lessened. Dyllon picked up a rock. I crazily thought he was going to do me in with it." She laughed a little, a sad, sad laugh, and shook her head. "Absurd."

"I didn't want to chance the gun," Dyllon threw in, absently. He still sat with his head hanging.

"He edged back to the formation, and the next patrol that had happened by, he smacked him on the side of the jaw. The guy went down with a *thump* that seemed to echo louder than the gunfire."

Trista stepped away from Dyllon and waved her hand down the side of her body. "My uniform. As I said, there was no time to pick and choose."

Ripples of silence washed away the last of Trista's words while everyone stilled, contemplating what she'd just told them. Ellyssa watched the captain, who seemed content to stare at his twisting hands.

During Trista's recounting of events, not once had Dyllon feel regret for his new choices, or anything that felt like he betrayed his society or planned to betray the resistance. All he felt were utter guilt, sorrow, and shame. A saturation, really. In that instant, at the site of the massacre of her family, everything he had once believed in had bled out onto the stony ground with the blood of the Renegades.

Ellyssa prodded deeper, sinking tentacles into hidden crevices and caches of his mind. Nothing sinister to alert her. Gating off the stream of thoughts, she pulled her eyes from Dyllon and met the expectant eyes of Woody and Rein. She nodded once, indicating he was telling the truth.

Like a light breeze had blown in, the intense storm cloud lifted a little as muscles relaxed and jaws unclenched. Peeking through, the sunshiny feel of the kitchen tried to reclaim its territory.

"What does that mean?" asked Trista, breaking the silence. She watched Ellyssa through narrowed lids, light eyelashes brushing her cheeks.

"It means," answered Woody, "we believe his story."

Trista's head snapped toward him. "So, what, does that mean I'm in the clear, too? And how would you know?" she said, facing Ellyssa. "What's with the freaky episode?"

Unbelievably, Rein chuckled, a sound that wasn't filled with happiness, as if he had just remembered everyone, besides he and Woody, was in the dark about her ability. "That's a long story, too."

Trista didn't try to pry any other information from them. She stared at them for a long time until she finally broke the silence. "Well, to continue, what is good about Dyllon's involvement with us is that they don't suspect him as of yet." She lifted her chin in pride. "His knowledge of the patrols is why *I* was able to check the cavern one more time for you before leaving."

"And where would you go?" Rein asked.

"It's too dangerous to stay here," Dyllon answered.

"They were going to hide south of here," Tim broke in. "I didn't know what else to do. Communicating with any others has almost been impossible. And I have Sarah to protect." He glanced at his wife lovingly. The older woman smiled.

"Which reminds me," Dyllon said, as he stood. "I have to get back." He tried to straighten the creases Rein's hands had left in his uniform, then gave up, shifting his attention to the armband. It fell loose again and dangled from a seam.

Leveling his eyes on Dyllon, Rein stood, while at the same time Woody placed his hand on the captain's shoulders as if he were about to shove him back into the chair. "And what about the others?" Rein asked. "Not everyone was..." he closed his eyes.

Dyllon's shoulders tensed, and he clearly looked uncomfortable, as if he couldn't wait to escape outside. "I don't know yet. I think they've been taken to a camp. I've been trying to find out, but I don't have the security clearance." He cocked his head. "I'm trying."

For the first time since Rein had grabbed him, Ellyssa saw sympathy in Dyllon's eyes, instead of confusion or pain. She touched his mind and saw the attempts he'd made trying to locate the missing people.

"It is okay, Rein, Woody. Let him go. If we keep him, they will send someone looking."

Woody's hand slipped off his shoulder, while Rein sighed.

Ellyssa stood and leaned into Rein. "Trust," she whispered in his ear.

She could feel his warmth, and an underlying odor of fear mixed with his scent. He nodded.

She turned back to Dyllon. "Do something about the marks on your neck."

Dyllon reached up and touched his neck. His eyes flinched at the contact. Looking at Ellyssa in a weird way, he said, "Yeah." He pulled his collar up and faced Trista. "I will see you tomorrow." He leaned over and quickly pecked her on the cheek.

Rein and Woody noticeably bristled but remained silent at the show of affection. Reaching over, Ellyssa laid her hand on top of Rein's. He interlocked their fingers.

Trista touched the spot where Dyllon had kissed her as she watched him slip out the back door. Crossing her arms, she turned back toward the table. "The way you treated him was deplorable."

"You don't understand," Rein retorted.

Trista's eyes raked across Rein, before she exhaled and released her arms from their defensive position. "You're right, I don't. I'm sorry for everything you've been through, Rein. For everything you all have been through. But you can't imagine what I've been through, either."

"You're right," Rein said, his voice drawn and tired. He plopped back down in the chair.

Looking at Rein and Ellyssa, Trista grabbed Woody's hand and held it to her chest. "You have to understand; he saved me. He helped me get to you. For that, regardless of his past transgressions, we owe him a chance. Please."

Rein lowered his face into his hands. It was a long while before he spoke. Finally, he said, "Whatever."

"I think we should get something to eat and talk about something else for a while," Sarah said, removing the coat she still wore.

Ellyssa glanced at Tim, who sat silently in his chair, thoughtful. She wondered what he was thinking about, how all this affected him and his wife. Tim had mentioned how they needed to protect themselves, too. She entertained the thought of looking into his mind, then disregarded the notion. The invasion of privacy seemed wrong. If he wanted to share his thoughts, it should be by his choice, not by her curiosity.

The older woman went to the refrigerator and started to pull out packages of meat and cheese, while Trista, apparently already at home in the quaint house, went over to the cupboard and grabbed bread and mustard.

Ellyssa's stomach rumbled loudly.

# 6

The one Rein had called out to during his torture, Doc, lay curled in the corner of the low-lit storage room. Red welts marked his back, chest and face, and beads of blood formed along the angry ridges. Regardless of the punishment, the prisoner's lips remained pressed together in a tight line. Head hanging low, he looked between strands of his greying hair, hatred burning bright in his light-brown eyes.

Even with death threatening, the prisoner had remained loyal to the Resistance. The wounds Commandant Baer had inflicted should have at least elicited a scream, a pathetic mew, but the male hadn't uttered a sound. Of course, the prisoner hadn't even begun to feel pain yet. Soon he'd be given the opportunity.

As much as Aalexis hated to admit it, the stubbornness of the Renegades was a strong point of theirs. So were their devotion and loyalty to each other.

It would also be their demise. Ellyssa had already proven that when she'd risked her own life to save Rein's.

Aalexis had hoped the prisoner would succumb to the comparatively mild torture of the Commandant, but she knew such would not be the case. Doc had other welts in different stages of healing.

As much as Aalexis didn't want the Commandant to witness her ability—the greed for power the subhumans couldn't understand—it seemed there was going to be little choice. The thought angered her and, surprisingly, excited her at the same time. Aalexis was unsure if the excitement stemmed from the thought of hurting Doc or from the power surge from her ability.

Much had changed since Ellyssa had destroyed The Center.

Aalexis stepped up next to the Commandant. "Let me try."

Hans looked down at her, his eyes wide with surprise. She knew it was because such a request from a teen female was unheard of. His lips set firmly together as if he was thinking about denying her, but then he stepped back; the crop extended from his left hand.

Eyeing the primitive weapon, Aalexis said, "I have no need for that."

"Oh," the Commandant said, looking rather silly. He tucked the crop back under his arm.

Aalexis pointed to a corner of the room. "Stand over there," she ordered.

Once again, Hans' lips pursed into a tight line and his posture went rigid, but he still didn't say anything. He walked over to the corner, his leather boots smacking against the linoleum.

Aalexis returned her attention to the pitiful creature, who eyed her with trepidation, as if he knew something terrible was about to happen. If Ellyssa had shared the secrets of The Center, most likely he had an inkling.

She settled onto her haunches, at eye level with the prisoner. "I will ask you only once," she stated. "What news do you have of Ellyssa? Where has she gone?"

Doc's pleading gaze swept from her to her brother, then to the Commandant, who stood obediently where Aalexis had sent him.

Finally, Doc looked back at her. "I don't have anything to tell you," he mumbled, his voice firm. Defiantly, he pushed himself into a sitting position.

"That is an unfortunate answer for *you*," she emphasized, standing. "Xaver."

She felt the air disturbance as her brother reinforced the energy bubble that cocooned them from outside forces, then created a small hole for Aalexis to focus her energy through. She squared her shoulders and stared deep into the betrayer's eyes, locking him within her gaze.

Powerful tingles coursed through Aalexis and tickled her skin as her sight blurred and the room transformed. Everything shifted into simplicity as she zeroed in on the subatomic particles. She couldn't actually see them, per se, for even *her* eyesight was too weak, but within her mind, they formed and, with the formation came understanding of their inner workings, their vibrations. Billions upon billions, the air hummed with the particles.

Twelve years ago, it'd been a simple connection when she'd first moved the block with the letter *A* with nothing more than wishing it so. How everything was made up of energy. Once she'd made the association, it'd been a matter of time to train her mind to visualize and manipulate, to send the commands. Because even thoughts were energy, nothing more than electrical impulses twitching with potential.

Unfortunately, it was that same energy which had allowed Ellyssa to slam the door onto the burning inferno Aalexis had created in her sister's mind when Ellyssa had stupidly risked her life for the inferior being, Rein. An unfortunate setback.

The purr of the vibrations brushed against Aalexis' sensitive skin, making the hair on her arms stand on end. But she was looking for a distinct vibration, and quickly discarded the particles with the wrong atmosphere until she found the familiar repetition of the atoms that made up the molecular structure of the inner thermal nociceptor. She saw it clearly in her mind—the soma, the dendrites that forked into tree-like limbs, the axon that stretched into the spinal cord. Sending out her own energy stream, she latched onto the cellular body. Within a second, Aalexis' force surrounded the pain receptors of the inadequate human.

Afterward, Aalexis' vision cleared, and her lips hid a smile. *Burn,* she commanded, her thought mimicking damaged tissue.

At one moment, Doc was looking at Aalexis with confusion and fear; the next, his face contorted, his mouth tightened and his eyes bugged. He struggled against the phantom pain, tried to fight it by covering his face with his hands and biting his palms. But fighting something that wasn't really there, a hallucination, was impossible. The prisoner couldn't hide from his own mind.

Aalexis knew his struggle wouldn't last long; Rein had also tried that with little success. In the end, Rein had screamed.

Aalexis tweaked the neurons a bit more, the imaginary flames growing to an inferno. Slowly, the inferior being slid from his upright position and writhed on the floor, back arching. Screams followed, echoing around the cement bricks.

Watching the male squirm on the floor like the worm he was, Aalexis' heart accelerated at the release of dopamine and endorphins. Such feelings were forbidden, but even her father had felt excitement. She'd seen the way his eyes had lit when he'd studied her, even though he'd tried to contain the feeling. Why shouldn't she, also, take pleasure on her quest to complete his work? Her father should be proud.

Sweat beaded on Doc's forehead and ran into his greying dark hair, forming matted clumps. His tanned skin blotched with red.

Disgust for the creature twisting in agony sickened her. How could such insects flourish within their society? Walk on the Earth? One day soon, all inferiority would feel pain. And afterwards, they all would be exterminated. Including the ones acceptable by society's standards, like Commandant Baer. She glanced over her shoulder.

Face slack, eyes wide, jaw hanging open like a simpleton, Hans stood frozen. The crop hung from his lax hand.

Since Aalexis had first walked through Commandant Baer's door, she'd witnessed his feeble attempts to hide his anxiety, gathering bits of courage to defy her. It served him well to be put in his place, to know true *perfection*. Finally, he understood he was nothing. How could he not? The corner of her mouth curled.

Facing forward, she released her grip. Doc curled on his side, chest heaving with rattled breaths. He didn't call any names as Rein had, but then again, he hadn't even begun to taste the pain Rein had endured.

Doc moaned, arms wrapping around his midsection; the aftereffects of her torment still burned, like embers of a dying fire. Still, he said nothing.

"Would you like more?" Aalexis asked.

Doc shook his head, then looked at her in desperation. "Please."

"Talk."

He shook his head, again. "I can't. Please."

Doc's plea landed on deaf ears. Aalexis was incapable of feeling pity for the creature. The brief stint of pleasure and disgust had left. She felt hate, though. An urge to finish him off.

But it wasn't time for that yet. If the creature refused to divulge the information she sought, then she had other plans for him. Her sister's devotion to the one called Rein had enlightened her. Maybe Ellyssa's allegiance extended to other members of the Renegade family. Until then, though, she could make Doc wish he had done what she'd requested.

Tears dropping onto the floor, Doc reached out to her as if seeking help. Aalexis stepped back. Of course, the insect couldn't actually touch her; Xaver's shield protected her, but she still didn't like the thought.

"Unfortunate."

Aalexis ignited the flames once again.

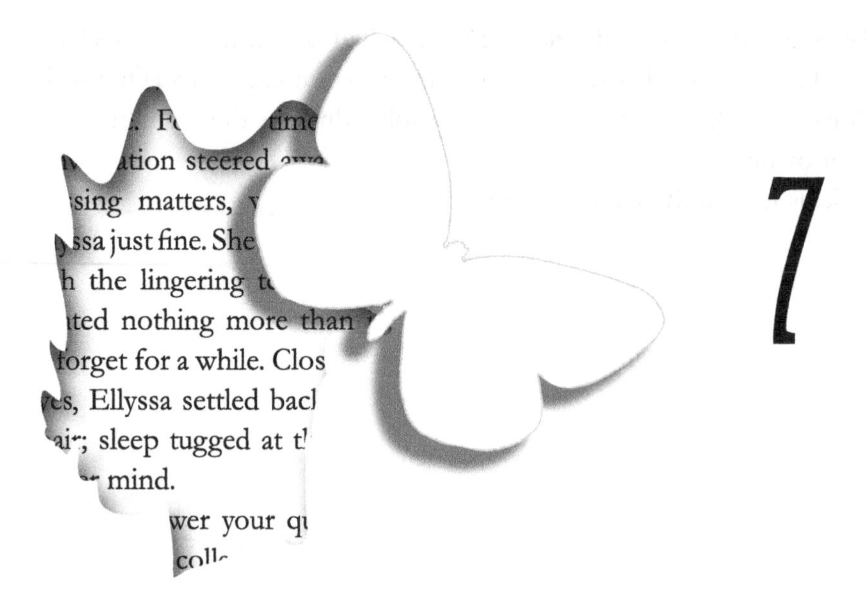

# 7

With stomachs full and dishes cleared, everyone sat around the table. For the time being, conversation steered away from pressing matters, which suited Ellyssa just fine. She felt awkward with the lingering tension. She wanted nothing more than just to forget for a while. Closing her eyes, Ellyssa settled back in her chair; sleep tugged at the edges of her mind.

"To answer your question," Trista said, collapsing Ellyssa's reverie like an imploding star, "no, but he is trying."

Apparently, the moment for relaxation was over. "Who's trying what?" Ellyssa inquired.

"Dyllon is searching for survivors," she answered. "And by the way, I still want to know what's up with all the freaky *he's telling the truth* stuff?"

Exhaling, Ellyssa deflated. The moment had come, and all she wanted to do was slip into a bed and mull over everything, alone. Or, better yet, forget and sleep. She glanced at Rein, who squeezed her shoulder, then at Woody, who gave her a "go ahead" nod.

"It's hard to explain," she started. She didn't know how to continue. She still remembered the way Rein had reacted, although, Mathew, Jordan and Woody had accepted the truth rather easily.

Raising her eyebrows, Trista prodded. "And?"

"I can read minds," she blurted out. The finality of it all blanketed the kitchen with silence.

After a moment passed, then two, Tim broke the silence, a frown tugging his brow. "Have you always had this ability?"

Nodding, Ellyssa responded, "Since I was a child."

The older male eyed her for a moment longer, thoughtfully, then looked at Sarah. "It's true."

"Seems that way."

Shocked, Ellyssa leaned forward. "You knew?"

"Kind of, but we didn't know it was you—at least, not one hundred percent certain. We wondered, with you being from The Center and all. The contacts in Chicago had sent word of the experiments at The Center. It was mostly whispers here and there, nothing concrete. It seemed they had a—a double agent, for lack of a better word, working with one of the doctors."

Ellyssa nodded. "Yes, Leland. He worked with my father, Dr. Hirch."

"I believe those were the names, weren't they, Sarah?" he said, looking at his wife.

"I believe so."

"Yep, there isn't much more than that, except... Do you have brothers and sisters?"

"I *had* brothers, and only one sister."

"And they had abilities, too, I take it. Moving things without touching them, able to tell the future, stopping people from moving, things like that?"

"Not completely accurate, but, yes. It doesn't matter now; they are all dead."

"And it's a good thing, too," said Rein, "with what Dr. Hirch had planned."

For the next fifteen minutes, Rein and Woody gave them a shortened version of the events leading up to the destruction of The Center, her father's plans, and how she and her siblings were prototypes of an Aryan breed that was even more superior and capable of destroying them all.

Not wanting to relive the past, or revisit the guilt still tingeing her mood, Ellyssa sank back in the chair, trying to make herself invisible. Finally, Rein finished. The worst was over. Everything lay before her extended family to pick through and examine.

Thoughtful, Tim pulled at his beard. He stopped and locked eyes with Ellyssa. "You don't happen to have any files or anything left, do you?

Sighing on the inside, Ellyssa shook her head. "Everything was destroyed with The Center."

Tim's hands caressed his beard again. "It's better that way. No one should mess around with the natural order of things. No one should play god. That's the downfall of Hitler's plan, you know?"

"Can you do it now?" Trista chimed, thankfully, breaking into the conversation before Ellyssa could answer her host.

Tired of talking about the whole ordeal, every word bringing up stabbing memories, especially when Rein had recounted the events of his torture, Ellyssa glanced at her friend. Trista flashed a smile and fidgeted in her seat.

"I could."

"Would you?"

Uncomfortable, Ellyssa looked at Rein. He just shrugged.

She shook her head. "I don't like to. It's like an invasion of privacy."

"So, what? You can control it?"

"I can block your thoughts."

"Why would you do that?"

"Trust," Ellyssa stated, simply. "That, and with thoughts streaming nonstop, I had to learn to build...a type of wall. People are loud."

"Oh." Trista looked disappointed for a moment. Slowly, her lips curled into a grin. "But, if I'm giving you permission, then it isn't an issue of trust. Tell me what I'm thinking."

Ellyssa couldn't help but smile. Trista's blue eyes lit with expectation. Concentrating on her enthusiastic friend, she opened the door. Good feelings thrummed inside Trista, all buzzy and excited. Trista concentrated hard on the number seventy-two, but, gradually, an image of Dyllon dominated over the digits. His sea-green eyes, his smile, the kiss they'd shared out in the barn the day before Trista had left to explore the cave and find them.

The way Dyllon had looked at Trista before he'd leaned over and softly brushed her lips reminded Ellyssa of Rein and they way he kissed her. Slightly embarrassed, Ellyssa closed the door.

"Are you sure you want me to tell you what you're thinking?" Ellyssa asked, cocking an eyebrow.

Confident, Trista folded her arms across her chest. "Go ahead."

"Don't you believe I can read your mind?"

"It's not that I don't believe; it's more like it's hard to believe."

"Suit yourself. You're thinking about Dyllon." Out of respect and definitely not wanting to cause anymore problems, Ellyssa left out the kissing part. A vein was already pulsing in Rein's temple at the mention of his name, and Woody didn't look too pleased, either.

"Nope. You're wrong. I was thinking of the number seventy."

Smiling, Ellyssa shook her head. "Actually, you were thinking the number seventy-two, then Dyllon came into your thoughts."

Red flushed Trista's face as her lips parted in astonishment. Woody chuckled, and amazement widened Tim and Sarah's eyes. Rein's chest puffed out in what Ellyssa assumed was pride, even with the pulsing vein. Dyllon was going to be a subject of controversy. Hopefully not tonight.

Trista narrowed her eyes. "Okay, you can get out now. You made your point."

Ellyssa put her hands up in surrender. "I told you."

Her friend's eyes shifted from side to side. When she made sure no one was watching, she mouthed, "Thank you." For not telling exactly what she'd seen, Ellyssa assumed. Apparently, Trista didn't want to get into it either.

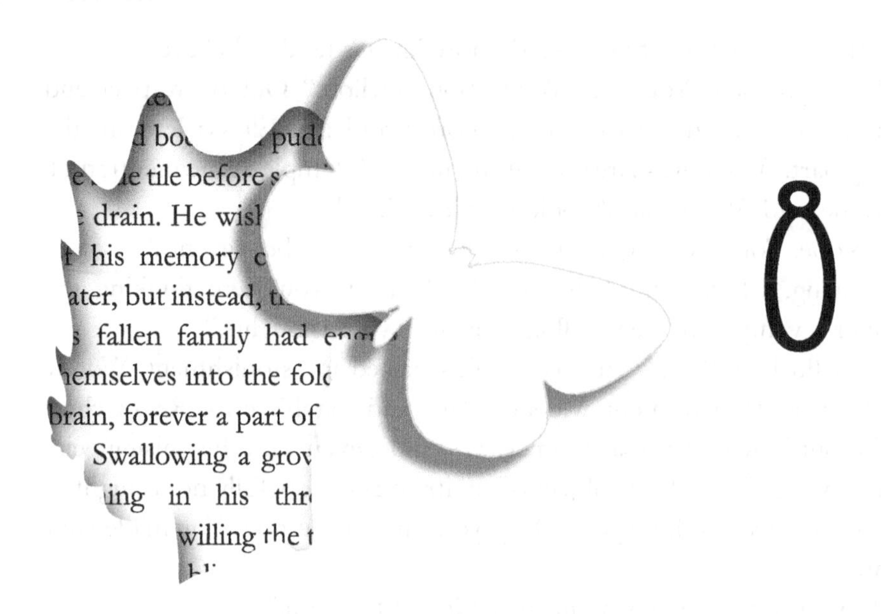

# 8

Rein stood in the shower. Hot water cascaded down his face and body and puddled on the blue tile before seeping down the drain. He wished the plague of his memory could join the water, but instead the images of his fallen family had engraved themselves into the folds of his brain, forever a part of him.

Swallowing a growing lump forming in his throat, Rein looked up, willing the tears away, refusing to blink. Steam rose in humid clouds and escaped over the glass door into the bathroom.

All his life, Jordan had tried to prepare him for the possibility of the demise of their band of Renegades, his family and friends. But nothing could have prepared him for the sight they'd found in the depths of their old home. All the faces frozen in surprise...in fear. Dead eyes staring into nothingness. Men. Women. The children. All had been gunned down as if their lives held no meaning.

Rein pulled his fingers through his wet hair, then rested his head against the tiles. Water fell onto the back of his neck and ran between his shoulder blades. He wanted the thoughts to stop. Of course, they didn't.

The whole thing with the captain was another chapter. Dyllon was very lucky Ellyssa had been there, or his corpse would had been lying in a shallow grave. Rein could still feel his fingers digging into the man's flesh, his intent to choke the life from Dyllon; he could still feel the cold satisfaction at the look on the man's face, his eyes bulging in their sockets.

At the sight of him, memories had flooded through Rein, like currents of a river. The blond bitch who'd captured him and turned him over to Dr. Hirch, then to...Aalexis. Even with the heat of the water, a shiver shot up his spine. The torture he'd endured; he'd never felt anything like it, and the blonde girl with the angelic features hadn't even laid a finger on him.

If Dr. Hirch had been able to carry forward with his genetic manipulation...

Rein shook the thought away. Dr. Hirch didn't pose a problem anymore.

He couldn't shake away the images of the lifeless bodies or the pain. Those were memories he wanted to leave buried, never to explore or think about again. He slid down the tiled wall to his backside, wrapping his arms around his knees.

Rein didn't know how long he'd sat at the bottom of shower, filing away all that had happened, but the water started to lose heat. He looked up into the cascade; cold drops plunked against his face.

*No more.*

If he was going to continue, he was going to have to accept that the ones who were gone were gone, and appreciate who he had left. And hope that somehow an opportunity would arise leading them to Doc, to Eric, to everyone else who was missing.

Hope.

Resigned, Rein stood, turned the water off and stepped free of the shower, stepped free of the chains of his sorrow. There was too much to do; he could not allow himself to wallow around in his regret and grief. The Renegades had always survived, somehow, always. Jordan had taught him to endure, to continue, and Rein would be damned if he didn't do whatever he could to make sure all who were left were reunited.

He dried off and exited the bathroom with a towel wrapped around his waist. The hallway was dark save for a night light leading the way to the room Tim and Sarah had afforded him and Woody. Ellyssa was one room over. Rein hoped she wasn't asleep; he wanted to feel her arms around him before he went to bed. He padded down the foyer and knocked on Ellyssa's door. When she didn't answer, he let himself in.

"Ellyssa?"

Ellyssa sat on a chair in front of a window, her head bent. Moonlight streamed through the glass panes and caressed her hair in spun silver. A slight shudder shook her shoulders.

"Ellyssa?"

She turned and looked at him, her cheeks shining and her eyes glistening from tears. She, too, had her sorrows, her regrets.

"Oh," Rein said, going to her. He lifted her chin with his hand and wiped away a fallen tear. Sadness floated in her azure eyes, shimmering pools of twilight.

"It's going to be fine," Rein murmured, wrapping his arms around her back. "I promise."

Ellyssa buried her face in his midsection. Something hard in her hand pressed against his backside, and he knew instantly it was the cave pearl the little girl had held in her death grip.

Silently, they held each other, his hand gliding over her silky hair. Her grief released in soft sobs; what remained of his left with hers. Time passed before Ellyssa looked at him, her eyes boring into his.

"I'm sorry," Ellyssa said, her voice as soft as the streaming moonlight. She sighed. "Things I've just realized were missing in my life are gone... again. It started with Jordan, which wrenched my soul, and now...everyone."

Rein pulled her up and enveloped her in his arms. "It's going to be okay. I promise. We *will* get through this. And if the few missing are still alive, we will find them."

Nodding against his chest, Ellyssa clutched onto his back as if she feared losing him too. Rein brushed his lips across the top of her head, her temple.

As Rein kissed her, Ellyssa's grip on his back tightened. She leaned her head back and found his lips. At first, Ellyssa's mouth moved with his, softly, almost hesitantly, then she pulled Rein closer as her tongue parted his lips. Her taste flooded his mouth as she explored; heat radiated off her. The urgency in Ellyssa's kisses increased, and electric tingles shot through Rein's veins. Like an addict, he savored it and wanted more. He walked her to the bed with her arms wrapped around him and gently pushed her down, breaking them apart.

Rein looked down at Ellyssa and pushed a strand of hair away from her eyes, the back of his hand cherishing the softness of her skin. The azure of her eyes burned bright, not with sadness or anger, but with ardent desire.

Since he'd first kissed Ellyssa in the field weeks ago, their relationship had been one Rein tentatively explored. They'd shared a kiss here, a touch there. He didn't want to scare Ellyssa off with a onslaught of feelings she couldn't comprehend or understand.

Rein definitely didn't want her to respond to him out of despondency. He feared it would only confuse her more.

Rein traced the curvature of Ellyssa's cheek; her skin pinked with desire. Closing her eyes, she pressed her face against his palm.

Rein sighed. Since he'd first found her in the store, all he had wanted, if he were to be honest was to be with her.

How he hated Dr. Hirch, not for the torture he'd put him through, but for what he had done to Ellyssa—trying to turn someone apparently so full of love and understanding into a robotic killer.

Ellyssa opened her eyes and looked up at him. Her bottom lip pulled into her mouth, seductively.

The love pulsed through Rein's body and wrapped around his heart, instilling life in him—a reason to continue. If it wasn't for Ellyssa, the need to be with her, to hold her again, he would've died the day Dr. Hirch had introduced him to Aalexis. Because of Ellyssa, he had found the strength to continue.

He owed her everything.

He wanted to be her everything, to share himself with her, to become one with her.

Did she?

Questioning, he raised his eyebrow.

Ellyssa looked up at Rein; green fire flickered in his eyes, but indecision made him hesitate. She knew it was because they hadn't ever explored this forbidden territory. They'd never had a chance. Being alone was not part of their lives. The moments they'd shared had been a few touches and gentle kisses that had only increased in passion once back in the makeshift hospital, before Rein had left to a fate she didn't ever want to consume her thoughts with.

But the opportunity was afforded now, and too precious to let slip through her fingers. Especially now when all Ellyssa wanted to do was forget. She'd tried when she'd first entered the bedroom, but the horror in the cavern had swept into her exhausted mind and dominated her thoughts with glazed-over dead stares and bloated bodies and a...cave pearl, until Ellyssa was a sobbing mess.

She had to move forward, and Rein was the means.

The unknown squeezed Ellyssa's heart and her pulse accelerated, carrying with it hormonal urges. Everything she knew about procreating had been clinical, something found in a textbook. The route her father had taken to create her and her siblings hadn't required that a male and female lie together.

*Only inferior beings participated in showing affection of any kind*, her father had said. *Emotions show weakness, and with weakness comes hesitation, and with hesitation comes death.* Ellyssa remembered the words as clearly as if he said them to her now.

But her father had been wrong about her, about all the things he had drilled into her since her childhood.

Ellyssa gazed at Rein. His dark hair was wet and mussed, bow-shaped lips set into a chiseled face, the towel riding low on his waist, his body lean, muscular and hard. He was the most beautiful person she'd ever seen, and *not* one part of him was her father's, or society's, idea of perfection.

Passionate heat radiated off Rein and mixed with her own. Unsure, her hand shaky, Ellyssa reached out and, tentatively, touched his stomach. She trailed over the indentations of his muscles and over his chest. His muscles twitched in response. His bare skin was smooth and rough at the same time. Every point of contact sent sparks.

"Come here," Ellyssa whispered.

Rein bent over her, his wet hair tumbling over his forehead, and his mouth found hers. She scooted back on the bed, her head coming to rest on a pillow as he leaned over her.

"Are you sure?" She could hear the careful hesitation in Rein's voice. "I don't want this to happen because you feel... I don't want to take advantage of you," he finished.

She thought for a moment. *Was she mixing up her feelings for him with the loss and sadness she felt?*

So what if she was?

Ellyssa loved him. From the time her eyes had first opened to Rein's angry face back when she'd been hurt in the coal mine, she'd been drawn to him, although Ellyssa hadn't recognized the foreign sensation at the time. And she knew Rein loved her.

Wasn't love enough?

As Rein watched her, moonlight curving around his body, excitement Ellyssa had never experienced before coursed through her. The fluttering in her stomach and her heart, she knew what she wanted—what she needed. It had nothing to do with the loss she felt.

Chewing on her bottom lip, Ellyssa nodded. " I'm sure." She paused for a moment, soaking in the happiness on his face. "I love you. I always have."

Rein dove down, his lips grazing the crevice of her shoulder and finding the hollow of her neck. Ellyssa sucked in a breath as he made his way up, sampling her jawline. Wherever his lips grazed, her body quivered.

Then, Rein found her mouth, his kiss deep and wanting. An explosion of intense proportions swept through Ellyssa. Her heart pounded inside her chest, and heat burned in her lower stomach. She matched his urgency.

"I love you, too," Rein said against her lips, his voice husky.

His warm breath washed over her, and she inhaled his scent. Losing herself, the door she'd always kept closed to his thoughts creaked open. Monumental sensations rushed in and tangled within hers. His love, her love, the touches of their skin, the electricity and tingles. All melded into one.

Rein shifted, and she felt his hand on her stomach, palm to skin. He pushed the borrowed T-shirt she was wearing up, and cool air caressed her, fueling the heat within. Ellyssa grabbed the back of his neck and brought his mouth to meet hers as his hand moved toward the swell of her breast. Powerful currents shot from his fingertips.

Rein stopped kissing her mouth and moved down over her throat before continuing to her midsection, each light nibble of his teeth making her stomach twitch in anticipation. He lifted her shirt up and over her head, and she lay exposed before him.

"You are perfect," Rein said, his eyes moving from her body to meet her eyes. "So beautiful."

Heart thudding, blood running lava hot, Ellyssa reached up and cupped his cheek. He leaned in to her touch and kissed the inside of her palm.

"You have my promise, I will always be with you. Nothing will tear us apart," he said.

Without another word, Rein was on her mouth again, deep, urgent, his tongue exploring. Ellyssa's pants landed on the floor next to her shirt and his towel.

The penetrating kisses and the hardness of Rein's body against hers filled Ellyssa with an emotional barrage that whirled through her so fast, she couldn't keep up, nor did she try. His hands ran over the curve of her hips and thighs.

With gentle care, Rein shifted above her and pressed his body against hers. Breath hitching in her chest, Ellyssa stilled, unsure, afraid. Then, foreign instincts surged, and her body knew what to do. She let it take control. Her hands clutched his back, trying to pull him closer as he carried her to the edge where she gladly fell over the precipice.

Rein moaned *Ellyssa* in her ear at the same time as she sighed.

# 9

Mathew's limp body was dragged across the compound by unseen soldiers who gripped him under his armpits. His body felt disconnected from his mind, as if his muscular integrity had been compromised, unresponsive to his mental commands.

The cold nipped through the thin cotton material and stung his broken flesh. Coals of the dying fire burned relentlessly inside him, the pain a constant reminder that his body was indeed a part of him.

The door to the barracks slammed open with a *bang*, and Mathew was dumped into the familiar hell, like a discarded bag of trash. The wooden floor of the barracks smacked his backside.

Through slitted lids, he peered at two soldiers. The shorter of the two blurry images stepped forward, and a sharp pain penetrated his side as the man kicked him. Grunting, he rolled over, out of the way of the door. It slammed shut behind him.

As soon as the soldiers had gone, another blurry face popped into his line of sight and cool hands touched his face. "Oh my god, Doc. What in the hell did they do to you?"

Mathew recognized the deep tenor of the voice, but the owner's name flitted away from his grasp. He opened his mouth to respond, to say anything, but the ability to form words seemed to have flitted away, too.

"You, go get some water," commanded the voice, "and you, rip up that sheet."

Mathew hissed as trails of pain followed behind fingers, leaving in their wake a throbbing discomfort. His head started to pound in cadence. He closed his eyes to the bombardment of dull colors and wavering images—to the pain.

Mathew couldn't close out the confusion that kept his brain working, though.

As soon the girl and the young man had walked through the door, Mathew had known. Their resemblance to Ellyssa was uncanny—the same blond hair, the same cold azure eyes, the same pitch to the German accent when the little girl had spoken.

Fear had pricked Mathew's insides when the little girl, who physically looked older than her young face showed, approached him. He'd remembered what Ellyssa had told him about her siblings, the abilities they wielded. But he hadn't been prepared for the pain that had followed. Ellyssa had said nothing about that.

Had she known?

Surely, Ellyssa wouldn't have deceived them. Not after all they'd been through together. He had witnessed her transformation.

Ellyssa had been the one to go after Rein, after all.

No. Something else was the culprit.

Had the epitomes of perfection evolved further?

Mathew screamed as sharp knives stabbed wherever someone touched him. His overtaxed brain screeched to a halt, and his train of thought muddled. Sweet endorphins released and swept through his bloodstream, dulling the stabbing to pricks.

Water wet Mathew's tongue. He fought the urge to gulp the steady stream. The coolness flowed inside him and quenched the remaining burn.

Suddenly, the hard planks no longer supported his weight, and he floated, blissfully. He wondered if he was dying; it felt like he should be after what he'd been through.

Black drifted in front of him. Sweet and coaxing.

Mathew went to meet it.

The aftereffects of what the Commandant had witnessed kept him stunned into silence. Slouched behind his desk, feeling insignificant, Hans watched Aalexis and Xaver. Postures straight, heads held high, they regarded him with disdain, their derision shadowed behind placid expressions, but there nevertheless.

Hans had been right. The two young people sitting in front of him were the epitome of perfection and well trained by The Center, but they were more. By all accounts, they were superior.

The *Führer's* poster children.

The Center had been busier than what the information Hans' security level had provided.

He wondered if the Colonel knew. *Of course he did.* How could he not? That had been exactly what he meant by the missing link. Though, he wondered if the Colonel had taken the time to consider the implications of what such superiority could mean, not just to the Renegades, but to all of them.

"You do understand?"

Aalexis' German accent broke through Han's musing. She still spoke to him as if he was a child, and she his superior. Then again, he supposed that was exactly how he seemed to her.

The commander of camp nodded. "Yes, I do."

"The male called Doc must be kept alive."

"I understand."

"Good," Aalexis said, standing. "Until our next visit." Without another word, she moved out the door. Xaver swung it shut behind them.

The Commandant stood and went to the window. Blackness had swallowed the light, and stars scattered across the sky.

It amazed him how dark the plains became during the evening hours. Of course, besides the camp he was charged with, there was no light pollution from any cities for hundreds of kilometers. Due to its isolation from other major cities, the city that had once been called Amarillo had been evacuated of its thirty thousand or so civilians, and they were relocated to a more populated area for better control.

The place had remained completely empty until the old Air Force base had been reopened as a isolated concentration camp fifteen years ago. *Isolated* was the keyword. Besides the hundred soldiers assigned under Hans' charge, his corporal, the sergeant-at-arms, and the political prisoners, no one lived within a four-hundred-kilometer radius.

In addition, the area was further desolate due to the lack of a sturdy infrastructure; the old highway, which had been newly paved before Germany won the war, lay in disrepair, just like the small city. After the initial raids and patrols, the Führer, apparently, had decided there were better ways to spend money. If not for the small airport being reopened along with the camp to transport the prisoners and supplies, traveling would've been almost impossible.

An arc of light from the office door caught the commander's attention and drew him from his thoughts. He watched as the shadows of the two teens moved against the wind to the Audi. The dome light flicked on as Aalexis climbed into it, then again as Xaver hefted himself into the driver's seat. Soon afterward, headlights sliced through the darkness.

Hans couldn't see the young girl or boy perched in the SUV, but he could still feel their eyes on him, drilling into him.

Hans' skin crawled.

# 10

The sky grew darker in the west as the sun threatened the night from the east, bringing the moment of twilight, the indistinguishable division between night and day.

Tiredness clung to Aalexis' eyelids, making them feel heavy and gritty. She hated the need to sleep, but it was something that couldn't be helped. Regardless of her superior genes, she still held ordinary characteristics, still had to maintain homeostasis.

Fighting the desire to lean her head back against the hard plastic of the chair and close her eyes, Aalexis stood just as Xaver entered the small room next to the hangar. Her brother's eyes were puffy and red, too, making their blue more prominent. His chiseled features sagged with exhaustion.

"They are ready to leave," he said, rubbing his face.

"Finally."

Aalexis grabbed her bag and handed it to her brother, then followed him into the early morning. Freezing wind whipped around and snuck up the bottom of her coat, sapping away any of the heat from indoors. She looked at the sky where oranges and reds streaked. Off to the northwest, angry dark grey clouds swirled. She hoped the weather wouldn't impede their return home. She wanted to check on the workers' progress.

"The pilot wants to leave before it snows," said Xaver as if reading her mind.

Aalexis boarded her father's private jet—no, it was now *hers*. Not everyone had the luxury of flight, usually only important people of the military or the state. Of course, no one had questioned when she and Xaver requested the privilege.

The jet could comfortably seat ten people. A television hung on the wall in front of the seats, and a stereo system was anchored to a table beneath it. At The Center, none of them had ever participated in watching television or listening to music, except for educational purposes. Her father had found such frivolous pastimes wasteful when there was an agenda of training and practicing and conducting experiments.

Aalexis agreed.

Xaver stored the bags away, then offered her a seat next to the window. As Aalexis walked past him, a whiff of a soapy, outdoorsy scent entered her nose. Inhaling deeply, she took her seat. The odor was pleasant, eliciting strange feelings in her midsection. It took her a moment to realize the scent came from Xaver. Her heart accelerated.

"Would you care for a drink?" Xaver asked.

Confused, Aalexis didn't respond and gazed out the window, trying to weed through the strange feelings. The sensation in her stomach was as unsettling as the dark clouds churning in the horizon.

"Aalexis?" Xaver asked, his voice deep. His voice didn't sound normal, robotic; it sounded concerned.

*Strange.*

Aalexis hesitated for a moment before she swallowed and turned toward him.

He stared at her; his eyebrows arched over his expressive eyes.

"Yes," she uttered, even she could hear the slight high pitch in her voice. Uncertainty?

Xaver's eyebrows drew together, which was very odd. She looked away from him, then back. His face now held its usual unexpressive placidity.

Aalexis didn't understand what was going on, but she didn't like it at all. Anger flared smothering the sensation in her stomach. "I said I want a drink."

Xaver studied her for a moment longer before he grabbed water from the refrigerator and handed it to her. Refusing to look at him, Aalexis snatched the bottle from his hand. She didn't know what was going on; she'd detected her brother's scent before, but not in an intoxicating way.

Not where it made her stomach feel strange. And the confusion? She didn't feel confusion. She was always sure of herself. She was bred to be sure, no hesitation.

Thoughtful, Aalexis unscrewed the cap and took a sip as Xaver settled down next to her. She scooted as close to the window as she could and watched the propellers spin.

"Things will be fine," Xaver said, breaking into her musing.

Aalexis whipped her head around, but Xaver wasn't looking at her. His eyes were closed, and his head leaned against the back of the seat.

The plane started to taxi down the runway, faster and faster, until the nose lifted, followed by the rest of the body. The ground grew smaller, and in the distance, she could see the ruins of a small city that soon shrank in the distance. As far as her eyes could see, the land lay flat below her, no mountains, nothing of interest. She leaned her head against the window and stared at the wispy clouds as the plane lifted into the atmosphere.

Slightly disturbed, definitely angry, Aalexis fell asleep.

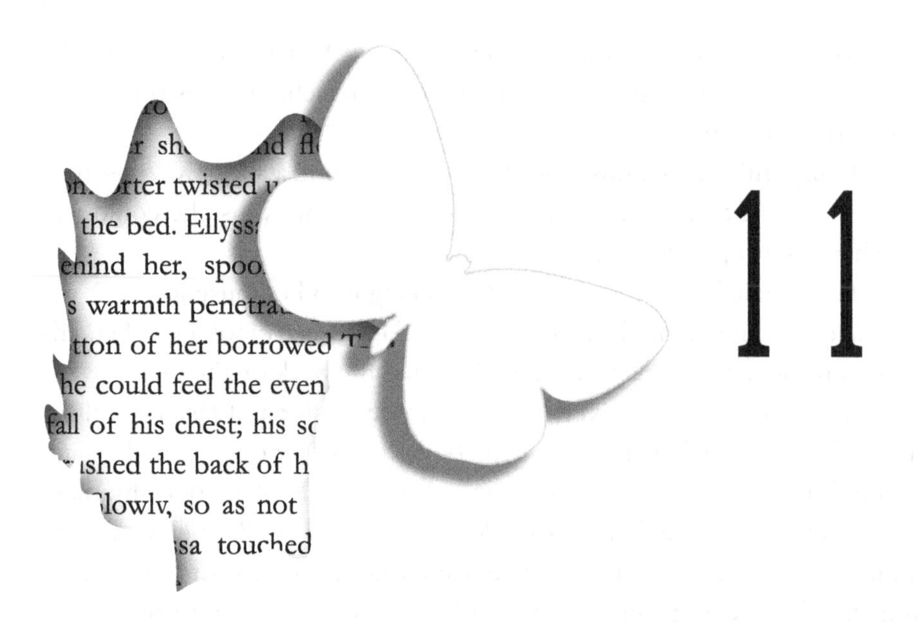

# 11

Early-morning sun peeked into the room and crept over the lavender sheets and floral-print comforter that lay twisted up at the foot of the bed. Ellyssa lay with Rein behind her, spooned together, his warmth penetrating the thin cotton of her borrowed T-shirt. She could feel the even rise and fall of his chest; his soft breath brushed the back of her neck.

Slowly, so as not to disturb Rein, Ellyssa touched her lips. They were swollen from his kisses and nips. Never in her life had she experienced anything like what the two of them that shared last night. Joy thrummed in her body, the afterglow muddling her mind. All memories of the last couple of days were fuzzy. All she could think about was the feel of Rein's body on hers, and the way his touch left her heart singing and her body craving.

How could her father believe emotions weakened people? The bond she shared with Rein felt strong and durable...unbreakable. The love Ellyssa held for him gave her reason. The bleakness she had felt last night seemed like a bad memory best left buried the past. They had a future to concentrate on. Their little band might be depleted, but if the missing were still alive, it was up to them to bring them back together and rebuild.

It was what Jordan's family, and the other survivors who had made it through the devastation of the War, had done. It's what Jordan would want them to do now.

Rein stirred behind her. A kiss landed on her earlobe.

"How do you feel this morning?" The question held undertones of worry.

Rolling over, Ellyssa looked at him, his chestnut hair mussed from sleep. His jade eyes held the same concern as his voice.

Ellyssa smiled; she couldn't help it. He looked like the fox who got caught in the henhouse. "I feel..." She chased after the right words "... complete."

Rein's lips curled up, lighting his face. "I wish I could express the love I feel for you."

She laughed. "I thought it is I who has trouble expressing."

He traced her lips with his finger. "Not when it comes to you. I love you, Ellyssa. I always will."

Ellyssa's heart fluttered, like a thousand butterflies launching into the air at once. Leaning over, Rein kissed her, softly. His full lips grazed hers, light as a feather. Her body responded, heart pushing molten heat through her body. Unable to control her innate response, Ellyssa slipped her arms around Rein and pressed her body into his. He pulled away, grinning slyly, knowingly. Warmth rose in her cheeks, but she didn't care. She did not want him to stop.

Ellyssa rested her hand on Rein's cheek. Morning stubble tickled beneath her fingers. "And I love you."

The grin Rein held started to grow, and he met her waiting mouth with more urgency. His tongue darted between her lips, and soon afterwards, Ellyssa found herself on the same precipice. This time, though, she flung herself over.

# 12

A soft knock at the door stirred Ellyssa from the light sleep she had slipped into, disrupting the dreams of Rein's soft touches.

"Are you awake?" said Sarah. "Breakfast is ready, and I cleaned your clothes." There was a brief hesitation. "Uh, I'll leave them on the table by the door."

"Thank you," said Rein.

Listening to the fading shuffle of the older woman's footsteps, Ellyssa rolled over and rested her head on Rein's chest. Her fingers lightly traced the contours of his chest. Right now, things seemed so peaceful, as if the troubles of the world no longer existed. She didn't want it to end. Why couldn't her life be like the insides of the little family homes she'd seen on her way to the railroad station when this had all started?

After a moment, Rein broke into her thoughts. "As much as I hate to, I guess we should get up."

"I know," Ellyssa sighed, moving off of him.

The bedroom door creaked as Rein retrieved the clothes and brought them back to her. They smelled like forest rain. Ellyssa slipped on the black T-shirt and camo pants and went to a dresser to use the brush she found resting by a mirror. She pulled the bristles through her clean hair, freeing the tangles. Ever since the ordeal in the Missouri woods a lifetime ago, the simple act of brushing her hair was something Ellyssa truly enjoyed.

Hair smoothed into a tight ponytail, she faced Rein. He was sitting on the foot of the bed, watching her.

"You're beautiful."

A light warmth reached her cheeks, and Ellyssa grinned. "Thank you."

Standing, Rein raked his fingers through his own hair and rearranged the chaotic strands into a new pattern. His hair was longer now, and the strands hung more limp than sticking straight up, but Ellyssa loved the feel of them wrapped around her fingers. Her body warmed at the thought.

Smiling, Rein held his hand out to her, and she went to him. He nuzzled her hair and inhaled. "You smell wonderful."

The warmth reached her face. Ellyssa wasn't sure how to respond. Was she to tell him how great he smelled, outdoorsy and manly? "Thank you," was what she finally settled on.

With his fingers laced in hers, they went to meet the day.

The scent of eggs and bacon greeted Ellyssa and Rein as they passed through the living room she'd admired the first time she'd been in there with Woody. With the chaos of last night, she'd forgotten how homey it'd felt. Like rest of the house, the room welcomed her, even with the cracks in the plaster from Dyllon's head.

"Um," said Rein, looking at the wall, "I guess I need to fix that." Sighing, he pulled her toward the French doors.

The sunny kitchen buzzed with activity. Her grey hair pulled into a tight bun, Sarah wore a plaid blue dress and was performing baking magic at the oven. She pulled out a hot pan of biscuits.

Still wearing overalls, Tim was hunched over a map, pulling on his beard thoughtfully. He looked up when they entered and beckoned to Rein. Woody was wearing the same black shirt and camo pants as Ellyssa and Rein, his ash-blond hair combed away from his face. He turned with a stack of plates in his hand and smiled when he noticed Ellyssa. Then, slowly, the grin fell as his eyes flicked to their hands.

Completely confused, Ellyssa stared back at him until he looked away and set the plates on the table. He placed one in front of every chair, not making eye contact with her.

Ellyssa's frown deepened as she watched Woody. She couldn't figure him out. Once in awhile, he acted like her pillar of strength; other times, he would give her weird looks and act like he was now—standoffish.

Didn't he know his friendship meant as much to her as Rein's love? Ever since the day Jordan had passed away, Woody had been there for her, understanding her when she hadn't even understood herself.

And if not for his help, Ellyssa's mission to save Rein would not have ended in success. She could never thank him enough. Maybe that was the problem; Woody didn't understand how grateful she was and how much he meant to her. She made a mental note to tell him the next time they were alone.

As Ellyssa took a seat next to Rein to listen in on the discussion he was having with Tim, Trista bounced in, exuberant as ever, as if all that'd transpired hadn't happened. Her braided blonde hair flipped with each step. She wore a purple knit sweater and blue jeans that hugged her shape and long legs.

Ellyssa looked at her drab black shirt. Never in her life had she been permitted to wear regular clothes. At The Center, they had worn white. When she had escaped, she had worn worker attire. And even now, she still wore a uniform of a black T and camos.

"Good morning," Trista said as she took a seat next to Woody.

"Where'd you get the clothes?" Ellyssa asked.

"Dyllon brought them to me." Her nose curled, looking cute, when she mentioned his name.

"I need to speak to you about him," said Rein.

Like a switch was flipped, in an instant all the cheerfulness melted right off Trista's face as her eyes cut over to Rein. "There is nothing to discuss. I've made myself perfectly clear."

Rein ignored her. "Woody and I discussed the...relationship you two seem to have developed."

"Which is none of your business."

Woody held his hand up at Rein. "Look," he said, diplomatically, "I know he has done a lot for you...for us. And we are grateful that he saved your life, but you have to admit, he has been trained differently than all the other defectors that we'd brought in. We've never had anyone with his background before. What if he changes his mind when push comes to shove?"

"Plus, with what happened, how do you expect me to trust him?" Rein asked, his tone calm, trying for Woody's approach.

It didn't work. Fury pinched Trista's face, and she sat there for a moment, speechless, eyes turning to ice.

Ellyssa had never seen Trista so angry, and that included last night. The same grey cloud of tension rolled into the kitchen again.

"The same way you trusted *her*," Trista snapped, an accusatory finger pointing at Ellyssa.

Like Trista had slapped her, Ellyssa recoiled. That was the second time Trista had alluded to her. Ellyssa sat shocked for a moment. Apparently, trust was something Trista wanted but yet still questioned. Without a second thought, Ellyssa shifted her wall to block the unwelcome buzzing and opened the door to Trista's thoughts, and then understood.

Trista blamed Ellyssa. Blamed her for their discovery, for her family being murdered, blamed her for everything. The lump of guilt stirred and reared its ugly head.

The blonde met Ellyssa's eyes. Comprehension flicked across Trista's face, followed by horror. She knew.

"Look, I—I'm sorry."

"No need," Ellyssa muttered.

Rein's gaze slid between her and Trista. "What?"

Ellyssa shook her head. "It doesn't matter."

Even with everyone around her, all eyes cast toward her, Ellyssa felt alone. Nothing more than a replay of when Jason had attacked her. Then, just like now, Ellyssa was the outsider. After all, Ellyssa was from the breed meant to destroy them. Why should any of them trust her? Ellyssa's sins exceeded Dyllon's.

Not only that, but Trista's sentiments matched her own. Regardless of what Rein or Woody said, it was Ellyssa who had brought death to the old coal mine the moment Rein had decided to save her life.

Hurt swelled in Ellyssa, and tears pricked her eyes. She couldn't take any more. The onslaught of emotions, the slithering guilt she couldn't shake, the love she felt for Rein, the sorrow, the confusion. Too much. She blanked, shoving away the swirling sensations, her soldiering instincts sliding into place. Comfortable skin.

"What is it?" Rein asked, his eyebrow dipping down in concern.

Ellyssa started to stand. "Nothing. If you will excuse me, please." She could hear the familiar monotonous tone in her voice, but she didn't care.

"No." Trista shot up and rushed around the table. "I don't really feel that way."

Ellyssa knew that was a lie. "You do not have to explain yourself."

"What did you do, Trista? What were you thinking?" asked Woody, apparently understanding that unspoken words had been exchanged.

Catching on, Rein pulled himself to his feet and wrapped a protective arm around Ellyssa.

His touch felt strange to her, foreign, and she felt herself go rigid. Part of her wanted to shrug his arm off, but deep inside the part she shoved down fought to break free. Despite her sloughing of the turmoil raging inside her, the one thing she didn't want to lose was the way Rein had elicited awareness in her, like he'd woken her from a deep sleep. Ellyssa struggled between keeping her guard up and letting the hurt consume her. She definitely knew she didn't want a repeat of last night, when she'd broken down.

"How could you?" Rein asked, directing his question toward Trista.

Ignoring them both, Trista reached down and wrapped her fingers around Ellyssa's. Ellyssa yanked her hand away.

For a moment, Trista stared at her empty hand before she spoke. "No, I do need to explain. I don't blame you. I swear I don't. It was just the heat of the moment. I just..." She sighed. "I just don't understand. You were born and raised at The Center. You were bred to be superior to all of us, a soldier to destroy us, and they're giving me a hard time about Dyllon. Despite what he did in the past, he's been helping us."

Trista's blue eyes begged for understanding. "Just like you are now. Read my mind now. You'll see. I don't blame you."

"No. I should not have pried to begin with."

"Please."

Ellyssa didn't know if it was the desperation in Trista's voice, or how strange Rein's touch had felt, which she didn't like, but her resolve slipped. The soldiering half of her would always be part of her, but not as armor whenever she felt overwhelmed. This new self was her true self. It had lain in wait to break free for years, responding to Jeremy when he'd been dragged in by the *Gestapo* back at The Center. Jordan had thought Jeremy reached out to Ellyssa because he could see through the thick barrier and into her soul. She'd believed Jordan to be right. There *was* more to her.

Ellyssa could understand why Trista felt the way she did. It wasn't fair. Dyllon had saved her life, and Trista felt a strong bond with him, not much different than the bond Ellyssa shared with Rein.

Of course, the strike Dyllon had against him was his involvement with the *Kripo*, Detective Angela Petersen, which had led to Rein's capture and ultimately his torture. The captain would definitely have to prove himself to Rein and Woody.

The devastation on Trista's face spoke volumes. She truly was sorry for what she'd thought, and Ellyssa had had no right to poke in her head. Dismissing her instinct to shut down, Ellyssa shed the pain, controlled the whirlwind of emotions.

"I'm not going to read your mind. I believe you."

Relief bled through the desperation as air rushed from Trista's lungs. She looked hopefully at Ellyssa.

"You read his mind, too. Tell them that he isn't going to betray us."

This time, Ellyssa reached down and took Trista's hand. "From what I read last night, he isn't. No betrayal, and no regret for the choices he made. He is completely devoted to you." A smug look climbed across Trista's face. She started to turn around to gloat at Rein and Woody, but Ellyssa stopped her. "But Woody is right," she continued. "He might not be planning anything now, but that doesn't mean he can't in the future."

Rein crossed his arms. "My sentiments exactly."

"Shut up, Rein," Trista said, whipping around, red glowing on her cheeks. "You're the one who started all of this."

"I have a better idea," Sarah said, dropping the pan of biscuits on the table. "All of you shut up." The corners of Sarah's mouth dipped in disapproval, deepening her wrinkles. Everyone, including her husband, stared at her, stunned into silence. "All of you should be ashamed of yourselves. How can you expect to work together when all you do is bicker? You can't act like this. Don't you young fools know the easiest way to be defeated is from within? Not just from within a group, but within yourselves.

"You hadn't seen each other for close to three weeks or so; Woody and Ellyssa brought Rein back, Trista's alive, and this is what you do. This is a time to celebrate, not fight. And that is exactly what we are going to do.

"There will be no more of this squabbling. Rein and Woody, you will give Dyllon a chance to prove himself. I know with what had happened it'll be hard, and you haven't been with him for as long as we have, but I believe he is a good man." She grabbed a plate of bacon and a bowl of eggs and placed them on the table.

"Now, you and you and you," Sarah said, pointing at Rein, Woody and Ellyssa, "dig in. You look like skeletons. And you"— her finger singled out Tim—"put that map away. There's plenty of time for that after breakfast."

Tim grumbled something about "Mrs. Bossy" but folded up the map before Ellyssa had a chance to see what he'd been showing Rein before the disagreement.

Proud of herself, Sarah planted her hands on her hips. "Well, what're you waiting for? Get to eating."

Everyone responded at once.

Ellyssa spooned German potatoes onto her plate along with bacon, a hefty helping of eggs, and two biscuits. The rest of the food disappeared off the table in moments.

Sarah looked pleased at the enthusiasm in which the food she'd made disappeared, even with the awkward silence that lingered over the table. As time passed, though, tongues loosened. The sunshine ambience broke through the cloud.

Ellyssa smiled. She was sharing a meal with friends and the man she loved. When she thought about it, and not counting the community dinners or the sterility and lack of conversation during The Center's meals, this was the first true family-style get-together she'd ever experienced. It reminded her of an American painting her father had once show her. "Freedom from Want, they called this," he'd said in a mocking tone. Ellyssa had never understood why she'd felt drawn to it—until that moment.

Enjoying the moment, Ellyssa observed everyone else. Rein and Tim were huddled over the map that had miraculously reappeared back on the table, folded into eighths. Trista laughed at something Sarah had said. Then her gaze met Woody's. She didn't know how long he'd been watching her, but his grey eyes examined her like she was an experiment.

Cocking an eyebrow, Woody popped a piece of bacon in his mouth. The right corner of his lips curled into a lopsided smile.

Ellyssa wondered what that meant.

Just a few minutes ago, before the big blowout, Woody had been aloof, refusing to look at her, and now he was watching her again. Once in a while, his mood swings seemed to slough and re-form faster than Trista's.

As Woody smile grew, defining his cheekbones, Ellyssa had a huge urge to slide inside his head and see what gears were turning. He closed his eyes slowly, then opened them, cat-like, the grey hiding unknown meaning.

He was an enigma.

Narrowing her eyelids, Ellyssa struggled with the wrongdoing of just taking a peek. Doing so would put a lot of unanswered questions to rest. Then again, with what had just happened with Trista... Before she had a chance to weigh the consequences, Trista's voice interrupted her thoughts.

"Ellyssa," Trista said. "I bet Dyllon brought something that would fit you."

"What? Really?" asked Ellyssa.

Trista nodded. "There's a blue cardigan hanging in my closet. It'll make your eyes go BAM."

"Bam?" The word felt strange on her tongue. Ellyssa couldn't help but smile. This was the Trista she'd grown to appreciate.

"Yeah." Trista nodded. "BAM. You'll see what I mean."

For rest of the meal, everyone seemed to have pushed away the problems that loomed ahead, like an ominous shadow lurking in the corner. Ellyssa watched the easy exchanges within the small group—the playfulness, the teasing, how they interacted with each other. It was beautiful, and different, and the perfect way to spend her first family-style meal. All these years, she'd missed out on so much, all because of her father's sick desires.

The thought pulled at her heart because the carefree moment wouldn't last long. It couldn't, in spite of Sarah's words.

Her father and siblings might be dead, The Center destroyed, but other members of *their* family were still gone, their whereabouts unknown.

Ellyssa would find them.

# 13

Ellyssa looked through the window and watched Trista and Sarah with their coats bundled tight around their necks slip into the garage to grab supplies. Nothing they needed her help with.

Behind Ellyssa, Tim had the map spread across the table again. For the last several minutes, he'd been discussing the locations of each of the concentration camps with Rein and Woody. She already knew where the camps were located; the problem was she hadn't a clue where to even begin looking.

Ellyssa's gaze drifted over the backyard. Patches of frozen grass poked yellow stalks through the thin layer of snow; a light breeze pushed the bare branches of the trees. Everything seemed peaceful, normal. Completely opposite of the anxiousness building in Ellyssa's stomach.

She reached inside her pocket and worried the cave pearl.

For the first time in weeks, her hands felt bound. Ellyssa wasn't accustomed to it. She was a person of action. The majority of her life, she'd trained. For the last couple of months, she'd fled, felt emotions, adopted a new family and lifestyle, and fallen in love. Even when Rein had been captured, Ellyssa had immediately responded. But now, there was nothing left to do but wait...and worry. The more time that passed, the chances of finding anyone grew closer to nil.

The thought drove her crazy. Releasing the round stone, Ellyssa fisted her hands in frustration.

"Ellyssa, what do you think?" Rein asked.

"I told you already, I don't know," she snapped.

Rein's and Woody's heads snapped up, and Ellyssa widened her eyes in surprise. Although anger was a sensation that was definitely ingrained in her, lying in wait like a snake ready to strike, it wasn't often her voice held the emotion. As a matter of fact, until recently, her voice had not held any type of inflection at all. Once in a while, it amazed her when she paid attention to the sound or the shifting manner in which she spoke...even the fading of her German accent.

"I'm sorry," Ellyssa stated, shrugging—her uncomfortable or unsure response. "I'm just feeling...useless." Inhaling deeply, she walked over to the table. "To answer your question, I don't know. At first, I would have assumed they would be sent to southern Missouri." She pointed to an area south of a small town previously known as Waynesville. "It's the closest. But then again, the police are probably leery of help from contacts because of all that's happened, which would cross out any of the camps near the Chicago area and around here." She sighed. "So that leaves basically everywhere else."

Rubbing his face, Rein leaned back in the chair. "I guess we have no option but to wait to see if Dyllon can find a location."

"Or," said Tim, "maybe we'll hear something from one of the other contacts."

Thoughtfully, Ellyssa pursed her lips together. "How many are there?"

"Haven't the slightest, my dear. There could be hundreds, thousands. The farthest we've ever ventured is Chicago, and it took us over twenty years or so to establish contact with them."

"When everyone is hiding, it's hard to find each other," Woody said.

"Renegades don't talk. We don't know things about each other, like who else our contacts helped...if anybody." Rein added. He reached up and grasped Ellyssa's hand, giving it a little squeeze of understanding. "Right, Tim?"

"It's true. You know I've helped others," Rein nodded at Tim's words, "but I can't tell you who or what or why. Most of the time, I don't even know. For instance," he said to Ellyssa, "your population was the biggest I knew about, helped with supplies and such for years, and

I still didn't know everyone there. Hell, I didn't know how many lived there...until recent events."

Tim stroked his beard. "Unfortunately, it takes a long time for a network to be established. If that has helped us or hindered us, I don't know. We have to tread carefully, though. So far, we've been lucky."

"Certainly, there are populations bigger than ours. Someone who knows of us, someone you report to?"

Tim shook his head. "No, no one we answer to. We just kind of worked together, learning bits of information here and there. Last night, I asked for any information leading to where new prisoners might have been taken."

"Who'd you ask?"

"Our contacts in Kansas City. They're our best source of information for the Resistance...even if it *is* usually outdated."

Ellyssa frowned. "Not by computer, right? The government keeps close tabs on all activity."

Tim smiled. "Nope. A radio. A low frequency that so far has not been detected. But we haven't heard anything from them. The last transmission we received was word about Chicago, and that was three weeks ago. Either the contacts in Kansas City have been discovered, or they are keeping a very low profile."

A radio? Except for handhelds used by the police during investigations, the out-of-date technology was obsolete. Ellyssa couldn't believe the technology they used to benefit their group. The only time she'd seen a radio was in a textbook. "You have a radio?"

Tim nodded.

"Aren't you worried that, if they've been captured, any transmission could be intercepted?"

"Nope," Tim said. "Thanks to Woody, the frequencies are short, and we use a code."

Woody grinned and tipped his head. "Plus, we change channels for added precaution. Of course, that was when we had Davis to relay the messages."

An image of a broken man emerged unbidden in Ellyssa's mind, one that she had retrieved from Woody's frantic thoughts when he'd escaped from Detective Petersen—when Rein had been captured.

Another death that'd happened during her father's relentless search for her.

"Can I see it?" Ellyssa asked.

"Sure. I'll show you tonight."

Ellyssa turned around as the back door opened. Sarah came in, lugging a box, followed by Trista's giggling.

"What are you four conspiring about?" asked Sarah.

Ellyssa took the box from the older woman and put it on a counter. "A lot of stuff. Mostly the other contacts."

Sarah washed her hands. "Oh. What about them?"

"I was wondering how big the Resistance was."

"I couldn't even begin to imagine," said Sarah. "We've heard so many rumors through the years."

The older woman went behind Tim and placed her hands on his shoulders. Although Ellyssa had rarely see them touch, the love they shared was evident. She wondered if she and Rein would ever enjoy the luxury of growing old together, peacefully, in a home of their own. If she was ever given an opportunity, she knew she was going to decorate the kitchen with sunflowers.

"Including the rumors about the facilities in Texas, DC, and California," Tim continued.

Ellyssa's eyebrows scrunched together. "Facilities?"

"Right before America entered the war, there were rumors milling about how to protect the ideology of freedom. Supposedly, huge underground chambers were built in Texas, DC, and California, each big enough to support the population of a small city. Of course, no evidence existed as to whether that was true or not. Just rumors."

Woody laughed. "Those are just Renegades' wishful thinking. Besides, DC is nothing more than a wasteland. The place is uninhabitable."

What Woody said was true. Washington DC, where the President at one time had resided, where the whole idea of democracy had gone up in a giant mushroom cloud, was nothing more than a field of blackened dirt. All the monuments and the White House lay in utter ruin after Hitler ordered the bombing, August first, nineteen forty-five. The devastation had been astounding, and it was the first and only time a fission bomb was detonated.

Since then, all atomic weapons had been dismantled. Of course, since Hitler had seized power, there had been no use for them. World domination had resulted, along with the mass killings of millions of people to make way for the perfect society.

D.C. was contaminated, and no population lived anywhere within two hundred kilometers. There wasn't any way a group of Renegades lived there.

# 14

Aalexis picked a chunk of plaster off the ground. Although the remnants of The Center were piled into big heaps of twisted metal, concrete and debris, the area was still a disaster. Track tractors and backhoes moved mounds of dirt around, clearing space for the new foundation. Bundles of steel beams were stacked next to the site.

The workers wearing dark brown carpenter pants and thick brown jackets milled around her and Xaver; their tools, dangling from leather belts, clinked together. As the inferiors strolled about, none made eye contact with her or even questioned why two young people were in such a dangerous zone. Rules set forth for regular humans did not apply to Xaver or her. Besides, this was their building now.

Disgusted at the slow rate of rebuilding, Aalexis dropped the piece of plaster. It broke into smaller pieces on impact, and dust plumed.

Ellyssa had ruined everything.

"Come," said Xaver.

Aalexis walked next to Xaver, his shield in place. Inside his protective cocoon, she could feel him, and his scent was overpowering. They were two things she chose to ignore.

"Where are you taking me?"

"I have something that should please you."

*Please?* Briefly, Aalexis entertained the idea of the sensation she'd felt on the plane as pleasing. Is that what the stirring had been? She quickly disregarded the insanity. She didn't feel pleasure. She didn't feel anything except anger...hatred. Those were the emotions that fueled Aalexis' life.

Xaver stopped at a modular building; the door was marked *Authorized Personnel Only* in bold, black letters. Two huge locks secured the building.

"What?"

"You will see."

Xaver's lips twitched, like he was trying to suppress a smile, and he pressed them tight together. He punched in a combination and opened the door to an office with a large metallic desk and a black leather chair. A computer sat on top of the desk. Light from the overhead fluorescents reflected on the polished white tile. The freshly painted walls held no paintings or decorations. The two bookshelves behind the desk were bare. A high-powered compound microscope, petri dishes, nano-sieves and electric field conductors waited on top of two metal tables pushed to the side of the room. The odor of disinfectant scented the air.

Everything was clean, sterile. Home.

Standing at the door, uncomprehending, Aalexis was unsure what her reaction should be. Everything inside her, everything she'd been trained to do, conflicted with a growing warm glow, different from the previous heat in her midsection.

No one had ever given her anything.

Ever.

Aalexis had an overwhelming urge to squeeze Xaver's hand.

She glanced at her brother; Xaver's face held no expression, but his eyes seemed alive as he watched her. Something was happening to Aalexis, to Xaver, to both of them.

These alien sensations, swirling and heating her insides, were forbidden. They brought weakness.

And Aalexis was not weak.

As a matter of fact, Aalexis' ability placed her even above Xaver, and definitely Ellyssa. Her father had instructed Xaver to protect her at all costs, not the other way around. That alone proved her superiority.

Tossing water on the building glow of the emotional barrage, Aalexis stepped into her small lab. Warm air greeted her. "This will suffice for the time being," she said, careful that her voice held nothing more than flatness.

"I thought it would do for experimental purposes, until we find Ellyssa." Xaver went behind the desk and flipped on the computer. "I have something else for you, too," he said, withdrawing a memory stick from his pocket. "*Der Vater's* notes."

Aalexis relieved him of the drive and slipped it into the port. "I am glad you were able to extract them from what was left of *der Vater's* hard drive." After taking a seat, she clicked on the computer icon, and the files of her father's livelihood filled the screen.

She highlighted the one marked *Subject 74*, her number, and double-clicked it open. There were several notes starting from the time she'd been born to the most recent experiments—her manipulation of weights, the frame-by-frame of bullets being fired at her, and then the torture of the human subjects, including Rein.

After clicking on Rein's icon, Aalexis watched as the male her sister seemed to care for writhed on the ground, finding no relief from the pain. She pressed the back button and he disappeared. Files filled the screen again.

Scanning quickly through the notes, she highlighted another subfile titled *Genetic Sequence*. She clicked on it. A movie link opened. Her father's image came into view, and she felt a tinge of a peculiar sensation. Loss? Anger flared. *Ellyssa will pay for his demise.*

Her father spoke in German as he explained the steps of how he'd isolated the genetic sequence responsible for Aalexis' ability. His voice sounded just the way she remembered it.

"Yes," she said, looking at Xaver, "this will be a start."

"You understand," he responded, "that we do not need Ellyssa. We can pick up from where *der Vater* stopped. Our abilities and intelligence will produce a more than adequate soldier. We can create the next generation."

"Yes, but *der Vater* wanted Ellyssa for a reason. We have already lost the abilities of Micah and Ahron's DNA in the destruction." She rolled her chair to the side so that he could see his image playing across the screen. "He wanted more than *adequate*. I think we should honor his wishes. Ellyssa needs to be brought home."

Xaver sat silently as he watched their father's instructions for the combination of the genes. The simplicity of the procedure was almost ludicrous. As much as Aalexis hated to admit it, her father had had his limitations. His genes were superior compared to society's, and he was a genius by normal standards, but he was inferior nevertheless.

Of course, if not for his intellect and his visions, Xaver and she would not be. He should be eulogized for that fact alone. Aalexis and Xaver would make sure Dr. Hirch's legend and vision would be honored next to Hitler's—founders who had orchestrated the purification of the human model.

After a couple of minutes, Xaver nodded once. "I agree. We will continue where he left off. We are his new evolution of humanity, and we will use our DNA to bring forth the next evolution."

"This will be appropriate for gene isolation," she said, waving her hand at the silver tables, "but we will need a full, functioning lab by the end of the month."

"I will contact the foreman."

"Make sure he understands the importance of the project."

"I will have them bring inferiors from a camp. They should be sufficient in cleaning the area, instead of hired workers wasting time with such a miniscule task."

Heat warmed Aalexis' fingers. She looked down and noticed how close her brother's hand was to hers, resting next to the keyboard. She moved away. Something, indeed, was happening to her. She glanced at Xaver, but he was studying the computer screen again.

Maybe she needed to train? Maybe that was the cause of the strangeness she'd been feeling. It made sense. Aalexis hadn't had the luxury of physical exercise and practicing her techniques since Ellyssa had destroyed their home. She harbored pent-up energy. Just the thought of releasing the tension made Aalexis feel better.

"I want another building erected for us to train."

"I think that is a good idea," Xaver stated. "We must maintain our physical performance. I will instruct the foreman."

He clicked another folder marked *Subject 71*. A picture of Xaver's DNA crossed the screen. A section of the genetic code set apart from rest of the structure, showing the exact location of his gift.

As Aalexis watched her father, she started to simplify his techniques. There were many steps he could've bypassed if he'd only understood the workings of molecular structures, the way they moved, the energy they held.

Aalexis' brain whirled with the mechanics.

Ellyssa stared in awe at her reflection in the dresser mirror. Trista had been right.

BAM!

Her eyes appeared even more blue—a darker blue—than usual, like the sky just before the sun disappeared behind the horizon. And Trista had fixed her hair so the blonde cascaded over her shoulders, like silken thread.

"I told you," Trista said. "Didn't I tell you?"

Dumbfounded, Ellyssa nodded.

The blue cardigan hugged her curves in all the right places and overlapped across her chest, where cleavage peeked shyly. A black belt secured the sweater on the right side. The dark jeans were slim-fitted and clung to her legs.

After all the years dressed in uniforms, drab and colorless, civilian clothes seemed almost sacrilegious. Everything within Ellyssa felt disjointed, so unlike her. But she liked it. A lot. Funny how something as insignificant as clothing could make such a difference in appearance. In a weird way, Ellyssa felt freed, as if this small change separated her further from the monster her father had tried to create.

"Now," Trista said, "go like this."

Ellyssa pulled her eyes away from the mirror and glanced at Trista. Her friend stood there with a gaped mouth and rounded eyes, all serious. She tried to mimic Trista, but Ellyssa's mouth kept curving in to a hopeless smile. She couldn't help it; Trista's expression was ridiculous.

"Come on, now. Haven't you ever worn lipstick?"

"Once," she answered, her memories shifting to the night when she'd escaped from The Center.

"I know what you mean. Makeup hasn't been a top priority, living underground. We better enjoy it while we can. So, go like this." Trista opened her mouth again.

Struggling to keep a straight face, Ellyssa did as instructed, and Trista applied the cosmetic.

"Now, go like this." Her friend rubbed her lips together, that made a popping noise when they separated.

Ellyssa copied the action.

"Now this." Trista puckered her lips together and made a smooching sound.

Ellyssa cocked an eyebrow, but did as requested.

Trista started laughing. "I'm just messing with you."

Chagrin colored Ellyssa's cheeks. "Oh."

"Now look."

At a glance in the mirror, red colored a pouty appeal on Ellyssa's lips. Trista peeked over her shoulder.

"You're beautiful."

Ellyssa blushed again. "You, too." She faced her friend. "Thank you for the clothes."

Beaming, Trista placed the lipstick back on the dresser, and then crawled onto the four-poster bed. She sat with her legs crossed beneath her. "So," she said, her hand running across the violet bedspread, "you and Rein, huh?"

Ellyssa couldn't help the sappy grin that seeped onto her face. "Yeah."

"I knew something was up between the two of you before...well, you know. He's a great guy."

She remembered the last time Trista and she had shared in "girl-talk," what seemed like ages ago. Ellyssa had enjoyed it, the normality, even with the danger that had lurked in the form of her father. Much had changed since then; danger still lurked, her adopted family lay within a earthen tomb, and the others were missing. Ellyssa pushed away the sadness that threatened to storm within her.

"I think so, too," Ellyssa said, sitting across from her. "You and Dyllon?"

Pulling a throw pillow onto her lap, Trista didn't answer right away. After a moment, she met Ellyssa's eyes. "I know it's silly; we just met, but I think I love him."

Ellyssa didn't know what to say. Should she congratulate her or condemn her? "Really?"

"Yeah. We've been through a lot together. I know you don't understand," she said, fiddling with the thick fringe on the pillow.

Trista was wrong about that. Ellyssa understood completely. That didn't make her feel any more comfortable, though. She liked talking to Trista, but words still failed her. "Um..."

Trista's hand shot out and grabbed Ellyssa's wrist. "Please, don't say anything to Rein or Woody. Not yet. I just don't want to hear it."

Ellyssa gazed into Trista's pleading eyes, the blue filled with apprehension. She couldn't blame her, but then again, Ellyssa could understand Woody and Rein's point of view. Dyllon had helped the detective. Whether or not the captain felt sorrow for his act now made no difference. Especially in Rein's eyes.

"Promise me."

"Okay."

A small smile flicked across Trista's lips. "Thank you."

"They're going to figure it out soon enough."

"I know. But I'm tired of arguing with them. Mostly because, no matter what they say, I'm going to do what I want. So arguing is pointless, right?"

Ellyssa nodded.

Trista's smile brightening, she glanced at the clock. The first number flicked from two to three. "He should be here soon." Then, in true Trista style, her face shifted from happiness to questioning. Her brows met at the bridge of her nose. "You don't really think he'd betray us, do you?"

Ellyssa shrugged. "It's impossible to tell, but as of yesterday, there was nothing to indicate betrayal. Dyllon was sincere in everything he said."

"I thought so," Trista said, the smile on her face again.

As if on cue, from the kitchen, Ellyssa heard Sarah greet the yellow-haired male.

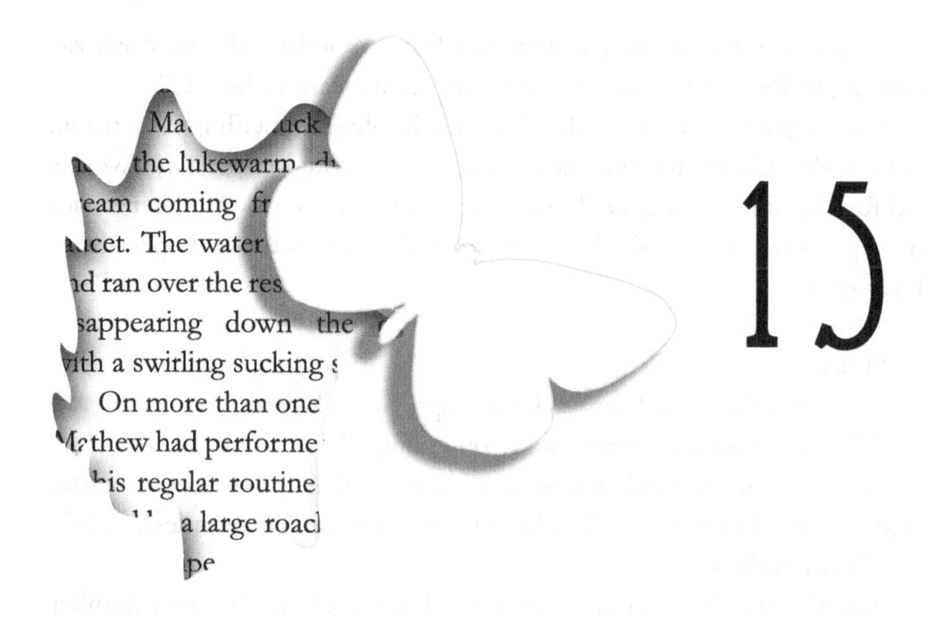

# 15

Gripping the edges of the metal sink bolted to the concrete blocks, Mathew stuck his head under the lukewarm, discolored stream coming from the rusty faucet. The water hit the crown and ran over the rest of his head, disappearing down the drain with a swirling sucking sound.

On more than one occasion, Mathew had performed this part of his regular routine and been greeted by a large roach crawling from the pipe. His gaze stayed locked on the gaping hole, just in case one decided to surprise him. How he hated the six-legged creatures, along with everything else in the living hell he now endured.

Mathew lifted his head and met his reflection in the lackluster excuse for a mirror. It, too, was made out of the same material as the sink, bolted to the wall, no glass to break off and end miserable existences. No, the commanders of such camps didn't want to be deprived of the joy of torture, of ending those miserable existences themselves.

Since Mathew had arrived, he must've lost at least thirty pounds. His cheekbones jutted from his face and the sides were sunken in, skull-like. Thin, cracked lips sliced a grim line.

He flinched from the distorted image staring at him with sunken eyes, the light brown dull and gaunt. Lifeless. No hint of the warmth or humor that once lived within the depths. It scared him to look into those dead eyes, knowing they belonged to him, but he forced his lids back and met the stranger in the reflection. Nothing more than a shadow of his previous self, his spirit on the verge of breaking.

There were times in the abandoned coal mine when food had been scarce, but Mathew would happily return to those times now. The pangs he experienced here gnawed constantly at his midsection as if trying to devour the lining of his stomach.

His head looked huge on his skinny neck and overly defined collarbone, like the bobble-head doll one of the group members had found during a food raid.

A slight pull tugged at Mathew's lips, reminiscent of a smile, as he remembered how happy the young boy—*what was his name? Darrel?*—Darrel had been when his father had given the toy to him.

It bothered him how hard names were to recall once in a while. Fading memories of better times. And, of course, Darrel was no longer.

Running his hand over his newly buzzed cut, the stubble rough against his fingers, Mathew rubbed the water away vigorously as he turned around. Fifty bunk beds, with filthy, stained mattresses so thin the springs poked through, lined the grey concrete walls. Forty-two mattresses were occupied, thirty-one by members of his family; the other eleven had already been there. Originally, there had been fifteen other occupants; four had been incinerated since Mathew's arrival.

Their misery was over.

Mathew assumed the female barracks held no special amenities and looked the same. Since the day they'd emerged from the bus, he hadn't seen any of the women. The guards kept them separated, divided by a four-meter concrete wall, dividing the old military base in half. He didn't know if any of them were alive, and didn't dwell on something he couldn't control.

He had to cope.

A chill wracked Mathew's body, originating from his toes and hitting his spine, probably from his cold head and the damp collar of his striped pyjamas. The barracks were drafty, icy air creeping in under the door and oozing through the porous cement. Needing to warm up, he walked over to the small potbelly stove.

Getting sick wasn't an option. With immunization against viruses, such as the common cold, disease really was a thing of the past for regular society, but not so for Renegades. They didn't have that luxury. Regardless of the threat of ailment, the prisoners were forced to work in the freezing cold until their legs crumpled.

Mathew laughed out loud, the sound more cackle-like than a real laugh.

After the hell the mini-version of Ellyssa had dragged Mathew through, worry over becoming ill seemed insignificant. The faux flames that had licked his insides, the constant burn, was beyond intense. He'd passed out more than once, his body's defense mechanism. Even after the true pain diminished, phantom fire, scorched into the memory of his brain, would shoot through his body if he thought about it too long.

"What's so funny?" Eric asked, drawing Mathew from his thoughts.

Mathew glanced over at the former councilmember, back when they'd actually had a council. His old friend clapped him weakly on the back. Light from the dim, buzzing fluorescents shone on his caramel bald head, the light brown stubble of his hair lost within the color. His skin pulled across his bony skeleton, and his prison attire swallowed his thin frame.

Mathew scanned the other inmates, the undesirables, shuffling from one place to the other or lying on top of the thin mattresses, like lifeless lumps. Misery hung over their heads, like ominous clouds of doom.

They all looked alike—same clothes, same buzzed head, same hollowed expression, same ghoulish lumber. If not for the differing hues of skin color, they'd be carbon copies of each other. Dehumanizing effect. More efficient to file them into the camp, then out to the incinerator.

If Mathew didn't stop it, he was going to take a ride on the train to crazy town, first class.

"Nothing," Mathew finally replied. "There isn't one damn thing funny."

Eric nodded in understanding, looking down at his feet. "You know," he said, "you can't let them win. If you do, then it's over for all of us."

For some unforeseen reason, the survivors of the group looked up to Mathew, as if he were the unsung leader of the dead-man brigade. That strange laugh bubbled in the back of his throat; Mathew swallowed it back down. Good God, he already had purchased the crazy ticket.

Mathew was definitely in no shape to be some form of spokesman.

The true leader, Jordan, lay in a grave back in Missouri; one candidate had been captured, the other had left to save him with Ellyssa. Mathew wondered if any of them were still alive.

"I never asked for this. Let someone else have the honor."

"They look up to you." Eric lifted his head and met Mathew's eyes before he turned and dragged his ragged body back to his bunk.

Eric was right. Whether Mathew wanted the honor or not, the responsibility burdened his shoulders. It was one thing to give up on himself, but to drag everyone else with him was more than his conscience could handle. If Mathew didn't pull out of this funk that threatened to swallow him, he'd never make it. And if he didn't make, a lot of the others would give up hope too.

Mathew rubbed his face with the palms of his hands, trying to scrub away the despair. He couldn't let hope slip through his fingers, not of his own accord. If he was to die in this desolate place, it'd be by the enemies' hands.

The door of the barracks swung opened and pounded against the wall. Icy air rushed through the opening, sapping away what little warmth the potbelly stove provided. Two soldiers walked in, wearing long, wool coats and helmets held secure with chinstraps; rifles hung over their shoulders.

Like Pavlov's dogs, everyone scurried to the front of their bunks and stood at attention. Fear of pain and death was what moved the inmates with more zeal than they showed when alone—an effective, albeit immoral, way to program people.

Mathew moved just as fast as the others and stood with his fellow prisoners. The guards moved through the line, then turned toward him. Their helmets cast half of their face in a shadows where their eyes hid.

"Are you the one they call Doc?" asked the broader one on the left.

Mathew's mouth dried at the question. Ellyssa's sister had been the last one to address him by his nickname, and then had led him into a storage room where she'd burned his insides. When he didn't answer right away, the thinner soldier on the right moved his hand to the crop he had holstered to his belt.

"Yes," Mathew squeaked. Actually squeaked, and the sound of his voice shamed him. He forced himself to swallow, then lifted his chin. "Yes," he restated, a bit more loudly.

A mocking smile spread across Mr. Broad's mouth, apparently finding amusement in Mathew's mouse-like behavior. If he had a gun, he would've blown the smile right off Mr. Broad's head, see what he had to smile about then.

"Come with us." Mr. Thin stepped to the side, affording Mathew room to step between the two of them.

This was it. He'd refused to play the informant, and these two soldiers were going to lead him to his death. Funny how life worked. Just a few minutes ago, he'd wallowed in his suffering, the idea of giving up tantalizing, and now, the thought of dying fed horror through his veins. He didn't want to die, not in this godforsaken place.

He lifted his chin and stepped between the deliverers of the dead man walking.

Mathew thought he'd been surprised when the guards led him past the old storage room, where pain had been lashed and burned into his mind. But when they'd led him past the little square building where smoke puffed from the small chimney—where four prisoners had fed the incinerator a few days ago—toward the rectangular building of the Commandant's office, surprise didn't even begin to cover how he felt. More like astonishment along with a deep-rooted sense of dread.

He couldn't imagine why they would take him to see the Commandant, but a dark corner of his mind screamed that death would've been a better alternative. Whatever the reason, it couldn't be good.

The two soldiers pushed him through the door, and Mathew stumbled into a warm room with a tiled floor polished to a glossy shine. A young man with honey-blond hair stood from behind a desk where papers were stacked in neat piles. Every metallic part, from the insignias to the buttons of his navy tunic, glinted under the lights.

Honey-Blond's mouth pulled into a grim line, and his look spoke disgust as his blue eyes flicked the length of Mathew's body. "Is this him?" he asked.

"Yes, sir," said Mr. Broad.

"He's filthy. Take him under the hose."

Rime coated Mathew's muscles and froze him in place. He'd been under the hose once before when he'd first shown up on the doorstep to hell. The pressure had filleted his skin, an experience he didn't want to repeat. And with the sub-freezing temperatures? An involuntary spasm shot up his spine.

By the look of the soldiers, they weren't too happy about it, either. Mr. Broad's jaw clenched as if trying to lock away choice words.

"Come on." Mr. Thin grabbed the scruff of Mathew's shirt and shoved him toward the door.

The smooth soles of his prison shoes slipped out from under Mathew, and his butt met the floor hard enough that his teeth clicked together. Before a punishment could be dished, Mathew scrambled to gain his footing, but the waxed surface of the tiles fought him every step of the way. His legs slipped out from under him again, and he found himself back at square one.

Mr. Broad's nostrils flared in irritation. "Get up, maggot."

Mr. Thin stepped forward and grabbed Mathew by his shirt collar, his eyes glinting with crazy sadistic joy, evidently enjoying the prospect of delivering pain. The larger soldier lurched forward, the riding crop already fisted in his hand, and swung. Pain exploded in a burst of stars when the soldier brought the leather handle down across the top of Mathew's head. Images spun in a blurry whirlpool, and bile rose in his esophagus. Mathew gagged.

"Stop it," a deep voice boomed.

The hand holding Mathew released him, and Mathew crumpled to the ground on his hands and knees, head hanging. The floor spun.

Leather soles shuffled, and a series of *Heils* followed.

"Your orders were to bring him unharmed."

Through the ringing in his ears, the voice sounded like the Commandant's, but that didn't make sense. Wasn't the concentration camp all about harming? Mathew shook his head and blinked his eyes. The floor slowly stopped the spin cycle.

"He was unwilling, sir."

"When I give an order, it is to be followed," The Commandant said in a dead calm voice. Mathew looked up at the man in the pristine uniform. He peered down at Mathew with steely blue eyes. Wrinkles crested his mouth as he sneered at him. "Corporal?"

"Yes, sir," said the man behind the desk.

"Go to the mess hall."

"Sir. Yes, sir."

More boot clicking and a short gust of wind blew through the lobby as the Corporal left.

"Bring him into the office, if you two idiots think you can handle the task." The commander performed an about-face and walked through the doorway.

"Yes, sir." The broader soldier reached down and yanked Mathew to his feet, forcefully. "Go on," he said, giving Mathew a push.

Dizziness still clinging to his peripheral vision, Mathew shuffled into the office. He stopped just inside the doorway and marveled at how civilized the office seemed. He didn't know what he'd expected. Some form of torture chamber? Definitely not the warmth of dark paneling and green upholstery, or the pictures hanging on the walls. It was hard for Mathew to imagine the commander as nothing more than a cruel monster, not someone with partially human characteristics, with family and friends who might actually miss him.

The Commandant went behind a elaborate desk, the grain a beautiful, deep reddish-brown, then extended his hand. "Have a seat."

Mathew glanced at the two soldiers standing behind him; they looked just as perplexed as him. Suspecting some form of retribution, Mathew hesitantly walked closer to the desk. The Commandant stared at him expectantly, which was different than his usual look of detestation. Mathew sat.

The Commandant flipped his head up. "Dismissed."

Mathew didn't need to turn around to know the soldiers were uncertain about leaving their commander unattended with a heathen such as himself. After a moment, though, they responded with a boot click and a *Heil*, then the door snicked closed, leaving Mathew alone with the superior officer.

As soon as the soldiers left, the commander sat across from Mathew. He leaned back in his leather chair and linked his fingers across his chest. "I assume you are wondering why I have commanded your presence."

Mathew's head throbbed from the crown of his head, down through his temples, into the back of his jaw, and the blood rushing from the thumping of his heart wasn't helping. "The question has crossed my mind, sir." He kept his voice steady, much different than the havoc running amok within his nerves. He gripped the arms of the chair.

"The girl, Aalexis, and her brother, Xaver, have taken an interest in you."

Wrinkles cut across Mathew's forehead. Of all the things he'd imagined, his imminent death included, he'd never expected that to come from the Commandant's mouth. A heaviness sank into the pit of his stomach. "Oh?"

"Do you know why?"

Mathew shook his head. "No, sir."

"Tell me about Ellyssa," he continued.

*Here we go again.* Lips pressing into a tight line, Mathew mentally rolled his eyes.

"Still not going to talk?" said the Commandant.

Face hardening into stone, the officer leaned forward in his chair, the desk, thankfully, separating the two men by a good meter. There was no doubt Mathew was afraid, but they could beat the hell out of him; they could unleash the blue-eyed demon child, but he wasn't going to talk.

Ever.

Before the uniformed man had a chance to further grill Mathew, a knock sounded. The Commandant settled back.

"Enter."

The door swung inward, and the corporal entered with a tray laden with two plates under silver lids, a bowl and a woven basket covered with a red cloth napkin. From his arm, a bottle of wine hung chilling in a container.

The scrumptious aroma of roasted potatoes and meat assaulted Mathew's nose. His stomach clenched, painfully, and his mouth started to salivate in expectations that would never be met.

"Set the table and go."

"Yes, sir." The Corporal carried the tray to a mahogany table and set the tray to the side. He placed one plate in front of a chair, followed by silverware, two stemmed glasses, the bowl and basket. Finished, he turned around, his gaze shifting uneasily from the commander to Mathew; confusion dipped his brow. "Will that be everything, sir?" he said, clearly unwilling to leave.

The Commandant didn't even bother looking at him. "I said, *go.*"

Without another word, the corporal left, but not before giving one more uncertain look toward Mathew. As soon as the door closed, the Commandant stood.

"Come," he said with a wave of his hand as he came out from behind the desk. He continued to the table and took a seat in a green chair trimmed in mahogany.

With the aroma still wafting up his nose, befuddling any coherent thoughts of anything other than food, Mathew slid off the chair onto jellylike legs. His stomach tightened again, and he cringed until the pain abated. Slowly, he walked toward the table, each step cramping the muscles in his midsection, and stood next to the table, unclear as to what the Commandant expected.

"Sit," the commander said, unfurling a napkin across his lap.

Wondering if food was the new torture, worse than feeling the lick of the riding crop, Mathew sat. The commander picked up his fork and knife and proceeded to cut a triangle section of the roast. Reddish-brown juice puddled under the cut of meat and ran into the melted butter dabbed between potatoes and green beans.

Mathew swallowed, hard.

"Aren't you hungry?" the Commandant asked, lifting the fork to his mouth and placing the bite inside. The commander flipped back the cloth covering the basket and pulled free lightly browned yeast rolls. With his knife, he sliced one of the rolls in half. "Eat," he commanded as he buttered the warm bread. "But I'd take it slow. The food is richer than what you're accustomed to."

Unable to shake the feeling that this was some sort of trick, which would end up with new bloody welts over his tender flesh, Mathew hesitantly reached for the utensils. He stabbed the meat with his fork and cut off a piece. The meat was tender, the knife slicing through it like butter. He brought up the fork, his mouth watering like a fountain, and warily glanced at the Commandant.

Surprisingly, the officer smiled at him. Not one that actually reached his eyes; Mathew still saw the hatred swimming within the depths, but a smile nevertheless.

The commander put a forkful of potatoes in his mouth. Mathew watched his jaws work as he chewed.

"It's delicious," the Commandant stated. "Eat."

Mathew slid the fork between his lips, and flavor exploded in his mouth. The roast actually melted in his mouth. Melted in a succulent array of flavors. After the first bite, it was over. He couldn't stop loading his fork with roast, then green beans, then potatoes. He stopped shoveling the food long enough to butter a roll, then that too joined the rotation.

"Wine?" the Commandant asked, filling the glass full.

Mathew nodded, taking the glass in his hand, and washing the food down with the slightly sweet liquid. He continued eating, ignoring the commander. The way he looked at the situation, if there was a trick involved, he would die with a full, happy stomach.

After a while, Mathew struggled to tear his eyes away from the diminishing food and looked up at the Commandant. The man was leaning back in his chair, swirling the wine around in his glass, watching Mathew with interest.

Feeling one level above a Neanderthal, but only because he wasn't ripping into the food with his bare hands, Mathew straightened in his chair and regarded his host with suspicion. This type of treatment was unheard of, and he wondered what the "good" commander's angle was.

"Good?"

"Yes, sir," he replied. "Um. Thank you?" He wiped off his mouth with a napkin. In his frenzy, he barely remembered dislodging his utensils from the cloth.

The Commandant stood, leaving the majority of his dinner on the plate. "Please continue," he said. "I'm not very hungry. Of course, I get to eat like this all the time." Humor dancing on his face, he tipped the glass up and took a long swallow.

Mathew shrugged and tore a roll in half. "No disrespect, sir, but why don't you tell me what all this is about?" he said, before popping the bread into his mouth.

The commander took another sip, then brought the glass down. "I already told you. I want to know about Ellyssa. You did know her?" he asked, the question more of a statement.

*And now comes the torture.* At least his stomach was full.

Tired of playing whatever game the Commandant was playing, Mathew leaned back, his full belly distending over the top of the thin pyjama bottoms. He felt a little nauseous and hoped the food would stay down, especially when the licks of the crop cut across his skin. He stared at the commander with locked lips.

The commander inhaled deeply. "You misunderstand me. I'm not asking for her or anyone's location. I'm not asking you to betray your kind." He said *your kind* like the Renegades were not of his species. "I just want to know about her. I want to know why she's so important."

"Why don't you ask the little girl?"

Surprisingly, the Commandant didn't fly into a fit of rage, like the last time he'd tried to pry information from Mathew.

"It's not that simple. Maybe you need to think about it." He went to the door and pulled it open. "Corporal."

"Sir," the corporal's voice floated in from the adjoining room.

"Summon the guards. The prisoner needs to be returned to the barracks." He closed the door and looked back at Mathew. "You can wait in the Corporal's office."

"Yes, sir," Mathew said, standing.

As Mathew reached for the doorknob, the Commandant plopped into his leather desk chair, wine glass still in hand.

"The enemy of my enemy is my friend."

The voice was so low, Mathew was unsure he'd heard the words right. Mostly, because it made no sense. "Sir?" he asked, peering from around the door.

"Get out," the Commandant said.

The last thing Mathew saw was the commander of the camp swiveling his chair around to stare out into the compound. Large snowflakes danced outside the window.

# 16

As soon as Trista had bounded into the kitchen to greet Dyllon, the captain pulled Trista in close and kissed her fully on the lips. After they'd parted, with a grin spread across his face, he'd informed them he had news.

Ellyssa thought Trista was going to explode. For the last hour, while they waited for the males to return, Trista had tried to sway Dyllon with fluttery eyelids and pleas, but he'd refused to talk. He'd just smile and squeeze her hand. Finally, with a pouty lower lip, Trista gave up, but not before she told Ellyssa she'd better not peek. If she wasn't in the loop, then no one was in the loop.

Since Trista had mentioned the peeking, Dyllon had watched Ellyssa from the corner of his eye. The expression on his face was hard to read—was it suspicion? Ellyssa wondered if Dyllon was aware of her capabilities. His past with the detective would have put him in a position of some knowledge.

Her curiosity piqued, Ellyssa had found it hard to contain herself and not glean the information from the captain. No one would be the wiser, and her nerves would be settled. Instead, though, she honored Trista's request, and passed the time watching Sarah's expertise with wielding a spatula, like an artist with a brush, while icing a chocolate cake. The older woman was the epitome of a mothering soul, at least what Ellyssa imagined one to be. She was going to miss Sarah when they left.

And they would have to leave, even without knowing their destination. Dyllon and Trista had already had plans before this reunion.

The thought saddened Ellyssa. She wished they could stay in the little home with the yellow sunflowers and the knickknacks, but she knew the time was drawing near when they would have to depart. As Tim said yesterday, he had to protect Sarah and himself. His job had been transporting, not harboring. The longer the reunited group stayed, the more dangerous it became for Tim and Sarah.

"Ellyssa?"

Dyllon's voice pulled Ellyssa's attention away from the spatula gliding across the top of the cake. She faced him.

"May I have a word with you?"

Trista's eyes narrowed. "Why? Are you going to tell her?"

He chuckled. "And what, be subjected to your wrath?"

Lifting her chin, Trista folded her arms across her chest. "Don't you forget it, either."

He looked aghast for a moment. "Never." Then a grin sliced across Dyllon's face, reaching his blue-green eyes, as he brought her hand to his mouth and brushed his lips against her palm. "It'll just be for a moment." He stood. "Please?" His question was directed at Ellyssa.

Both of the women looked at her—Trista with a look of reverie as her finger circled the part of her palm where Dyllon had kissed, and Sarah with a chocolate-frosting-covered spatula.

Shrugging, Ellyssa said, "Okay."

"In the living room?"

Her curiosity crested; she stood. "Sure."

With a quick glance at Sarah and Trista, Ellyssa followed the captain into the adjoining room. He closed the doors behind them, blocking the questioning looks of Ellyssa's two friends.

"Please sit down," Dyllon said, extending his arm toward the couch.

Ellyssa passed him and took a seat. She turned and looked at him.

Seemingly very nervous and definitely uncomfortable, Dyllon didn't move away from the door, as if he thought being close to an exit would prove useful. A hint of a smile curled Ellyssa's lips.

For a few moments, Dyllon didn't say anything. He rocked back on his heels, his hands shifting from folding across his chest to disappearing behind his back. His eyes would linger on her, then he'd quickly avert them as if he suddenly realized he was staring.

The whole thing was becoming a little irritating. If Dyllon didn't say something soon, Ellyssa was going to end the ordeal by grabbing what she wanted from his mind. Finally, Dyllon's hands fell to his sides, and he went to the couch and took a seat next to her, his knees pointing toward hers.

The Captain took a deep breath, then blurted, "What did you do to me last night?"

Completely taken by surprise, Ellyssa blinked. "What?"

"You did something to me," he accused.

"No..." She shook her head, her forehead creasing. "What are you talking about?"

"It's obvious you're the one the detective was searching for. You look just like that Micah. The resemblances are uncanny." He glanced down at his hands. "He was uncanny. The way he could...see things. He was the one who found the Renegades' stash." His eyes lifted and met hers. "I know you have abilities, too. All of you do. Angela told me."

"I didn't do anything to you."

He frowned. "But you do have abilities?"

"Yes."

Rubbing his hand over his chin, he stood. "What can you do?"

Ellyssa thought about not telling him. Technically, he was still employed by the Warrensburg police department. Maybe it was best they kept the information secret until...well, she didn't know. Until he proved himself? But, then again, she'd read his mind, seen his devotion to Trista, his horror at the slaughter in the cavern, his desire to change. Plus, after the captain told whatever news he had, she could keep a monitor on him without breaking her promise to Trista.

Ellyssa's decision made, she replied, "I can read minds."

For about a second, Dyllon's expression was one of perfect surprise—jaw dropped, eyes wide, astonishment paling his skin. Then he snapped his mouth closed and nodded. "That makes sense," he said, rubbing his chin in thought. "Perfect sense. That's why Trista said no peeking."

"Yes."

Dyllon sat back down on the couch and faced her. "That's it?"

Suspicious, Ellyssa asked, "Why?"

"Last night, when you touched my cheek and said, *calm,* it was like I couldn't help but to become calm. My mind was racing one moment, the next...things didn't seem so bad."

Ellyssa laughed, hard. The sound resonated deep in her chest and burst forth. Dyllon watched her, his face pinking, then he smiled and joined her. She could only imagine Trista's and Sarah's wonder at what was so funny and why they weren't included, which made her laugh harder.

After a minute, Ellyssa took in a deep breath and brought the giggling fit under control. "No," she shook her head, "I can't do anything as extraordinary as influence emotions. Just an average, boring mind reader." A snigger escaped from between her lips. She pressed them together.

"I guess the thought is ridiculous. It's just...I don't know." He looped his fingers together and let them hang between his legs. "It seemed like I had no control."

"You were under a lot of stress. I mean, you were dangling from Rein's hand." Ellyssa flinched at the same time he did at the reminder. "Sorry about that."

Dyllon touched his neck, an angry bruise peeked out from behind his collar. "No need. If I was in his shoes, I probably wouldn't have stopped. It must have been awful for him."

"It was." Ellyssa stood. "Are we done?"

"Yes," he said, reaching out and touching her hand. "Thank you for, you know, making him listen to you."

Something to what he'd said tickled the back of her mind. Something that wanted to click into place with other stuff, like puzzle pieces, but then Trista shouted, and the pieces fragmented again.

"They're back!"

Ellyssa stood on the threshold to the kitchen as the back door swung open. Tim came in, followed by Rein and Woody, who were both carrying boxes. Rein lugged his box over to a counter and plopped it down, biceps flexing as he made room for Woody's burden.

Tim marched right over to Sarah and planted a kiss on her awaiting cheek "Mmm, chocolate cake," he said, dipping his finger into the bowl.

Sarah made to smack his hand, but he dodged, sticking his index finger into his mouth as he turned toward Ellyssa. His brow wrinkled, which looked comical with no eyebrows.

"You look...different."

"Tim," shrieked Sarah, "your manners." She hit him with the dishtowel she'd used to dry her hands.

"No. No. You look great."

Blush rose in her cheeks as Rein turned around. A smile twitched the corners of his mouth, and a spark lit his jade eyes. With wide strides, he went to Ellyssa and wrapped his arms around her. She buried her face into the side of his neck and inhaled. Like always, he smelled wonderful.

"Wow," he said into her hair. "You really do look different. Beautiful."

"Thank you," she said, her voice muffled.

Suddenly aware of the eyes on her, she peered over Rein's shoulder. Dyllon had taken his previous seat next to Trista, who held a "told you so" smugness on her face. Tim's arm was wrapped around Sarah's waist, their expression full of happy approval. Woody stood silently, watching them. He pulled his fingers through his ash-blond locks, like he was agitated, and his mouth moved like he wanted to say something. Instead, he gave an approving nod, then started to open one of the boxes.

"I told you. Didn't I tell you, Ellyssa?" Trista beamed.

Rein pulled back, shifting his hands onto Ellyssa's upper arms. "BAM," he said, with a smile.

Pleased, more heat rushed into Ellyssa's face. She felt an urge to look away in embarrassment but couldn't; Rein had her locked with his gaze. Visions of their night together warmed her body as well, and then she definitely blushed with bright-red embarrassment. The smile on Rein's face turned to one of knowing, and he blushed as well. Maybe to hide his embarrassment, Rein pulled Ellyssa in and hid his face in her hair.

Dyllon cleared his throat. "I have to be going soon."

Every muscle in Rein's back seized tight at the sound of the captain's voice. He moved to Ellyssa's side, his arm sliding around to her waist where he pulled her in protectively. Ellyssa couldn't help but think how cute the act was.

"Don't let us stop you," Rein said, his tone clipped and unwelcoming.

Woody guffawed while Trista shot Rein a look that could've curdled milk.

"Don't start, Rein," she warned.

Rein held his hands up. "I'm not starting anything." He brushed a kiss across Ellyssa's cheek, then joined Woody. His back rigid, he started to pull out white boxes with red crosses on the lid.

"Rein, he has news for us," Ellyssa urged, looking at Dyllon.

"Oh?" he said, his voice couldn't have lacked any more interest. Without looking up, Rein opened the other box with MRE, 10 UNITS marked on the side.

Trista popped out of her chair, snatching her hand away from Dyllon when he tried to contain her. "Yes, you big ass."

Everyone's expression shared the same look of shock, except Woody, who snickered. Rein's head snapped up, as if he was about to say something, but Trista wasn't going to have any of it. She propped her fists on her hips and glared threateningly.

"We've been waiting all day for you guys to get back. He should have left twenty minutes ago, but he stayed, risking himself, because he wanted to tell us something."

"Risking all of us," Rein retorted.

"Scratch big ass. You're a *huge* ass."

"I agreed to work with him, but I never agreed to be happy about it."

"Trista, it's okay," Dyllon said, placing his hand on her shoulder.

"No. He shouldn't be—"

"Listen, I don't have time for this. I have to get back. Rein," Dyllon said, his gaze meeting Rein's furious glare, "I just wanted to tell you, all of you, I know where they took the others."

Anger bled out of Rein as his face fell slack and his hands dangled uselessly by his sides. "Wh-what?"

Within an instant, the kitchen buzzed to life, all the bickering of a few seconds ago forgotten. Words like *when?*, *where?* and *how did you find out?* blended together in a whirlwind of inquisition. Trista threw her arms around Dyllon and kissed him repeatedly on the cheek. Tim slapped him on the back. Tears swam in Sarah's eyes before they broke free. And Rein stood there, dumbfounded. Ellyssa went over to him and wrapped her arm around his waist.

Smiling in triumph, Dyllon swaggered under the pressure of the swarm. "Hey. Wait. I'll tell you what I know, but I have to be going. Shh."

After another moment or two, everyone settled down; all eyes turned toward Dyllon.

"All I know," he said, "is they are in the west part of Texas, in a concentration camp called Amarufoss."

"That's impossible," said Tim. "They evacuated everyone in that area. It's deserted."

"It *was* deserted. They opened up a concentration camp about fifteen years ago on an old military base."

"Fifteen years ago? And this is the first I've heard of it?"

Dyllon shrugged. "Communication."

The kitchen buzzed again with the new information, and it took another minute for Dyllon to quiet them down. His face turned grave as he prepared to tell the next part.

"The Commandant is a man named Hans Baer, and he is well known for his job. *Well* known," he emphasized. "I don't know how many survived, if any are even still alive. And that's all I got." He glanced at the clock. "I have to leave. I'm sorry for going with so many unanswered questions. I'll try to find out more information for you."

"Go, son," said Tim. "We've waited this long; another day or two won't kill us."

He leaned over and gave Trista a quick peck on the lips. "I'm sorry," he said, then opened the door.

"Dyllon," Rein called.

Dyllon stopped, his shoulders flexing. Tentatively, he turned around. "I really don't have time."

"I just wanted to say 'thank you."

"Don't thank me. I haven't done anything to deserve it yet. I will bring more information for you, though."

Dyllon left, leaving them all with their thoughts...and hope.

# 17

After Mathew's visit with Commandant Baer, things really changed. His assigned work details no longer included blustery wind, the portions of food he received from the mess increased, and just recently, he'd been called to the laundry, where the soldier had thrust a new pair of boots and clothes into his arms with contempt.

The new clothes lay across his bed next to Mathew while he turned one of the boots around in his hand. He guiltily sat alone in the barracks, his detail of polishing soldiers' boots completed. Everyone else was out in the compound pushing piles of snow from one side to the other, in thin jackets and worn boots with holes in the soles and tears in the seams.

Mathew didn't completely understand everything, but he wasn't stupid enough not to know the special treatment had something to do with Aalexis and Xaver, nor did he take for granted that it had something to do with the information the Commandant wanted.

Every night since then, Mathew had lain awake in his bunk, listening to the snores and occasional cries from nightmares of his forty-one roommates, and thought about what the commander had said.

*The enemy of my enemy is my friend.*

Mathew's mind struggled with the words. Certainly, he'd mistaken the Commandant's mumbling, but another part of him was pretty damn sure he'd heard the commander right.

And if Mathew had heard him right, what in the hell had he meant?

A bitter wind gusted through as the door opened. Shuffling steps approached Mathew. He didn't look up until a pair of battered boots came into his field of vision. Shame dug a ravine through Mathew when he looked at Eric. First, his detail consisted of him polishing ten pairs of boots to a glossy shine, indoors—something that took him about two hours—and now, he had nothing to do, indoors.

"Hard day at work, Doc?" asked Eric, sitting on a bunk across from him. The former councilmember shook off a chill that clacked his teeth together hard. He took his thin knit gloves off, the same grey as their uniforms, and briskly rubbed his hands together.

Mathew couldn't help but notice how red and cracked the tips of his fingers were, along with his cheeks and lips. More guilt split the gully wider. "I guess." He placed the boot down.

"New boots?"

"Yeah."

"And clothes, I see."

"Yep."

Eric reached over and fingered the material. "Well, aren't you lucky?" Jealousy dripped from his words.

A tinge of anger briefly flared inside Mathew. He understood why Eric felt resentful, but it certainly wasn't his fault. What was he supposed to do? Refuse his details? End up in the chamber?

Mathew sighed. "I don't feel lucky at all, Eric. I feel a little irritated and a lot confused." He flipped the clothes to the side. "Do you think I asked for these things? Maybe I *should* refuse and let them kill me."

Looking as if Mathew had reached out and popped him one, Eric looked away. Hurt and anger pulled at the man's face, glistened in his eyes. "Don't be ridiculous." He stood.

"Wait," said Mathew. "Wait a minute. Please sit back down."

Eric's gaze flicked toward the door. Fear replaced the other emotions, his face paling somewhat as if he just remembered where he was. "I can't. You know I can't. I should have already returned."

As if on cue, a soldier whipped open the door and marched in, the hard leather soles clacking across the floor. The fabric of his heavy coat and pants made a hissing noise where they came together as he walked. His green helmet bore the single circle of a private.

Without a moment of hesitation, he came right for Eric, grabbed him by the arm, and yanked him back. Eric stumbled and landed on his backside, his head bouncing off the floor.

Mathew leapt to his feet and started toward Eric, but the guard held him off with a point of his finger. A pointing finger? Below pathetic. But, once again, what could he do? If he interfered, the consequences would be worse...for both of them. Mathew stilled.

His upper lip curling, the private said, "You, stay back. And you," he sneered at Eric, "get up."

Rubbing the back of his head, Eric groaned. Blood smeared a trace of red across his palm. With effort, he managed to get his elbow under him, but when he tried to shift his weight to his feet, he swayed, his face paling.

The private swung the rifle off his shoulder and around so the butt aimed at Eric. He raised the rifle.

"Stop," yelled Mathew. His feet moving before he even realized it, Mathew skidded on his knees and bumped into his friend's side. He shielded him.

The soldier stopped just before he released the blow meant for Eric, fury contorting his features. "Move out of the way, you despicable abomination. Or I'll get to him through you."

"Go right ahead. Afterwards, we'll have a talk with the Commandant."

Behind the hatred, fear flickered, and the rifle lowered minutely as the private hesitated. He glanced at the door for a second before returning his eyes to them. His grip on the weapon tightened. The soldier's teeth locked together in a snarl, and the butt rose higher. Mathew closed his eyes, waiting for the contact that would blur his consciousness with stars, but before the threat could be played out, a life rope was tossed. The door opened.

"What in the hell is going on in here?"

The soldier dropped his rifle to the side and stood at attention, his chin lifted and arms rigid straight. "Was trying to retrieve the prisoner, Sergeant."

More clacking leather soles made their way to Mathew, and he looked up at a man who wore the same clothing as the private, only his helmet was adorned a circle flanked by two diamonds. Under the helmet, Mathew looked into the square face of the sergeant-at-arms. The sergeant was a young man, no more than mid-twenties, with a blond high-and-tight and dark blue eyes. His cheeks cut savagely across his face and ran almost a ninety-degree angle to his jowls. His nose was crooked and bent slightly to the left.

Running a close second in the sadistic department, right under the Commandant, the sergeant was known for cruelty. Once, when Mathew had first became a resident of the camp, soldiers had dragged him, kicking and screaming, into the Storage Room of Pain, where he'd been introduced to the lashes of the sergeant's cane that extended to three times its closed length with a flick of the wrist. The cane was infamous—at least in their corner of hell.

Mathew held no doubt the nature of the sergeant was what had propelled him to his position of power at such a young age.

"And why haven't you?"

The private pointed at Mathew. "That prisoner interfered, Sergeant."

The dark blue of the sergeant's eyes cut a path to Mathew. "I see." His cold gaze flicked back to the private. "Does he have a weapon?"

"No, Sergeant," answered the private, a slight faltering in his voice, as if careful to answer the question correctly.

"But he detained you from your duty?"

"No, Sergeant. I was about to take care of the situation."

"With the butt of your weapon?"

"Yes, Sergeant."

"Were you not given a direct order during formation that no harm was to come to that particular prisoner?"

"No...I mean, yes, Sergeant."

"Which is it, boy?"

"Yes, Sergeant. I was given a direct order."

"And you decided to take it upon yourself to disobey?"

"No, Sergeant. I wasn't going to harm the protected prisoner, Sergeant," the private lied.

Mathew could hear the untruth in the private's voice as well as see it on his face. The shine of light perspiration on his forehead, the minute movement of his eyes to the side, the slight hesitation right before he answered. By the sergeant's squinting lids, Mathew knew he read the telltale signs as well. According to what little information had flowed their way, higher military personnel were well-trained to detect such falsehoods.

The sergeant-at-arms regarded the private for a moment longer, his face remaining as deadpan as Ellyssa's when she had first come into Mathew's neck of the woods.

"Get back to your post," he ordered.

Relief washed over the soldier's features. "Yes, Sergeant." In little less than a blur, he left.

As soon as the door closed, the sergeant turned his unwanted attention back onto Mathew. "I told the Commandant that you all were as likeminded as children. Give you a little leeway and you steal a kilometer. He refused to listen."

The sergeant dropped to his haunches, leaning close where Mathew could hear his breath and see the pores littered across his bent nose. "Tell me what he wants with you."

Along with the other fringe benefits he'd been receiving, the Commandant had ordered him unharmed. The courage he'd found to help Eric, who remained frozen and quiet and safe below him, strengthened with that realization.

"As I've told you before, I have nothing to say, Sergeant."

Red rose to the surface of the sergeant's face, and his hand clenched into a fist. The cold in his eyes froze to deadened pools.

For a moment, Mathew thought the sergeant was going to ignore the Commandant's order too, and his heart pounded beneath his ribcage in a irregular *thump, thump, thump*. This time, perspiration beaded on *his* forehead.

Instead of beating him to a bloody pulp, the sergeant stood and turned around. "He just doesn't understand you creatures like I do." Mathew assumed he meant the Commandant. "He's around for the interrogations. Even rather renowned for his cruel nature, but he has never worked with you as I have." He flipped around, his chest puffed beneath his coat. "I, too, was at one time nothing more than a private. I clawed my way to the position I'm in now."

*Did he want a compliment?*

The sergeant paused and stared at him intensely. Mathew squirmed a little under his gaze.

Eric moaned and struggled to sit up, breaking the hold the sergeant had on Mathew. His gaze cut to the injured man.

"Take him to his bunk, then report to the Commandant."

"Yes, Sergeant," Mathew replied, hunkering down and helping Eric to his feet.

"Be sure to wear those nice new clothes," he sneered before executing a ninety-degree turn and going to the door. "I'll send a soldier for you, and for your injured friend, too."

Eric wobbled a little but was able to remain upright. Mathew led him to the thin mattress popped by rusted springs and helped him onto his bunk. Running fingers through Eric's hair, Mathew touched the tender spot on his head. His friend flinched.

"Ouch."

"Only a small cut," he said, "and a nice-sized goose egg, but you'll live."

Eric lifted his head, a small smile gracing his lips. "Is that your professional opinion, Doc? Or should I seek a second diagnosis?"

Mathew laughed. It felt good in a place as dismal as this, like a thin ray of sunshine breaking through a charcoal-grey covering. For a moment, just a small moment, but enough to bring light into his withering hope, things seemed almost normal.

"Hey." Eric grabbed his hand. "Thank you."

Patting his hand, Mathew said, "No problem."

"I owe you."

"When we get the hell out of here, I'll make sure you pay up."

Eric groaned and lay back on his pillow. "Chop. Chop. You've been summoned," he said, closing his eyes. "And don't forget to put on those nice new clothes and shiny boots."

Unlike the chilling temperatures of the barracks, the Commandant's office was toasty warm. Almost too warm. Or maybe the heat Mathew felt was because of the commander's hate-filled glare. Seemed the officer wasn't used to not getting what he wanted, when he wanted it.

The Commandant sat across the desk from Mathew in his leather chair. Everything about the man was rigid, from his posture to his crisp, dark-blue *Waffenrock*, right down to the shiny brass buttons.

After a moment, the commander leaned against the back of his chair. "I was hoping after a few days to think things through logically, you would have some answers for me."

Mathew felt deflated. For the last hour, he'd repeated over and over again the same words he was about to say now. "I have nothing to say."

"Why? It isn't giving any valuable information to betray your beloved family." The Commandant spit the word *family* out like it tasted bad on his tongue.

Mathew scooted closer to the edge of his chair. "Why don't you tell me exactly the reason you have an interest in Ellyssa?"

His face hardening into stone, the commander of the camp's lips formed a rigid line under his nose. "Regardless of other parties' interest in you," he seethed, "let me remind you I run the show here. You are dangerously close to crossing the line."

Careful to keep his poker face in place while a rising tide of worry washed onto his shore of courage, Mathew wondered how much further he had to go before he toed that line. Not that it mattered. Whether or not the requested information would compromise the Resistance, the Commandant was barking up the wrong tree. For all the people who had died for the cause, more than he could probably fathom, he would honor them.

"Are we done now?" Mathew asked.

The Commandant's ears shaded red. "Get out," he said in a low, dangerous voice.

Mathew thought it wise not to press his luck. He rose from his chair and went to the door.

"Oh, and Doc?"

Hand on the knob, escape within a turn of his wrist, Mathew stopped.

"There is more than one way to inflict pain."

The Commandant's voice was low, like before, only this time there was no mistaking his words. Fear trickled into Mathew's blood. He wasn't exactly sure what the Commandant meant, but he figured he'd find out soon enough. He also figured he wasn't going to like it. Twisting the doorknob, Mathew went to meet the soldier who would escort him back to his drafty barracks.

Wind whipped outside, rattling the metal door against the frame with a hollow, eerie sound. Cold crept under the crack of the door and across the floor, meeting the cold that had seeped through the walls.

A chill crawled along Mathew's spine and jabbed into the back of his skull. He shivered under his thin blanket. Pulling his legs into his stomach, he lay on his side in a fetal position, looking toward Eric's empty bunk. He could see just barely see the outline of the metal legs and thin mattress, courtesy of the low, flickering flame burning in the stove.

When Mathew had returned from his meeting, the barracks had been empty. He'd assumed Eric had been ordered back to the ever-important job of pushing piles of snow from one end of the compound to the other. But when the crews returned with no Eric, a deep foreboding had taken root. Then when no one had known where Eric was, and when he hadn't shown up during mess, the foreboding had sprouted and continued to flourish as the night progressed.

He'd kept hoping his old friend would show. Maybe he'd been reassigned to another detail that required a late night to make up for his absence earlier in the day. But every time the door had opened, followed by the progression of soldiers for the seven o'clock count, the eight o'clock count and the nine o'clock count, and still no Eric, the hope sizzled into an ashen lump.

Guilt slithered in Mathew's midsection. His friend was gone, and it was his fault.

The Commandant had been right. There was more than one way to cause pain.

And it sliced Mathew deeper than any riding crop.

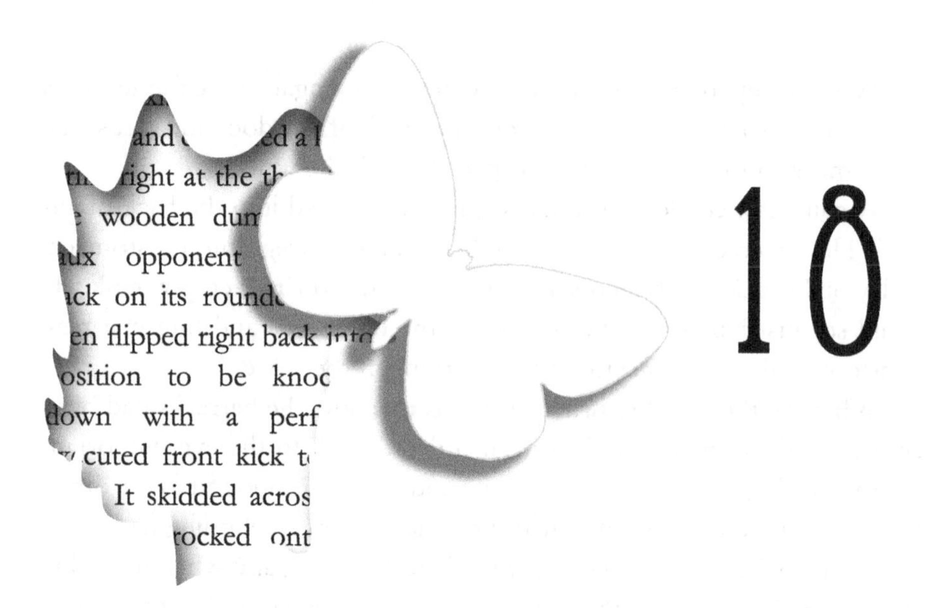

# 10

Aalexis stiffened her fingers and delivered a knife strike right at the throat of the wooden dummy. The faux opponent wobbled back on its rounded butt, then flipped right back into position to be knocked down with a perfectly executed front kick to the chin. It skidded across the mat and rocked back again.

The well-ingrained movements were performed with little thought, one flowing into the next into the next, by now ingrained into her. Her *gi* snapped at each execution. A right punch followed by a left uppercut, followed by a spin kick to the gut. Already, the dummy was showing wear, just like the sand-filled punching bag she'd knocked off the chain the day before.

Aalexis had always found quiet in the performance, the feel of her taut muscles twitching under the exertion, the tendons moving under her skin, her deep and even breaths. It freed her mind for other pursuits, like what atrocities her sister had committed, and how she and Xaver would extact revenge.

Spinning around, Aalexis finished with a back kick hard enough to lift the dummy off the ground, then, dropping down on her haunches, she whipped around and swept what would have been legs out from under her wooden opponent. It landed on its side with a crashing thud before it rounded back upright.

"The bait has been set," Xaver said.

Xaver's voice wasn't a surprise. Her brother had been watching her for the last five minutes. Not only did she feel the difference in temperature when he opened the door, but his scent cloaked the exercise room as soon as the door shut.

Looking at the rocking mannequin, Aalexis stretched her neck from side to side and spread her arms wide, releasing the tightness in her chest and biceps. She strolled back over to the bench and picked up her towel. Slowly, as she wiped her face and neck, Aalexis faced Xaver.

Xaver stood next to the treadmills, his body lean and muscular under the white tank top that clung to his midsection, defining every line of his stomach. The *gi* bottoms hung low from his hips.

Aalexis' insides quivered.

She didn't understand the feelings he elicited in her, the warmth in her midsection or the how pleasing his outdoorsy scent was, but eventually she'd have to confront them. If she could say she feared anything, it would be to break down like Ellyssa had, and end up a feeble creature, unworthy of her father's brilliance. Aalexis forced her eyes back to Xaver's face.

"The location has been released?"

"Yes. If Ellyssa is still in the area, the news will carry with the traitor."

"Good," she replied. "I am growing impatient. What of construction?"

"Proceeding ahead of schedule."

"Finally, things seem to be moving."

"Also, the Commandant reported. He assures us that the prisoner is still well."

"We might need him if we do not apprehend Ellyssa right away. Her love for the Renegades will work against her." She started to turn away.

"Emotions weaken."

Halting, a chill crawled over Aalexis' skin. Did Xaver know her about her lapses?

Lids narrowed to slits, Aalexis turned back toward him. Xaver stared at her, but nothing in his posture alerted her to a challenge. Instead, his face held a look of...of fondness? Maybe? It looked somewhat like an expression that had crossed her father's face on occasion, soft and relaxed; the corners of his lips slightly curled upward.

The display was alien on him, confusing to her, but that didn't stop her heart from accelerating or warmth from spreading. For a moment, time seemed to slow as she tried to decipher what was happening.

"Would you prefer a live opponent?" Xaver asked, breaking the spell, his face now blank, his voice lackluster.

Aalexis averted her eyes, reining in the eerie whirlwind inside her. She shoved it into the deepest, darkest recesses of her being. Under control, anger—the emotion she understood, even if it was caused by the disorder her body was experiencing—surfaced.

"Brother," she stated, her voice amazingly calm under the circumstances, "I might be younger, but I have grown stronger. I will prove to be a most formidable opponent."

A wicked smile flicked across Xaver's face and disappeared as if never there. "I know."

Without another word, Xaver barreled toward her, his bare feet slapping against the mats. He was nothing more than a blur of movement, and Aalexis barely had time to drop the towel she'd been holding before Xaver was upon her. Within a blink of the eye, he stepped left and dropped, swiping his right leg out. Aalexis felt the swish of air as she flipped over his extended leg and landed on her feet a meter away.

Relentlessly, Xaver came at her. Aalexis scarcely had time to move to the left as his fist blazed toward her, overshooting above her shoulder. She twisted to the side and executed an elbow strike, clipping his wrist as he was pulling back.

Somewhat proud, if Aalexis was to name the exuberant feeling, she met his eyes. She wasn't sure, but she thought she saw pride on his face, too, right before they hardened to an icy blue. Xaver unleashed an merciless series of *uchis* and *tsukis*. Aalexis countered with *ukes*, knocking his strikes and punches away from her.

He advanced, and she backed up under the fierceness of his attack. Her brother's skill matched and, if she were to be truthful, exceeded her own with age and weight. But that didn't make Xaver impossible to defeat. Aalexis kept her eyes peeled for an opening.

As he pulled his leg in for a roundhouse kick, Aalexis seized the opportunity and went on the offensive, easily avoiding his foot and retaliating with strikes as powerful as he'd just exhibited. He blocked them, one after the other. With him on the defensive, her strikes sure and precise, Aalexis stepped forward, pushing Xaver back.

Like a graceful choreographed dance, they continued moving back and forth across the mat, matching strikes with blocks, agilely evading kicks and sweeps, each holding their own against the other.

Then, Xaver moved to the right, and Aalexis countered, but not before he struck her in the ribs. The pain was excruciating and refreshing at the same time. He stepped in, putting his left foot behind her, grabbed her by the neck, and she landed on her back. Before Aalexis had a chance to recover, Xaver was on top of her, his knees on each side of her, rendering her incapacitated.

"Do you know your mistake?" he asked.

Aalexis was speechless, liking and hating the feel of his weight against her. His muscular chest rose and fell with short breaths. He leaned closer, a perfect brow raised over one eye, and his scent assaulted her nose.

"Well?"

Anger at letting him get the best of her, but more so for the barrage of incomprehensible sensations now, licking through Aalexis' veins. She bucked, hard, and flipped him over her. Xaver landed on his back, and before he had a chance to move, Aalexis sprang to her haunches and pinned his neck under her knee. Minutely, he moved as if readying to counter, but she pressed down harder, cutting off his air supply.

For a moment, she thought how easy it would be to end all the conflicting feelings storming around in her. A slight movement of her knee and his neck would be broken. Easy and over with.

But she couldn't.

Besides the protection Xaver afforded her, his intelligence or her father's wish of them being inseparable, Aalexis couldn't imagine the absence of him from her life. A detail she chose to ignore for the time being.

"Do you know yours?" Aalexis asked.

He gazed at her, his eyes no longer flat or cold, but flickering with something she couldn't quite identify. Something that made her insides twitch in response.

"Indeed I do."

# 19

Ellyssa wiped away the condensation from the frost-covered window and watched Woody cross the backyard. He moved hunched over, his ash-blond hair and the parka whipping in the wind. He opened the door to the barn and disappeared inside.

Things had been fine, normal even, until Rein and Tim had gone into the radio room and Trista went to take a shower, leaving the two of them alone. Soon afterwards, Woody had mumbled something and escaped into the grey day.

"I think I'll help Woody," she said, turning around as Sarah entered the room.

"Be sure to bundle up," Sarah answered.

The older woman went to man her regular post, the stove, and stirred spaghetti sauce in a big black pot. The air smelled heavenly with garlic and oregano. Ellyssa's stomach made itself known.

"I'll be right back," Ellyssa called over her shoulder as she shrugged into the parka.

Harsh, icy wind clawed at Ellyssa's cheeks as soon as she opened the door. Taking a deep breath, she rushed over the threshold and into the frozen air of the Missouri winter.

The hood of the coat caught by the drawstrings in her fist, Ellyssa quickened her pace across the path, each step a struggle against Mother Nature's forces. Ominous clouds swirled angrily in the sky, holding the promise of a cascade of snow. Tim had said blizzard-like conditions were possible in the evening, and it seemed the possibility was more than likely.

Reaching the barn, Ellyssa opened the door, only to have the wind snatch it out of her hand and bang it against the siding. Woody flipped around on his heels, his arms flung upward as if to protect himself. He visibly relaxed when he noticed it was her.

"Close the door," Woody said. "It's cold enough in here."

The door slammed shut without much effort on Ellyssa's part, the blustery weather's way of lending a helping hand. For a moment, she stood unmoving, the cold knob in her hand. Words fumbled around in her brain. She knew what she wanted to say but was not sure how to say it. Ellyssa wanted him to know how much he meant to her for all the things he did, for the things they shared. Since they'd blown The Center into a skeleton of its former self, things had spun into their future so fast, leading them to this point of time.

Most of all, though, Ellyssa wanted to know what was up with his mood swings, something she'd thought about over the last couple of days. If what she kind of thought was true, the air needed to be cleared between the two of them.

She owed him that much.

Ellyssa loved Woody. Not the same way she loved Rein—of course she could distinguish the difference—but she loved him nevertheless. Funny how, just a few months ago, sitting in her sterile room of her old home, the thought of love or friendship, or family for that matter, had never crossed Ellyssa's mind. Her joys and sorrows she had carefully filed away into a box, never to be exposed. Now, Ellyssa stood in a cold barn, hiding in Missouri, preparing to launch another expedition into an unforeseen future with hope of finding missing friends alive, as the feelings she'd denied so long curled and writhed and heated inside her.

"So, did you leave the warmth of the house to stand in the cold?" Woody asked, his voice holding the same irritation she'd heard in the dilapidated old store where she'd taken refuge after she'd escaped, what seemed a lifetime ago.

Taking a deep breath, she looked at Woody's back as he wiggled a box with a red cross marked on the side free from the shelf. Ellyssa lowered her head as she moved to the middle of the floor. "Woody, may I have a word with you?"

He paused for a moment, careful to avoid eye contact with her. After a second longer, he lugged the box over to a table and opened it without saying a word.

Life would have been so much easier if Ellyssa had just swung her gate open to Woody's thoughts. At the very least, she would be certain what he was thinking, instead of playing a guessing game that she really didn't excel at.

A thank-you seemed to be the best way to start. "I've never really had a chance to offer you a proper thank you."

This time, when he stopped, his grey eyes met hers. Woody's eyebrows dipped over the bridge of his nose. "For what?"

"For helping me. With everything. For Rein. If not for your insistence on coming with me, he wouldn't be with us today." She swallowed a lump that'd formed after the words came out. "I would have failed alone. You risked your life and saved all of us."

"No need to thank me, Ellyssa. He would've done the same for me...as I'm sure you would've, too."

Ellyssa took a step forward. "Without a second thought."

A brief smile tugged at the corner of Woody's lips. "That's what we do for each other," he said, before he averted his gaze back to the box. "Was that all?"

Ellyssa watched as he pulled out a small plastic container filled with bandages, antiseptic cream, lip balm and other first-aid supplies. The group already had ten stored away, along with boxes of MREs, tents and sleeping bags, and other goods, in the white van parked behind a copse of evergreens. It was another vehicle Tim had used for emergency transportation of Renegades, and had given to them for their trek into Texas. For precaution, Tim had replaced the plate with numbers untraceable back to him and Sarah.

"No."

Still not looking at Ellyssa, Woody paused again for a moment before he started to rifle around in the box as if searching for something. "Then what?" he snipped. "Why else are you here?"

She was a little hurt at the way he sounded, and mad because she was pretty sure he knew why but was going to make it difficult on her. "This is why," Ellyssa blurted. "You. Why do you act like we're friends one moment, then like you're trying to avoid me the next? A minute ago, you smiled at me; now you won't even look at me." She waved her hand at the box. "We don't need any more medical supplies. You just came out here to avoid me, and don't think I don't know it, either."

"I don't know what you're talking about."

She went around the table and stood next to him. "Yes, you do."

Sighing, Woody gave up the pretense of looking for something. "It's my problem, Ellyssa," he said. "Don't worry about it."

Part of Ellyssa wanted to just let it go, but she had to know. She exhaled, her chest deflating with the release. "I don't want you to hate me," she whispered.

Woody's head whipped up, his face bewildered. "I don't hate you."

"I don't understand, then. All your actions are so confusing, but the one I can definitely comprehend is that you don't really care for me. Maybe for my sake, or for Rein's, you act like you like me because we're all in this together. It's the only solution as to why you smile at me one second and then refuse to acknowledge my presence the next. I might not be a master of emotion or body language, but I'm far from stupid." Bottom lip quivering, Ellyssa turned away. She couldn't stand the thought of him feeling sorry for her.

Unbelievably, Woody laughed. Full and hearty, the sound filled the air around her. Here she was, exposing herself to him, exposing her fear, and he found humor in it. Her lip stopped trembling as embarrassment slithered under her skin, heating her cheeks. Anger followed close behind.

"Just forget it," Ellyssa snapped and started for the door.

The laughter died as abruptly as it had started. "No, don't." Woody caught her by the upper arm.

Briefly, she entertained the thought of knocking his hand away. Maybe twisting his arm behind his back, incapacitating him. Of course, she wouldn't. That was an instant reaction of her old self. But her old self was still a major part of her. After eighteen years of living and breathing under certain conditions, she couldn't help the times when she felt uncomfortable or insecure or angry for those types of thoughts to emerge. Instead, Ellyssa shrugged out from under his hold.

"It's fine, Woody." She started for the door again.

"Ellyssa, stop," he said, coming behind her. "I listened to you. Would you please give me the same courtesy?"

Against every instinct, old and new, she did as Woody requested but refused to look at him, to even turn in his direction. "What?"

"Do you remember back in the cave, before the whole thing with Rein getting captured, when I told you that I liked you?"

She did remember. He had looked at her all weird then, too. He also had made her feel all weird.

"My feelings haven't changed."

Tentatively, Ellyssa faced him, her gaze lifting to meet his grey eyes. Woody's lips were slightly curled down, as were the corner of his eyelids. Shadows angled under his cheekbones, and his straight nose twitched as if he needed to sneeze. The back of his jaw clenched and unclenched, not in anger, but indecision.

"I really don't understand."

He stepped forward, his hand brushing a strand of hair behind her ear. He was close, his full lips mere centimeters from Ellyssa's. The back of his fingers lingered against her cheek. Foreign tingles, like what Rein left behind but not quite, trailed from his touch. She remembered the feeling from the last time he'd touched her, back when he had told her he'd liked her.

"I know you don't," Woody said, his voice low and husky, his eyes blazing like Rein's when he was about to kiss her. "In some ways, you are so innocent."

His breath washed over her, and she inhaled his unique male scent that teased her senses. Her heart accelerated; blood pulsed through her veins. Suddenly, Ellyssa didn't feel the cold anymore. Confused, she stepped back, breaking the contact.

Woody slowly lowered his hand. "I like you, Ellyssa. As I told you before, I like you a lot. More than I should."

"More than a friend?" she asked, although now she finally understood.

"A lot more. I—I love you. Ever since that night after Jordan died, I knew. I'd even say before then." He lifted his hand, like he wanted to touch her again, but he stopped. Instead, he pulled his fingers through his hair and turned around. "Rein is my best friend. My brother. I would never do anything to hurt him."

She shook her head, trying to quiet the mounting discombobulated thoughts. "I love Rein." Ellyssa's voice didn't sound as convincing as she wanted. "I really do love Rein," she restated, stronger.

He spoke with his back to her. "I know you do. So, please understand when I seem standoffish, it has nothing to do with you. It's me trying to cope the best way that I can."

Even though Woody couldn't see her, Ellyssa nodded her understanding. He was jealous. "I think I should go."

"Please don't say anything to Rein."

"I think it's best that I don't." She paused for a moment, unsure of what else to say.

Shoulders sagging under the weight of his confession, Woody didn't move. Not knowing what else to do, Ellyssa opened the door and sprinted across the yard back into the kitchen.

Luckily, the room stood empty. Everyone was off doing their own things, none the wiser. She leaned against the door, tears threatening to spill over her cheeks. Not because of what Woody had admitted, but because she liked the feel of his hand on her cheek. Because she couldn't understand *why* she had liked it.

Her love for Rein was undeniable, incontestable, no question about it.

So, why did she feel as if she'd betrayed him?

# 20

Running a brush through her hair, Ellyssa sat between Rein's legs on the edge of the bed they'd been sharing since the first night. The usual effect of the brush did little to calm her nerves that were coiled in anticipation, Woody's revelation nothing more than a distant memory she'd filed away for the time being.

They were leaving tomorrow. The thought filled Ellyssa with excitement, sadness, and dread. Every day that passed diminished the possibility of survivors. Camps were not known for their compassion, especially with what little information Dyllon had provided. Amarufoss was under the control of a Commandant named Hans Baer, a male not well renowned for his hospitality.

"Relax," Rein said, followed by distracting kisses on the back of her ear, his fingers running down the curve of her neck. Shivers accompanied his soft caresses. She leaned against his chest, and he wrapped his arms around her.

"If you keep that up," Ellyssa whispered, "breakfast will get cold."

Rein slipped around to her side, lowered her on to her back and lay next to her. His hand slipped under her shirt, his warm palm lying against her stomach; he leaned over and kissed her.

"Would that be so bad?" he breathed.

His scent jumbled any coherent thoughts she might have had; her breath hitched in her chest. "I—I—" was all she could manage. Ellyssa licked her lips, tasting him.

Knowing perfectly well the power he held over Ellyssa, Rein's delicious lips curled upward as the jade eyes sparkled, mischievously. He leaned over and tantalized the sensitive spot within the groove of her collarbone with light kisses. His nose traveled along her neck to her ear, where his teeth gently teased her lobe. He trailed along her jawline and ended back where he'd started, his lips against hers.

Tingly current from his touch pulsed through Ellyssa's veins, fed by the pounding of her heart. She reached behind his neck and, moaning, crushed her mouth against his. She pulled back long enough to tell him how much she loved him before her mouth moved against his again.

He broke free, his lips trailing down her neck, his tongue flicking against her skin. "I love you, too," Rein mumbled before his teeth nipped her.

Her chest fluttering, she moaned softly. He was driving her crazy.

Ellyssa tugged at the back of his shirt and pulled it over Rein's head. She stopped for a moment, mesmerized by the muscles lining his chest and the bulge of his biceps. She touched the indentation below his ribcage and ran the tips of her fingers across his stomach.

"You're beautiful," she said, looking into his eyes. "I love you so much, Rein."

He smiled. "Words cannot even begin to describe how I feel for you."

"You promise, no matter what happens, that you will always stay by my side?"

A slight frown pulled his eyebrows together. "I promised you that a long time ago."

"I know. I just wanted to hear it again."

Rein lifted her hand and kissed the tip of each of her fingers. "I'm not going anywhere, and that is a promise."

Ellyssa smiled just as Trista's voice boomed into the room. "What the heck, guys? We're starving out here. Would you stop the smooching and come eat?" There was a small pause as footsteps clicked down the hall followed by her voice. "Good God. Come on."

"I guess that's our signal," Rein said, pushing himself off the bed. He took Ellyssa's hand and pulled her into his arms. "You ready?"

Looking in the mirror, Ellyssa sighed. Her hair was disheveled all over again, as if she'd just crawled out of bed. "Let me finish brushing my hair."

Her gaze flicked to Rein. His brown hair was just as bad. One side lay smashed to the side of his head, while the other stuck out, as if he'd poked his finger in a socket. She giggled.

An exaggerated frown surfaced before disappearing inside the black T-shirt she'd recently freed him from. "What's so funny?" he said as his head popped through the neck hole.

"Maybe you should think about doing something with that incriminating evidence," she said, pointing at his hair.

He pulled his fingers, once, twice, through his hair and presto, a perfect array of spikes. "There," he said. "Better?" He poked one of the spikes. "I really need a haircut."

Males had it so easy. "Still better than mine."

He beamed and that spark lit his eyes again. "Let's go."

"I need a couple more minutes. You go ahead before the food police comes back."

He kissed the tip of her nose. "Okay. Hurry."

"I will."

As soon as Rein departed, Ellyssa's nerves twisted into tight wires.

She grabbed the brush off the floor where it had ended up and went to the mirror. She was going to miss the simple things, like a mirror, the warmth of a home, good food set on a table, the sweater and dark jeans she wore. She was going to miss Tim and Sarah. She wondered if she would ever see them again.

Ellyssa didn't want to leave, but at the same time she felt like they shouldn't wait until tomorrow. Every day brought unknown consequences to their group at the concentration camp. *If* any members were still alive. As much as she hated to think about it, the odds were not in their favor. And unfortunately, Dyllon's security clearance and the need to be inconspicuous had hindered any further helpful information.

Her hair tied back in a loose bun, she started toward the door. Footsteps filtered from the hall.

*Trista, so impatient.*

Narrowing her eyes, Ellyssa sidled to the door with cat-like stealth and waited to pounce. Knob in hand, she prepared to whip the door open and pop out, but the sound caused her to hesitate. They didn't belong to Trista.

Woody lingered outside the door, the thickness of the wood separating them. She could feel his presence, hear his breath. Closing her eyes, Ellyssa pressed her back against the wall, waiting for a knock, but one never sounded. Instead, he sighed and continued to his room next door. As soon as she heard the *click* of the door closing, Ellyssa released bated breath.

Since the day of his confession, they hadn't been alone together—thankfully. Ellyssa's lack of experience made her feel uncomfortable at the prospect. She didn't know what to say or how to act. Even though in some ways things were better between them with the air cleared, at least for her because she understood now. But at other times, a thick wall of tension settled between them. Then there were instances, like now, when the ghost of his touch breathed across her cheek.

Guiltily, she rubbed her cheek until her pale skin glowed, as if to erase the phantom presence.

Sitting on his bunk, alone, Mathew leaned forward on his elbows, his hands hanging between his knees. A pile of dull boots was stacked next to feet, the unused cloth and unopened polish next to him. Unshed tears stung his eyes as he stared at the cold ground. Guilt crushed his chest, his being, like a ton of bricks were dropped on him.

A week had passed, and still no Eric. Mathew had known the first night his friend was dead, Eric's body shoved into the incinerator like trash. The following morning held more proof; puffs of dwindling smoke had curled from the chimney on top of the square building with the vent, but he had held on to hope like a life preserver.

Mathew had to let it go, accept his friend's demise. Sink or swim.

The Commandant wouldn't touch him—*couldn't* touch him?—but the man wasn't beneath making Mathew pay anyway. Eric's disappearance had proven that. What was worse was that he would care less if it had been his own life. That was something he'd come to terms with a long time ago. None of the Renegades sacrificed the safety of their group for themselves. What he couldn't come to terms with was a group member being sacrificed anyway. All on account of him.

Fury and despondency wilted what was left of Mathew's optimism. He couldn't stand to face the dismal cloud of death anymore. He stood and kicked the boots he was supposed to be polishing. Black leather rose and fell to the concrete ground with unsatisfying thumps. He stomped over to a boot lying by Danny's bed—a young man of about twenty, wafer-thin and sickly now—and ripped it up off the floor. With all his might, he launched it at the metal mirror, angered even more because it just bounced off the polished surface without so much as a crack. Mathew carried on with his tantrum, kicking and throwing the boots, smashing them into walls and bunks, each attempt to destroy as unsatisfying as the next.

Suddenly, Mathew stopped, the coals of uncontrollable rage fizzling into ashes, his paroxysm ebbing.

Chest rising and falling irregularly, Mathew looked around at the chaos he'd created. Boots lay around everywhere—on the bunks, on the floor, one tottering at the edge of their pathetic source of heat.

All he'd managed to do was cause more trouble if a soldier happened to appear. Actually, Mathew was surprised that, with all the noise, someone hadn't burst through the door. Then what would happen? More people dying because of his outburst. Punishment and more punishment. Before the nightmare was realized, Mathew rushed around the room, picking up the boots and tossing them into a pile next to his bunk, until he stooped to grab one at the foot of Eric's old bunk.

Mathew tried not to pay attention to where he was, but it was useless. His eyes were drawn to where his friend, up until recently, had slept. The thin mattress lay bare with no grey, scratchy blankets to hide the yellowed stains of fear from previous occupants.

With the boot dangling from his fingers, Mathew crumpled to his knees, tears coursing down his face.

As much as he hated the fact, he knew what he had to do.

Ellyssa waited until Woody's bedroom door closed, and his steps faded down the hall before she peeled her back off the wall. She couldn't explain why she was so afraid if he happened to knock. So what if Woody's love for her was different than the love she felt for him? She still felt close to him for all he'd done, for being her best friend. Eventually, a time would come when they would be left alone. The problem was, when she'd tried, she couldn't rub away the feel of his touch. Still it haunted the side of her face.

Plucking up her courage, Ellyssa straightened her sweater and opened the door to an empty hall. She stepped over the threshold, closing the door behind her.

Voices carried from the kitchen, the clinking of dishes. They had started without her.

"Is Ellyssa feeling well?" Sarah asked, motherly to the core.

"She's fine," replied Rein. "Fixing her hair."

"Maybe you should stop messing it up," Trista said with a giggle.

Ellyssa felt red rush into her face.

"Shut up." Rein's words.

Trista giggled again.

Slowly, waiting for the heat to diminish from her cheeks, Ellyssa started a slow pace to the end of the hall and stopped at the small room where Tim kept the out-of-date radio. A short burst of static resonated within the room, along with what sounded like a single word.

She swung the door open. Dead air greeted her. The gun-metal-grey longwave radio sat silently on top of the scarred desk. The slatted-back chair was pushed into the space under the single drawer; unconnected headphones lay draped across the scarred arm. A black wire led from the radio to the beat-up microphone. The dial rested to the left.

Ellyssa reached out and fingered the volume knob, turning it to the right. Nothing. The band stayed still.

Thinking she was mistaken, hearing things, she dropped her hand. She started to turn around when the tuner band pegged and static erupted from the speakers.

"Base One," the electronic voice said followed by silence. Interference marred the voice, making it hard to understand.

Ellyssa backed out of the room. "Tim. The radio. Someone is trying to contact you."

Abruptly, silence swept away any conversation. Less than a second later, excited words and chairs scraping across the floor answered. Rushed steps galloped toward Ellyssa.

Tim burst into the hall first, his bald head shining with perspiration. Rein, Woody and the rest were on his heels.

"What did they say? Did you respond?" Tim asked as he moved past Ellyssa, not giving her a chance to answer. He plopped onto the chair and started turning dials back and forth. White noise squelched. He depressed the button on the microphone. "Base One to Control. Go ahead, Control." Static answered and Tim turned another dial.

Rein's hand slide into Ellyssa's, and she turned to look at him. "What did they say?" Rein repeated Tim's question.

"They said, 'Base One.'"

"That's our radio name," Sarah said, excitement lighting her face in a beautiful glow. Her hand intertwined with Trista's, whose face shone, too.

"Was that it?" Woody asked.

"That's all I heard," Ellyssa replied, turning back toward Tim. "I was walking down the hall when the static started."

The older man pushed the button again. "This is Base One. Go ahead, Control. Over."

Buzzing squelched, loudly, like fingers across a chalkboard. Ellyssa cringed. More white noise transmitted, then a single word came through, clear as a cloudless day. "Run."

Dead air settled from the speaker and blanketed the room in an ominous cloud and, for a second, time seemed to crawl as things focused crystal clear.

Rein's face darkened as his hand tightened, squishing Ellyssa's fingers together. Trista's and Sarah's faces dimmed. Woody's muscles twitched as if he was going to take off any moment.

Tim glanced back, his forehead bunched into horizontal lines. "Did I hear him right?"

As if to answer his question, the back door banged against the counter. Heavy footfalls stormed across the linoleum.

*They found us*, Ellyssa thought, tendrils of fear constricting her heart.

"Trista?" Dyllon's frantic voice echoed through the house. "Trista?"

Time sped up.

All at once, everyone exhaled as Dyllon flew around the corner without his parka. His uniform was crumpled, and sweat circled under his pits and dripped from the side of his face. His breath came in gasps as if he'd been running.

"Oh my God, there you are," Dyllon said, his voice mixed relief and fear.

Dyllon pulled Trista into his arms, smothering her against his chest. She said something, but her voice was muffled.

Pulling back, Dyllon covered Trista's face in kisses. "What?" He didn't give her a chance to speak before he yanked her back to his chest.

"You're freezing," Trista mumbled.

Dyllon laughed, but not a happy one, more of one teetering on the edge of panic. "You're safe. You're safe."

Releasing Ellyssa's hand, Rein stepped forward, his gait stiff with alarm. Fear breathed from his pores. "What's happened?"

"It's time to go," Dyllon answered over Trista's head. "Now."

"What do you mean?" Woody asked.

"They know. They're coming" was all the answer Dyllon gave.

Tim leapt from his chair faster than Ellyssa had ever imagined the older male could move. After unplugging the radio, he handed it to Rein, then grabbed the microphone and headset. "Showtime," Tim said, dashing out the door.

Ellyssa wasn't exactly sure what that meant, but she had a fair assumption that there was no waiting for tomorrow. Like roaches, everyone scattered. Woody bolted toward his room. Tim's hand appeared from behind the wall and grabbed Sarah's. He pulled her into the living room.

Rein looked at Ellyssa, his face marred with worried alarm. "It's going to be okay," he said.

Ellyssa was unsure if he was trying to convince her or himself. "I know." She squeezed his hand. "We're together."

Trista started to pull Dyllon down the hall toward her room, but he stopped her. "No time." He raised his voice. "No time for anything. They were about thirty minutes away when I intercepted the call. That was about fifteen minutes ago."

Dyllon turned, pulling Trista as he went into the living room where their hosts stood off to the side. For the first time ever, Sarah's youthfulness had disappeared, and she looked like a fragile old woman. Even Tim seemed to have aged.

The older man called out, "Everything is ready. Just go." His voice was frantic, edging toward hysterical. The change in his usually calm demeanor was terrifying.

"Let's go," Tim repeated.

Woody reappeared, a knapsack slung over his shoulder. Three more dangled from his hand. He handed one to Ellyssa, one to Trista, and the last to Rein. When Woody's hand was free, he took Ellyssa's, their differences forgotten, and squeezed reassuringly. Fear tightened his face, his pupils dilating.

Rein led the way, lugging the radio and pulling them through the living room toward the kitchen door. Ellyssa knew the destination was the van hidden somewhere to the south within a copse of trees. Avoiding the roadways meant going through the backyard, over the fence and across the frozen barren field.

"Rein, there is no time. They'll catch you," Dyllon said, moving toward them. "You'll never make it."

Rein flipped around. "What would you have us do?"

"I—I don't know."

"So, no help from you."

"That's not fair," interjected Trista. "He at least gave us warning."

"There is no time for this crap," Tim charged. "Dyllon, do you know which way they will be coming from?"

"Everywhere. The alert went across the channels."

Tim's gaze flicked to Sarah, an unknown message exchanged between them. She nodded.

"Okay, everyone down to the basement."

"That pops out right on the side of the house. Anyone coming down the road will see us," Woody said.

"Son, trust me. I never put all my eggs in one basket. Plus, there are weapons you need to take. If they find them during the search..." Shuddering, he glanced at his wife, then faced Woody. "I will protect her at all costs."

"Let's go."

Tim opened the door and disappeared down the stairs, the headset cord flapping behind him. Woody took the radio from Rein and followed. Trista shook free of Dyllon's grip and ran to Sarah, throwing her arms around her.

"Thank you," Trista said. "I would have never found them without you."

Tears sparkling in her eyes, Sarah patted her back. "Get going now."

Trista pulled away, her hands enfolding Sarah's. A small smile flitting across her unlined face, she let go and went down the stairs without looking back. Dyllon trailed behind.

"Sarah, thank you." Rein said, giving their hostess a quick hug. "Stay safe."

"You, too."

Rein draped his arm around Ellyssa and started to lead her toward the mouth of the basement. "One second," she said, breaking away and going over to Sarah. "I want to thank you. For all you and Tim have done. For sharing your home."

"My pleasure." Then, like the first time when she'd met the old woman, Sarah yanked her in for a big hug with hidden strength. "I know you," she whispered. "Keep them safe."

Blinking back tears, Ellyssa nodded.

"I know you will, dear." She dropped her arms. "Go."

Ellyssa went.

Yellow light arced across the floor from a hanging lamp, reflecting off the concrete walls. Like before, the basement was well-maintained, free of debris and dust, but a slight wet, mildew scent fragranced the enclosed space. The radio sat off to the side.

"Come here," Tim said to Rein.

Tim and Woody were under the stairs where shadows reigned away from the light. A metal shelf full of tools and boxes piled upon boxes occupied the area with them. They were moving the boxes and handing them to Dyllon, who stacked them against a wall. Trista was tossing cartons of ammunition into a large duffle bag. Barrels stuck out from between the folds.

"Get that." Tim pointed to a metal trunk.

Repositioning his pack, Rein ducked under the stairwell and pulled the trunk out by its handle.

"Shove it under the workbench."

The metal scraped across the concrete floor, leaving behind marks.

"Ellyssa, grab those rifles on the bench. Let's go, folks. Woody, grab on that side, and on the count of three, lift."

As Tim started the count, Ellyssa swung two AK-47s over her free shoulder. Trista zipped the duffle back and dragged it by the stairs. Dyllon bent down and grabbed the handle.

"Argh," grunted Tim, followed by a popping noise and more scraping.

Mostly hidden in the shadows, a door swung outward, creating a gap large enough for them to slip inside. Darkness waited.

"What?" Rein said, completely surprised. "Where does it lead?"

Hunched over, Tim came out from under the steps. Stretching back, with his hands on his lower hips, he groaned.

Sarah came down, a broom in hand. "This house is over two hundred years old, passed down through my family," she said. "The tunnel was part of the Underground Railroad."

Ellyssa had read long ago about the Underground Railroad, network for slaves to escape their owners with help of the abolitionists. Technically, the routes were not underground or railroads, but it seemed that was not always the case.

With nothing learned, history was doomed to repeat itself.

"You never said anything about that," Woody said, astonishment coloring his words.

Tim chuckled, a dry sound without humor. "As I said, I never put all my eggs in one basket. In our business, we have to keep some things a secret. Now go." He went and grabbed the radio, handing it to Rein. "Set this on the other side of the door."

Einstein had said time was relative. It was true. Like back when Ellyssa had slunk through the vents in The Center, time crept by in her anxious fear of it running out. Here, in less than ten minutes, they had gone from horror in the radio room, to clearing under the stairwell, to revealing a door. Now their time had come to an end, and something new awaited them.

Taking the bag from Dyllon's hand, Woody slipped through the opening. Darkness swallowed him whole.

Trista turned toward Dyllon, tears glistening in her eyes. "I guess this is goodbye." She swallowed hard, as if to take away the sorrow lodged there.

Dyllon reached out and touched her cheek. "I can't stay here. I'm coming with you. If they haven't found the car yet, they will. I parked it in a grove after the call came through."

"Like hell," Rein said, his tone rumbling in anger.

Sea-green eyes slicing toward Rein, Dyllon countered, "If I'm caught here, they will kill us all. I have to go with you."

Ellyssa nudged Rein. "He's right. And we don't have time. Let's go."

Muttering something indecipherable, Rein slipped through the gap. Enveloped in a cocoon of hope, Trista led Dyllon into the tunnel. Ellyssa sidled through and turned around. Tim thrust a flashlight into her hands.

"Good luck," he said.

The last things she saw were Tim's face and Sarah behind him moving the broom back and forth. The older woman stopped for a moment, and with a shaky hand, she wiped her cheek. A knock banged from above. Fear widening his eyes, their host pushed the door closed, cutting off the source of light. An earthy smell and darkness closed around them.

For a second, only the sounds of breathing could be heard, in and out, in and out. No one moved, no one said anything. Another knock, louder this time, put Sarah and Tim in motion. Thumping and scraping came from the other side of the door. A *thud* echoed against the door that Ellyssa guessed was the shelf getting moved back into place.

"Coming." Sarah's muffled voice drifted into the enclosed space. Soft thuds clumped above them.

Tim started to hammer something.

"We have to go," Woody said, his voice barely a whisper.

"Okay," Rein answered. "Be careful of the radio." He relieved Ellyssa of one of the rifles and grabbed her wrist. "Let's go."

Ellyssa switched the flashlight on and pointed the beam down the enclosed hole. Black scampered and took up residence further away. Wooden beams and posts, rotten with age, buckled precariously. The radio rested in a groove next to the door where Rein had placed it. More clopping of leather soles sounded from above. Sarah yelled down to Tim. The hammering stopped, and his heavy footsteps moved up the steps.

In a straight line, as silent as possible, all of them stepped with care, following the light into the unknown.

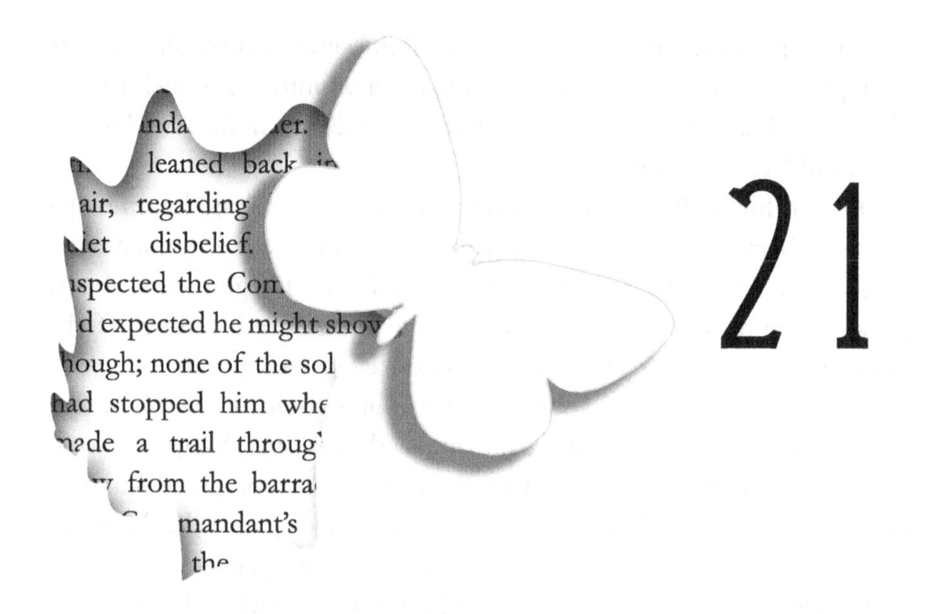

# 21

Mathew sat across from Commandant Baer. The officer leaned back in his chair, regarding him with quiet disbelief. Mathew suspected the Commandant had expected he might show, though; none of the soldiers had stopped him when he made a trail through the snow from the barracks to the Commandant's front door. Even the corporal had just gazed up when Mathew had entered before waving him on through.

A couple of minutes of silence later, Commandant Baer leaned forward. "I'm assuming the reason you barged into my office has something to do with the information I requested."

Mathew stared at him. The commander wore his pristine uniform with the shiny adornments, his hair parted meticulously to the right. The huge desk sat between them like a river of betrayal.

What was he doing here? Did he really think he could sway Commandant Baer?

Mathew ignored the officer's question and asked his own. "What happened to Eric?" He already knew the answer but needed finality to ice the top of his cake of guilt.

Commandant Baer frowned. "Eric?" He actually had the audacity to sound innocent.

"The man you murdered the other day."

A smirk played across the Commandant's lips. "I didn't murder anyone. Insubordination requires punishment. Punishments are dealt in the appropriate manner according to the crime." He placed his elbows on the desk and leaned closer, his teeth showing gloatingly. "You were all informed of the rules. In essence, when one breaks the rules, they are punishing themselves."

"I think you killed him because of my refusal."

The commander waved the accusation away. "As I said, you were informed of the rules."

Anger licked through Mathew, like a raging fire. Fearing the words that dangled on his tongue, he looked away, composing himself. Nothing would be accomplished if he goaded the Commandant until his composure snapped and he sent Mathew to the chamber.

*Would the commander harm him?*

*How much influence did Ellyssa's sister wield?*

After a moment, Mathew's gaze met the Commandant's. "We will discuss my reason for coming here. But first, I want answers."

Commandant Baer seemed to consider his request for a moment before he finally settled back into his seat. "Go on."

"How many women are left?"

"I'm assuming you mean from your group?"

"Yes, but I also want the total number."

Pivoting his chair to the side, the commander looked out the window. Mathew followed his gaze. In the background stood the metal gate; two armed men stood at their posts. Closer toward the compound, glimpses of disembodied, skeletal heads popped in and out of view as the prisoners slaved away in the cold. Feeling guilty that he sat in warmth, Mathew averted his eyes.

While the Commandant stared out the window, seconds dragged into minutes. Mathew started to think he wasn't going to answer. Finally, he swiveled back around.

"I want make perfectly clear to you that any attempt to try to escape or help anyone else will only prove to be fatal for you...and the rest of your group. Like your *friend*, their deaths will be on your hands." Mathew cringed, and the guilt that he already harbored tore a chunk out of his heart. "My first priority is the security of my establishment. Do you understand?"

Mathew held no doubt of the truth in the Commandant's words. He nodded.

"Out of the twenty females who came in with you, only nine remain. There are a total of seventeen women."

Shocked, Mathew fell back in his chair. "Only nine?" he muttered.

"Women tend to be more troublesome."

Mathew didn't reply. Tears building in his eyes, he turned away.

*Nine? In less than a month, eleven had perished in this hellhole. Alone. With no one by their sides.*

Anguish shattered in Mathew's chest, heavy and unyielding. A knot formed in his throat, one he didn't think he would be able to choke back down. He couldn't bear to even look at the commander, much less talk. If he tried too soon, he'd crumple in despair. Surprisingly, the Commandant sat in silence while Mathew tried to put himself back together.

After a long while, hatred overshadowed sorrow, and within it he found bits and pieces of strength to pull himself together. But like weak glue, the binding threatened to dissolve.

With dry eyes, he faced the officer. "You killed them all."

The commander's face didn't show a hint of regret. Nothing at all. Just as stone-faced as before. How could a being kill innocents without feeling something? Then, he remembered the look of glee as the Commadant's crop had come across his Mathew's face and flesh, and he understood. Any members below society's standards were nothing more than animals. When the Commandant punished, it was no different to him than stepping on a bug was to Mathew.

"I've already explained the process of punishment."

"Can you give me their names?"

He shook his head. "None of you have names."

That was something Mathew could understand. Easier to kill when your victims were dehumanized. No identity. Just the face of the enemy.

"I see." The glue started to liquefy. He had to get away before his composure turned to jelly. Mathew stood.

For a moment, the stony countenance shattered as Commandant Baer rose to his feet. "I believe there are more things to discuss."

Mathew's gaze held his. "I will provide the information you seek, but I can't right now."

Once again, Commandant Baer seemed to consider, and once again, he surprised Mathew. "Do not come back until I summon you."

Knowing he had to grab on to as much of the upper hand that he could, Mathew straightened his back and lifted his chin. "Summon me tomorrow."

A vein pulsed on the Commandant's forehead, but he didn't comment. He gave a curt nod, dismissing Mathew.

Mathew opened the door and wasn't surprised to see the same two soldiers who had brought him for his first visit with the Commandant standing in the front office. He stepped between them.

Time stood still, almost nonexistent, as Ellyssa jogged through the earthen corridor, stretching into forever, unendingly. Light arced back and forth, bouncing off the walls and the ground, under the guidance of Ellyssa's swinging arms. The only sound that had accompanied them were soft pants of exertion and the clinking of rifles.

The sweater and jeans Ellyssa wore stuck to her uncomfortably, constrictingly. Sweat dribbled from her hairline and ran down the back of her neck. Unlike the cold temperatures outside, the tunnel was relatively warm, like an early spring day. She eyed Rein's loose-fitting camo pants, riding low on his waist, and T-shirt, wishing she'd also worn what she considered the Renegades' uniform.

They must have jogged at least three or four kilometers; probably about fifteen minutes total had elapsed, but it seemed longer—much longer. Every time Ellyssa had thought the "Underground Railroad" ended, she was disappointed when it instead curved to the left or the right, coiled like the body of a snake.

The tunnel just kept going and going and going.

Not knowing what had become of Tim or Sarah made it worse. She comforted herself knowing that her hosts had been through this before. That they were prepared for anything. The surprise of the tunnel had proven so. Tim was ready for any possible scenario.

*They will be fine.*

Woody's voice broke into Ellyssa's reverie. "What's that up ahead?"

Slowing down, Ellyssa steadied the beam ahead. Something wooden and long leaned on its side against the dirt wall. "I think it's a ladder."

"Is that the end?" Trista asked, her words coming in short bursts.

"I hope so," Rein replied, facing Ellyssa, his face pale with fear, his hair a drooping mess. Somehow, he managed a smile, trying to reassure her. He brushed his lips against her cheek. "Together."

Ellyssa moved closer and was partly relieved to confirm they were finally at the end of the tunnel. And partly disappointed as the beam revealed the condition of their escape.

Woody set the duffle bag he'd been carrying down and pulled the ladder off the ground, He held it at a slight angle so that it wouldn't bump into the earthen ceiling. Frayed rope held dilapidated rungs in place. One of the rungs broke off in his hand. "Well, I guess at *one* time it was a ladder."

"Ellyssa, shine the light up there." Rein pointed above his head.

Ellyssa pointed the flashlight upward. Slats covered a square opening about three and a half meters over their heads. No sunlight filtered through. She wondered where the hatch led, and if they'd even be able to move it. There was no telling what covered it.

"That's our way out," Rein concluded.

"How are we going to get up there?" Trista huffed, bent over, her hands resting on her knees, clearly unused to jogging long distances, something that would remedy itself if this first leg of their journey was any indication.

"We'll make a human ladder," Woody stated. "First Rein, followed by you, Ellyssa, me, then Dyllon."

"I don't think so," Dyllon remarked. "You'll leave me down here."

"They will do no such thing," Trista said, straightening. Her hands moved to her hips.

Rein chuckled. "I might not care for you, but I'm not that cold."

Ellyssa swung the flashlight down. "Do you think we can use the ladder to prop the door open?"

"I think so," Woody replied. "Rein, come help me balance. Be careful. This thing has seen better days."

Grabbing the rail opposite Woody, Rein positioned the ladder under the hatch and pushed up. Surprisingly, it opened with ease. As daylight crept into the tunnel, dust and clots of dirt fell.

"Cover your eyes," Ellyssa said.

"A bit more," huffed Rein, his lids scrunched tight.

They pressed upward; the door swung back with a dull *thud.* Woody replaced the ladder in its previous location.

"Okay," Woody said. "Rein, crawl up on my shoulders."

Ellyssa shook her head. "I have a better idea," she interjected. "You and Rein clasp your hands together and swing me up."

"I don't think so," Rein said.

Woody nodded his head in agreement. "Don't be ridiculous."

"You'll get hurt."

The thought of her getting hurt was what was ridiculous. This was something she'd been trained to do since she'd been a toddler—bred into her, actually. "Thank you, but you two have a better chance of getting hurt trying to balance on my shoulders." Placing her hand against Rein's cheek, she said, "I promise."

"I don't know." Rein glanced at Woody for help, but he just shrugged and looked away. Rein sighed.

She leaned closer to him. "Don't forget who I am."

The flicker of unease in Rein's eyes dimmed a little. In the back of Ellyssa's mind, a tidbit of conversation with Dyllon emerged. It flashed, then extinguished as Rein drew away from her hand. Time for pondering later.

"Okay," he agreed, disheartened, but still in agreement. "What do you need us to do?"

Ellyssa set her bag and rifle down. "You and Woody overlap your arms, grabbing each other's forearms, like this." She demonstrated. "Then you will hunker down and on three, you both push up while you swing your arms upwards. Understand?"

Rein took in a deep breath. "All right, but I still don't like this."

Woody came up and faced Rein. Grabbing each other's arms where Ellyssa had indicated, they crouched.

"Just be sure to keep steady," Ellyssa said, stepping into the cradle they'd created.

Her heart accelerating, unease settled. She wobbled for a second before she breathed out, releasing the anxiety. Calm spread through her, her emotions fleeing. Her face fell flat as she stood straight. Any swaying on their part she easily counteracted.

"When I say three, push." She swung her arms back into position. "One...two...three!"

In harmony, both males thrust upwards, their arms swinging above. Ellyssa launched herself, like springing from a diving board. She burst through the gap into the sunlit world. An icy breeze pushed her hair and jabbed freezing fingers through the damp sweater. Tucking her chin and knees in, she flipped around and landed lightly on her feet about fifteen centimeters from the gap.

*Exhilarating!* She grinned.

"Ellyssa? Ellyssa? Are you alright?" Rein's frantic words chased after her.

She looked over the edge into four upturned faces, lids scrunching against the late-morning sun. All of them wore looks of astonishment. "I'm fine."

"That was remarkable," Woody exclaimed.

The others nodded.

Beaming, Ellyssa's smile grew.

"How about the rest of us?" Trista asked.

"One second."

She stood and turned around. Evergreens and firs encircled her, their needled branches high and wide, like a natural fence. From Ellyssa's peripheral vision, a brief flash of white glinted. She focused on the source.

"Rein, I think we're at the van."

A brief pause later, Rein answered, "Really? That makes sense."

"Why?"

"Tim disappeared for a few minutes while I was situating things. He must have come and loosened the hatch just in case. Smart man," he concluded.

"Tell me there is some rope in the van."

"Of course."

"This is going to be easier than I first thought. I'll be right back."

Jogging, Ellyssa popped into the clearing where the vehicle had been parked. Boxy, white, nothing to draw the eye, the van was unremarkable. Just an ordinary delivery van used for transporting materials. Perfect for them. She opened the swinging back doors.

Less than two minutes later, she returned, a coil of rope hanging from her shoulder. Tugging on the thick cord—nylon, strong—she tied a loop at one end and dropped it through the hole.

Taking the length in his hand, Rein gazed up at her. "Are you sure you can pull me up?"

Pulling the corner of her mouth back, Ellyssa gave him an "are you kidding me?" look.

Rein threw his hands up. "Of course." He swung both rifles and a bag over his shoulder. Giving the rope a quick pull, he slipped his foot into the loop.

She stepped away from the mouth. Using one of the trees, Ellyssa braced herself. "Ready?"

"Ready," Rein's disembodied voice answered.

She pulled, her hands alternating back and forth, and the rope grew in length behind her. Soon, Rein's brown crop popped into view. He grabbed the edge with one hand and yanked himself up. Wiggling, he dragged the rest of his body onto the ground.

He stood, brushing dirt off his shirt. "Here," he said, his hand held toward her. "Let me."

"I can do it," she said.

"I know. Let me do it anyway."

As Rein handed her the weapons and bag, Ellyssa gave him the rope. He dropped the nylon escape route down the hole, and soon afterward, everyone was safe on the ground. Their bodies trembled in the cold. Puffs of warm air escaped from their mouths.

"We need to leave," Woody stated as he walked toward the van. His hands were full with a duffle bag and knapsack.

Rein dropped the hatch back into place and kicked dirt and leaves over the wood. Dyllon helped him.

Trista gazed toward the north where Sarah's and Tim's house lay obscured by the dense forest and distance. "Do you think they're okay?" she said, her voice squeaky.

For a moment, no one answered. Rein, finally, broke the silence.

"I'm sure they're fine. Tim and Sarah are resourceful."

"But what if—?" Trista started.

As if the Fates themselves had slithered through the forest, Trista's unfinished question was answered. An explosion rolled across the earth, the ground rumbling in its wake. At once, everyone's heads snapped toward the north where a mushroom cloud ballooned over the trees. Tim and Sarah's threads, snipped before their eyes.

Stunned, Ellyssa's thought process jammed. Things played out in slow motion. The woods quieted, and the air stopped blowing. Somewhere, as if separated by a vast distance, she heard Rein gasp and Woody yell, "What happened?" Above the jagged line of firs and evergreens, a fire and smoke ball hung, as if in suspended animation, where she knew their hosts' house had stood. Hazy, dream-like, comprehension fled from her grasp, her brain failing to make sense of what her eyes saw. Her gaze stayed locked on the billowing umbrella of destruction.

It was Trista's scream that caused time to slam back to normality.

"No!"

The single syllable stretched until Trista's voice broke into a heart-wrenching sob. The next moment, Trista was bolting toward the treeline, her feet pounding against the ground. Dyllon was the one who stopped her, his arms wrapping around her midsection as he tackled her. He flipped around an instant before they hit the ground so that she landed on him.

Still, Ellyssa couldn't move as reality played out before her. She understood there was an explosion, but couldn't quite connect that with the meaning of Tim and Sarah's life. All she knew was her heart sank with dread, like a dead weight, through her belly, down into her feet.

"Ellyssa," Rein said. "We have to go now."

She didn't respond. She didn't move. She did nothing but stand there, her feet frozen.

"Ellyssa," Rein said again. His face popped into her line of vision, wan and dulled with grief. "We have to go." He pulled on her hand.

"I—" Ellyssa started, but any other words failed her. She didn't know what to say. Tears collected in her eyes, blurring her vision, and rolled down her face.

Rein's face crumpled in grief. "I know." He encircled her in his arms, his warmth penetrating her freezing skin. "I know. But we can't do this right now. We have to go."

Within the safety of his embrace, Ellyssa saw Trista bucking and kicking as Dyllon dragged her toward the van. She screamed over and over again until he put his hand over her mouth, shushing her with words that did little to soothe. Free of the items that had burdened him earlier, probably deposited in the van, Woody went to help Dyllon. Trista was relentless in her fight to free herself.

Numb, Ellyssa let Rein lead her to the van.

# 22

For the last four hours, Ellyssa had been staring out the back window. Her thumb worried the black cave pearl grasped in her hand. She found comfort in the rock and was glad she had had the forethought to slip it into her pocket. A constant reminder of the toddler and of the family members they had to rescue.

The rutted road that hadn't been used for years unfolded below her. Tires slowly crawled over the broken asphalt that jutted in uneven patterns, jarring them uncomfortably. Winter-savaged plants bent under the wind.

Ellyssa hadn't spoken a word—no one had. Her mind endlessly looped on a perpetual replay of the mushroom cloud blooming in the sky, the knowledge of Tim and Sarah's death eating at her until her insides felt raw. Except for the occasional whimper from Trista, the slosh of gasoline in the two plastic containers next to Ellyssa, and the contents of boxes rattling, silence reigned within the confined space.

During the whole time, Rein had sat beside her on a crate, his hand folded around her free one. Dyllon was driving while Trista sat in the passenger seat, her knees pulled to her chest and her face hidden in her arms. Woody sat behind her. Once in awhile, Woody's hand would rest on her shoulder, trying to comfort her, then he'd let it slip away.

Emotions were a twofold contradiction. Ellyssa knew they strengthened; she'd felt the difference in herself since she'd allowed bonds to form. She had no regrets, but it was times like these when her father's words rang true—emotions weakened. No one was thinking clearly, not even her, if she were to be truthful.

In the back of her mind, Ellyssa knew all of it was wrong. They weren't doing anything according to plan. Trista was supposed to be driving, since her identity remained relatively hidden and the false credentials Dyllon had provided at least had her picture. Dyllon wasn't even supposed to be with them, which created a whole new problem. If they were pulled over right then, all their hard work, Tim's and Sarah's deaths, would be in vain.

It would be so easy to slip into her soldiering skin right now, to separate herself from the pain; Ellyssa looked around the van at all the long faces filled with grief and loss. What good would it do?

*Worry. Worry. Worry.* Her thumb rubbed faster against the little round rock.

She—*they*—needed to pull themselves together. Ellyssa wanted it all to change. Not to forget, but to react. Somehow she needed to help, but her inexperience, her awkwardness, kept the right words out of reach.

She glanced at Rein. His face sagged in intense sorrow and his eyes glimmered with wetness. Gently, his hand tightened around hers. He returned her gaze. His lower lip quivered.

"I love you," he said, his voice soft.

She closed her eyes. Those three words burned through her despair, finding their rightful home in her heart. She hadn't realized how much she needed to hear them. Rein was her support. Her reason. Her hope.

Opening her eyes to Rein's face, Ellyssa saw faith flicker beneath the sadness. He hadn't given up.

"I love you," she breathed.

His lips curled into a sad smile as he draped his arm over her shoulder. "Welcome back."

"I really didn't go anywhere."

"I know."

Shoving the little cave pearl into her pocket, Ellyssa took a deep breath and stood. Her arms splayed under the rocking motion, she made her way past the containers to Trista, not saying anything; Woody gave her a wistful look and scooted over. Ellyssa took the offered space.

"Trista, I don't want you to hurt," Ellyssa said, placing a hand on Trista's shoulder. A shudder swept through her friend as she whimpered. "I understand how you feel."

Trista turned her head to the side and shot Ellyssa a glare through wet eyelashes. "No, you don't," she stated. She hid her face back in the crook of her arms.

Chewing on her bottom lip, Ellyssa sought the right words. None came. "We have to continue," she tried again. "You have to find the strength."

"Just leave me alone."

Letting her hand drop, she returned to Rein.

For the next hour, time lost meaning with the drone of the tires; Ellyssa felt the air begin to change. As Dyllon continued driving down the old farm-to-market road, Trista's sobs became less frequent, and Woody started to chamber rounds into the AK-47s, magazines, his shaky hands fumbling with the cartridges. Minutely, life had started to push away the oppressive gloom of death.

Unexpectedly, Trista's head whipped up, her eyes red and raw. "Pull over," she ordered.

The suddenness of Trista's voice punctured the weakening bubble of despondency, and it seemed as if the van breathed out a sigh of relief.

"What?" asked Dyllon, his head swiveling back and forth as he looked into the side mirrors. "What's wrong? Did you see something?" His voice edged on panic.

She turned to look at him, her face set stubbornly and her eyes burning with a fire of determination. "No. I'm supposed to be driving. What if we get pulled over?"

"Are you sure?" Dyllon asked. "Are you feeling better?"

"No, I'm not feeling better. Two more of my friends died. But I'm not going down like this. None of us are." Her eyes turned toward Ellyssa. "We have to continue. Now stop the van."

Dyllon did as instructed, tires grating on the pebbles as the van came to a halt. Trista slipped out the passenger side. Dyllon climbed out and met her up front. She paused as he said something, his deep voice carrying on the wind, then Trista flung herself into his arms. Stroking her hair, Dyllon's mouth moved against her ear and she nodded. By the time she pulled away, a small smile softened her face. He grinned back at her, and in that moment, Ellyssa saw what Detective Angela Petersen had seen, although the detective had refuted her attraction. The male had a wonderful smile that reflected in his eyes. With a renewed bounce in her step, Trista walked to the driver's side and looked into the back of van.

"What?" Trista said, popping onto the seat. "Why are you all looking at me?"

Ellyssa couldn't see Woody's face, but she knew her and Rein's jaws had gone slack.

"Nothing," Rein said, a hesitant smile surfacing.

Maybe, for the moment, Rein had forgotten his dislike for Dyllon. The way Trista had turned seemed to do wonders for them all, as if the sun shone through bleak clouds carrying a ray of hope.

Trista waved him off and started to bark orders. "We have things to do, and bastards that need to pay. They have to pay." She pointed at Woody. "Change places with Dyllon. If they found his car, they might be looking for him. His picture is probably plastered all over by now." Woody scrambled up front as she motioned to Dyllon. "Grab the K100 out of the bag. No, not that one. The one with the suppressor. Load it. Wait, you need to strip. I need your clothes."

Pride lifted the rest of Ellyssa's spirit as she watched Trista transform from someone sinking in a sea of despair to someone with a take-charge attitude, completely Trista-style, her emotions an ever-changing tide. Her friend had gone through a lot, witnessing her friends murdered in cold blood to losing the people who took her in during her time of need and, yet, she'd managed to climb out of the pit of sorrow.

Dyllon sputtered, "What?"

"I don't think my pink sweater and jeans are regulation."

"What am I supposed to wear? And the credentials have you as an inspector, not area police."

"Don't you like my outfit?"

Dyllon just stared at her.

Woody snickered, and a little more of the cloud evaporated. "Trista," he said, "there is no reason for anyone to give up their clothes." He reached into the knapsack and pulled out a black roll. "Here." He handed it to her.

Flashing Woody a grateful smile, Trista said, "You think of everything."

She popped out of the van for a couple of minutes and returned wearing a wrinkled uniform of the *Gestapo*. Two bars on the collar glinted under the light.

"It looks terrible," Trista said, poking the pink of her sweater inside the collar as she looked in the rearview mirror. "And I don't have the overcoat or the gun. I'm guessing you don't have either of those shoved in the bag."

Woody shook his head. "Nope, sorry. I was kind of in a hurry."

"Well, we will just have to make do. And people will still be losing clothing. You and Dyllon need to switch."

Dyllon glanced at Woody. "She's right. You could pass for one of the patrols if they don't look too closely."

Woody opened his mouth, but then clamped it shut. He yanked the T-shirt over his head and handed it to Dyllon. The muscles in his stomach and arms rippled as he stood to unbutton his pants. Warmth creeping up her neck, Ellyssa averted her eyes and kept them focused on her hands as the males switched clothing.

"This smells," Woody stated, the tunic pulled up to his nose.

"I had to run through the woods and a dark tunnel. Besides, your clothes don't smell like a basket of roses either."

"Are you guys done?" Trista asked. "We need to be moving. And I still don't have a loaded gun." She nodded at Dyllon, her eyes dropping to the weapon.

"One sec." Rein stood and crouch-walked toward the front of the van. "I have something to show you," he said to Ellyssa. "With everything..." He paused. "It just didn't happen. You remember how I told you about the hiding place?"

"Yes."

"It's under here." He pushed a box over and a panel slid back. "It will fit three."

Hunched over, Ellyssa moved toward him and looked at the enclosed space. *Another coffin,* she thought with dismay. The Renegades seemed to move supplies easily, years of hits and misses and learning, but when it came to people, their solution was shoving them in cramped places like sardines.

Ellyssa hated having her freedom to move, to react, restricted. And this was worse than the box Tim had hidden her in, or hiding under the seat when Trista had taken them to Tim's and Sarah's. The false bottom hidden in the floor of the van called for entering feet first and sliding downward, like slipping between sheets. It would be easy, if they were discovered, for the police, or whoever, to open the compartment and shoot them all in the head. Not wanting to think what would happen if they ran into trouble, Ellyssa moved back to the rear of the van.

"As my father used to say, time to blow this Popsicle stand." Trista moved the lever to drive. The van jolted forward at a slow, steady pace.

Rein's deep laugh broke through the remaining clouds. It was a beautiful sound. Woody's and Dyllon's mingled with his.

Ellyssa had no idea what Popsicles or stands had to do with anything. But she laughed along with everyone else, and it felt good, a stress relief.

At that moment, Ellyssa held no doubt that their missing family was alive and that they would find them. And when they found them, Ellyssa would make sure they were all reunited. As Trista said, there were people who had to pay.

Their group was strong, fueled by emotions.

Ellyssa squeezed Rein's hand.

# 23

As Mathew walked between the two escorting soldiers, he felt the eyes of fellow prisoners follow his trek across the compound, their heads staying downcast so not to be caught. In their thin coats and ragged boots, they carried rocks and stacked them in a field adjacent to the Commandant's office.

At least the day was warmer, even with the grey wispy clouds that floated across the sky, fracturing the sunlight in bent rays. Patches of snow littered the walkway, slowly transforming into slush. A constant drip sounded as drops of water fell from the gutters to the ground below.

A line of soldiers stood watch over the slave labor, rifles cradled in the crooks of their arms. Next to them, shadowed within the overhang of the building of death—the vent clear of smoke for the time being—stood the sergeant-at-arms. Mathew wasn't a hundred percent sure, but his skin crawled as if the steely blue eyes of the sergeant raked over him. He faltered, which earned him a poke with a muzzle.

"Get going," said the soldier.

Tearing his gaze away from the shadowy figure of the sergeant, Mathew's eyes settled on the thick stone barricade that separated the females from the males. Behind the wall, he could hear a female yelling orders to her wards. The voice held a hard, authoritative edge.

Mathew wondered if his plan would work. If he'd be able to save any of them. His gaze shifted away.

The building housing the Commandant's office loomed at the end of the pathway, and Mathew was on his way to become a traitor.

Commandant Baer was leaning back in his chair when Mathew entered. Without looking up, he waved Mathew toward the chair. "Sit," he said.

Mathew took the proffered seat and watched the Commandant shuffle papers into a neat, orderly pile. "Well?" said Commandant Baer, leveling his gaze at Mathew. "Have you decided to provide me with the information I seek?"

Nausea rolled in Mathew's stomach, but he lifted his chin. He was going to do what he had to do, and technically, he wasn't providing information about the Renegades or their contacts.

He still felt like a traitor, though.

"You wish to know about Ellyssa?"

Leaning back in the chair, the Commandant folded his hands across his midsection. "Yes."

Mathew studied the officer for a moment. As always, the Commandant wore his dark blue *Waffenrock* neatly, the red piping lined straight, the armband bearing the swastika wrinkle-free. He knew Commandant Baer wanted the information. He just hoped the want exceeded his so-called moral duties. Mathew swallowed.

"I will provide the information to you. But it will come at a cost."

Commandant Baer shook his head, his eyebrows rising in amusement. Mathew guessed this was the first time any prisoner had had the audacity to offer information with a price tag. Hell, it was probably the first time a prisoner had offered information ever.

"No deals."

"Okay," Mathew said, shrugging. "Then I guess there is nothing to talk about." He started to stand.

"Remember, Doc," the Commandant said, his eyes cold and calculating, "you might be safe, but your friends are not."

Lids narrowing, Mathew boldly placed his hands on the Commandant's enormous desk. "You do what you have to do," he stated with a lot more courage than the sinking feeling in his chest should have permitted. "I will not cave. Most would be better off dead than the conditions they are living in now." He turned away, the door his next destination.

"Wait," the Commandant said.

Mathew stopped, his heart pattering like mad. He kept his back to the officer.

"Maybe we could reach some form of agreement."

"I'm listening."

"Sit," the commander ordered. "Let's talk."

Facing the Commandant, Mathew walked slowly back to the green chair, the thumping in his chest deafening to his ears. This was it. Sink or swim.

"What do you propose?"

"First, tell me if any more women have...been put out of their misery."

"None."

Settling into a false air of confidence, Mathew scooted back in the chair, his eyes never leaving the Commandant's. If he flinched or look away, the cards would shift sides.

"Then my proposal is this. No one else dies."

"Is that all?"

"No. I want everyone to have warm clothes and new boots. I've seen the stacks of clothes you have; there is plenty, especially with the depleted numbers. And more food. There is no reason to starve a man."

"And is that all?"

"In exchange for the better living conditions, I will answer questions about Ellyssa as long as you understand I will not, no matter what, divulge any information that might compromise the Resistance. And I won't answer anything until new clothes show up on the backs of my friends."

Commandant Baer swiveled in his chair and stared out the window; his arms folded across his chest. For several long minutes, the man said nothing, and the nerves started to bundle in Mathew's stomach, giving rise to nausea again. He hoped he hadn't blown his chance to help his fellow inmates, to stop them from dying, but he meant what he had said—he wouldn't give.

Finally, the Commandant turned around, his face hard as stone, and the hope Mathew held on to plummeted.

"Fine," he said.

Mathew felt his eyes bug. He really hadn't expected the man to agree. Deep down, he had assumed he would be walking back to the barracks, his bargaining chips revoked.

"Let me make something perfectly clear to you," Commandant Baer continued. "No one is to know about our...arrangement. If any word leaks out, everyone will visit the chamber. Yourself included. To hell with the consequences."

"I understand," Mathew said, somehow keeping his voice steady.

He opened a drawer and pulled out blueprints. "I have need for a recreation center for my men. Your people will build it. It gives an excuse for the extra clothes and food. Of course, I would want them healthy until the work was completed."

"We wouldn't want your reputation tainted."

He folded his hands across his midsection again. "It seems I have found a reason to keep you filthy Renegades alive for a bit longer."

Mathew let the insult roll off his back. It wasn't like they were friends now. Each of them was working for his own agenda, but that didn't mean they couldn't be on the same side of the fence. "One more thing."

"I'm sure that is all you are going to get from me. That was the deal."

Mathew shook his head. "I'm not asking for anything. Just some information for my benefit." He readjusted in his seat, leaning forward. "Why? Why are you so interested in Ellyssa?"

Commandant Baer moved his hands to under his chin, his fingers lacing together. "That is none of your business."

"But I think it is," Mathew stated. "And I think you know it. *The enemy of my enemy is my friend.* Weren't those the words you used?"

The Commandant glared at him through slitted lids. "I think we're done for now."

# 24

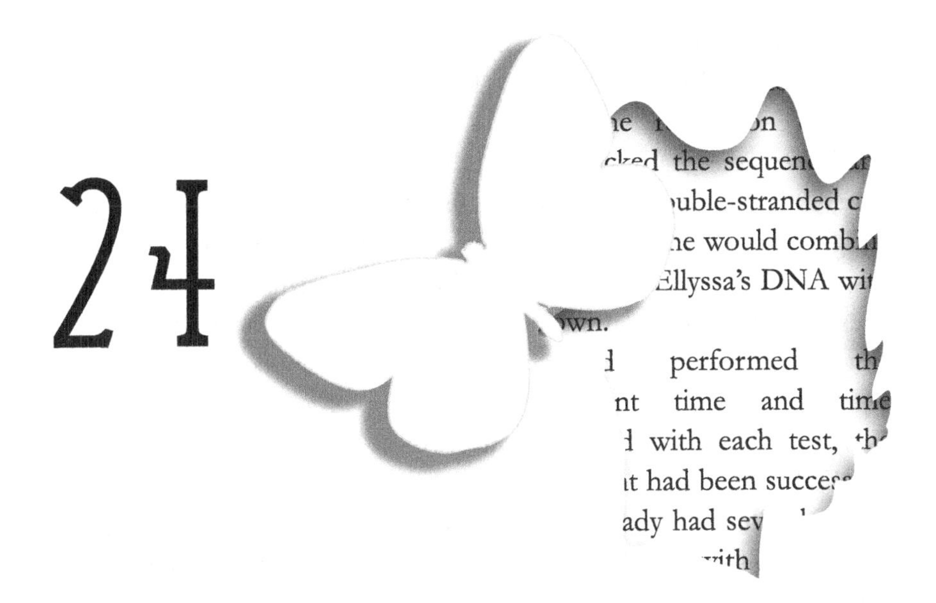

Aalexis turned the fine focus, bringing the DNA into sharper view. The restriction enzyme had attacked the sequence and produced a double-stranded cut. It was there she would combine Xaver's and Ellyssa's DNA with her own.

She'd performed the experiment time and time again, and with each test, the attachment had been successful. She'd already had several partial combinations with her and Xaver's DNA frozen.

Besides the return of her sister, what Aalexis really needed was a lab with a medical facility so that she could conduct the somatic cell transfer and implant the blastocyst into the surrogate. The complications of the procedure had grown past the use of the temporary lab.

The door opened and Xaver stepped into the sally port to be disinfected. She watched his tall frame as he slipped on the white surgical coveralls, shoe covers and mask. When he was dressed, he pushed through the heavy plastic flaps and proceeded inside the lab.

"What progress have you made?" he asked as he approached her, his blue eyes peeking at her from above the mask.

Even with the strong odor of disinfectant and the surgical attire covering him from head to foot, Xaver's unique scent still cut through, all clean and male. She pushed the mask tighter around her nose and turned away.

"As we already have discussed," Aalexis stated, "we need Ellyssa. With her, we can finish combining the DNA and start the replicating sequence inside a cell."

Xaver sidled up next to her and his heat penetrated through to Aalexis' skin, as if she stood by a roaring fire. His scent invaded her nose again. Tingles surged where his hand dangled closest to hers and her heart responded. She felt the blood pulse through her veins. Too aware of Xaver's presence, Aalexis felt an urge to escape. Taking the petri dish, she moved toward the freezer where the other specimens were contained.

"The contact led the police right to her," Xaver said following behind her. His heat radiated from him in waves.

Did he know? Was he torturing her on purpose?

"But she escaped, of course." she said, somehow maintaining a steady monotonous note. Aalexis opened the freezer, using the steel door to block him from sight. Cold air rushed out, brushing against her skin.

"As predicted."

"I assumed as much. The information about the Renegades has reached her."

"It seems a Captain Dyllon Jones is missing. The same one who aided the detective during her search. He is either dead or an informant."

"Perfect. If they are incapable of capturing her within the next few days, we will have to go back to Amarufoss and wait for her. The people in charge are imprudent."

"I agree. I have also contacted the Commandant and instructed him to reinforce his patrols of the area, in case they happen to bypass the roadblocks."

"As I am sure they will."

Aalexis placed the dish inside the freezer and closed the door. When she turned around, Xaver stood right behind her. Surprised, her eyes widened minutely. Not enough that an average human could have registered, but Xaver was not average. Ignoring him, she pushed past, her destination the door.

"I have something I want to discuss with you." He was following her again.

"What?" she asked on her way to the decontamination port. All she wanted to do was go to the gym and think about what was happening to her. She wondered if Ellyssa had experienced the same symptoms.

"Would you stop for a moment?"

"I want to work out."

"Aalexis. Stop," Xaver commanded, his voice deep.

The muscles of her neck constricting, she halted her progress, her escape route just within reach. "When will the lab be completed?"

"In less than three weeks. But that is not what I want to talk to you about."

Turning, their gazes met. Xaver's mask was pulled down and his blue eyes, shelved over his angular cheekbones, glimmered. A lock of platinum hair escaped from the hood of his coveralls and hung on his prominent forehead. A strange fluttering tickled the inside of Aalexis' stomach and rushed to her chest. Fighting to maintain her composure, she swallowed.

"When Micah returned after he had located Ellyssa," he started. With magnetic force, Aalexis' gaze was pulled to the movement of Xaver's full lips. "He told me some things that at the time had meant nothing, but now I wonder."

"Wonder?" she stated, her voice dead.

He took a step toward her. "It concerns Ellyssa and the emotions Micah sensed through the music box. They were so strong that he actually felt them."

Aalexis stepped back. Whatever foreign affliction she had been feeling she shoved down. She would not be like her sister. Anger forged forward. "I do not wish to talk about Ellyssa's breakdown," she said, the deadpan tone no longer a fight to maintain.

"I think we should. I have developed a theory."

Taking another step back, Aalexis shook her head. "What theory? Emotions weaken. There is nothing to theorize. Now, if you will excuse me, brother, I have training exercises." She spun on her heel and escaped through the flap. Without looking at Xaver, she removed her coveralls and shoe guards. Her hair fell around her shoulders in blonde waves. She pulled it back into a bun.

"If you care to join me," Aalexis said, her hand on the knob, "you may. I feel a need for a worthy opponent."

Aalexis walked out into the evening and inhaled, welcoming the cold that sharpened and focused her mind. Whatever she had felt would not control her. She would not succumb.

*What had Xaver meant when he said Micah felt the sensations?* Aalexis shrugged off the uncomfortable thought. It didn't matter. What mattered was seeing her father's plans come to fruition.

To the right, a bright round moon hung directly over The Center—*her* Center. Rat-a-tat noise and machinery sounds drifted on the Lake Michigan breeze. Beams of yellow light spotlighted the three-story building. Bricks and concrete climbed up the skeletal frame in colors of grey and red. The building wasn't as tall as her father's had been, but she didn't have to hide behind false training schools and eugenics used for more conventional means. Nor would she hide her experiments down in the basement for training purposes.

Aalexis was meant for more.

The rocking motion wasn't soft, but it was hypnotizing. Sleep pulled at Rein's eyelids, but he couldn't grab hold of the bliss to lull him under. Instead, his eyes remained wide open, alert, as he amazingly stayed still. A metal latch poked relentlessly at his back, but he refused to move. Ellyssa rested in the crook of his arm, her head on his chest.

Except for the dash lights and a full moon grinning from above, darkness clung in the back of the van. Woody was driving, his hands aligned at the two and ten positions, his back ramrod straight. Red from the dash lights reflected off his hair. Next to him, curled in the passenger seat, Trista slept, her head leaning against the vibrating window. Dyllon leaned against her seat, his eyes closed, and soft snores pushed from between his lips.

Rein still didn't like the man, even with all of Ellyssa's reassurances. He just couldn't get past the fact that Dyllon had helped the detective, which had led to a pain he'd never forget. As the fire had licked through his veins with just Aalexis' thought, it'd also burned into Rein's long-term memory. But he thought, at least with all that had happened, he might be able to tolerate Dyllon. He seemed to really care for Trista, and Ellyssa had confirmed his devotion.

"How are you doing?" Rein asked Woody.

"I'm pretty wired right now. The nap I took earlier helped."

"Do you know where we're at?"

"I'm thinking we're somewhere close to the Oklahoma border. Hopefully past it. I know we slipped into Kansas, but it's hard to judge."

"Mmmhmm," Rein mumbled, closing his eyes.

The van jolted back and forth. The tires scraped across degrading pavement. Mesmerizing. The prospect of sleep was finally catching up.

"You know," Woody said, his voice soft, "she's special."

Rein's lids fluttered open. Although he never acknowledged it, Rein was pretty certain he knew how Woody felt about Ellyssa. Something a little more than friendship? At the very least, a big-brother syndrome. How could he not? Woody had been there for a fundamental awakening in Ellyssa, a transformation to an extent, when Jordan had passed away. At that point, Woody had seen through the soldiering exterior, the danger she imposed, and into the innocence of Ellyssa's heart. Rein never vocalized it, but jealousy flared on occasion when he thought about Ellyssa opening up to Woody. Regardless of the connection between his friend and the woman he would die for, Rein knew what he and Ellyssa shared was something much more.

With heavy lids, Rein looked down at Ellyssa, her pale hair under his nose, her scent tantalizing. With every rise and fall of her chest, her even breaths, the twitching muscles in her sleep, his love for her grew. He felt the expansion in his chest, like his heart would burst.

"I know," he answered.

"If I only had the insight."

"Not all of us can be winners."

Woody peered at him in the rearview mirror, a light mischievous grin on his face. "You're lucky I didn't."

"Whatever."

Ellyssa mumbled. Her hand twisted in his shirt. Lightly, he placed his lips against the top of her head and inhaled. Nuzzling against his chest, she relaxed again, sleep reclaiming her.

Leaning his head back against the metal, Rein said, "A lot has changed."

"Yeah."

"Promise me something."

"What?"

"If something happens to me, you will take care of Ellyssa."

Woody didn't reply, his eyes remaining focused ahead. As the seconds swept into minutes, Rein began to wonder if his friend was going to answer at all. After a while, he didn't care. He felt himself teetering on the edge of the slumber abyss, only to be savagely yanked from the edge when Woody answered.

"Don't talk like that. Nothing's going to happen."

"If it does."

"With my life."

Rein settled back again, his lids sliding shut. The next thing he knew, a blazing light pierced through the dark, blinding him. The sleep that had tried to seal his lids scrambled away.

"Shit," Woody said, applying the brake. "We have company."

Life sizzled in the van. Trista bolted upright, as did Dyllon. The light haloed around the passenger seat, making his wide eyes seem sunken like a skull's. Ellyssa's head jerked up, but that was the only move she made. Her breath stayed even and, except for a cold flash within her blue eyes, her face became an emotionless mask. Rein wondered if she could feel the pounding inside his chest. He certainly could.

"How many?" Rein asked.

"I see two cars," Trista answered, her hand shelved across her forehead, "but I can't tell how many people. It's too bright."

Ellyssa closed her eyes. "There are five. Two in front, two on the left, one on the right. They are looking for Renegades and they know about Dyllon."

Rein shuddered. "Figures."

As the van came to a stop, Ellyssa reached up and broke the mini-bulb in the dome that came on when a door opened. Wondering what she was doing, Rein blinked, and she was suddenly crouching behind Woody's seat. He didn't even hear her move.

As Trista straightened her uniform, Dyllon reached to pull the box hiding the compartment. A *click* sounded as the panel slid back.

"Get in," Ellyssa said in an inflectionless voice without looking at Dyllon. Her face was pressed between the paneling and the side of the driver's seat.

Feet first, Dyllon slid in and disappeared from Rein's sight.

Ellyssa looked at Rein. "You are next."

Something told Rein, the way she looked, the way she spoke, that Ellyssa had no inclination of crawling inside the compartment. That was why she'd broken the bulb; she didn't want to be seen. She was in soldiering mode.

"What about you?" he asked, his eyes narrowing.

She glanced away and shook her head. "We do not have time. Please."

"I'm not getting in there without you."

The beam of light expanded, their unwelcome company drawing closer.

Ellyssa pulled the box back into position as Dyllon said, "Wait." She cut off his protests.

"No time for us," she said, looking at Rein. "Hide."

*Where?*

Woody's gaze flicked to the rearview mirror, a grim line pressing his lips together. With as little movement as possible, Trista reached between her legs. She shifted to the side and slid the pistol Rein knew she had into her pocket.

The beam of light swung back and forth as one of the soldiers approached. Soon afterward, he heard a male's voice from directly in front of the van

"Papers," the man yelled.

"What am I going to use?" Woody asked.

"Dyllon's," Ellyssa whispered.

"This isn't going to end well." Woody reached into his pocket and withdrew a black wallet.

As Woody started to roll down the window, Ellyssa reached under the seat, and the K100 appeared in her hand. Rein reached for the AK-47. He slid the bolt back. As quietly as possible, he lifted the door handle. The latch released with a *snick*, drawing Ellyssa's attention. She looked over her shoulder, fear replacing the blankness. She shook her head.

Rein had no intention of listening to her. He paused, his fingers wrapped around the edge of the door, as he waited for the perfect opportunity.

Woody stuck his hand out the window and waved the wallet.

"Both of you, get out of the van with your hands extended in front." A different voice with an accent that held a familiar twang. The words sounded more like, *both joo, get outtah d'vahn wit yo hahnds extended in fwont.* He sounded a little like Mike had, Rein thought with a pang, when Mike had first joined the group. If he remembered correctly, Mike was from the Northeastern coast.

Trista leaned over to speak out of the driver's side. "I'm Inspector Klein. We are in a hurry." She tossed a look over her shoulder. Panic stressed her face, but her voice remained surprisingly calm. "I have a Renegade."

"I'm sorry, Inspector, but we have to follow orders. Please exit the van with your hands where we can see them."

"I understand," Trista said.

As Trista and Woody opened their doors, Rein swung his open. He turned back toward Ellyssa, the blankness faltering as her wide eyes begged *no.*

For a moment, Rein considered staying with her, but he couldn't. He had to protect them. His eyes darted from her to the box covering the hidden space. "Stay here," he mouthed.

The last thing he saw was fear melting away the last of Ellyssa's vacant demeanor before he slipped through the gap. Kneeling behind the bumper, he listened to the tap of boots on asphalt. Slowly, he edged to the corner and peered around it. Two floodlights illuminated the night. Woody wisely hung back, close to the corner of the van.

"Papers, please," said Mr. Northeast. Luckily, he hadn't asked for Woody's yet.

There was rustling, then silence. "Inspector Klein."

"Specialist," Trista answered with disdain, "as I told you, I have detained a prisoner, and you are interfering."

Trista kept talking, holding their attention, her intonation commanding with no-nonsense authority. Rein was impressed.

"It's late, I'm beyond tired and I don't have time for this delay."

"I'm going to have to ask to inspect the back of the van, Inspector," No-Accent said.

Trista sighed dramatically, and Rein used the opportunity to sneak to the left side of the road. He lowered to his belly behind a bare bush and long-dead grass. The plants crunched under his weight. The frosty ground served as a reminder of the freezing temperature—adrenaline had held it at bay until now. The glacial cold seeped through his thin T-shirt. A shiver gripped his spine.

The two men, dressed in thick olive-green coats and grey breeches bloused into black leather boots, faced Trista as she ranted. Woody stood as inconspicuously as possible, keeping his grey eyes averted—a dead giveaway that he wasn't part of society. Rein couldn't see the others, but he knew that Woody and Trista were both targeted in their sights.

Trista threw up her arms. "Of course you do," she replied irritably. Her hand kept going toward her pocket as if to ensure the pistol was within reach. "The prisoner is locked in the back."

"Thank you, Inspector," No-Accent said.

*Ellyssa.*

A sinking feeling, like a boulder, crashed through Rein's stomach. He felt sick as he leveled the rifle at No-Accent as he broke away and walked along the side of the van. At the back corner of the van, the soldier paused and swung around, looking past Trista, who was still raving, and unobtrusive Woody, toward the tree line. There, Rein was sure he saw a shadowy movement. The soldier gave a nod and the shadow slipped behind the tree.

Three accounted for. Rein had no idea where the other two were, but he knew Woody and Trista were the ones in immediate danger.

With No-Accent centered between the crosshairs, Rein's finger tensed on the trigger, the cold metal curving smoothly. The soldier pulled down on the handle. Abruptly, the door swung outward, almost knocking into the unsuspecting man. The soldier didn't even have time to step back. In a white blur, two hands struck out of the van, and in less than a second, No-Accent dangled limp, the hands holding him by the side of the head. Ellyssa dragged him silently inside.

Relief washed through Rein, but only for a moment. Ellyssa popped from the back of the van. Crouching, her face hidden within the shadows, her head whipped left, then right. With predatory speed, she darted to the opposite side of the road and disappeared into the leafless vegetation.

*What was she doing?*

Rein's heart slammed into his throat. Fighting every compulsion to go after her, Rein stayed put, his muscles twitching defiantly. It was against every instinct, but deep down, Rein knew Ellyssa could take care of herself and was better equipped to do so.

A long time ago, she had told him how emotions weakened people, how they could get in the way of rational thought. In the effort to ensure her safety, he could understand. Following Ellyssa would be a mistake, one that would end up in death for them all.

Rein swallowed his trepidation. In the distance, Trista kept Mr. Northeast's attention, her words hollow, like crossing through a tunnel. Woody shuffled, his head hanging down, keeping his telltale eyes away from the spotlight.

As the pounding in Rein's chest subsided, his head cleared. If Ellyssa went to the right, she had gone to dispose of the single soldier. Rein glanced toward the tree where he hoped the other still hid.

Planning to belly-crawl deeper into cover, Rein dropped onto his elbows, the AK-47 snug against his underside. A sharp jab to the back stopped him.

"I would stay real still if I was you," said a female.

Rein's heart jumpstarted to overdrive, his mind becoming a jumbled mess. Fear, not for him but for his love and friends, almost incapacitated him. He had to get a grip. Rein inhaled deeply, trying to calm his nerves, which was hard with a barrel digging into his spine. Given little choice, Rein did as requested.

"I knew I saw something crawl out of the back of the van. Put your hands to the side and roll over, real slow-like. Let's see what you got under you."

"What's going on over there?" said the specialist from the northeast.

"I got one of the sneaky bastards, Sir," the woman answered.

"What?" Specialist Northeast asked disbelievingly. There was a pause. "You," he pointed his weapon at Woody, "over there." Woody went next to Trista. "Private Stoker, bring your prisoner here."

"Get up," Private Stoker said with a painful jab. "Keep your hands to the sides where I can see them."

The pressure of the muzzle slightly lessened as the private took a step back, the sole of her boot crunching the ice-laden grass. Without a second thought, no real plan of what to do next, Rein flipped over. He swept his arm to the side, knocking the barrel away just as a round slammed into the ground next to him. Slivers of frozen dirt spewed in the aftermath and the crack rang deafeningly in Rein's ears.

Slightly disoriented and with a consistent buzz in his head, Rein followed the motion with his leg. The private landed on her backside with an *oomph*. Leaving his rifle where it lay, Rein managed to clamber on top of her when the gates of hell broke open.

A scream resonated from somewhere up the road. A short burst of gunfire sounded. Someone—Trista?—yelled. Another barrage, closer this time, rattled. Pings sounded as the van was hit. More yelling.

Rein's head snapped to the side as pain exploded in his lower jaw, adding to the discomfort of the buzzing. As his vision tunneled to a pinpoint, the private bucked hard, almost sending him to the side. He grappled, finding his balance, and had barely repositioned himself when fingernails raked the side of his face. Private Stoker pitched beneath him again. This time his balance was completely thrown off. Reeling, Rein's face met the cold ground.

The private spun out from under his legs and scrambled for the rifle lying a meter away. Rein grabbed her ankle and she stumbled, but not before her hand clasped the butt of her weapon. She swung the weapon around and he pulled back, the muzzle zipping in front of his face in a black blur. Grabbing the barrel, he tried to pull it free from her grasp. She yanked back and pulled the weapon free as Rein toppled forward. The private kicked and screamed, her hands everywhere, the rifle slamming into his backside.

Then, suddenly, Private Stoker stilled, the rifle clacking to the side as her finger relaxed, her lids peeled back in a look of surprise. It took a moment for Rein to realize the woman was dead even as he watched a thin stream of red lazily seep from a bullet hole in her temple. In his frenzy to stay alive, he hadn't even heard gunfire.

Surprised at the sudden turn of events, Rein turned, thinking Ellyssa or Trista would be standing by the road, but his eyes rested on a figure clad in green and grey. A rifle rose and he found his eyes locked on the gaping hole of the weapon.

Moving as little as possible, Rein felt behind him. His fingers curled around the butt of the woman's rifle and he moved just as the flash lifted from the barrel. Air disturbance lifted his hair as the round zipped by. Instinctively, Rein brought the weapon up at the same time he fell. He squeezed the trigger, and the rifle, recoiling, slammed repeatedly against his shoulder. Cartridges went wild. Gunpowder scented the air. He was thrown off-balance. Silence followed as he landed on his side behind the dead private.

As the smoke, weighted by the icy air, lifted, Rein heard Ellyssa call his name.

The world shifted and everything faded away.

# 25

As puffs of breath escaped Ellyssa's mouth, she squeezed the freezing water from the cloth, then dabbed at the scratch over Rein's right ear, where the bullet had skimmed his head. He lay on a blanket; his head was propped on another, and he was covered with the thick coat of the dead soldier, warding off the early-morning cold with little effect. Besides the wound from the bullet, three long scratch marks marred Rein's cheek.

White noise squelched annoyingly, catching Ellyssa's attention. She turned to look at Dyllon, who still hovered close to the soldiers' ATVs, waiting to respond if anyone called for updates from the patrol. His stance was rigid, still angry at being shut inside the human stash alone. When Woody had finally opened the panel, Dyllon had scrambled out, spewing words Ellyssa had never heard anyone say, though she caught the gist of the meaning. He'd gone directly to Trista, alternating between pulling her close and checking her for injuries despite her reassurances.

Ellyssa didn't blame him. She couldn't image the turmoil he'd endured, locked away in a metal box. She could have at least stayed connected to Rein on a mental level. Dyllon had had nothing to reassure him.

Trista huddled safely within his arms. Constantly, Dyllon would touch her cheek or press his lips against her forehead, as if to reassure himself.

They were sharing moments Ellyssa wished she was sharing with Rein.

Inhaling deeply, Ellyssa went back to caring for the reason her heart continued beating, refusing to acknowledge the worry that kept trying to wiggle through the cracks of her carefully constructed wall.

Rein was going to be fine. She'd examined his wound a dozen times. The edges were smooth and blackened from the heat. The blood had already coagulated, sealing out any infection. The round hadn't done any permanent damage, nothing Rein wouldn't recover from. Just a scratch. It could have been a lot worse, if the soldier had moved the muzzle a millimeter to the left. She could have been covering his corpse with her body, crying tears of hurt and rage and loss, depleted of the will to live instead.

A chill not from the cold sent a shiver quaking up her spine.

Ellyssa didn't want to think about what could have been. What mattered was he that was safe.

She resealed the cracks in her mental wall.

"How's he doing?" Woody asked as he bounced up and down. He alternated between blowing warm air between his hands and vigorously rubbing his palms together.

"He's fine," Ellyssa answered, gently applying the cold compress.

Sensing Woody's hand hovering above her shoulder, Ellyssa reached into the cup of water to wet the cloth again. A moment later, she felt his hand. He squeezed her shoulder reassuringly, and she relished his touch, his friendship, the fact that he was there. The awkwardness between them a couple of days ago seemed to evaporate in that moment. Although different, they both carried a love for the other.

Ellyssa looked up at Woody. The floodlights circled his head like an aura.

"That was pretty intense," he said.

"It's going to get worse."

"Yeah, I know." Woody squatted next to her. He grazed his fingers across her cheek, leaving a streak of warmth. "He's going to be okay."

"I know." Ellyssa smiled. "Thank you."

"I know I've been acting weird lately. Just me trying to deal."

"I understand."

"I do love you, though."

"I love you, too."

Sighing deeply, he said, "I know." He pushed a lock of hair from her eyes; his soft touch grazed her skin. He dropped his hand to his knee. "Friends."

"Always."

A comfortable silence wavered between them for a moment until Woody asked, "Did you get a read from any of them?" He motioned to the dead bodies.

"Just that there are other patrols. I think mostly south of here. I couldn't catch the exact locations."

"Do they know our destination?"

"I don't think they did," she answered, raising her chin toward the dead bodies. "Someone is tracking us, though."

"I think now would be a good time to start heading west."

Groaning, Rein's lids fluttered open and Ellyssa's heart jump-started with relief. He looked at Ellyssa, then, eyes widening, he swung into a sitting position. The color in his face bleached away, and he fell back on his elbows. "Whoa."

Ellyssa reached out to him, her hands fluttering about, unsure what to do. "What's the matter?"

"Dizzy." He paused for a moment before attempting to right himself. "Where are they?" he asked, remaining upright this time, pink recoloring the paleness.

"Dead."

"Oh," he said, looking relieved for a brief moment. Suddenly, Rein's gaze flicked to Ellyssa, fear touching his eyes. "You're not hurt, are you?"

"Not a scratch."

His shoulders relaxed. "Good. I wish I was as lucky," Rein said, touching the spot above his ear. His breath hitched. "Damn. What happened? My brain feels like it got caught in a vise."

"You were shot. Nothing serious. Barely a graze," Woody reassured.

"Shot!" Rein winced again as he touched the side of his head.

The expression on Rein's face was comical, a mixture of confusion and surprise. Ellyssa couldn't help but smile, more with relief than anything else. She handed him aspirin and a canteen of water.

"You're going to live," she said as he swallowed the medication.

Mouth twisting into a lopsided grin, Rein brushed her cheek with the back of his fingers. "Is that your professional opinion?"

He was so beautiful, his eyes shining with humor even when in pain. Ellyssa captured his hand in hers. "I promise."

"I guess I have little choice than to go with your diagnosis, but remind me to duck next time."

Woody knelt next to them. "I don't know," he said, eyeing the side of Rein's head. "Looks like you're going to have a small bald patch."

"Great."

"You can comb it over like old Mr. Wilson used to."

Ellyssa surmised that it was a name belonging to a Renegade she hadn't met.

"I'm not taking any styling advice from you."

From the direction of the ATVs, static sizzled followed by a female voice. "Patrol four, status update?"

After waiting a couple of seconds to make sure no one else responded, Dyllon answered the call. "Patrol four. Clear."

"Wrap it up. Bring it in. Over." The radio silenced.

Grabbing Trista by the hand, Dyllon walked over to Ellyssa. "I think that's our invitation to bug out."

With Woody's help, Ellyssa pulled Rein to his feet. She wrapped her arm around his waist to keep him steady. "We should hide the bodies and vehicles."

"Good idea," Woody said. "Let's get the injured man over to the van and make it happen."

The sun peeped over the horizon of the flat land and spread its rays out in a spectacular display of oranges and reds. The puffy white clouds reflected the brilliant light and tinted the plains. Unfortunately, the sun refused to warm the air.

The chill bit the tips of Mathew's fingers as he toted an armload of pickaxes—apparently his new job—to the area next to the Commandant's office where the rec center would be erected. The new detail would prove to be challenging, as the ground was hard and frozen, but at least his fellow inmates were more warmly dressed.

As agreed upon, the clothes and boots had arrived soon after his talk with the Commandant. Dinner had proved to be a treat with a bit of protein in the form of peanut butter and two pieces of bread each. Breakfast came complete with cups of cold milk and wedges of cheese.

Mathew couldn't help but feel surprise. Deep down, he'd expected the commander wouldn't follow through, the sadistic need to torture those he believed beneath him proving too great to deny. It seemed the information Mathew could provide about Ellyssa was more tantalizing.

After Mathew dumped the pickaxes on the ground, the prisoners in their new but still too thin grey-striped coats, each grabbed a tool, one at a time under the scrutiny of the soldiers because of the potential for using them as weapons. The worry was needless. Even with the added protein, the inmates were too weak to withstand the cardiovascular exertions of a fight; they could barely lift the axes. Such energy would take a lot more than a dollop of peanut butter and a glass of milk.

Even with the pickaxes, that didn't account for the double patrols Mathew had noticed over the last few days. Enlisted men in six groups of four, wearing olive-green coats and armed with rifles, walked the perimeter of the fence. The metal gates had been sliding back and forth on clattering wheels more often than when Mathew had first arrived, as more soldiers reported to duty.

Mathew stepped away to return to the tool shed for shovels. Down the path stood the sergeant-at-arms, his crooked nose and square jaw visible beneath the visor of his military cap. A momentary pause later, Mathew kept his present course until he stood face to face with the formidable man.

"The Commandant requests your presence," the sergeant sneered.

"Yes, Sergeant," Mathew mumbled.

He started to turn back toward the office when the sergeant grabbed his arm. His fingers dug in painfully.

"I want to know why the Commandant has such interest in you."

Glancing down at the sergeant's hand, fingertips lost within the folds of his grey-striped coat, Mathew fought the urge to defiantly yank away. It wouldn't be a smart thing to do. He couldn't risk bringing further attention to himself or the jeopardize the fringe benefits his fellow inmates were receiving. Instead, Mathew looked into the younger man's eyes with a lie on his lips. "I'm not sure I understand, Sergeant."

"Do you not think I haven't noticed the changes around here?"

"From what I understand, the prisoners are building a new rec center for the men stationed here."

The sergeant-at-arms ripped his grip away, almost yanking Mathew off his feet. Folding his arms across his chest, his jaw set and his eyes narrowed dangerously. "I find it interesting how one day your hide was being ripped off your bones with the Commandant's crop and the next you're polishing boots, warm inside the barracks."

"I perform the details I've been assigned," Mathew said with growing disquiet. "Perhaps this conversation is something you should take up with your commander."

"Perhaps I will be keeping an eye on the situation." The sergeant executed a perfect one-hundred-eighty degree turn and strode away.

Mathew watched the sergeant until he stopped by the wall separating the two camps. He flipped around and grated Mathew with a hooded glare soaked in animosity. Muffled by the thick stones, he heard sharp tinks of metal on stone. Offhandedly, he wondered if the Commandant had kept his end of the deal and provided for the women too. There was no way to tell; Mathew had little choice but to take the commander's word and hope lies didn't taint Nazi lips.

Shoving his hands in his flimsy coat pockets, Mathew started down the walkway toward the Commandant's office. Curious stares of soldiers and downcast gazes of the prisoners followed him. Trying to ignore them, Mathew kept his head down and ascended the steps onto the porch.

He was going to have to inform the Commandant of the sergeant's inquisition, although he doubted the sergeant cared; his job was to police the camp, and that was exactly what he was doing.

After opening the door, Mathew stepped inside the colorless, immaculate office with the corporal, who was perched over the computer, tapping away. He glanced up at the intrusion, then popped out of the chair to escort Mathew into the Commandant's office.

As the corporal straightened his pristine dark-blue tunic and smoothed his grey breeches, he ordered, "Come with me." The single diamond insignia on his left collar sparkled under the fluorescents as he turned his back on Mathew. "The Commandant expected you five minutes ago."

"I was detained."

The corporal stopped with his hand on the knob. Sidling to the left, he glared at Mathew, his blue eyes colored with disbelief. "I highly suggest the next time you are summoned, you come immediately." He opened the entrance and stepped inside. Extending his arm, the corporal said, "Heil."

Mathew heard the Commandant's voice as he repeated the salutation.

"Your ward has arrived."

"Send him in and then you may go."

The corporal stepped back, allowing Mathew room to walk into the warm interior of the Commandant's office and all its homey browns and greens. As soon as Mathew went by, the corporal backed out, closing the door behind him.

Mathew stood just inside the door as the Commandant rose from his chair.

"Mathew," he said with a single nod, "sit."

Mathew hesitated. All the misgivings he thought he'd smashed down and disregarded plummeted down on him at once, leaving a sinkhole where feelings of betrayal and treachery tumbled. Technically, he wasn't supplying any information to compromise the Resistance. But divulging Ellyssa's secrets might prove to be worse.

"Second thoughts?" Commandant Baer asked as he regarded Mathew. Amusement danced in his eyes, Mathew's discomfort clearly entertaining him.

Mathew studied the Commandant, meticulous to the most minute detail from his combed silver hair parted on the right, to his crisp blue *Waffenrock* where the black swastika was arrogantly displayed on his left arm to the shiny medals and insignias gleaming with pride.

"Remember, Doc, you will either keep your end of the bargain," the commander continued, placing his hands on top of the mahogany desk, "or I will torture each of the women, slowly, until their screams echo throughout the camp. Then I will move to the men." He smiled, a terrifying skeletal smile. "You will have a front-row seat."

Nausea percolated in Mathew's stomach at the thought.

For whatever reason, Commandant Baer wanted the information he could provide, confirmed by the fact that the commander had agreed to Mathew's conditions in the first place. He was going to have to get a grip and play the game he'd agreed to and do so well, or he would lose the upper hand.

"No second thoughts," Mathew denied, covering the sinkhole with renewed faith that if he could keep everyone alive a bit longer, a miracle would present itself. Piecing together the nerve with which he had started the endeavor, he went and took his usual chair across from the commander. Mathew causally leaned back and leveled his gaze. "I will remind you, Commandant, to me, death is not a threat." His tone managed to remain steady while voicing the untruth. Mathew didn't want to see anyone tortured to death.

Commandant Baer grinned. "Very good."

"I think we should start with your sergeant-at-arms."

# 26

An hour after passing a toppled town sign with letters starting with an A and ending in NY that had somehow managed to hold its place against the passing of time, the van had coasted the last meters before coming to a stop amidst the flattest land Ellyssa had ever seen. There wasn't any natural cover to hide behind. Besides a scraggly tree or bush defiantly poking through, the land was barren. No towering buildings stretched toward the sky, no cars, no people; absolutely nothing moved. In a way, it was peaceful; it was also eerie and definitely freezing cold. The blustery air thrashed across the expanse with freedom to move as it pleased.

Their vehicle stood out in the open like a sore thumb. The only solace was that it blended with the kilometers and kilometers of fresh snow that blanketed the area for as far as the eye could see, until white met blue on the horizon.

Luckily, they were inside the van for the time being. Ellyssa wasn't looking forward to battling the icy wind whipping from the northwest, bringing with it dark grey clouds.

As Rein and Woody hunkered over the antique map that Tim had donated, debating where they were, and Dyllon rolled the sleeping bags, Ellyssa and Trista packed the gear into knapsacks. They needed enough food and supplies to last at least a month. Once they reached their destination, they would need every ounce of strength to penetrate the concentration camp and rescue their family.

Based on the information she'd mentally received from the soldiers they had killed, she wondered if Amarufoss would be expecting them. Why else would patrols be stationed on unused roads?

Ellyssa just hoped it wasn't a ruse to flush them into view, a thought she hadn't yet shared with the others. The whole thing with Tim and Sarah being discovered after years of clandestine operation, then the roadblocks, niggled the back of her mind.

Deep down in her consciousness, a little voice would whisper her insecurities. That the military and the *Gestapo's* involvement was because of her and not because of the Renegades' hideout and the discovery of citizens sympathetic to their cause. That she was the one imposing the danger again. But that couldn't be right. Her and her siblings' existence had been kept secret as far as she knew. Her father, sister and brothers were dead, The Center destroyed.

Who else would be looking for her?

*No one*, Ellyssa answered.

Concentrating on the task at hand, she shoved five more MREs into Rein's pack.

"I think we're east of this town here," Woody said, pointing at the paper.

Rein picked up the map. "In Kansas?" He sounded disappointed.

"It's not that far."

"What the hell are you talking about? That's a long way off."

"Nah. It's only this far." Woody held his thumb and forefinger a few centimeters apart.

Absentmindedly touching the bandage over his ear, Rein rolled his eyes.

"Look," Woody said, taking the map and laying it on the dashboard, "if we are about here"—he placed the compass on the area—"we should keep a bearing of about two hundred thirty degrees. That should get us near the place."

"Or a hundred kilometers away."

"You are just a ray of sunshine. We can use landmarks. There are plenty of roads to help guide us. We just have to keep a lookout for signs."

"Are you guys about ready?" Trista asked, zipping up a backpack. "There's only a few more hours of sunlight."

Ellyssa gazed through the window at the rolling clouds, again. They were an angry grey, the type that promised more than a light dusting of snow. "I'm not sure. Maybe we should wait until morning. If there is a blizzard, the tents won't hold up against winds out on flat ground like this. We'd be exposed." As if to confirm her suspicion, an icy blast rocked the van.

"But what about patrols?" Trista questioned.

Tossing the last sleeping bag on top of the other tight bundles, Dyllon answered, "We haven't seen any since our last encounter."

Woody plopped back into the driver's seat, pinching the bridge of his nose. "That doesn't mean there won't be any."

"I'd rather face a patrol than the subzero temperatures, though," Rein said.

Trista looked out the window next to Ellyssa, her gaze on the impending clouds. Worry etched the lines of Trista's face, making them more prominent around her mouth and between her eyebrows. "I'd rather not face either one."

Dyllon hunched, walked across the van to Trista and sat on the corner of one of the unopened supply boxes. Taking her hand, he said, "I agree. Neither is promising, but we would be safer in here. At least we'll be in shelter."

"And what if we get trapped in a blizzard out there? What about then?"

Dyllon kissed the back of Trista's hand. "We'll worry about that *if* it happens."

Still staring at the upcoming storm, Ellyssa felt a hand stroking her hair. She turned and met Rein's jade eyes, a small reassuring smile in his face. He mouthed, "I love you."

She returned his grin. "I know," Ellyssa mouthed back.

"Okay," Woody said, clapping his hands together. "Let's get the empty boxes piled in the front and the sleeping bags out."

Dyllon groaned. "What a waste of time."

Ellyssa swung the doors open to a surprisingly clear, crisp morning, not even the stir of a breeze. The sun hovered above the eastern horizon in a pure azure sky the color of her eyes. The snow, which she had been sure would be a meter deep, barely covered the ground. The storm that had pummeled the van, rocking it back and forth and rattling the windows to the point that Ellyssa thought the van was doomed to go tumbling across the vast plains, seemed nothing more than a bad nightmare.

Ellyssa dropped to the ground and watched as the others followed her, like a line of abominable snowmen, dressed in identical snowsuits that clad them from head to foot in white. She couldn't help but smile as she remembered Trista's declaration of that fact. The males had seemed less than delighted at the observation.

As far as clothing went, though, the snowsuits were remarkable pieces of gear. The thermal lining was specifically designed to use body heat through a fibrous insulation and flexible coils, which vented the suit and maintained the temperature at a constant twenty-one degrees Celsius. The same went with the sleeping bags each of them had strapped to the top of their knapsacks. Regardless of the milder weather, it was still bitterly cold.

With the three tents, food, water and limited medical supplies, they would be fine as long as the calm weather continued. The problem was what would happen once they reached their destination.

Closing her eyes, Ellyssa faced the sun, enjoying the feel of it against her skin. Rein came up from behind and folded his arms around her waist. He pressed his lips against her cheek. "Are you ready?" he asked.

Ellyssa nodded. He handed her her backpack. After a quick check to make sure the cave pearl was still in the side pocket, she slipped her arms through the shoulder straps and adjusted the weight on her back. "Let's go."

"One second," Woody said, positioning the compass steady in his hand. "Two hundred thirty degrees." He started to move southwest.

Their small band followed him toward a vast white and blue unknown.

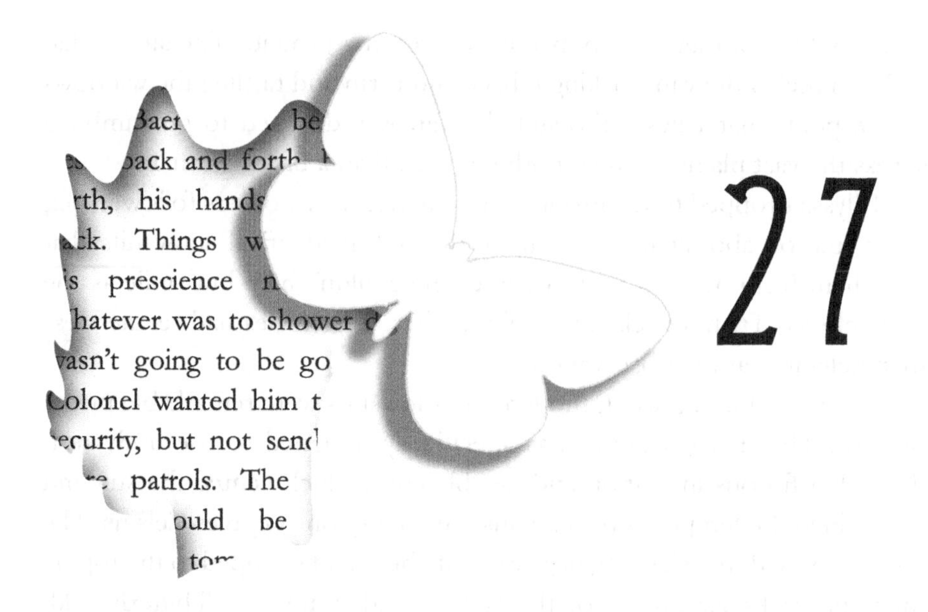

# 27

After hanging up with Colonel Fielder, Commandant Hans Baer paced behind the desk, back and forth, back and forth, his hands behind his back. Things were brewing; his prescience naggled him. Whatever was to shower down wasn't going to be good. The Colonel wanted him to double security, but not send out any more patrols. The two faux angels would be returning sometime tomorrow or the next day. All of this, and Hans' superior officer still refused to divulge anything further than a "need to know" basis.

Basically, Hans didn't need to know.

Hans knew somehow everything circled around the female, Ellyssa. Especially after the information Doc had provided him about the girl.

According to the Renegade, The Center had been more vested in eugenics than was previously known; Alexis and Xaver were byproducts, as was Ellyssa. Apparently, the Colonel and possibly other leaders knew some of the surreptitious experiments that had gone on. If not before, then definitely now. That was why the Colonel had ordered Hans' cooperation.

What disturbed the Commandant the most was that, if The Center hadn't been destroyed and Dr. Hirch killed then, based on what Doc had said, a paved highway would have been opened for complete annihilation of the human populace, replaced by a super-being, a soldier, created from a test tube to populate the earth.

It stood to reason Aalexis and Xaver had plans to continue the doctor's work. That was why Aalexis sought Ellyssa.

Hans paused at the corner of the desk, his hand twitching over the phone. What would he say to the Colonel? How would he explain his acquired knowledge? Tell the Colonel the deal he'd made with a *prisoner*? Besides, Hans had a sneaking suspicion the Colonel already knew of Aalexis and Xaver's *gifts*. That was what the Colonel had meant when he'd said something about the missing link.

As his mother used to say, *Narren nicht erkennen.*

Colonel Fielder was a fool.

Letting his hand drop to his side, Hans moved to the window. He stood a little ways back and to the left, where he was hidden in the shadows. Across the compound, the sergeant-at-arms stood. The cap hid his face, but the hair stood on the back of Hans' neck as if the man's eyes scoured him.

He was going to have to do something about the sergeant. He had to give him credit, though; the sergeant was very astute, one of the reasons Hans had requested him in the first place.

As Commandant Baer watched from the warmth of his office, for the first time ever he had an inkling of understanding how the Renegades felt.

# 28

Aalexis couldn't help but feel excitement as she walked into the new lab. Her heart thumped and elation swelled in her chest. She tried to hold the feeling at bay, but she was unsuccessful, her body tingling with the forbidden sensation.

Everything was metal grey or white, clean. Disinfectant scented the air. Freezers, computers, incubators—everything was there and ready for use. From the shiny, state-of-art equipment to the simplest table, her father's vision of a truly perfect world would be realized. Aalexis reached out and gently touched one of the atomic force microscopes, her fingers running along the base.

All she needed now was Ellyssa, and from the intelligence Xaver had brought her, her sister would soon be reunited with her biological family. Days had passed since the dead soldiers south of the contact's house had been found and the van recovered to the west. She'd even had the Colonel call in his troops and the State call in the *Gestapo*. She knew where Ellyssa was headed. Besides, the incompetent humans wouldn't have caught her, anyway. But she and Xaver would. The day after next, they'd be heading south to the barren wasteland.

The trap had been laid; Ellyssa just needed to spring the trigger.

"Are you pleased?" Xaver asked.

Aalexis turned toward her brother. Xaver leaned against the frame of the decontamination port, his arms folded across his chest; the white lab coat he wore opened in the front over surgical coveralls. There was a slight grin on his chiseled face that reached his eyes.

Her heart missed a beat as she studied him. He seemed completely at ease, as if unaware of his emotional display.

Forcing the excitement at her new toys into check, Aalexis' face sank into an emotionless mask. "You are smiling, Xaver," she observed.

"I believe I am," he replied.

His nonchalance was a little disconcerting. That was, if she actually could experience such an emotion. Which she couldn't.

*Incapable.*

Aalexis hoped he wasn't going to break down like Ellyssa had, although she had begun to wonder. On more than one occasion, she'd had to redirect him from talk about her sister or Micah's revelations. She had no interest in such matters.

"Emotions weaken," she reminded as if he didn't already know.

"Are you weak?"

"Certainly not."

"But yet"—he pushed away from the frame and walked toward her—"I can see you."

In an unexpected response, she stepped back and had no clue why. "See what?"

"More than you want to reveal."

Aalexis took another step away. A lab table pressed into the small of her back. "I do not understand."

Xaver stopped midway. The grin remained on his face. "You do know what today is?"

"Yes. December seventh."

"Your birthday."

"It is your birthday, too, and Ellyssa's. I do not see why we are having this conversation."

He looked around at the elaborate setup. "This is quite the birthday gift."

"We do not celebrate birthdays."

His eyes found her again. "Do you not find it strange *der Vater* used the same birthday for all of us? A weakness on his part, perhaps?"

"*Der Vater* found significance with this date. It was a time of great change. The turning point that eventually led to the conquering of all the great superpowers of the time. As we are to be a turning point, a time of great change."

"A connection made from emotion. Would you not agree?"

Aalexis' mind whirled as she tried to see where her brother was leading. She was unsure whether she wanted to follow, to play into Xaver's trap. Especially if it led down the road toward Micah. He stood there, the unsettling grin still displayed under his straight nose. She didn't like any of it. After a moment, she answered, "I do agree. *Der Vater* was not completely like us, but his genius compensated. Like Hitler, he was a visionary."

Standing perfectly still, her brother regarded her. She felt her pulse quicken, her nerves tweak. She had to maintain control.

Finally, Xaver spoke. "After Ellyssa is brought back into the fold, would you have the same birthday for *our* creations? Our perfect soldiers?"

"No. Dates mean nothing. A tradition which has no effect on the beings we will create. We do not feel emotions to assign importance to dates."

"Yet, I can still see you."

"I do not know to what you are referring."

"Your eyes, they sparkle when you are pleased." His grin grew.

Aalexis didn't respond. All words escaped from her thought process.

Xaver started toward her again, and Aalexis' chest squeezed. If she didn't know better, she'd say she felt fear. But that was impossible. She was not afraid of her brother. There was no reason to be. Xaver's whole world centered around ensuring her safety. Even with the shortcomings she'd been experiencing, fear was unfeasible. A complete waste. Yet, as he approached her, her heart felt like it was going to depart from the cavity surrounded by her ribcage, and her stomach felt a little uncomfortable.

Moments like this, Aalexis wished she had Ellyssa's capability. That way, she'd always know what was coming. Her sister's gift would benefit the future superior beings greatly.

Xaver stood in front of her, and she stared at his chest. The coveralls and lab coat hid muscles he wouldn't have possessed if he had been born from inferior beings. Their physiques were much more mature and had accelerated since they'd reached puberty.

His scent was overwhelming, the heat radiating off his body. The table pressed against her back. Aalexis felt trapped. Anger stirred within her.

She tipped her head up and met Xaver's eyes with hers. "What is your point, Xaver?"

"We feel," he simply stated.

"We do not," she denied. "I do not."

"Although you try to hide it, I can see it in your eyes." He reached up and cupped her cheek. "The change in you."

At his touch, the stirring anger abated, as easily as water dousing a fire. A fluttering sensation burst in her midsection. Before Aalexis knew what was happening, she found herself leaning into his hand, but only for a moment. Her breath seized at the realization of what was happening, and fury burned away the flutter. She pushed him away, hard. A normal man would've been thrown back. Xaver wasn't normal; he stumbled back a couple of steps and his smile fell away.

"Do not touch me. Ever," Aalexis seethed.

He moved forward.

"I mean it, Xaver."

He stopped. "Or what? Will you send your pain through me?"

The thought had crossed Aalexis' mind, to protect herself, the innate carnal side of their beings. Unfortunately, her ability would be rendered as useless against Xaver as it had been against Ellyssa. His shield would protect him.

"Please." She could hear the plea in her own voice as the anger sucked away, like a black hole and caught the one feeling she was comfortable with. She felt weak, out of control. She felt herself caving.

"It will be fine," Xaver comforted as if he could sense her distress. "We need to discuss this...change. Or it might consume us like it did Ellyssa."

No," Aalexis said. "Emotions weaken."

Another telltale emotion surfaced on Xaver's face. An inquisitive one. His left eyebrow rose. For a moment, he looked like *der Vater*. "Do they?" He moved forward, his hand extending toward her, where he hesitated. "May I?" he asked.

While looking at Xaver's hand, Aalexis' twitched, as if her fingers longed to entwine within his. She balled her hand into a tight fist and shook her head.

"Very well." He looked disappointed. "Will you agree to listen to me, at least? To talk? How can we proceed if we do not look at this situation from a logical perspective? You can deny it all you want, but I do see." His gaze leveled at her. "And I know you feel."

She didn't want to talk. She wanted it all to go away. Instead, she agreed with a curt nod.

The slight grin crossed Xaver's face, again. His eyes seemed to dance. As much as Aalexis didn't want to admit it, he was truly beautiful. Then again, they were all beautiful; they were perfection.

Maybe Xaver was right. If there was a flaw within her father's programming, the intelligent thing would be to embrace it and use to their advantage instead of fleeing.

Ellyssa had fled. Ellyssa had been wrong.

With an elaborate gesture for her to go first, Xaver stepped to the side. Keeping a stoic face, Aalexis went over to a metal table with a pristine shiny surface. Her face reflected back at her. Then, she could see what Xaver meant. There was something in her eyes. A spark? Small, undetectable to the a normal human's eye, but there nonetheless.

She perched on the stool and turned toward Xaver. Unable to look at him, her eyes remained trained on the incubator, a part of their future, comforting.

Pulling a stool over, the metal legs scraping against the white tile, Xaver took a seat across from her. He launched into the story as if unable to contain the words he so long had wanted to tell. "Before Micah died, he came to me. He told me of what he saw when he touched the music box. The box had belonged to the Renegade who had feelings for Ellyssa, and Ellyssa had touched the box." He paused for a moment. "But instead of just seeing past events, Micah felt emotions. He tried to explain the onslaught he felt, a rush of emotions, a fluttering sensation in his heart, in his stomach. He said he felt the love Ellyssa held for the subhuman. Overpowering and very strong. The rush of emotion had changed something vital in Micah, like it opened a door that had been sealed shut."

Aalexis' gaze jerked toward Xaver, her lids narrowing. "You had an opportunity to tell *der Vater*. If he had known, he might have been able to develop another program for us. Something to right the flaw. Why did you hide this?" she demanded.

"Micah had asked me not to tell *der Vater*. He was...afraid, I think."

"You should have told him anyway," Aalexis reiterated.

"If *der Vater* had known, he might have had Micah eliminated."

"As well he should have."

"What if it was you? Would you go so willingly?"

"Yes." The lie left Aalexis' lips freely. The truth was something she didn't want to admit. Her father had instilled self-preservation well, at all costs. Had that been the reason Ellyssa had left? She quickly dismissed the idea.

Xaver watched her for a moment before he started again. "Honestly, I do not know why I did not inform *der Vater*. He was consumed with Ellyssa." He shrugged, Aalexis noted his ease of using body expressions as if he'd been practicing. "The more I thought about the conversation, the more curious I became. I began to examine other humans, the ones with whom we were allowed to come in contact, *der Vater* and his assistants. Yes, they are inferior to us in all ways, but maybe emotions have their use."

Xaver's face took on a faraway look as he considered the possibilities. All Aalexis wanted to do was block out everything, including those same possibilities.

After a moment, he came back. "Then Ellyssa came. She came for that...despicable human." Anger tinged his voice and, and for a moment, he sounded like the Xaver Aalexis knew. "Throwing out self-preservation as if the Renegade's life was worth more than hers. That was stupid of her."

"Exactly," Aalexis agreed.

"No. Putting the Renegade's life before hers was stupid, but the emotional bond she had formed with the Renegade was strong."

Aalexis hated the words her brother spoke, the possible truth in them. She'd agreed to listen, but she didn't agree to accept. Aalexis started to shake her head. She was done, but Xaver would not shut up.

"Undeniably strong. It strengthened her."

"No. No. No."

Xaver leaned toward Aalexis and placed his hand under her chin, forcing her to look at him. "Listen. It *did* make her strong. The connections she had formed with the substandard humans made them come together. Two are better than one. Do you not see, Aalexis? Because of their beliefs, because of their bonds, they came into an armed building and defeated us. *Us*," he repeated, as if he still could not believe the outcome.

"That detective helped them."

"Propelled by what?"

She tried to look away, but he held her chin firm.

"Propelled by what?" he asked again.

"Emotions." The word rushed out of her like a breath of tainted air.

"Exactly. The emotion she felt, jealousy I believe, made her unpredictable. We did not see the betrayal in her."

Slowly, Xaver moved his hand to her cheek. This time, Aalexis did not fight it. His touch had a calming effect; there was no denying that.

"I will have to consider what you have told me."

"I have something else to say," he said, his thumb tracing the contours of her cheek.

Tingles left in the wake of his touch, his breath washed over her like a soft breeze, his scent filling her nose. Incontestably, Aalexis' heart responded. "What?"

"I love you."

Although Aalexis had been attempting to conceal the turmoil raging inside her, there was no hiding what happened next. Her mouth opened with an audible pop.

An eternity seemed to unfold before Aalexis had the sense to close her mouth. When she did, her teeth clicked together.

She didn't know what to say. Her mental processors had jammed. Not in a million years would she have ever thought those words would flow past Xaver's lips with such ease.

Several minutes later, she uttered, "We cannot love."

The words seemed not to have an effect on him. "Ellyssa loves."

"She is broken."

"I thought we already established how bonding with others strengthens."

What in the hell did he want from her? Aalexis didn't know how to love. She didn't want to know how. "Maybe it does, maybe it does not," she stated, irritated. "I would not even know what love would feel like."

The corner of Xaver's mouth tilted into a smirk. "Do you hate me?"

Aalexis blinked. Hate was something she did know. The taste of detestation flooded her mouth whenever she thought about Ellyssa, or anyone else for that matter. Everyone...except for her father and, with the exception of her sister, her siblings. But because she didn't hate them, did that equate love? "I have never thought about it," she whispered. "I do not know."

"I have."

"Clearly." She paused, looking at the incubator again. "How do you know you love me?"

"When you are near, I feel it here," Xaver said, placing his palm against his chest. "Even when I think about you, my heart...it flutters. When you touch me, my whole body buzzes."

Aalexis' pulse increased as he described what happened to him, the same physiological effects she had felt. Maybe she did love him.

"When we are apart, I cannot stop wondering if you are hurt. I cannot wait to return to you."

Maybe everything would be jeopardized. Too much.

She covered her ears. "Just stop it," Aalexis said, shaking her head. "I do not want to hear any more." Her mind whirled as she tried to grasp on to anything with which to refute his argument. Then she found it so easy, she felt a little stupid for not thinking of it earlier. She blamed her moment of obtuseness on the inexperience of dealing with the sensations. Like a lifesaver, Aalexis seized hold of her salvation at the same time he gave her another excuse.

Xaver reached up and pulled down one of her hands and didn't let it go. "I would protect you no matter the cost."

Dropping her other hand, her eyes flicked to him. Her pulse quieted. Her face became smooth, slate-like, as she slipped into her emotionless skin. Comfortable. "Even if it meant your life?"

He nodded.

"Then that is where we differ, brother. I would not sacrifice my life for yours." Xaver flinched as if Aalexis had slapped him, and she reclaimed control. For good measure, she tossed in her other reason, logically blocking him further. If their discussion had been a game of chess, she would have won. "Besides, it is wrong."

"Wrong? Why is it wrong?"

She slipped off the stool and started toward the decontamination port. "A millennium of taboo. You are my brother," she said without looking at him.

"All we have is each other." His feet hit the ground followed by the muffled padding of covered shoes as he moved closer. "Besides, *sister*, you know as well as I do, we might share a common strand of DNA from *der Vater*, but we are far from being genetically brother and sister. Our DNA comes from several sources, sliced and spliced together. We are more like distant cousins."

Aalexis stopped, her shoulder blades pulling together.

"I know you feel for me. I can see. If you continue to try and fight something that is overwhelming a part of you, you might break like Ellyssa did. Maybe like Micah was about to. I told you something changed in him."

Xaver edged closer, and Aalexis could feel his presence behind her.

"With the acknowledgement of this inevitability, we could become stronger."

She was tired of discussing, tired of listening, and she was going to put an end to the nonsense, whether Xaver was right or wrong. She wanted no more of the madness. Fists clenched, Aalexis spun around.

An infuriating smile graced his full lips, one she desired to permanently remove. Her body coiled, preparing to strike; her arm pulled back, full of potential energy for knocking away the emotion he proudly displayed.

Surely, Xaver knew what was coming, could identify the fury in her, yet he didn't react.

"But if you want to take the sibling angle, the most powerful in history and mythology were brothers and sisters. Kings and queens. But are we not more, *sister*? Are we not gods?"

Flummoxed, Aalexis' tightly wound body uncoiled like a stretched spring, her previously cocked fist dangling useless at her side. Fury fleeing, her tongue held no retort.

Xaver had checkmated her.

# 29

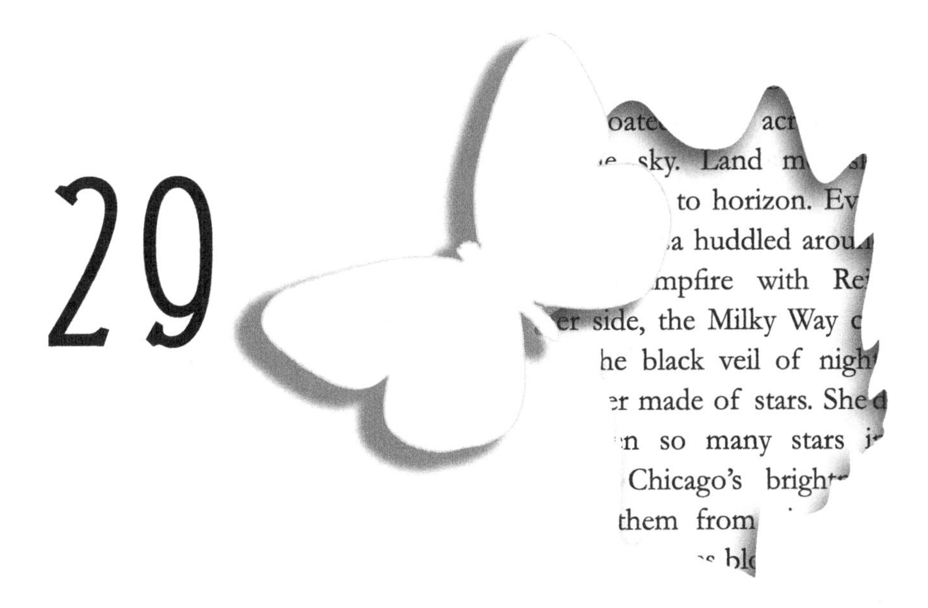

The Great Plains held an unmistakable beauty. Big, puffy clouds floated lazily across the vast blue sky. Land met sky from horizon to horizon. Even now, as Ellyssa huddled around a warm campfire with Rein by her side, the Milky Way cut across the black veil of night, like a river made of stars. She'd never seen so many stars in her life. Chicago's brightness had dimmed them from view and the Missouri trees had blocked them from view.

The low flames ate hungrily from the breeze that blew into the canyon where Woody had directed them using the old map. Amarufoss was located about thirty-two kilometers north. The walk had increased the timetable by two days, putting them south of their intended target, but hopefully, the added precaution would prove beneficial. Besides, they couldn't just go storming into the camp.

"Any ideas on what we should do next?" Woody asked as he stood. Orange from the flames played along his face and reflected in his eyes. He pushed the mop of his hair back off his forehead.

"I think we should consider sending two of us for reconnaissance like Dyllon suggested," Ellyssa answered.

"I think that might be a good idea."

Surprised, Ellyssa faced Rein. "Really?"

Shrugging, Rein poked the dying fire with a stick. The flames crackled back to life. "Just because I don't really care for the guy doesn't mean he has nothing to contribute."

"We already discussed that. Any new ideas?"

Ellyssa shook her head. Rein stared at the fire.

"Let's figure it out tomorrow," Woody said as he stood up. He stretched his arms above his head and lengthened his body, yawning. "I'm bushed."

"Good night," Ellyssa and Rein said simultaneously, then giggled.

Rolling his eyes, Woody disappeared inside the mouth of a nearby cave where Trista and Dyllon had already settled in for the night.

The cave wasn't deep, more like an indentation in the side of the cliff at the bottom of the canyon, but it was wide enough to accommodate all three tents, blocking out the elements. A rocky overhang helped to hide the flames of the fire, which had been a great concern during their flight. Fortunately, and surprisingly, they'd only seen one plane, a faraway dot moving across the sky. That fact alone fed Ellyssa's concern that camp personnel, and possibly the *Gestapo,* were lying in wait for them.

When Woody left, Rein sat behind Ellyssa and leaned against the red wall. He wrapped his arms around her, pulling her against him. She rested against his chest, the beat of his heart whispering in her ear, and closed her eyes.

The sounds of nature denoted a peaceful exquisiteness, wind whistling through the scraggly mesquite and dramatically twisted juniper trees, their branches and leaves rustling eerily in the darkness. A rabbit or deer crunched along in the brush. Somewhere far to the north, a coyote bayed at the moon.

Yesterday, when they'd first approached the edge, which seemed so out of place amongst the flatness, Ellyssa's breath had been captured by the view. Kilometer after kilometer of foreign terrain unfolded across the expanse. Years of evolution had painted the sides of the cliffs in a geological treasure of magnificent reds, yellows, browns and greys caused by millions of years of erosion; hoodoos rose in a forest of towers, and tufts of prairie grass and xeric shrubs poked through patches of diminishing snow. The descent into the desert-like valley had been just as magnificent.

Early in the morning, Ellyssa had woken early to take in the sunrise. The experience had been stunning. A sea of yellows, oranges and majestic purples flowed across the azure sky, casting soft pink rays through the drifting clouds in a warm glow that defied the freezing cold. She'd already planned to enjoy the dawn the next morning, too. She sighed in pleasure. For the time being, everything was perfect.

"Thinking good thoughts?" Rein murmured. His breath was warm against her skin.

"We've been lucky."

There hadn't been any more snowstorms since they'd left the van somewhere northeast of them in Kansas. No more patrols. Just the relentless cold and the sudden wind that had pushed and pulled them like marionettes. Ellyssa thought it ironic that Chicago had been dubbed the Windy City.

"It's peaceful here," Rein said. "Almost as if our troubles stayed at the top of the cliffs."

Twisting around and placing her legs over Rein's thigh, Ellyssa looked at him. His snowsuit was unzipped to his waist like hers, the heat of the fire comfortable. His dark hair lay flat atop his head, the strands too long to stand up, the ends curling lazily.

Ellyssa reached up and touched the spot over his right ear where the bullet had skimmed him. Short hair scratched her fingertips where it had started to grow back. Not that anyone would've noticed the wound; his hair covered the scar. The scratches on his cheek had already healed. Things could have gone so much worse.

Rein's eyes watched her intently, as if reading her thoughts. Shadows from the fire danced across his face, waxing and waning. Orange flames danced within his green irises. He smiled.

"Do you know what the date is today?" Ellyssa asked.

"Um...the days have kind of blurred. Should I?"

"December seventh."

"The day Japan bombed Pearl Harbor."

Her eyes widened. "You know about that?"

"Of course. Pearl Harbor. The beginning of the end. We cave people know our history." He chuckled.

She loved the sound of his laugh, deep and throaty. "Nineteen years ago, I began on this date."

His eyes lit. "It's your birthday."

Nodding, Ellyssa said, "Ironic, isn't it? All of us were born on this date. Perhaps Father saw us as a different type of beginning to a different type of end."

Reaching out, Rein pushed strands of hair behind her ear. His fingers grazed her cheek. "Happy birthday," he whispered. He leaned down and touched his lips against hers. The kiss was sweet, gentle, his breath warm.

"No one has ever said those words to me," Ellyssa said when he pulled away.

Cupping her cheek, Rein didn't reply. His eyes bored into hers; love burned within their depths. Love that she returned. He leaned forward again and pressed his lips against hers. Heat rose in waves across her skin, in her body. Her pulse quickened as did his breath. Rein's hand slid behind her neck, where he held her firmly. The softness grew urgent as her lips parted, inviting him in to explore. His taste exploded in her mouth.

Someone moaned. Rein pulled back. "That wasn't you," he said, his voice a whisper.

Chest rising and falling raggedly, Ellyssa shook her head.

"Give it a rest," Woody said, his deep voice thick with the promise of sleep.

A new warmth blushed Ellyssa's face as she looked away, but not before she saw a hint of humor glinting in Rein's eyes.

"Sorry," Rein said to Woody. He brought her hand up and kissed the tips of her fingers. "Later."

Ellyssa flipped back around and rested against his chest again. Rein's arms circled her waist, and she ran her fingers along the back of his hand.

The fire flickered lazily. A deep quiet settled as the night pressed forward.

Closing her lids, she inhaled the scent of burning wood. She felt the rise and fall of Rein's chest, the push of his breath against her hair.

"Rein," Ellyssa said.

"Hmm."

"I know who you are. I know I love you. I know Jordan raised you. What I don't know is anything about your past. You've never shared."

"There really isn't anything to know." He paused for a moment. "What would you like to know?"

"When were you born? What happened to your parents?"

"Don't know," Rein replied before kissing the top of her head. "A woman named Sybil—she died way before you came along—found me at the entrance of the cave. Bundled up in blankets and left in a carrier. No one knew who left me there, no one saw anything. It actually frightened them for someone to know the location of the cave, and they didn't know who. For three months after my arrival, they patrolled the area, but no one found any clues. Anyway, Sybil took me to Jordan, and he kind of adopted me as his own, like he already had with Jeremy. There was about a ten-year gap between mine and Jeremy's age."

"How old were you when they found you?"

"Doc said I was around three months, give or take a few days. Jordan made my birthday February fourteenth."

"I know that date. Civilians celebrate it as Valentine's Day?"

"He used to tease me, saying I was his love child."

"I don't understand."

"I didn't, either. Jordan never married or, as far as I know, had been with any woman. Ever." Rein moved as if shrugging. "When I was about nine or ten, Woody came along, and Jordan was blessed with the two of us." Rein chuckled. She felt the rumble deep in his chest. "We were a handful."

Interest piqued, she said, "Like how?"

"You know. The usual things boys do."

"No. I don't know."

"I guess you wouldn't." He sighed. "We did stupid kid stuff. Like hiding snakes or spiders inside blankets." He laughed lightly. "One time, Woody had the bright idea to help with cooking. We dumped a whole container of garlic inside a big pot of soup. Garlic was a priceless commodity we didn't get often. Needless to say, people were *not* happy."

"You ruined dinner."

He nodded. "Yep."

"Was Bertha cooking?"

"No. Another lady held the duty then. We ended up having powdered eggs that night. I think that was the maddest I had ever seen Jordan. For punishment, he made us organize and clean the storage room. Of course, we ended up having a water fight instead. Ruined two boxes of bandages. Woody's fault entirely."

Thinking back to the day in the field when the toddler had held the bouquet of wildflowers, which tinged Ellyssa's heart with pain, then to her own upbringing with her brothers and sister—backs straight, no talking, learning, and practice, practice, practice, Ellyssa found it hard to imagine children being mischievous.

"Do all children act like that?"

"We did. Woody was a bad influence."

"Lies" came from Woody's tent.

"You threw the water on me first."

"You have an amazing knack for selective memory."

"Whatever."

Smiling at their banter, Ellyssa asked, "What happened afterward?"

He tightened his arms around her. "Jordan definitely didn't punish us with chores anymore after that. He made us stay inside our holeys the whole day whenever we got in trouble. It was beyond torturous. The worst thing you could ever do to two little boys. When anything happened, Jordan always knew it was us."

"How?"

"We hung around to watch how things played out." Rein's lips pressed against the top of her ear. "Criminals should never stay at the scene of the crime."

Still smiling, Ellyssa curled around in Rein's lap and nuzzled against his chest. Warmth cradled her and the *thump, thump* of his heart mesmerized her. She yawned.

"Since you had a bedtime story, are you ready for bed?"

Ellyssa nodded.

"Let's go."

Cradling her in his arms, Rein stood. For someone not crafted together in a sterile lab, he was strong, amazingly so, his chest muscles bulging under her weight. She found it extremely tantalizing. A deep want stirred within her. He must have felt it too, his lips grazing her ear. Rein's steps crunched along the loose gravel as he carried her to their tent.

Woody's voice followed them. "It's about time."

# 30

Ellyssa woke. Darkness clung to the tent, like a thick spider web.

She listened. Rein's breaths were deep and even. Leaves whispered in the wind. The dying embers of the fire crackled. An owl hooted in the distance.

Farther off, faintly, a stick snapped. The *tink* of a pebble that had been kicked.

Ellyssa stilled. Her training thundered forward.

Blocking the dreams of her friends, she expanded her *hearing*, searching. In the distance, minds were awake, thinking, nervous.

Five people, two females and three males, stole closer.

Soft murmurs floated in the current of the breeze. Too soft for a normal person's ears. Ellyssa could hear them, though. Her hand moved to wake Rein. Then Ellyssa stopped.

*Members of the Resistance?*

The strangers knew about them. Something about an intercepted message.

Ellyssa had been right all along. Someone was trying to pull them into a trap.

Since Ellyssa and the others had arrived in the canyon, the unknown Renegades had had them under surveillance. Too far away for Ellyssa to have sensed them, it seemed they had use of a telescope. They had been sent by someone named Loki—*a doctor?*—to bring them back.

Quietly, she scooted to Rein's side. "Rein," she breathed.

He stirred.

"Rein." She squeezed his forearm. "Do not talk," she ordered, her voice low and monotonous, her soldiering instincts in overdrive. She sensed the people didn't want to cause harm, but she also knew they carried weapons.

"Wh-what?" Rein said, his words thick with sleep.

"Shh. Renegades are coming."

One second barely awake, the next Rein bolted into a sitting position.

Ellyssa's hand snapped out and clamped around his mouth before he could utter a sound. "Shh," she repeated. "Renegades."

He nodded and pulled her hand away.

"They came to get us," Ellyssa breathed in his ear. "I think we will be fine."

He nodded again, his hair tickling her cheek.

As quietly as possible, Ellyssa grabbed their snowsuits and handed one to Rein. He shrugged the clothing on; the ruffling of the material seemed to echo around them, not even close to being as quiet as she would've liked. Fortunately, the visitors were still a few meters away.

Through the material of the tent, barely distinguishable, a soft glow permeated the distance. A flashlight. After a moment, the light extinguished and a twig snapped, followed by hushing.

Rein leaned close. "What are we going to do?" he asked, his voice as soft as the light breeze.

"Wait," Ellyssa answered.

A few moments later, the sound of footsteps crunched on loose gravel. The Renegades' stealth left much to be desired. Hushed whispers and more crunching. Rein's shallow breath. Woody stirred. Trista mumbled.

Then, finally, the announcement of the visitors' arrival. A powerful beam of light flashed inside the rocky nook.

"We have you surrounded," said a male; his tone sounded sure. His nerves were frazzled, though. Mike—that was his name.

All at once, there were surprised mumbles, unzipping of bags, swishing of fabric, thumps of movement.

"What the hell?" Woody's voice carried over.

"We have you surrounded," Mike repeated again. "Come out with your hands showing first. Leave your weapons inside. I want to see five sets of hands."

"Do as they say," Ellyssa said. She opened the flap to her and Rein's tent and put her hands through.

More thumps and swishes. Someone—Ellyssa thought Trista—zipped her snowsuit.

"Okay, that is enough; come out now," said one of the females, authoritative. Her name was Ann. "I only see six hands. If four more don't show within the next two seconds, we'll open fire."

Ellyssa knew she was lying. Their orders were to bring them back alive. "Rein," Ellyssa said, as she slipped her hands through the flap of the tent. His hands joined hers.

"Okay. Keep your hands in view and come out of the tents. Slowly."

Hunched over, Ellyssa moved into the biting cold, flinching away from the beam of bright light. Rein followed.

"That's right. Keep your hands where we can see them. Careful now."

Woody, Trista and Dyllon crawled out to the right of Ellyssa, their arms extended in front of them. Before Ellyssa stood three shadowy figures standing in a triangle formation, the two females and one of the males; the other two males hid behind a rock formation off to the right. Ann, the team leader, stood at the point. All carried rifles trained toward their quarry.

"Who are you?" Ann asked.

"Who wants to know?" Woody countered.

The woman stepped toward Woody. "I'm the one with the weapon. That means I get to ask the questions."

"Woody, it is fine. I am Ellyssa."

"Ellyssa," Ann mimicked. "And you." She pointed the barrel at Rein, who answered. She went down the line asking the same question.

"Woody, apparently," Woody said, finishing the mandatory under-threat-of-weapon question with a thickly sarcastic tone.

"What are you doing here?"

Ellyssa took a step toward her.

"Hey! Hey!" Ann said, swinging her weapon toward Ellyssa. "Stay where you're at."

Ellyssa couldn't see the female's face, the light staying trained in her eyes, but she was growing weary of standing still while being questioned. Questions that would be asked by Dr. Loki in the underground facility where this group hid. A very technical place Ellyssa wanted to see.

"We are not going to hurt you. Apparently, you have come for a reason. Either shoot us or take us to your camp," Ellyssa said, calling her bluff. "Either way, let us proceed."

With the muzzle still facing Ellyssa, the team leader stepped back to confer with her friends. A moment later, Ann said, "Okay. One at a time, starting with the loud one at the end." She indicated Woody with her rifle. "Step forward and move one behind the other. If any of you try anything, I *will* shoot you."

Ann tried to sound convincing, but her tone hitched toward the end, revealing the lie. From the subtle frown and downward curve of Rein's mouth, he detected the untruth, too.

Ellyssa's group moved in a straight line, Woody in front, Rein behind. Their captors escorted them in a jagged triangle formation with Ann leading, Mike midway on the right, and the quiet female, named Loreley, behind and a bit to the left. The other two males had emerged from hiding and trailed far behind all of them.

As they hiked down a game trail, a soft azure washed away the midnight blue as the sun rose and rays streaked across the sky, extinguishing the stars in their wake in a brilliant orange and royal purple. The dark silhouettes of the canyon's landscape started to define in uneven lines and different hues. The group's shadows lengthened.

All Ellyssa could tell about Ann was that she had flaming red hair twisted in a tight bun. Mike's hair covered his ears in a curly orange. And Loreley had caramel-colored skin, black hair also tied in a bun, and blacker eyes. They all wore tactical fatigues and thick jackets, perfect camouflage for the terrain, unlike the white snowsuits Ellyssa's group wore, easily visible against the reddish-brown backdrop.

Nerves pricking, keeping the captors on high alert, they kept surveying the sky and behind them. None of them were accustomed to being out in the open during the day.

Approximately five kilometers later, they reached their destination, a rust-colored canyon wall on the west side. Mesquite trees and thick brush grew abundantly where the morning and afternoon sun fed the plants.

Ann faced them, her pale face hard with suspicion. Freckles sprinkled across her nose and cheeks, and bow-shaped lips pursed as she regarded Ellyssa and the rest of her group with pale green eyes. Ann's thoughts were angry. She wasn't sure why Ellyssa and her group were there, or why Dr.

Loki had organized the team to fetch them. She hated to be exposed when everything they'd worked for could be so easily discovered. "Line up over to the side. There," Ann said, using the weapon as her pointing finger.

Moving as a unit, Woody led them to file down the side of the cliff, while the two other males, Keith and Gus, the ones who'd trailed behind, kept them targeted, Ann moved behind thick brush and pulled away a heavy, rust-colored fabric. Lying behind it was an entrance to the facility Ellyssa wanted to see. From what Ellyssa could gather, their soon-to-be hosts lived in a place almost as technologically advanced as The Center had been. Maybe two or three years behind.

Woody muttered in amazement at the proficiency with which they hid the tunnel, the way the colors of the curtain blended within the walls of the canyon and the shadows of the indigenous plants. Completely undetectable to any patrols who didn't know where to look.

"This way," said Ann. She gestured with her rifle.

"What about our equipment?" Rein asked.

After exchanging a glance with Loreley, Ann directed Keith and Gus with a nod of her head. When the two males retreated down the path that had brought them to the cave, Mike took over their positions and raised his muzzle. Loreley joined him.

"They will bring your stuff back," Ann said.

Woody watched as the two men left, his face bunched in mistrust. "It better all be there."

"Now you make threats. You really don't get the whole 'I carry the gun, so I'm in charge' thing, do you?"

Woody's sharp gaze jerked toward the redhead. "I'm with Ellyssa. If you wanted us dead, you had your opportunity."

Ann glared at Woody. "As I see it, as long as I hold this," she said, weighing the gun in her arm, "my opportunities are endless."

Ellyssa narrowed her eyes as anger, as much a part of her as the beat of her heart, thrummed like a live wire, making her muscles respond in anticipation. Although she knew the redheaded female was supposed to deliver them unharmed, she couldn't predict the future, and the female was weighing her options.

After years of never coming into contact with anyone from the outside world, Ann feared them and the dangers Ellyssa and her group possibly posed. Ellyssa hoped Ann wouldn't try anything stupid. She'd hate to end their welcome with the death of one of Dr. Loki's people, but Ellyssa wouldn't hesitate if the need called.

"Now, this way." Ann indicated with her rifle, again.

With Rein's hand in hers, Ellyssa found herself entering a wide tunnel large enough to accommodate four people walking side by side. White dust motes danced in the filtered, arced sunlight. After letting the curtain fall back into place, Ann switched on the flashlight, shining the beam in front of them.

"Follow the tunnel until I tell you to stop," Ann ordered.

"This is man-made," said Rein, his hand running over the sharp cuts made by a pickaxe.

"It took five years to clear out," responded Mike.

"Shut up," Ann ordered as Loreley shot the male a death glance.

Mike promptly obeyed.

"Move," Ann ordered.

Ellyssa and Rein followed behind Woody, Trista and Dyllon. Their three captors trailed them. A couple of meters down, silicon ribbon solar cells were stationed on rollers, for easy movement, and lined against the rocky wall; based on what Ellyssa had captured, their hosts left them out during the morning hours every other day to recharge. Thick cables hooked to the wooden supports at regular intervals and disappeared into the darkness, their source of electricity.

"Wow," uttered Trista, her soft voice loud in the enclosed area.

"Keep going," Ann directed when they stopped to marvel at their solar technology.

They had shuffled forward another thirty meters when Ann called for them to halt. The redhead maneuvered around them and shone the flashlight into a gaping hole carved into a section of the tunnel. Five red four-wheelers with black wheel covers were parked inside the earthen garage.

"Do you know how to drive an ATV?" Ann asked Woody.

Dumbfounded, Woody shook his head. "Where did you acquire these?"

"Don't worry about it." Her gaze moved from one to the other. "Any of you?"

"I do," Dyllon said.

"Okay. You and that blonde," she indicated Trista, "ride together." She went and stood in front of the group and started to point out all the levers and pedals. "This is the clutch. This is the brake. These are the gears." She put her foot on a lever. "One click down is first, up is second, so forth. Got it?"

Not waiting for an answer, Ann stared to point and direct again. "You two," she said to Ellyssa and Rein, "will ride together. And you," she turned toward Woody, "will ride with Mike. Try anything funny and the dark-haired girl behind you will put a bullet in the back of your head."

Woody's jaw clenched. Ellyssa didn't invade his thoughts, but she still could see the words that slithered around inside him, wanting to strike out.

Ann straddled one of the vehicles and Loreley climbed behind her, leaving the fifth for the two males who had gone to retrieve their stuff.

"Let's move out."

As Ellyssa looked over Rein's shoulder, her arms strapped around his waist like vises, the passage of air swept her hair back and twisted the strands into tangles. The engines roared deafeningly, and the rumble vibrated through her thighs and clicked her teeth together. Headlights illuminated the twisting man-made passage. The destination was a lot farther than she had expected. At least thirty minutes, if not a bit longer, had passed by the time Mike, with Woody as his passenger, slowed and pulled the ATV into a garage-type room dug into the side of the tunnel.

The silence felt out of place after the long minutes of the rumbling noise. Even with the engines shut off and free of the four-wheelers, Ellyssa's ears rang, and she still felt the vibration in her legs.

Ann took the lead again. "Come on."

Around the next bend, a thick metal door divided the tunnel from what lay on the other side. Ellyssa had a good layout of the schematic, and was very impressed, to say the least. The others would be just discombobulated. She wondered how Renegades could have accumulated such technology. Ellyssa grew anxious to meet this Dr. Loki.

Ann pushed the orange button on the intercom. "Status good."

"Roger," said a male voice.

A moment later, the door slid back on its track and revealed a steel wall.

"What the hell?" muttered Rein. He tore his eyes away from the scene and looked at Ellyssa.

She squeezed his hand. "Just wait. You aren't going to believe it."

Ann stepped through the door and went to the right. They followed.

Except for the wall and floors being constructed from steel, the corridors reminded Ellyssa of The Center, sterile and cold. The metal hall twisted and turned. Closed doors led to rooms. People, dressed either in tactical gear or white lab coats, rushed to unknown destinations. Some passersby glanced at them with surprise; others seemed too preoccupied to acknowledge their presence. All the while, Ellyssa and her group soaked in as much as they could.

"I can't believe this," Trista said. "Can you believe this?"

"Shut up back there," came Ann's answer.

The section of the hall ended at stairs leading down. Without even a glance back, Ann descended. Ellyssa looked over the railing. The steps went down four flights without any stories between.

"Let's go," Ann called. "I want to be done with you."

Still holding Rein's hand, Ellyssa went.

A cacophony of metallic clanging echoed throughout the stairwell, sounding more like a whole platoon charging instead of just eight people walking down steps. At the bottom was only one door, a room completely separated from rest of the complex. Ann pushed numbers into a keypad, 6-1-7-4, then placed her thumb on a scanner. A red light read from right to left. The door clicked and popped open. Stepping off to the side, Ann waved them to enter.

Towing Rein with her, Ellyssa stepped over the threshold and into a small room containing a long table surrounded by eight chairs and a desk with a computer. Perched behind the desk was an older male, about fifty-five, with dark blond hair greying on the sides and, wearing a white lab coat. He looked up at the sound of the door, his eyes a teal blue, and his thin lips pulled into a warm smile.

The door already opened to Ann's and Loreley's thoughts, Ellyssa knew the doctor was adored and respected. He had been the leader of their community for the past thirty or so years, which led Ellyssa to believe he was older than his outward appearance. More along the lines of her father's age? Her father had looked deceptively young too, a specimen of eugenics.

Ellyssa gated off their random thoughts as she zeroed in on the doctor. Warmth exuded from him, his curiosity overwhelming and genuine, but behind all the cheerfulness and rambling questions about the newcomers into his facility was something else, not quite identifiable, as if a door was closed to her probing.

A well-guarded secret? Possibly.

Ellyssa felt her inner soldier writhing beneath her skin, waiting to leap forth at a moment's notice. The doctor seemed harmless enough, his forefront thoughts nonthreatening, but she didn't like not being able to get a full read on him. His mind was a maze of winding corridors and hidden doors, much like his steel complex. Whenever Ellyssa thought she found the right passage, a dead end awaited her.

"I was wondering when you were going to get back," Dr. Loki said, standing. He approached Rein with an extended hand. "Welcome to Sirus, our home. I'm Dr. Loki. It isn't often we have...visitors here. Renegades like us. Part of the Resistance."

Glancing at Ellyssa, Rein took the proffered hand. "Rein." He shook once and let go.

"Nice to meet you, Rein." After introducing himself to the others, shaking hands and repeating the same greeting he'd given Rein, Dr. Loki said. "Please, please, have a seat. I'm sure you are all curious and have many questions. As do I."

With a lift of his chin and an unspoken exchange, he dismissed Ann and Loreley. The redhead gave a wary glance before she retreated. After the dark-haired female closed the door, and the lock clicked into place, Dr. Loki took a seat at the head of the table.

"I hope Ann and Loreley or any of the team weren't too rude. You must understand—when I say we don't often have visitors, we really don't. You are the first Renegades to come into this facility since..." he paused for a second, thinking, "about ten years or so. Now, where shall we begin?" he said, rubbing his hands together. "So many things. So many things."

"How about this?" Woody said, leaning forward. "Who are you?"

A small frown bunched the doctor's brow. "Dr. Loki."

"Yeah, I get that. But *who* are you?"

"And what is this place?" chimed in Dyllon.

"Why did you bring us here?" asked Trista.

"One question at a time. Only one." Dr. Loki thought for a moment, his gaze landing on each individual. "I think it will be easier if I try and start from the beginning."

Despite Ellyssa's reservations about the male doctor, she found herself mesmerized as an amazing story unraveled.

# 31

Dr. Loki's mind was like reading a book with blurry words as he gathered his thoughts. Some images came in sharp and crystal clear, others were fuzzy and would disappear, filed away behind the mental blockade. The secret remained hidden. For right now, Ellyssa gave up on trying to uncover the enigma, interested in hearing the story she'd seen in his head. He didn't pose a threat for the time being. Besides, she knew she'd eventually find the right synapse to ride toward the truth. A leak would present itself.

Dr. Loki studied his audience, his eyes moving from one to the next, but Ellyssa noticed that his gaze lingered on her more than anyone else. He wondered about her, her platinum hair and azure eyes, the epitome of Aryan perfection. He had heard, or learned, about The Center; things blurred in the process. Ellyssa poked around in the vagueness but found nothing defined.

After a few seconds, Dr. Loki swept his hand in an arc. "What you are looking at is the completed clandestine operation that went under construction at the same time as Pantex, a bomb plant for the United States Army in nineteen forty-two, almost three months after the bombing of Pearl Harbor. Of course, Pantex was long ago disassembled, after D-Day. We thrive under the ruins."

Rein leaned back in his seat. "So, it's true?"

"What?"

"If you are really here, then there are others. Washington? California?"

"Ah, yes. The rumor mill. As far as I know, yes, they've survived. This complex is *Sirus*, codename, The Pit." He grinned at the reference. "The one in California is *Hypogeus*, and the one in Washington is *Infernus*, which, considering what happened to DC, might be appropriate."

"All Latin?" Ellyssa said.

Dr. Loki shrugged. "The founders thought the names appropriate."

Woody's forehead crinkled. "You don't know if the others have survived or not?"

"No. I have no idea. I would say the one in California might have survived. I haven't heard any different. Washington DC is iffy. The Capitol is a wasteland. But, as I've already said, as far as I know they all survived."

Questioning the doctor's honesty, Rein glanced at Ellyssa. She gave a quick nod. "How can that be?" Rein asked, facing the doctor.

The doctor inhaled deeply. "It was part of the rules that were agreed upon."

"Rules?"

"It's complicated," Dr. Loki stated. "During the nuclear arms race, some top men in the government started construction of the three underground facilities. You understand, just in case. We were lucky, because the *just-in-case* became reality.

"The development and construction of each of the facilities was hidden behind something else to throw off any suspicion. For instance, this facility went under construction during the erection of Pantex. Of course, it took a lot longer to complete than the nine months of construction the bomb plant underwent.

"When it became clear the Allies would not be victorious, we closed the doors and, for the most part, remained self-sufficient. We had our orders. Knew what to do. The risk of contact was too high."

"But," Ellyssa said, "you have technology. You have outside sources. Others know of your existence."

Dr. Loki nodded. "Just like your camp of Renegades had. Let me finish. Back when we started construction, some news leaked out. Probably from the workers. After the War had concluded, people came looking for us, the Germans as well as survivors seeking salvation from the threat of extermination. They didn't find us, though."

"What happened to the survivors?" Trista asked.

The doctor shrugged. "I'm sure that, if they didn't find cover, they were executed."

Her jaw slack, Trista stared at their host. "You just-just let them die?" Disbelief colored her voice.

"Once the doors were closed, we didn't open them again for ten years. Those were the orders."

Trista's mouth moved as she struggled with words. "You...could have saved them."

"We don't take in outsiders."

"Ever?"

"No."

Like a bright red blinking sign, Ellyssa saw the lie in the doctor's mind. A small leak had sprung. All she needed to do was widen the hole. "That isn't true, is it Dr. Loki. At one time, *you* were an outsider."

The doctor's eyes widened for a moment then narrowed. "I am not an outsider."

"You were not born here," she countered.

Dr. Loki's thoughts reeled as he tried to process her ability to have such knowledge. Something about truth. Ellyssa found herself coasting along the stream that led to his secret, to her answers. A mental picture of a male started to form before it dissipated like smoke on a breeze. The words and images dwindled and distorted. A mental wall blocked her view.

Dr. Loki had stopped the stream himself. On purpose.

Did he know of her ability?

Stubbornly, his lips pressed together as he regarded Ellyssa. Dr. Loki wasn't going to say anything, or think anything useful, for that matter. Ellyssa suspected his knowledge of The Center was on a more grand scale than just hearsay.

Narrowing her eyes, she poked around a bit more. As if he knew, their host's mind filled with the periodic table.

Ellyssa tossed him some bait, trying to strengthen the feed to the doctor's hidden thoughts. "Although very subtle, I can detect a slight German accent."

Dr. Loki didn't bite. "Yours isn't light at all," he replied calmly.

"Touché," Ellyssa said.

They stared at each other until the doctor broke contact and turned his attention away from her and back toward Trista. The line Ellyssa had been riding completely snapped as he directed his thoughts toward her friend.

"We would've risked everything if we brought in the poor souls. In the beginning, it was all about survival. And this establishment *had* to survive."

"Why?" Dyllon asked, breaking his long silence.

A proud smile broke across Dr. Loki's face. "It would be easier to show you."

The Pit was huge, a labyrinth of unending sterile corridors, turns and stairs. During their maze run, they passed by the sliding steel door that led to the tunnel where they'd been escorted through into a different section of the underground structure and up to another story.

Finally, the doctor paused at yet another steel door. "I think you will find this impressive."

Like Ann, he punched in a code and scanned his thumb. The door popped, letting them gain access. The doctor stepped aside while his visitors entered an open room, much like the observation deck of Ellyssa's father's at The Center. The grey metal walls housed a line of tables pushed against a large picture window. Each table held two computers. A variety of people with different skin tones and hair colors manned the stations, watching through the glass and documenting their observations.

When they'd entered, some of the observers had glanced over their shoulder, flashing different shades of green, brown, and blue eyes, before disregarding them, their attention captivated by whatever was on the other side of the window.

"Come and look," invited Dr. Loki.

Below them was a group of about fifty people, all lean and muscular, dressed in white tank tops and roomy pants. Before them stood three teachers Ellyssa immediately recognized as *sensei.* Loreley and Ann were two of the teachers. The master was of Eastern descent, his hair black as night. He barked orders in Japanese, and the students started a string of *katas.* From what Ellyssa could tell, the *katas* were a combination of several different disciplines like what she'd practiced at The Center, containing strikes, kicks and throws to invisible enemies. Ellyssa's body ached to join them.

"What is this?" Rein questioned.

The corners of the doctor's lips lifted slyly as he watched his people perform the dance of a conglomeration of the ancient arts. "This place started off with thirty people. Fifteen males and fifteen females. Each a genius in their own right. They didn't care about nationalities. They cared about expertise.

"When the War broke out, even before the United States entered it, six scientists, two for each of the facilities, scoured the earth for the most intelligent, the best, doctors, scientists, mathematicians, tacticians, arms experts, strategists, even high-ranking military personnel.

"Today, our population stands at two hundred fifty." The doctor's chest puffed out and his chin lifted. "The people below are Alpha Group One, our best. We have an Alpha Group Two and Three, and our Beta Group consists of twenty-three children between the ages of five and sixteen."

Ellyssa stared at the group of people. Their lean bodies moved with precision, the execution of the *kata* perfect, their stances flawless. They reminded Ellyssa of herself, her sister and her brothers. With growing alarm, she realized that, in a roundabout way, the Resistance, lurking beneath Pantex, had accomplished the exact same thing that her father had, just not on as grand a scale.

Soldiers meant to execute.

"You asked about us being in contact with the other facilities." Dr. Loki said. "One day, when we are ready, we plan on taking back what is ours."

"With two hundred fifty people?" Woody asked, dubiously.

"We have our contacts, too. The few are...let us say...important people in high places. The Resistance is like a surreptitious organization within an organization." Dr. Loki's gaze landed on Ellyssa, then shot away. "I'm sure you have a lot more questions. And I have several of my own. But I do have work to do." He walked toward the door, where two men waited on the other side. "Oliver and Glenn," he introduced, nodding in respective order. "Please show our guests to their quarters."

Turning, Dr. Loki gestured with his arm, inviting them out. "If you please."

"No, I will not please," Woody said, pointing his finger in the doctor's face. "You brought us here against our will."

The one he called Oliver stepped forward, but the doctor stopped him with a wave of his hand. "I am sorry to inform you of this, but I do have other duties. Our discussion will have to continue after dinner tonight. Then, I'll show you the rest of The Pit."

Glowering, Woody looked like he was going to say something else. Actually, he looked like he was about to demand answers, but before he did, Ellyssa placed her hand on his wrist.

"Woody." She shook her head. "Not now."

Surprisingly, Woody's demeanor cooled and he backed away. "After dinner, then," he said tersely. He glanced at Ellyssa, a strange look on his face.

"Of course. I assure you I do understand your interest. I am just as interested in you. Now, if you will excuse me." Dr. Loki ushered them out and shut the steel entrance, leaving them outside with their new escorts.

"Come with us," the one called Oliver said.

Oliver was a smaller man, about Ellyssa's height, defined and wiry, with black hair pulled into a ponytail, amber eyes, and exotic light-brown skin. Glenn was much taller, big and bulky. His skin was as dark as Jordan's, his hair curled tight to his scalp. Reminiscent of Rein, his arms crossed over his muscular chest as he watched Ellyssa and the others file behind Oliver to another section of the clandestine structure.

Oliver and Glenn led the group down one long corridor to another. Ellyssa assumed they were taking the scenic route to keep the newcomers confused. She didn't blame them. If her own group had had a technological goldmine such as this, keeping any guests confused and lost would be an integral part of defense for them as well. Unfortunately for them, Ellyssa had a tight grasp of exactly where they were. And if she knew Rein and Woody, they too had the maze memorized. Their whole lives had been living in a network of dark passages where the development of such skills was necessary.

Bottom line, the place was still impressively huge. Layer upon layer of levels and a labyrinth of passageways.

Oliver led them down four flights of stairs, then down a very long passageway. Ellyssa could hear the thoughts of the occupants behind the closed doors as they passed, pleasant thoughts of companions or of work that needed to done. Nothing sinister. The family seemed to be as close-knit as hers had been. Living together, working together. But toward what end? Something more than just surviving?

Oliver stopped at the end of the hall. "You two," he said indicating Trista and Ellyssa, "are in here." He slid the door back on a track.

Ellyssa gave Rein a reassuring smile before she entered the room behind Trista. Unlike the other rooms she'd seen, the walls had a type of cream-colored padding—noise reduction?—and there was a thin brown carpet. A little more homey than rest of the institution. Two small beds, with thin mattresses and army-green blankets and a small bedside table nestled between, made up the furnishings. Off to the left was a wooden door left ajar. A sink and part of a shower were visible, leading her to believe there was a water treatment process somewhere within the steel structure.

On the beds lay their backpacks and one of the three tents rolled into a tight cylinder. Ellyssa went right over to her bag and reached inside the side pocket. Her fingers enveloped the smooth cave pearl. Relieved, she left the little pearl where it was and faced Oliver and Glenn.

"Where are our weapons?"

Glenn was the one to answer. "They've been stored away. You have no need for them."

Scanning his mind, an image appeared of a rather impressive arsenal—pistols, rifles, grenades, launchers and crossbows for hunting, two floors above them, one level directly below the entrance to the tunnel leading back to the canyon.

Behind him, Rein clenched his fist. Ellyssa tossed him a comforting smile and shook her head. Rein's hand relaxed.

Oliver opened the door directly across from Ellyssa and Trista's room. "You three in here."

With reluctant glances, Rein, Woody and Dyllon ventured into their room, which had the same décor as the girls' room.

"The showers are on timers. Five minutes. I suggest you use them." Glenn grimaced, flaring his nostril. "The doctor requests you to stay in your rooms until dinner."

Rein's worried eyes were the last thing Ellyssa saw as their escorts slid the doors closed. Only one set of steps left.

"Oliver is our guard," Ellyssa stated.

# 32

Commandant Hans Baer stepped out onto the deck in front of his office. The morning was warmer than usual, but a chill still bit his skin. Anger gnawed his insides.

Blue skies housing an afternoon sun did little to brighten his mood. Not after the phone call he'd received from Xaver. He was to expect them later in the day, unfortunately before the blizzard the radar predicted.

Off to his left, prisoners walked into the newly finished rec center carrying gallons of paint, brushes sticking out of their pockets. A few stayed out in the cold, fingers sticking through thin gloves, finishing final touchups. Although still underweight, their steps bounced with a renewed vigor, and their frames looked less like scarecrows drowning in grey stripes and more like humans.

Doc stood among the ones outside, still on light duty as had been ordered, carrying a canteen of water to his fellow inmates. Doc glanced up at the Commandant when he stepped outside. He flicked his head to the side toward the sergeant-at-arms, and Hans' gaze shifted to the enlisted man.

Like most of the soldiers, the sergeant stood along the stone wall, his arms crossed in front, a rifle slung over his back. Only, instead of observing the working prisoners, the Sergeant was staring at him.

Taking Xaver's hand, Aalexis stepped out of the SUV. His touch still left a mixture of confusion and comfort. She was growing accustomed to their new arrangement, though. To embrace the emotions she'd felt for her brother had settled the unease, the anxious feeling. No longer did she fathom the insanity of such sensations or fear them weakening her. Aalexis' head remained clear and focused.

As soon as Aalexis had agreed to stop fighting the innate urges, Xaver had embraced her with a fierce hug. He fell into the role of loving her just as easily as he had protecting her. Perhaps because Xaver had already accepted the feelings way before her.

Aalexis looked over at her brother. Xaver rummaged in the back of the SUV and pulled out their bags. The coat he wore hid muscles she knew bulged under the weight. Hands full, he straightened, his azure eyes catching hers. His full lips lifted briefly, then fell back to their previous placid state.

They'd agreed that what happened between them would not show to the outside world. Only inferior beings were stupid enough to wear their hearts on their sleeves. Excluding Xaver, she'd found the barrage of feelings did not include the lowly creatures, anyway. Aalexis' detestation of them remained as active and strong as ever.

A cold breeze lifted her hair from her shoulders and fanned it around her head. She pulled the hood of her parka up and gazed out across the camp. Prisoners milled around a building that hadn't been there at their last visit, folding tarps and cleaning paintbrushes. They seemed stronger, the clothes they wore newer, gaunt expressions lessened, and hope seemed to spring in their steps.

Guards stood watch, bored looks on their inferior faces. Except one, whose face remained shadowed under the cap he wore, a square jaw set tight. Although he wasn't facing her, his eyes were on her, watching.

For a moment, Aalexis played with the idea of sending the male to his knees, the mere thought of pain incapacitating him. Removing his cap, the male turned toward her. Blond hair cut short shelved over a hardened face. Fearlessly, his eyes carved into her. Aalexis recognized the look. She'd seen it enough times in the mirror.

"Who is he?" Aalexis asked Xaver.

Xaver glanced over and subtly curled a nostril. *Was he jealous?* "I do not know," he replied, turning away.

Keeping her eyes firmly set on the male, who didn't carry the good sense to flinch away, an idea started to take shape.

"There might be a use for some of the subhumans. The detective proved to be useful to a certain extent."

"She betrayed *der Vater*."

"Yes. He did not have the insight we do now. We could rectify the problem."

Xaver turned and studied the male. "I see," he stated, understanding Aalexis' train of thought.

"The Colonel has been helpful."

"He is thinking with a narrow mind of how we might be able to benefit him and the State."

"Yet he has his uses for now."

"I agree. The Commandant will not be happy."

"He will cooperate or die," Aalexis said with no inflection, still looking at the soldier. "Some inferiors might prove useful while we prepare."

"They will need to be young. Strong. Have a bit more intelligence than the average."

"We could formulate an extensive training program. One to help eradicate those who are too weak."

"Until our creations are of age."

"Of course."

"We can help them achieve an even higher state."

Tearing her gaze away from the male who stood his ground, Aalexis looked into Xaver's eyes. "Exactly what I was thinking."

As Xaver processed the possibilities, he held a faraway look. "I see where we could utilize such a person while we are preoccupied with our creations. A substandard human better trained, enhanced, would prove beneficial and quite effective against those who are not."

"I think we should start formulating the process tonight."

"I agree."

Aalexis' fingers itched to entwine with Xaver's. Fisting them instead, she turned and headed up the stairs. She wanted to be done with the business with the Commandant and start on the new project as soon as possible, their first candidate already chosen.

Foreboding tumbled and ground in Hans' gut even before he watched the gates clank shut behind the SUV. It'd started thirty minutes earlier when he'd spoken with Colonel Fiedler. The Colonel had ordered him to cooperate fully with the children.

*What in the hell did he mean by the order, anyway?*

*Cooperate with children!*

Regardless of the symbols of Aryan purity, they hadn't the experience to do...what? What were their plans? He knew Aalexis and Xaver wanted the man who'd shared information about Ellyssa kept alive.

But why? A trap of some form? Did they expect their sister to come to this establishment and rescue the Renegades?

Laughable.

*Was it?*

After what he'd seen Aalexis do and what Doc had told him about Ellyssa and Dr. Hirch's plan, Hans could see a trap being set.

The SUV coasted to a stop in front of his building. Xaver got out. The boy looked even bigger than the commander remembered. Maybe the thick pea coat created an illusion.

*Doubtful.*

The coat certainly didn't add centimeters to the teen's tall frame.

He turned around before Aalexis emerged from the passenger seat, then returned to his desk. Never in his life had the Commandant felt such apprehension. The unknown plagued him. He pulled opened his desk drawer and retrieved a bottle of pink antacid.

He had to gain control. After pulling a long draw from the bottle and returning it to its drawer, Hans dragged in a deep breath, slowly let it loose, and waited. After a few minutes, much more time than should've passed, he heard the outside door open and Corporal Kraus extend a tentative greeting. The next second, his office door opened.

The Commandant stood, straightening his uniform as the corporal entered. "*Heil.*" Hans returned the greeting. "*Fräulein* Aalexis and *Herr* Xaver, sir."

"Yes. Thank you, Corporal Kraus." He nodded as Aalexis and Xaver entered. "Please come in."

Commandant Baer extended his arm, offering the seats across from him. As before, they dressed in civilian clothes, she in a bright red coat that hung to her thighs, and him in the black pea coat, no expressions troubling their faces, their eyes bright with danger. They seemed to float across the floor and took the proffered chairs.

"Should I bring some tea?" Corporal Kraus asked.

"No, thank you," Aalexis answered. "We have other pressing matters. Our meeting will be short."

"That will be all, Corporal."

Relief flashing across his face, the young man backed out of the office and closed the door. Hans didn't blame him. The young people in front of him had that effect. The commander took his seat, grateful for the expanse of the desk. Silence entered the room, blanket-like, as four azure eyes studied him. Uncomfortable under the heavy stares, Hans adjusted himself in the chair, leaning back in his chair and trying to appear relaxed.

"As you requested, Doc is still alive," he said, unsure of what information they wanted. "I have reassigned him to lighter duty."

Holding Hans' gaze, Aalexis said, "I noticed how everyone seems more...comfortable. Better fed. Is there a reason for such treatment?"

Forcing a relaxed smile, which felt anything but relaxed, Hans replied, "I had need for a new recreation center for my men. I wanted to make sure it was completed." The lie coated his tongue.

Aalexis seemed to buy the untruth. Then, again, he couldn't have detected otherwise; the void on her face remained unchanging. "Yes. The new building. It will be perfect."

"Excuse me?"

"My brother and I require quarters during our stay."

"Oh?" He couldn't keep the surprise out of his voice. "How long do you expect to stay?"

"For as long as is needed. I assume the Colonel has notified you."

"Yes," he answered tersely.

Studying him, Aalexis paused for a moment. "I understand your reservations. Let me assure you, though, Xaver and I are quite capable of running the camp."

"What?" The Commandant balked, taken aback. He started to stand, but the tension in Xaver's jaw reminded him to stay seated. "I do not understand. I was asked to cooperate. There wasn't anything said about you..." He couldn't even complete the sentence; anger held his tongue. To hell with the Colonel. "I will contact the General about this."

Unaffected by his outburst, Aalexis removed an envelope from an inside pocket. "You do as you see fit," she said handing him the paperwork. "I do assure you the Colonel and the General understand our arrangement. I think you will find everything in order."

Hands shaking, Hans opened the envelope and produced a white sheet of paper and a yellow copy. The official seal, an eagle over the SS bolts, was pressed onto the top. With growing fury, Hans' blood pressure reddened his cheeks as he read the orders. At the bottom were the signatures of General Richert and, below that, Colonel Fiedler. He forced his eyes away from the scrawl at the bottom of the page and looked at Aalexis. For the briefest of seconds, Hans was sure he saw pleasure fleeting across her face before it disappeared under the impassiveness.

No longer caring about the repercussions, Hans stood. "I will not stand for this. This is an outrage."

There. He saw it. The corner of Aalexis' lip atypically twitched as if she found his infuriation humorous. Whether or not she realized the subtle hint of emotion, it quickly disappeared. Both she and Xaver rose to their feet, their faces stone.

"You," Aalexis emphasized, her tone calm, but Hans heard the implication, "do not have a choice. Need I provide a physical reminder?"

Aalexis didn't say of what, but she didn't need to. Hans clearly remembered the pain Doc had endured, as if the incident had happened yesterday. Glancing at Xaver, who remained still by his sister's side, the commander sank back down, defeated.

"I thought you might see things my way. You are hereby relieved of your duties as the Commandant of Amarufoss."

"Yes."

"My next question to you is, do we have your support?"

What else was there to say?

"How may I be of assistance?"

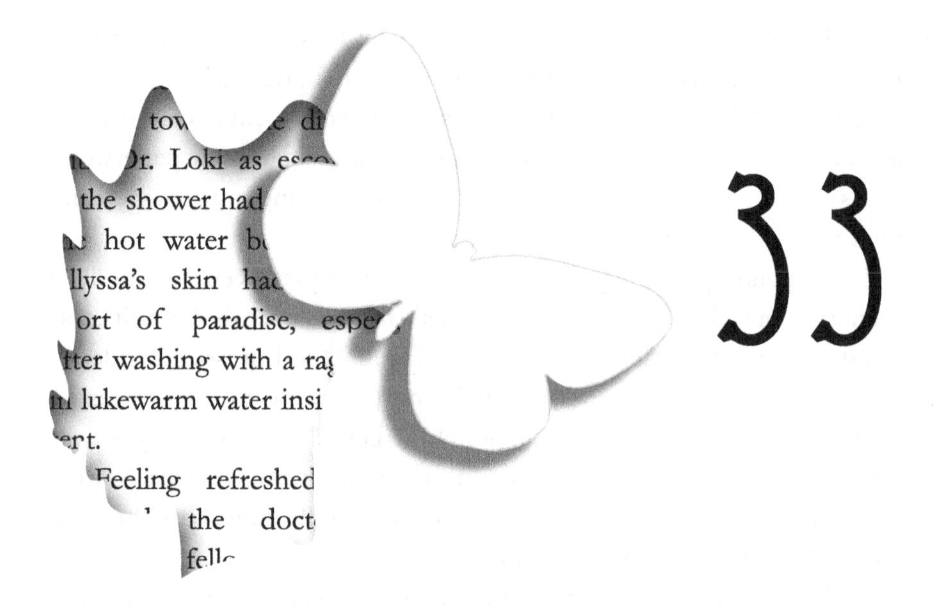

# 33

The scent of soap surrounded the group as they headed toward the dining hall with Dr. Loki as escort. Even if the shower had to be rushed, the hot water beating against Ellyssa's skin had been just short of paradise, especially after washing with a rag soaked in lukewarm water inside a cold tent.

Feeling refreshed, Ellyssa followed the doctor, who greeted his fellow inhabitants' curious stares with a warm smile. Rein walked next to her, his hand in hers, and Woody was on her other side, his hair still damp. Dyllon and Trista were behind them, whispering to each other.

Woody kept glancing at her, a weird look on his face, then his eyes met Rein's. The two males shared some sort of silent exchange she could have easily picked up on but didn't. After a moment of them looking at each other, Rein nodded.

"I need to talk to you," Woody said in her ear. His clean smell invaded her nose.

Ellyssa's brow dipped. "About?"

Woody's eyes jerked toward Dr. Loki, then back to her. "Why don't you just look?" he mumbled.

Eyebrows arching, Ellyssa glanced at Rein. Whatever it was, he was in the know, because he dipped his chin.

She looked back at Woody, who widened his eyes and gave several short nods with his head, hurrying her along. Even with Woody's permission, the act felt wrong. Over the last few months, she'd made it a point not to peek. But whatever floated within his head must be important. Rein wanted her to, Woody invited her to, and judging by Dyllon's anxious expression, he knew, too. Taking in a deep breath, Ellyssa formed a gate within her mental barricade and swung it open. So attuned to his distinct signature, Woody's thoughts easily filed in, clear words and images, one after the other.

*Can you hear me?*

Strange to have a one-way conversation with someone inside her head. Ellyssa usually just went incognito, snatched what she wanted and left. A smile lifted her mouth as she nodded.

*I think you can influence our emotions.*

That shocked her, so not what she'd been expecting him to say. "What?" she thought. A snicker bubbled in her chest when Ellyssa remembered the dialogue wasn't like an expressway.

Irritation lined Woody's face. *Look.* She could hear the exasperation in his nonverbal word.

The lines in Woody's forehead deepened as if he was trying to jam his thoughts into her head. Picking someone's brain didn't work that way. Ellyssa rolled her eyes and shook her head.

Chagrin coloring his cheeks, Woody's face smoothed and, as if a vein had been opened, his thoughts flowed. A conversation he'd with Rein and Dyllon in their newly acquired rooms about the calming effect she had on him when he was about to confront the doctor. In Woody's head, Rein's jaw dropped, but Dyllon nodded as if he already knew.

Then she remembered the incidents back at the farmhouse. Rein had stopped beating Dyllon after she'd touched him, a confused and frightened Dyllon calming down during the same incident. The time in the van after Sarah and Tim had been murdered—Trista's anguish had dissipated after Ellyssa had touched her, too, when she wanted the grief to go away.

Had her ability evolved like Aalexis'?

Was it possible?

Could she change how people felt by a mere touch of her hand and a flow of her emotions?

All at once, everything shut down as her mind tried to wrap around the possibility. Ellyssa stumbled forward, struck by the implications of such a development. Rein placed his hand on the small of her back to steady her, his touch sending a zing of electricity up her spinal cord, jump-starting her neurons to complete the synapses.

Just as Dr. Loki turned around as Ellyssa corrected her step and offered him an embarrassed smile to hide the astonishment her expression had to have been carrying. He returned the smile and continued on his way.

As Ellyssa followed the doctor with her group, her mind flipped through the memories over and over; the change of emotions did seem to be reactive to her mental want. Dyllon had even questioned her back at Tim and Sarah's, and she'd laughed away the idea as nonsense.

But it wasn't nonsense, and Ellyssa should've known better. She was a product of a fairytale. A fictional character born from between the pages of a novel.

Her gift progressing was just as likely as her sister's. Like the mental blockade she'd learned to build to keep out the nonstop bombardment of people's thoughts and the gate she'd learned to open to specific people's. This new ability required her to learn to flex another mental muscle.

As the doctor stopped at a set of metal rungs and turned to face them, her countenance blanked. She filed away the information to examine later, which wasn't going to be an easy task, but she had other pressing matters. And as much as the new light that had been shed on her ever-evolving ability, Ellyssa wanted to know more about The Pit and their host.

"Before we head to dinner, I'd like to show you something," Dr. Loki said. "I think you will be impressed." He climbed up the ladder and pulled a lever that held the door shut. A plate moved to the side and the hatch opened inwards. From above, moist air and the scent of earth drifted down.

"Follow me, please," the doctor said as he pulled himself through the hole.

Ellyssa was awestruck as soon as she poked her head through the opening. Smiling, Dr. Loki offered her a hand and helped her up onto the metal grating.

Her widening eyes soaked in the architectural astonishment as Ellyssa turned in a circle. In a steel-encased room, greenery stretched before her. Below them, plants and trees flourished. Overhead, grow lights hung from beams stationed six meters above, swathing the area in the light and warmth of a mild summer's day. Beads of perspiration formed on the tip of her nose from the humidity. She wiped them away.

"Wow," said Rein as he joined her.

Dr. Loki beamed. "I know."

"How?" asked Trista, her voice swaddled in disbelief.

"Brought here by the founders," Dr. Loki answered simply. "This concept had been around even before the war. The scientist who founded The Pit utilized it. Of course, improvements were made through the years." He moved down a grated walkway. "Come."

The doctor stopped at a small grove of orange trees, their tops pruned to perfectly round. An abundance of oranges hung from the branches. On one side, the fruit was still green; on the other, the fruit was ripe. "We are able to produce more fruit by keeping the trees trimmed. The technique directs more nutrients to the fruit instead of the growth of the tree. Plus, we save space for growing other food."

He started to move again, and they all followed. Pointing at the variety of fruits and vegetables, he continued. "Over here we have corn and potatoes. Here are the apple trees. Beans, bell peppers, onions, strawberries, lettuce, cauliflower." He stopped and looked at them. "The list goes on and on."

"Do you rotate the crops?" Dyllon asked.

"No need. We treat our waste and reuse it for fertilizer and irrigation."

Looking at the overhead lights, Woody frowned. "There is no way the solar panels we saw in the tunnel produce enough electricity to power all of this, *and* your computers, *and* your water heater."

As soon as he spoke, Ellyssa heard the real source of their power. A gurgling bubbled over by the far wall.

"Water?" she asked.

"Exactly. Let me show you."

Ellyssa didn't need to catch a read on him to know how much pride the male had in the establishment. She herself was beyond impressed. Keeping with the doctor's pace and wishing he would walk faster, excitement grew as the gurgling became louder.

Finally, their host stopped at an aqueduct. Clear water rushed through the canals, pushing a row of cylinders with paddles in a circle. Wires connected to nodules at the ends of the cylinders and joined together at different conductor boxes. From the top of the boxes, a single thick cable protruded and ran toward a red door.

"Our electricity," he presented with a wave of his hand. "We built a series of underground canals from the Red River." He paused for a moment. "The river in the canyon you stayed in. It wasn't an easy feat, but we did it. This is how we power our establishment. The computers, the grow lights, our water treatment. Everything."

"Impressive," said Dyllon.

"You haven't seen anything yet."

# 34

"Put that over there," Mathew said to Marcus, a prisoner of about eighteen with light-brown hair and dark brown eyes. His nose had been broken on more than one occasion, and a scar marred his left cheek from the corner of his mouth to his ear. Overall, a good-looking young man who deserved a better life than the one that'd been dealt to him.

Marcus had been at Amarufoss a few months before Mathew arrived and, at the time, had been nothing but skin wrapped around bones. In the last few weeks, though, since Mathew struck the deal with the Commandant, Marcus had plumped up like a teenager should. Marcus was the last of his group still alive, caught by area police five years ago during a routine trip to get food. His father had been with him. The last memory Marcus had of him was the back of his head disintegrating when a bullet exited. His father had been trying to protect him.

Marcus smiled, which wasn't something he did often, but over the last few days had become more frequent. "Why are we rearranging this... again?" He dropped the bed frame on the floor.

Casting a glance over to the two soldiers standing guard by the door, Mathew immediately started to assemble the metal pieces of the frame. When held prisoner at a concentration camp, loitering wasn't allowed.

The soldiers didn't seemed to be paying much attention to them, though, as neither of them posed a threat. Besides, both men were probably happy they'd been assigned to indoor detail instead of weathering the wind. Within an hour, the temperature must have plummeted into negative numbers.

"Visitors," Mathew answered. He'd seen the blonde demon child come through the gate.

After the bed was completed, Marcus grabbed the new mattress still in the packaging. "Visitors? Who in the hell would want to come here?"

Mathew shrugged. He didn't see any reason to worry the boy. After all, Marcus had been in the system too long, the evidence marring his young face. Mathew had to give the teen credit; the boy had endurance. A strong will to live. Like most of the others, Marcus should've died within months of being captured.

They hefted the mattress onto the springs. "I think that's it," Mathew said, rubbing his hands together. He looked around and lowered his voice. "I bet the Commandant's men aren't happy."

The recently assembled pool table and games had been disassembled and stored away. Beds had taken their place. The only things left were the gym equipment and the mat over by the fire escape that had been chained for security purposes. By the look of things, the soldiers weren't going to get enjoy the rec center anytime soon.

Marcus nodded in agreement.

Turning toward the soldiers, Mathew said, "We're done."

"You," the one on the left said, pointing at Mathew, "pick up the mess. And you, take the tools to the shed and report back to your barracks."

"Yes, sir." Marcus grabbed the tool belt and departed. One of the soldiers left with him.

As Mathew swept the floor under the scrutiny of the remaining soldier, the door opened. Freezing wind swirled through the room and brushed its icy fingers through his hair. A chill creeping along his spine, Mathew turned to see the Commandant and Ellyssa's siblings. Nausea rose in his stomach.

Aalexis and her brother entered, their gait confident. She wore a bright red coat, a hat covering her blonde strands, and Xaver wore a black pea jacket.

The soldier stood at attention, his arm extended. "*Heil.*"

Xaver turned toward the enlisted man, disgust evident. "Dismissed," he said.

Confused, the soldier faced the Commandant. The commander tossed his chin up and the soldier departed without a further word.

"I guess this will do," Aalexis said, looking around the Rec Center.

"We aren't running a hotel."

Aalexis shot the Commandant a glare and fear crossed his face, clamping his mouth shut.

Starting toward the beds, the young girl walked right past Mathew. He held his breath, hoping she didn't notice him. The hope fizzled after she paused and turned around, her unsettling gaze locking onto him. Mathew recoiled under the intensity of her stare. He had no control over the reaction. Remembered flames licked through his veins. Someone had once told him the memory of pain fades with time, but Mathew would never forget the fire.

Her face remained unemotional, no hint of recognition appearing. Lurking behind her eyes, though, he saw a glint of delight and amusement. Always at her side, Xaver stood behind her. Amusement twinkled behind his stoic look, too.

"Doc," Aalexis said, stepping toward him.

Mathew's leg muscles tensed with the desire to flee. Somehow, he managed to stay put. Probably because his feet felt like they had been encased in cement.

"I understand you have been treated well."

"Yes," Mathew managed, his gaze cast toward the floor.

"Food sufficient?"

"Yes."

"I think we should talk again."

Lifting his head, Mathew met her cold azure eyes, identical to Ellyssa's. "If we must, but I have nothing new to offer the discussion."

Her lids lowered as a subtle flinch ghosted her face. Mathew went down, flames devouring him, fire consuming him. He couldn't think; he couldn't see. All he could do was feel the extraordinary pain. He was pretty sure he screamed. Then it was gone, and he found himself curled into a tight ball on the ground, a low burn still casting heat. A groan escaped his lips.

"Doc," she said.

Struggling, Mathew opened his eyes and managed to lift his head.

"Maybe that reminder will prompt a reconsideration on your part. I will allow you time to mull it over."

Aalexis turned away and left him on the floor as if he was a roach she'd just stepped on. Actually, Mathew felt like a roach she just stepped on.

Xaver followed as they went to examine the exercise equipment. Mathew turned his head and saw the Commandant looking at him, his face pale with horror, useless arms dangling at his sides.

"Commandant Baer," Aalexis called, "I will require that additional items be brought in."

"Go," the commander mouthed, then turned his attention to the young blonde demon. "Of course. I will have one of *your men* make a list for you." He emphasized the key words as he walked past Mathew.

*Your men? Had she taken over the camp?*

He knew the answer.

She had.

Things were going to change, and not for the better.

Mathew rose on shaky legs that rebelled under his weight and stumbled out into the welcoming, freezing cold.

# 35

After following Dr. Loki down the four flights of steps into what Ellyssa assumed was his office, Ellyssa and the others took a seat at the rectangular table. As usual, Rein sat next to her, his hand on her knee, Woody on her other side. Trista and Dyllon sat across from them. The two leaned close together as couples often do. She'd noticed more than once Rein and her doing the same thing, like a magnetic force with an eternal pull.

"I hope you enjoyed the tour," Dr. Loki said, sitting at the head of the table.

When Dr. Loki told Dyllon that they hadn't seen anything yet, he wasn't joking. For an establishment beneath the earth's surface, these people didn't lack. Besides electricity and an indoor garden, the establishment housed a hospital, a communications room used for receiving any ground patrol's interactions, a soundproof firing range, and leading off the training room was a weight room that had left Ellyssa's muscles twitching with longing.

Even their computers were capable of connecting to the network. Dr. Loki's associate had assured them, though, that messages were only received. The computer was strictly used like a flytrap. With virtual fingers, it'd reach out, snatch information, and dart away, leaving behind an undetectable computer-generated dust in its wake, impossible to find unless someone happened to be looking for the specific signature at a specific time.

The reach the doctor had hinted at delved far and wide, which made her question how he couldn't know if the other Resistance organizations had survived. Actually she questioned a lot. But every time she'd probed through his mind for answers, she'd kept looping back around to his block. Somehow, Ellyssa was going to have create the leak she needed to bust through his wall and let his memories pour through.

She certainly hadn't learned anything from The Pit's residents. During dinner, she'd singled out individuals from the mass, flexing, shaping and bending her wall to open the gate to grab bits and pieces of their thoughts. Some questions about the newcomers, easy to pick out because they'd cast furtive glances their way. Mostly, though, the inhabitants thought about specific elements of training, and some performed *katas* in their heads, replaying the flow and technique. Ellyssa had enjoyed those the most, watching their mental images dance.

She'd gleaned nothing that caused her soldiering side to tingle with suspicion. The inability to read Dr. Loki did, though.

Woody answered the doctor. "It amazes me that you are able to acquire such technology. It's very impressive."

Dr. Loki beamed. "Well, now that you've had a look at all we've accomplished, I'd like to ask you some questions."

The five of them exchanged looks before Rein took the lead. "What would you like to know?"

"Basics first. Who are you?"

Rein squeezed Ellyssa's knee. "Go ahead," she said.

He faced Dr. Loki. "We're from Missouri," he began.

Besides leaving out Ellyssa's identity and The Center, their story unfurled through Rein's words. Certain parts still wrung her heart and reopened wounds. By the pained looks of the others, they were bothered by the recounting, too. Ellyssa entwined her fingers with Rein's, grateful he was there. She pulled strength from him.

As Rein spoke, Dr. Loki leaned back in his chair, captivated. All the while, though, his eyes kept drifting to Ellyssa. Setting aside her pain from the ones she'd lost, she entered the doctor's mind. The capture of the Missouri Renegades was not a surprise to him—old information. His concern was genuine, his horror of the tale being spun, but that wasn't what she wanted to know. Ellyssa dug deeper and found herself again with the wall, towering over her. Only this time, a hole had appeared, a small leak. Bits and pieces of thoughts dribbled, familiar images. She prodded.

"We came to rescue our friends," Rein finished.

"That won't happen for a few days," Dr. Loki said, his voice thoughtful. "Blizzard conditions have been forecasted. As of right now, the temperature is negative seventeen and that doesn't include the wind-chill factor."

"No," Trista whispered, her shoulders slumped. Dyllon wrapped his arm around her and pulled her close.

Closing his eyes, Woody massaged his temples. "Do you know how long?"

"At least three days. You will be safe here."

Rein ran his free hand through his hair. "Thank you." His tone was weighed with disappointment.

Dr. Loki waved the sentiment away. "We'll be delighted. Besides, I already expected you."

"Why?" Ellyssa asked, her gaze trained on the doctor. The more she kept the doctor focused on her, the better. Her mental probe continually picked at the hole, widening an escape for the flood. Disturbing but indistinct information puddled before her. She had to keep him focused on her. "Why would you be expecting us?"

The doctor propped his elbows on the table. Agitation darkened the teal in his eyes and twisted the corners of his thin lips down. For a second, Ellyssa saw the true age that hid behind the male's youthful appearance. "About a month ago, we picked up bits and pieces of communication about a band of Renegades heading this way. All of you," he said with a sweep of his hand, "could have jeopardized our whole operation. You must understand, besides an occasional routine patrol, there has been little to no activity here for years. Even when they reopened Amarufoss, there was only a basic sweep of the area.

"Then, about three weeks ago, the heavy patrols started. Even the *Gestapo* were called. We were on full alert. No one ventured out, not even to hunt. The ramifications of being caught... It could bring our whole cause down—at the very least, cripple the Resistance for generations."

He leaned back in his chair, peaking his fingers under his chin. His eyes leveled on Ellyssa. "What's strange is that the patrols suddenly stopped. The *Gestapo* left, the soldiers returned to their posts back at the camp. Nothing. Then you came along, as expected."

Suddenly, a crack zigzagged up the doctor's mental block. The wall crumbled, chunks falling down like a rockslide. Everything the doctor had worked so hard to keep caged poured freely, pieces and bits of memories broken like glass. Things weren't in chronological order, but Ellyssa had seen enough, including a glimpse of the female subject, Ida, whose file Ellyssa had stumbled across before she'd escaped, images of The Center, her father only much younger. Dr. Loki had worked with her father, had been part of the experiments. Like a tsunami, Ellyssa's soldiering surged forth enveloped in anger and hatred. Her hand tensed, squishing Rein's fingers until she felt bones rub together.

Rein winced. "Ellyssa?"

Dropping his hand, Ellyssa shot from her chair. Everyone's heads turned toward her. Fear snapped the doctor's lids into circles.

"You knew *der Vater*," she accused, fighting every instinct to clamber over the table and wrap her fingers around his throat. "You worked at The Center. You worked with *der Vater*." Ellyssa heard the monotonous tone of her voice, knowing her expression was just as vacant, and the way she'd reverted to her father's name. She didn't care. She had to protect. Survive. She'd seen the capability their host possessed.

Four sets of eyes whipped back toward the doctor.

"What?" Rein said, raising from his chair.

Dr. Loki squirmed as disbelief dropped his jaw. "I— It's true. Leland was right." he muttered.

The mention of Leland's name came as a surprise; Ellyssa hadn't caught that in the shards of his memory. Not that it mattered how Dr. Loki knew Leland, who had worked as her father's assistant and with the Renegades. Nothing mattered but the hatred squirming in her gut, the innate desire to act upon the anger coiling snake-like, ready to strike.

"Leland?" Woody sputtered, pushing his hair out of his eyes. "How do you know Leland?"

Fury bled into Ellyssa, feeding everything her father had designed her to be. She kicked the chair out from behind her and prowled around the table. She could feel the apprehension roll off her family's skins, their eyes widened with confusion. She didn't care. "You performed experiments. You killed. I saw the file. Subject 20. She was put to death," Ellyssa snarled, the robotic-like tone evaporating in her anger.

*A flicker of Ida's corpse lying on a gurney.*

"I didn't," Dr. Loki denied, his voice shaky.

"You were part of the whole design."

*An image of her father and Dr. Loki formed. Both men had smiles on their face as a child was born with fine blonde hair and deep blue eyes.*

Sweat beads popped out of Dr. Loki's forehead and the tip of his nose, his anxious eyes twitching from side to side as if seeking an escape. He started to get to his feet, but Woody, who had come up behind him, put his palm on the male's shoulder. The doctor plopped back down in the chair. The chunks of long-ago memories evaporated as if a sudden drought dried his mental progression. Fear replaced everything except for her advancing form.

Ellyssa loomed over him, red coloring her vision, her fists clenching and unclenching. Fury worked her jaw. She bent her chin down and dangerously glared at their host through slitted lids. "Why would you keep this from us?"

"I—I didn't know who you were."

"You lie. You recognized me."

He shook his head. "No. No. I wasn't sure."

Ellyssa's hand shot out and clutched Dr. Loki's throat. His hands wrapped around her wrist, futilely trying to set himself free.

"Please." His voice pinched within her grip.

"Now you can be sure. I am what *der Vater* created."

"Ellyssa." Rein stepped next to her. He placed his hand on her cheek. "Let him go."

Ignoring him, she jerked away from Rein's touch and squeezed harder. A satisfying shade of blue tinted the doctor's face. His lips opened and closed like a fish's. His eyes bulged within their sockets.

*Just a twitch of my wrist*, she delighted, *then dead.*

Rein grabbed her wrist, not gently either. "Let him go now, Ellyssa," he ordered.

*Orders.* She scoffed. *None of them are a match for me.*

The words charged through Ellyssa's head and scurried away before she had a chance to fully comprehend what she'd just thought. The implications. Her grip loosened, and the doctor took in a ragged breath. In an instant, she'd changed into the monster that her father had created. How easily she became his creation. Shocked, Ellyssa's stoic expression crumpled into horror.

Rein let go of her wrist. "What are you doing?" His voice sounded far away, hollow, like a long tunnel separated them.

"I..." Having no answer, Ellyssa's words faded. Two opposing forces warred inside her. Rage sizzled defiantly, willing her hand to stay locked around the doctor's tender flesh. Revulsion at how easily anger took over. She released Dr. Loki.

Sputtering, chest desperately heaving, Dr. Loki tried to claim much-needed air.

Recoiling, Ellyssa backed away until her back pressed against the wall, and she slid her mental wall back into place, cutting off the images from his splintered memories.

Everyone stared at her. Dyllon's and Trista's faces were colored the same, bleached white. Neither of them had ever seen her in full soldering mode before. Their eyes held concern as well as incredulity and fear. Even Woody, who had witnessed her soldier side before, stilled, his stormy grey eyes as wide as his mouth.

They were afraid of her. The air oozed with fear.

Rein stood in front of her, blocking out everyone. Concern in his eyes, his hand traveled the length of her arm, over her shoulder, and stopped as he cupped her cheek. "What happened?"

Ellyssa shook her head. "I do not know. His memories were... The things they did..."

"Are inexcusable," Dr. Loki finished, his voice cracked and harsh. He exhaled a rattling breath.

Ellyssa peered over Rein's shoulder at the doctor. The blue tint on his face had changed into red blotches. Bruises the shape of her fingers flared angrily on his neck. Even now as she looked at the male she'd almost broken, hatred twisted in her midsection. And shame coated it.

The doctor's eyes met Ellyssa's. "Please give me a chance to explain," he said, painfully grimacing with each word. "I withheld information, but so did you," he pointed out. He inhaled another noisy breath. "My wall is down. You can look for yourself."

Afraid her instincts would kick in again, afraid she wouldn't stop next time, Ellyssa said, "I cannot."

Rein's fingers, feather light, traveled back down her arm and he laced their fingers together. "It's okay."

"I do not think it is."

Her voice was robotic-like, monotonous, her old voice. Rein heard it too, a frown dipping his mouth.

"Breathe, Ellyssa."

She did. Once. Twice. Three times. Cool air rushed into her lungs, settling the tension in her stomach, calming her soldiering side. She expelled the breaths through her nose.

"Better?"

Ellyssa nodded.

"Do you want to...um...scan him?"

Still unsure if she had a grasp, she shook her head.

"Come and sit down." Rein pulled her arm.

Hesitant, Ellyssa willed her feet to move and let Rein take her back to the table. Woody slid into the seat next to her. Between Rein's comforting caress as he trailed his thumb along the back of her hand and Woody's soft touch as he drew little circles at the base of her neck, she felt the creature her father had made withdraw back into the recesses of her being.

Worried, Ellyssa chewed on her bottom lip as Dr. Loki's breaths evened out. She'd felt anger and hatred before, but nothing like what the doctor had invoked. She feared what she could do, what she could become. She knew the soldiering side of her, the monster, still lurked within her depths, but the way it had sprung forth, unannounced and uninvited, uncontrolled, it terrified her. If push came to shove, she would always do what she needed to do; that was something she'd come to terms with, but she wanted to make the conscious decision to do so.

"I know this is a surprise for all of you, and I'm not even sure where to begin," Dr. Loki said. His voice was scratchy, and speech was a struggle.

Ellyssa bore responsibility for the male's condition. Remorse started to take playful nips in her. Guilt bared its gnarly teeth.

"How do you know Leland?" Woody asked.

"That's a start," Dr. Loki said. A slight smile curled the left corner of his mouth. "I found Leland."

"Why?"

"That's a long story. How this all came to be. But first, I want to tell you how sorry I am, Ellyssa."

Her head snapped up at Dr. Loki's words as his teal eyes, flavored with regret, examined her. "Sorry," she muttered; strands of anger woke, peeking between the layers of remorse and guilt. "Sorry doesn't even begin to cover what I glimpsed inside you."

"Did you glimpse everything?"

Ellyssa opened her mouth to respond, but the fact was, she hadn't. The memories that had spilled from the crack were fragmented, incomplete. Regardless, she had seen enough, the forerunner being Ida's corpse being fed to the incinerator. Hatred sidled over next to the anger. She took in a deep breath. Control. "I saw enough."

"No, you didn't. If you had, you would know."

Tension knotted Ellyssa's muscles. Rein's grasp tightened and Woody's hand stopped massaging and splayed across the back of her neck as if he could stop her if she decided to rise.

Refusing to lose control, Ellyssa relaxed. She was different now. Not an animal, and definitely not a monster. Her father had failed.

"Then explain yourself," she muttered between tight lips.

The doctor removed his hand from his throat and placed it on the table. Round, angry bruises from Ellyssa's fingertips still glowed an accusing red.

"Your father was a genius, his IQ remarkable. As you know, he was a child of The Center, as was I. His physical attributes were...well, more defined than mine. His eyes were more pure, his physique within the acceptable guidelines. He was a remarkable specimen.

"We worked together, trying to perfect the Aryan bloodline. To create a superior being, strong, incredible reflexes, off-the-chart intelligence." He paused, his eyes moving from one face to the other. "You look at me as if I'm lower than an insect. Perhaps I am," he shrugged, "but I am nothing more than a product of what I was bred to do, what I was trained to do." His gaze moved to Ellyssa. "Much like you."

"Ellyssa's nothing like you," Rein seethed. "Nothing. She never killed because someone wasn't perfect."

"Neither did I. That is what you failed to see, Ellyssa. I was there, but I didn't kill her."

Ellyssa understood. In his attempt to keep his secret hidden, the doctor's memories, when they bled through, were bits and pieces, as of a shattered vase. At the time, she'd known the doctor's memories were fragmented, but she had reacted before she'd had a chance to puzzle the pieces together. The death of the female she'd found on the computer before her initial flight and her own detestation for her father had brought forth natural instincts. Fight or flight. One thing Ellyssa would never underestimate was that she'd always fight. Always.

Under regular circumstances, Ellyssa would've thought things through. Her dark side had been unleashed before she had a chance, though. That scared her.

Taking a chance, Ellyssa lowered her mental shield, sending the tendrils of her mind to soak up the doctor's thoughts. As if understanding what she was doing, Dr. Loki sat still, his gaze unwavering. His mind freely opened to her, the recollections unfurled. For a minute or two, she watched. The stirring creature inside Ellyssa fell asleep.

"You were her father?" Ellyssa said, not really a question.

"I loved her."

"And Leland."

"Yes."

"Others?"

Sadness enveloped Dr. Loki's mind as he looked down. "Yes." A few seconds passed before he found the courage to meet her eyes again. His throat moved visibly as he swallowed, followed by a grimace. "People change. *You* changed."

Rein's head swiveled back and forth between the two of them. "Would one of you like to let us in?" he said, voicing what the others wanted.

"Go ahead," Ellyssa said, her tone soft, thoughtful, normal. The robot had disappeared. "It's your story."

Dr. Loki repositioned himself, straightening his spine before he started. "As I was saying, I worked with Dr. Hirch. Our goal was to unlock the genetic sequence to develop a superior human. We found it, as you can see," he said with a nod in Ellyssa's direction.

He studied her for a moment. "As much as I've grown to hate your father, I must say his brilliance is awe-inspiring. You are truly beautiful."

"I fell short. My father had other ideas."

The doctor nodded. "I understand. The problem with your father was an incredible god-sized ego.

"Anyway, to simplify things," he said, returning his attention to the rest of his audience, "after we found the correct sequence, we sliced and diced DNA from both of our sperm samples, from other males', and from different females' eggs containing the desired qualities, then spliced them together. Amongst our discoveries were several genes that, once enhanced, brought about...special abilities, like Ellyssa's gift.

"We had hits and misses, Mother Nature's interferences. Most babies aborted naturally, some died in infancy. Some were born deformed. You understand society's take on deformities."

No one said anything. The practice of euthanizing severe imperfections was a practice that had been accepted for decades.

"The female Ellyssa was speaking about, Ida, she was one who I considered, my daughter." His gaze grew distance as he reflected into his past. "By all accounts, my genetic makeup is not perfect. My eyes, you see. Yet she was the first to overcome all odds. She was extraordinary, strong, beautiful, always laughing. I loved her as a father should. I bought her pretty dresses and dolls."

The doctor stopped, his eyes moist. Dropping his chin, he wiped away the unshed tears. The group remained quiet, too stunned for speech.

"Average intelligence," he continued, "which disappointed your father, but she was gifted with the ability to start a fire with nothing more than a thought. Our first to possess such a talent. At first, we didn't even realize it. Small fires would start from nothing. After a few more mishaps, we realized it was Ida, and a series of tests began.

"Ida hated them. But she was a good daughter and sat through them regardless. What we discovered, though, was she had no control over her gift. It seemed anger triggered the ability, but that wasn't always the case. One day she killed a nurse by accident. It devastated her. It thrilled Dr. Hirch.

"Against my protest, he locked her up and forced her to use her gift on test subjects while he remained safe behind the lines. Finally, she just curled into a ball and no longer responded to any stimuli. That was when he murdered her. That was when I changed my whole outlook on life.

"The night my daughter died, I fled and hid. I just couldn't take it. I was weak, I guess. I became a Renegade." He chuckled a little, humorlessly. "Eventually, I met a contact. Eventually, I gained his trust. Eventually, I ended up here. Since the War, no one had been brought into The Pit to live. The consequences of such actions were too much to risk, but my expertise in the training Dr. Hirch and I developed wasn't something they could pass up."

Subconsciously, Dr. Loki brought his hand back to his neck. "I don't know what brought about the existence of humans from the primordial soup, but I do know this; we were not meant to mess with it. Through evolution, we constantly change, moving toward this broad term called perfection. One day we may reach the ultimate goal; maybe we are closer than we think."

Woody's mouth opened. Dr. Loki held up his hand, stopping his unspoken words. "Let me finish. Through the Resistance network, I learned about Leland, who had been created the same as you all were, many years after I had left. I contacted him and you know the rest."

"He told you about me?" Ellyssa already knew the answer, but asked for the others' sake.

"Yes. About you and your siblings."

"They are dead. So is my father," she said.

"I know."

"How?"

"Word reached us about The Center being destroyed. Before Leland... died..." Dr. Loki paused for a moment, pain etching a deep line in his forehead. "...he contacted me. I didn't really think such an undertaking could ever be accomplished. You prevailed, though."

"And my ability?"

"As I already said, we knew Renegades were coming because of what little information we gathered and the increase in patrols. I didn't expect you, though. When I first saw you with your group, your physical characteristics, I knew you were the one Leland had told me about. The one who'd escaped. That is why I let you in."

"Wait," Woody said, leaning forward. "How did you block her?"

"A technique Leland told me about when I questioned him about you. Dr. Hirch was afraid Ellyssa would discover his true plans. Leland feared she would find out what side he really worked for." He smiled. "It didn't work well."

"My siblings and I were prohibited from using our gifts against any personnel. I had obeyed. As for the wall you created, it was impressive, but there is always a leak."

His story done, Dr. Loki slouched in his chair, seemingly exhausted from the recounting. Quiet settled over the group huddled around the rectangular table in the underground steel structure. No one moved, no one said anything. Minutes ticked away.

Finally, the doctor spoke. "I want you to understand that we will not help you get your friends back. We can't."

"We understand," Woody said.

"But in the meantime, you are free to roam around the facility. No more guards." A sad smile appeared. "There are no more secrets between us. When you are ready to go, you can retrieve your weapons and leave."

"Thank you."

The doctor rose. Angry blue and red splotches colored his neck. Ellyssa looked away from her shame.

"The hour is late, so if you will follow me, I'll take you back to your quarters." Dr. Loki moved toward the door as everyone got to their feet. He paused after he punched in the code and turned around. Glancing at the hands being held between the two couples, he said. "We will make living arrangements more suitable for your needs."

"Wait," Woody said, standing. "One more question."

"Yes."

"With all the contacts working together, the Resistance in its entirety, how do you not know about the survival of the other underground communities?"

Dr. Loki smiled. "The same as your failure to realize."

"I don't understand."

"You had contacts helping you, right?"

"Yes."

"Did you know where your contacts got supplies from?"

"Ordered them?"

"All of it? Really?"

Pausing, Woody mulled for a moment. "Probably not?"

"Did your contacts help others of the Cause?"

Woody shrugged. "We never knew exactly what the others did."

"There's your answer. We do our job. We don't talk. We don't ask questions."

# 36

As the wind howled, shaking the windows in their frames, Aalexis stared out the window. Not that she could see anything. It was like looking at a white wall, a complete whiteout. Even the spotlights from the towers couldn't penetrate the thick sheets of unrelenting snow with nothing more than a dull glow.

On the window, Xaver's reflection joined hers, his scent reaching her nose. He wrapped his arm around her waist. She leaned into him, his warmth caressing her. His lips brushed the top of her head; tingles cascaded through her body.

The intimacy of such an act felt strange, but good. Two parts struggled within her, one repulsion at the act, the other relishing every touch. As Aalexis became acclimated to the familiarity, the relishing was winning.

Xaver had been right. Once she'd embraced the connection instead of burying it, the apprehension had departed, the fear of becoming like Ellyssa. Plus, since she'd conceded, Xaver seemed to be even more devoted to her. More protective. A quality she would need if things didn't go according to plan.

At all costs, Aalexis must live.

"Do you think she will come soon?"

"After the blizzard, I am sure," Xaver responded.

A burst of wind rattled the glass. Snow continued to pound down across the plains.

"What if she does not survive this?"

"Do you think we would survive if exposed?"

"Of course."

"She will, too. I would not be surprised if her inferior company froze to death, though. There is no shelter for them."

The thought of them dying sent a forbidden pleasant thrill through Aalexis. Without the inferior people Ellyssa had formed relationships with, she would come alone. She would be vulnerable.

That was another thing Xaver had been right about, relationships had strengthened the vile Renegades. Unfortunately, Ellyssa had formed a bond with the wrong class of humans. If Ellyssa would've waited, her emotional connection could have been shared with her real family. Once Ellyssa returned home with them, she would learn.

Their father's work would come to fruition. And born from her father's vision, another experiment to accommodate them while they waited for their superior creations to reach adulthood. Aalexis was a little surprised her father hadn't tried. An easy concoction to formulate to suppress the substandard humans' emotions, so they could act as guards until his work was completed. Her father certainly would've benefitted from such an endeavor, instead of trusting an emotional, insane person such as Detective Petersen. If the female hadn't interfered, Aalexis' father might still be alive.

Anger twinged with her. Xaver noticed.

"What bothers you?"

"*Der Vater*," she stated. "We have a lot of work to accomplish when we return home. I will not have someone like that detective in charge of security. We are capable of so much more."

Aalexis had already handpicked the male to take part in the first trial, the one she'd seen before her meeting with Commandant Baer. She wondered if he would be honored at such a prospect or try to refuse. Either way, it didn't really matter. Aalexis would have things her way.

"I cannot wait to get started," Xaver said. "I actually feel excitement at the prospect. Strange, is it not?"

Aalexis heard it too, as the thump in his chest quickened. Xaver tightened his grip on her waist, and she rested her head against his broad chest. His heartbeat echoed in her ear. She felt her hair move under her brother's soft breaths.

A loud thumping on the door disrupted the calm.

Xaver dropped his arm and moved away. "Come in," he yelled.

Whoever was on the other side of the door didn't respond.

"I do not think they can hear you."

As if in affirmation, the wind moaned noisily as it beat against the building. The knock came again.

Xaver opened the door. Wind whipped through the entrance and cold spread across Aalexis' skin.

"Who are you?"

"Sergeant-at-arms, sir, here with the report," a male said, his voice deep and rough.

"Let him in, Xaver."

Her brother stepped back, and a male wearing a long olive green coat with a matching bomber hat and scarf entered, dark blue eyes peeking over the knitted material. Snow covered the male from head to foot; his boots were caked in frozen ice. He took off his gloves as Xaver shut the door.

"Heil," he greeted, arm extended.

"At ease," Xaver ordered.

The male pulled down the scarf, exposing a crooked nose and a fierce square jaw. Coincidence that the male Aalexis had seen earlier in the day showed up just as she had thought about him. Of course, her father had always said coincidences don't exist, only science and facts.

"I apologize for the intrusion," the male said. "I was just informed you have relieved the Commandant of his duties."

"That is correct," Xaver said.

"This is rather unusual." He paused, his gaze moving between the both of them. "I'm not sure I understand."

Lifting his chin, Xaver stepped closer to Aalexis, fully in protective mode. She thought it unnecessary. The male was no match for her. If she chose not to use her gift on him, she could just as easily break him with her own hands. Xaver was aware of this fact, but he was insistent he be the first line of defense. Aalexis didn't argue. Her brother was simply carrying out *der Vater's* wishes.

"I do not believe your understanding is necessary to carry out orders. Who are you?" Xaver challenged.

The male stilled, his lips parting. Impressively, he did not succumb to fear. Of course, he hadn't the slightest clue about either of them.

After a moment, he seemed to compose himself. "Yes, sir. I am the sergeant-at-arms. My duty is security of the camp. I have come to deliver to you the daily rosters and report." He unbuttoned his coat, then reached inside and produced a set of papers that were clipped together.

Aalexis stepped forward, under her brother's watchful eye, and took the papers. "What is your name?" she asked as the sergeant took an at-ease stance.

The sergeant studied her for a nanosecond, apparently unaccustomed to answering to a young nonmilitary female before he responded, "Sergeant Lukas Gersten."

"I see." She walked around him. "Security, you said?"

"Yes, ma'am."

Perfect.

"So part of your duties is to keep the Commandant informed of any unusual activity?"

"Yes, ma'am."

"Please continue" she urged.

"Yes, ma'am. Since the camp is under your command, I should report to you. No unusual activity reported."

"What of the prisoners?"

"There are a total of fifty-six prisoners. Forty-one males and fifteen females. Two females perished today," Sergeant Gersten said, smugly.

"I do not care about the number. How have they been treated?"

"I don't understand."

An impulse to send the sergeant to the floor reared in Aalexis. To watch him writhe. So inferior, even if she wanted to use him as part of her select team. "It has come to my attention they seem well-treated here. Do you understand now?" Aalexis asked, keeping her voice steady.

"Yes, ma'am. Their food intake has increased by fifty percent and they were recently assigned new uniforms and coats."

"Why?"

"It was my understanding the Commandant ordered the improvements due to the new Recreation Center."

"How nice of him."

"May I speak freely?"

"If there is more."

"Yes, ma'am."

"Please," she invited.

"One prisoner has been lifted above the others. The name he goes by is Doc. He has had several meetings with the previous Commandant of the camp."

Aalexis didn't respond, her expression remaining blank, but the mention of Doc's name both piqued her interest and stirred her anger. Why would the Commandant seek meetings with a lowly prisoner, even if she wanted him kept alive? Unless an agreement had been reached between the two.

Apparently, the Commandant hadn't been truthful with her. Not entirely. If the former commander had withheld information about Ellyssa, he would pay.

With her hands behind her back, Aalexis started to move around the sergeant again. Melted snow puddled under his black boots. He remained rigid, as if her presence didn't bother him. His stoicism was rather impressive for someone of his standing. Plus, he seemed to remain loyal to those over him.

Pausing behind the sergeant, she looked at Xaver. Her brother's gaze flicked to her, then back at the male named Lukas.

Lukas continued. "His treatment was the first to improve. The only reason I was given was that Commandant Baer had been ordered to do so."

She continued circling the male, then stopped in front, a lot closer. The top of her head reached a little below his chin. She stared at him, hard. He didn't blink.

Impressive.

"How old are you?"

"Twenty-seven."

"How many years' experience?"

"My promotion came into effect six years ago."

"Your record?"

"Exemplary. I graduated at the top of my class and have received leadership commendations and service medals."

"Your experience?"

Even under his thick coat she noticed his chest puff out in pride. "I have been at Amarufoss for five years. Recommended by Colonel Fiedler and requested by Commandant Baer. I am the best of the best, ma'am."

The Sergeant's conceit was laughable. He had no idea of what the best of the best consisted of. But Aalexis was impressed with his attitude and his loyalty. He would serve as a perfect test subject that, hopefully, would lead to a spot on her own elite security team if he survived.

Aalexis flicked a glance over her shoulder. "What do you think, Xaver? Should we offer?"

"I think he will do."

Aalexis faced the Sergeant, and his first real show of emotion etched two vertical lines over the bridge of his nose.

# 37

A deep sense of foreboding made a home in Ellyssa's psyche as she stood in the steel corridor. Harsh fluorescent light sputtered menacingly, casting eerie flickering shadows. The low hum of electricity sizzled in the air.

She looked around.

Something was amiss. Familiarity surrounded her, but at the same time, The Pit held an alien ambiance.

Ellyssa cast a glance over her shoulder to confirm that she was right. Sure enough her room was behind her, the door closed. Frowning, she looked straight ahead and took a step. The tap of her shoe echoed loudly, bouncing down the metal hallway. Then she understood what was wrong. Besides the fading ring of her step, emptiness filled the entire facility.

Someone had to be there. Rein wouldn't have left her alone. Neither would the rest of her family.

Sliding her eyelids closed, Ellyssa opened her mind to Rein. She couldn't find him. Maybe he was too far away? She shifted her concentration to locate Woody. Nothing.

She lowered her entire wall. Like a fisherman, she cast the mental net to latch onto anyone's signature. Nobody. She was alone.

Her pulse elevated as anxiety poured in her veins. Ellyssa's heart responded in her chest cavity.

How could she be alone? Not including Ellyssa's group, there were two hundred fifty inhabitants. They couldn't have all slipped away without her knowing.

Ellyssa opened her eyes to a changed scene. She still stood in the same corridor, but now the hall ended at a large grey door. Yellow light seeped through the crack at the bottom.

She felt foolish.

*Nothing more than a dream.*

Silently laughing at herself, Ellyssa started toward the door, her footsteps echoing with a lonely, hollow tone. With each step closer to the door, the ominous premonition returned and burrowed into her stomach. She tried to brush it off—*it's just a dream*—but it haunted her.

The door loomed ahead like a presence in itself, large and dominant in the dreamscape. The sides seemed to inflate and deflate as if breathing. Cool air brushed by, catching strands of her hair in its breezy grasp, and carried with it a whisper. She stilled, the beat of her heart in her ears and the hairs on the back of her neck standing erect, and sent her mind outward.

Silence.

Fear flowered in the pit of her stomach and incapacitated her muscles.

She had to get a grip. This was just a dream. A dream and nothing else. Clinging to that knowledge, Ellyssa willed her feet to move, and with a flash-forward moment, she suddenly stood at the beckoning entrance. She reached for the knob.

A shadow disrupted the flow of light, followed by the familiar voice of her father. "Come in, Ellyssa."

"*Thump, thump, thump*," her heart responded.

Ellyssa fought the urge to retract her outstretched hand and retreat back down the hall. How could her father's ethereal voice bring such anxiety? She swallowed the fear, the flight instinct, and unleashed anger. Her skipping heart slowed to its normal patter. Without another thought, she put her hand on the doorknob and twisted. The latch slid back and door swung inward.

She stepped into her father's office. The same white walls and tile shone clean, no designs or pictures to mar the purity. On the other side of the room, she could see Lake Michigan's grey waters through the picture windows. The only difference was that the room was completely empty of furnishings.

Ellyssa's father stood where the furniture should have been, wearing his white lab coat, his silver hair combed neatly back. Delight showed on his face. His hands were hidden behind his back.

"*Der Vater*," Ellyssa said. Her voice held no inflection. Her face felt hard and smooth like polished stone. Familiar hatred joined the anger. Together, the two sensations twisted and folded into each other, becoming one.

His blue eyes twinkled with amusement as he regarded her.

*Father never could hide his emotions as well as he wished he could.*

"You have returned to the fold," he said.

"No. I have not."

"But you will."

"No. I will not."

"You must join your siblings," he said, raising his arms outward as if about to present a magnificent show.

Her father didn't disappoint.

From behind him Aalexis and Xaver stepped out, flanking Father. Behind them, farther away, Ahron and Micah appeared out of thin air, like ghosts.

Ellyssa felt her muscles' desire to recoil at the sight. She refused and raised her chin. "You are all dead," she stated matter-of-factly.

Her father paused, bringing his index finger to his mouth as if in thought. A slight frown produced two lines between his eyes. He considered for a moment before he spoke. "Are we?"

"Yes. My family and I exterminated you." Although her voice remained robotic, she accentuated "my family" to grind the point home.

He arched his eyebrows. "Did you?"

"Yes."

Tucking his chin in slightly, an unsettling grin pulled her father's lips. "Are you sure?"

His menacing smile evoked nothing in Ellyssa. The doctor was dead, as he should be. "I am."

"Yet, here I am." He moved his hand from his head downward in presentation of the obvious. "As I always will be. You are my daughter, my creation. I will always be a part of you."

A small string of resolve snapped. Ellyssa tied it back together. "No."

"Always. As your sister and brother are."

He didn't reference Micah or Ahron farther behind him. Neither had moved, but they seemed to be floating instead of standing on two feet, their images wavering and unclear.

Ellyssa's father moved out from between Xaver and Aalexis and stood a little off to the side, examining them. His chest inflated with self-importance. "Are they not beautiful? Just look at them."

Ellyssa did. Both her siblings stared at her with deadpan eyes. Somehow, Aalexis seemed taller and older than when Ellyssa had fought her back when she'd rescued Rein a few months ago. Xaver definitely was bigger; his boyish stature had filled out with defined adult male muscles and length.

The doctor studied them for a second longer before he returned his attention to Ellyssa. "As are you," he said, gliding toward her.

Ellyssa wanted to move, her feet twitching with the anticipation of backing away, but she couldn't. They were glued to the floor.

*Wake up. Wake up. Wake up,* she commanded.

Dr. Hirch stood before her, his blue eyes boring into hers. She could feel his warm breath against her skin.

"You almost killed my old associate." Ellyssa's eyes widened at the revelation. *How could he know?* "The satisfying feel of his flesh beneath your fingers—it must have been hard to stop." The doctor's white teeth gleamed between his smiling lips. "You cannot fight who you truly are, Ellyssa. That is why you lost control. First and foremost, you are a killer of those beneath you. That is what you were bred to be."

Ellyssa shook her head. "No."

"It is, and you will join your brother and sister."

"I am not dead."

"Neither are they."

Ellyssa's eyes popped open.

Rein had felt the soft shudder of Ellyssa's shoulders, but it'd taken awhile for the meaning to sink into his sleeping mind. He opened his eyes to darkness and a whispering sob.

"Ellyssa?" he said.

She didn't answer.

"Baby?" Rein reached over and flipped the light on. A bright white washed the black away. He lifted up on his elbow and touched her arm. "What's wrong?"

"Nothing," Ellyssa answered, wiping away the tears she didn't want him to see.

"Look at me."

Rolling over, she stared at him; her eyes were red and a little swollen. She blinked, trying to keep the moisture trapped behind her lids. He touched a tear she'd missed glistening on her cheek.

"Don't tell me nothing's wrong."

"It's silly," Ellyssa said, looking away. "I just had a nightmare."

"A nightmare. It must've been one hell of a nightmare, then."

She rolled over, her back facing him. "It was, and I don't want to talk about it."

Rein's lips parted, words of comfort teasing his tongue. He closed his mouth instead. When she wanted to talk about it, she would. Slipping his arm around her waist, he pulled her close to him, letting her know he was there—that he would always be there. Her body was warm and soft against his, and the scent of her hair tantalized his nose. They lay like that for a few minutes, her chest rising and falling.

Finally, Ellyssa shifted onto her back so she could look into his eyes. Even with swollen lids, she was so beautiful. Her platinum hair spread across the pillow like spun silk, her flawless skin glowed, her full lips pouted. Rein smiled down at her, his lips preparing to brush against hers.

"Do you think I'm a monster?"

The smile faltered, then fell. Rein frowned at the question. "Of course not."

"But I am."

"Don't be silly."

"I almost killed Dr. Loki. I could have easily killed him. Just a twist of my wrist." Ashamed, she glanced away.

"Is that what your nightmare was about?"

"No." Ellyssa paused. "Sort of. It's complicated."

Rein shifted so she was forced to look at him. Misery and irresoluteness clouded the clear sky-blue color of her irises. "You are the most loving, caring person I've ever met. What you experienced was nothing more than a normal human emotion. You felt betrayed and angry."

"I lost control."

Rein pulled his fingers through his hair. "Do you think *I'm* a monster?"

A scoffing laugh burst from her mouth.

"Yet, if it wasn't for you, I would've beat a hole through Tim and Sarah's wall using Dyllon's head as a battering ram."

Lips pursing together thoughtfully, Ellyssa sat up. The sadness started to melt away. "True."

"You are who you are, Ellyssa. Nothing more, and nothing less." He cupped her face in the palm of his hand and stared into her eyes. "I love who you are, exactly the way you are, and everything that has made you the amazing person that you are."

Leaning against his touch, Ellyssa uttered, "Thank you."

Rein dipped his head and put his lips against hers, softly. He lingered there for a moment, inhaling her scent, memorizing the feel of her mouth, before he pulled away. "Now, what about the dream?"

The lifting sorrow sank right back onto her face. A light shudder trembled through her body. "I had a dream about my father. About all my old family. They were alive." She stopped for a moment, a crease forming between her eyebrows. "Well, my father, Aalexis and Xaver were alive. Ahron and Micah were in the background, floating like spirits." Her lids slid closed. "He told me that I was a killer and that I couldn't deny who I was."

Rein traced his thumb along the curve of her cheekbone. "It was just a dream."

"It just seemed so real," she breathed. Ellyssa opened her eyes and moisture shimmered. Rein leaned over and kissed her.

"But it wasn't. He can't touch you, can't hurt you. He has no hold over you. He never did. You're free. And you're with me," Rein said, followed by a kiss. "And I'm not going anywhere."

Reaching up, she folded her fingers around his hand. A small smile surfaced. "I love you."

"I love you."

Ellyssa leaned over and placed her mouth against his. Her kiss was warm and sweet...and electrifying. As he parted his lips to slide his tongue to hers, tingles swept through him, and warmth hummed in his veins.

What she could do to him with a mere look, touch, kiss still amazed him—the expansion in his heart, the stirring within his lower midsection. He wrapped his hand around the back of Ellyssa's neck, locking her in place.

"Can I try something?" she asked against his lips.

"Anything," Rein whispered, hoping whatever it was would be quick.

Hesitantly, Ellyssa placed her hand against his face. "Tell me what you feel."

Rein gazed at her for a moment, wondering what she was trying to do.

"Please."

Nodding, he closed his eyes. At first, he felt nothing but the excitement of her touch. Then gradually, his heart slowed, and he felt...calm. "I feel relaxed," he said. "I feel very relaxed."

"What about now?"

Tension flowed from Ellyssa's palm. He felt it. Not just from knowing her, like the uncomfortable tension when things got weird, but really felt it in his heart, his muscles, his bones. He felt frustrated and wanted to throw things and punch something. "I feel angry," Rein said, his teeth clenched together. His eyes snapped open to her surprised face.

"It works," she muttered. "And what about now?"

The anger released from Rein's jaw, and once again, he felt calm. Ellyssa dropped her hand. At the release of her gift, Rein felt normal. Not calm, not angry, just normal.

"Wow," he said, astonishment coloring his tone. "What did you do?"

"At first, I thought about relaxing things, like being safe in your arms. Then I thought about my father and Aalexis and the things they did to you."

Rein flinched at the reminder. Even now, he remembered the pain that had flowed through his mind with nothing more than Ellyssa's sister wanting it to be so.

"I'm sorry. But it was the only thing that I could think about that really evoked anger in me."

"I understand. Besides, that's all over with now." He smiled at her. "We were right about your ability to influence our emotions."

"Yes, it seems that you were."

His lips upturned into an sly grin. "I can think of other things I'd rather feel."

"Such as?" Ellyssa blinked innocently.

Rein wasn't sure if she was flirting, Trista's influence or not. Ellyssa was innocent in so many ways.

"Shall I demonstrate?"

Before Ellyssa had a chance to answer, Rein brushed his arm under her knees and flipped her onto her back. She squealed. Settling over her, he propped up on one elbow and slid a finger down the side of her face to her parted lips. She was so beautiful, flawless skin blushing with want, azure eyes shimmering with love.

He brushed his lips against hers once, twice, then deepened the kiss. Afterward, Rein broke away from Ellyssa's inviting lips and worked his way down her jaw. She lifted her chin, giving access to the hollow of her neck, her breaths coming in short pants.

"I'm never going to leave you," Rein breathed against her as he moved his hand under her shirt. She gasped, and her stomach twitched in anticipation.

Ellyssa wrapped her fingers in his hair. "I never want you to."

# 38

After breakfast, Dr. Loki met Ellyssa and the others at the tunnel entrance. They all wore their snowsuits in preparation for the weather. The doctor disappeared inside a room, then popped back out in a thick parka.

"You ready?" the doctor asked, slipping on black leather gloves. "I don't think you will be pleased."

"Let's just go and see it," Woody said.

Dr. Loki entered the code, and the door popped open. He stepped through and went into the side room, where the quads were kept. "Take your pick." He turned the engine, the roar shattering the quiet, and rolled out into the long passageway.

Pulling out in the same arrangement as last time, Ellyssa with Rein, Trista with Dyllon, and Woody by himself, the five followed behind Dr. Loki. Cool air swept by, and as they closed in on the entrance, the temperature dropped. Ellyssa ducked her face behind Rein's back to ward off freezing air.

Before they reached the opening, Dr. Loki glided to a stop and climbed off the four-wheeler. Quiet returned as the roar of engines died down one by one.

"Follow me," the doctor said.

He went to the entrance and pulled the camouflage curtain back. Glaring white bounced into the tunnel, as if the sun itself rose within the rocky walls. Wind blew in with the white and brushed its icy fingers against Ellyssa's exposed flesh.

Blinking back the light and cold, Ellyssa followed behind Rein to the drape and joined the crowd. A thick blanket of snow covered everything. The scrub brush and trees had disappeared under the white. Big, fluffy flakes fell and blew across the canyon.

"There has to be at least a meter of snow on the ground," Woody uttered in disbelief from over Trista's shoulder.

"And it hasn't stopped yet," the doctor confirmed. "The worst of the blizzard is over, though." Dr. Loki stepped away from the wintery scene. "Until it stops, you are more than welcome to stay with us."

"Thank you," said Trista. "I'm definitely not in any hurry to go out in that."

Disheartened, Ellyssa stepped away. Each day passing was a day that their family couldn't afford...if any of them had survived thus far at all.

Dr. Loki must have read the look on her face. "From what we gathered, the snow should taper off by tonight. You should be able to continue within a day or two. Plus, you won't be leaving from here. It's a two-to-three day hike, depending on the weather. You can leave from the original entrance."

"Oh," Ellyssa said, after taking a peek inside the doctor's head. The elevator, she gleaned, was large, with huge hydraulics that lifted and lowered a floor. On top of the roof of the machine was basically groundcover used to keep it well-hidden. Which apparently had worked.

"What?" Dyllon asked.

"An elevator," Ellyssa said, a little dumbstruck over the ingenuity of the people in an effort to stay alive. She'd thought it before, how her father really had underestimated the Resistance.

With a look that said he knew she had taken the information, Dr. Loki smiled. "We don't use it often. As a matter of fact, it probably hasn't been used for over a year, maybe closer to two. We keep it well-maintained, though. Always prepared. We have other tunnels that pop out all over that had been built over the years, but none as close to your destination as the elevator."

"That will be perfect. Thank you," Ellyssa said.

"The only thing is, when you leave, you will have to wait for a windy day. We can't chance your trail being traced back through the snow."

"I understand."

Mathew glanced up when the Commandant entered the barracks in his regular attire. Giving him a wary glance, Mathew went back to sweeping the floor. "Do you think it's a good idea for you to be in here?"

"It's my camp."

"Not anymore," Mathew retorted, knowing that had to sting. He didn't care; it wasn't like they were friends. Actually, Mathew would have liked to beat the hell of the commander with his own crop.

The Commandant didn't say anything for a moment. "I'm performing routine checks, accounting for inmates. Nothing out of the ordinary."

"Even with your sergeant-at-arms watching you. Surely you have noticed."

"I have. He isn't on the grounds right now."

Mathew looked up from his assignment. "Where has he gone?"

Frowning, the Commandant stood in front of Mathew. "I don't know. He doesn't report to me anymore." Pausing, he turned away and looked at the door, as if expecting someone to come through it at any moment. "I haven't seen much of him the last couple of days. It seems he has other orders besides his regular duties."

Moving the broom back and forth, Mathew waited for the Commandant to continue.

After a few seconds of staring at the door, the Commandant turned back around. "Do you think your friend Ellyssa will attempt a rescue?"

Mathew didn't hesitate to answer. "If she is alive...yes."

"I think Aalexis intends to carry on Dr. Hirch's work."

"That's the way I see things."

Silence followed again, except for the swishing noise of the bristles against the linoleum floor.

Finally, the Commandant said, "That's how I see things, too."

The former commander positioned his feet to execute a right-angle turn, but suddenly faced Mathew and backhanded him, hard. Just as Mathew stumbled back and tripped, and his backside met the floor with a *thud* that resounded in his teeth, Corporal Kraus stepped through the door.

"Don't ever speak to me that way again, you inbred scum."

The corporal glanced down at Mathew, a glint of sadistic humor in his eye. "*Fräulein* Aalexis requests your presence, sir."

"Please inform the *new* Commandant I am en route."

After the door closed behind the corporal, the former commander looked down at Mathew without a bit of remorse. "We have to prevent Aalexis' plans from happening."

Rubbing his cheek, Mathew didn't know what to think. The surprise of such a statement rendered him speechless, especially coming from a member of the military. Mathew had thought perfection was their highest goal. Wasn't that why they executed the people they saw as inferior?

Without another word, the Commandant exited the barracks, leaving Mathew with a red cheek and confused thoughts.

Commandant Baer's eyes locked on Aalexis sitting behind his desk with Xaver at her side. Irritation twitched the muscles in his face.

"Have a seat, Commandant," Aalexis said, pointing to the visitor's chair.

Although she didn't show any change of facial expression, Hans knew the little girl was rubbing in the switch in their positions and enjoying it. Locking his jaw to stop the tic, he proceeded to the offered seat, where he tried to appear relaxed by crossing his legs and resting his hands on the arms of the chair. The two faux angels didn't buy it any more than he did.

"You requested my presence?" Hans tried to keep the sarcasm out of his tone, but failed miserably.

Aalexis looked at the commander with a blank face, but Hans could see behind the façade. He could see the demented anticipation swirling like a cyclone behind the placid demeanor.

"Yes," Alexis said to Hans. Then to Xaver, "If you please."

The man-sized teen walked around the desk and stood behind Hans' chair. Hans couldn't see him, but he could definitely sense him as if Xaver was breathing down his neck.

Keeping his gaze steady, a remarkable feat, the former commander addressed the new commander. "How may I be of assistance?"

Cocking her head slightly to the side, Aalexis said, "It seems you have not been completely truthful with us."

Confused, Hans blinked. "I beg your pardon. I have answered all your questions."

"With half-truths," Xaver said. He placed his hand on Hans' shoulder.

Hans couldn't help it; he flinched as soon as the boy touched him. In the back of his mind, a little voice screamed a warning, and he understood why—he could feel the tension roil off Xaver's palm. Anxiety grabbed the reins and thundered through Hans' blood-stream, and the telltale signs of perspiration started to bead along his forehead. "I'm not sure I understand," he said, moving his eyes back to Aalexis.

"Tell me," she said, "why have you been meeting with the prisoner named Doc?"

*That's it?* "Oh." Breathing out pent-up air he didn't realize he'd been holding, Hans relaxed. He knew the sergeant-at-arms had been a busy little bee. "I was hoping to persuade him with extra promises of further livable conditions for the prisoners," he said, executing the well-rehearsed words without any glitch to show the lie in his voice. "Since he was already getting preferential treatment as per your orders, I thought he might be more open to...communicate."

"I see. And was he?"

"Of course not. If I had anything to report, I would have already told you."

"Interesting."

"Not really. I do apologize for the misunderstanding."

"Explain to me again why the other prisoners have benefitted from the arrangement."

Xaver's finger flexed minutely as Aalexis spoke, and Hans glanced down at the stiff fingertips digging into his shoulder. He didn't like the way the conversation was going. He had to tread carefully.

"They haven't. As I told you, I wanted the Rec Center to be completed."

"There was not a deal reached?"

Without warning, Hans' insides started to warm. Ever so slightly, like when sipping on warm tea. At first, he didn't understand what was happening. Had no clue. But as he watched Aalexis, comprehension dawned. He pulled at the collar of his shirt, trying to alleviate the heat as fear climbed up the rungs of his spine.

"I assure you, *Fräulein,* I have told you all that I know."

Stupidly, Hans tried to stand, the need to escape the rising temperature inside his body nullifying logical thought. Both of Xaver's hands latched onto his shoulders, keeping him firmly in place.

Saying nothing, Aalexis moved around the desk and stood in front of Hans. A malicious glimmer showed in her eyes as she regarded him. "That is not the information your clerk has loyally delivered. He could not catch everything, but he was able to hear about the deal you struck with the prisoner."

*Niklas? Niklas had betrayed him?*

"It did not take much convincing on my or my brother's behalf either. All I had to do was ask."

Hans knew what was coming next, and his heart tripled its beat. Then suddenly, acceptance engulfed him as the former Commandant made a life-or-death decision, a choice of the lesser of two evils. The little bitch could do her worst; he wasn't going to give her information about Ellyssa. To do so could help Aalexis and Xaver's plans, then the world would pay. Besides, if the lowly inferiors of the Resistance could withstand the torture, so could he.

The last thing Hans physically felt was Xaver's hands tightening on his shoulders a nanosecond before ice and lava entered his veins simultaneously.

# 39

Dr. Mike Ito, the resident *sensei* and weapons expert of The Pit, stood at the head of the Alpha Group while Ann and Loreley walked between the straight rows. The redhead kept glancing at Woody, and for some odd reason, Ellyssa didn't like it. Woody did, though; he flashed a smile every time he caught Ann's eye.

"*Ichi*," the *sinsei* barked.

On cue, the class executed *tsukis* to an invisible opponent's diaphragm. Ellyssa had to commend Dr. Loki and Dr. Mike. The students' precision was almost as fine-tuned as hers.

"*Ni*."

The same process with the opposite hand.

"*San*."

"Why don't you join them?" asked Rein.

Ellyssa wanted to. The urge twitched her muscles, but she shook her head. "Class is almost over. Those are cool-down exercises, then they will stretch."

"They are amazing. I wonder what Dr. Loki is waiting for," Woody said. He shot Ann another grin, and she turned away, her cheeks shading to the color of her hair.

Ellyssa shrugged. "Maybe some sort of sign."

"But from who? He doesn't even know if the other facilities still exist." Woody paused. "I wonder, if they do exist, if their people are as well trained. I mean, look at them," he said, flicking his head toward the students. "They are soldiers."

Nodding, Rein added, "And their arsenal is amazing."

Ellyssa watched as the class finished the series of punches and got on the ground to stretch. "But to do so, they would have to work together. Two hundred fifty people aren't going to be able to put a scratch on anything as big as the State."

The class had finished and started to make their way toward the door. Ellyssa, Rein and Woody stepped aside to let them pass. As Ann went by, with Loreley behind her, her gaze worked from Woody's toes to his head, as if undressing him. Woody puffed his chest out a little, like a rooster. Out in the hall, Ann whispered something about Woody being cute and Loreley said she was insane, then they giggled. Ellyssa rolled her eyes.

"You should have joined the class," said Dr. Ito. "I would've enjoyed seeing your technique. I understand you got your training from The Center."

Ellyssa glanced up at the thirty-year-old man. His dark brown hair matched his almond-shaped eyes. His skin was a yellowish bronze. He smiled at Ellyssa as he tossed a hand towel over his shoulder, his well-defined biceps twitching with the movement.

"I didn't want to interrupt."

"Maybe next time," he said, flashing ultra-white teeth at her.

"I would enjoy that. Thank you."

"Feel free to use whatever," he said, going into the passageway.

Excitement peaked in Ellyssa. "Come on," she said slipping her hands into Woody's and Rein's. She dragged them behind her over to the punching bags.

Dull thumps of fists hitting leather and grunts from exertion filled the huge room, and Ellyssa's muscles sang with satisfaction. It'd been days since she'd been able to work out, to practice her techniques. After thirty minutes or so, Ellyssa paused to watch Woody and Rein. Perspiration glistened on their foreheads as they concentrated on the bag. Their form was not as disciplined as hers, but still effective. The bags hefted under their strikes.

*Good enough*, Ellyssa thought. Adrenaline flooding, she bobbed up and down on her feet. "Okay. Who's first?"

Both Woody and Rein stopped to stare at her.

"What do you mean?" asked Rein.

"Let's spar."

A nervous laugh escaped Woody as Rein shook his head. "I don't think so."

"Why not?"

"I'm not sparring with you," Rein said.

Woody confirmed the sentiment with a shake of his head.

Ellyssa studied Rein for a moment, confused. "Why not?"

"I know you're well-trained, but what if I get lucky and accidently hurt you?"

Ellyssa laughed at the idea. "You're not going to hurt me. We need to practice. It will be good for the both of us."

"That's true. My money's on Ellyssa," Woody said, pushing Rein toward her. "Go ahead."

"Why don't you give it a whirl?" Rein protested.

"I'm not stupid."

"That's a matter of opinion."

"Please, Rein," Ellyssa begged. She tugged on his hand. "Your worries are unwarranted."

Hesitantly, Rein stepped into the middle of the room with Ellyssa. The look on his face was a little comical, yet glum.

Ellyssa said, "I promise, no accidents."

"It's not you he's worried about," Woody called from the sidelines.

"Shut up."

"Talk like that, and it won't be Ellyssa you have to worry about."

"Any time, little man."

Laughing, Woody said, "Listen to that trash talk. I get my turn after you, Ellyssa."

With a smile on her face and the vibration of anticipation humming in her muscles, Ellyssa faced Rein. "Take a swing at me."

Getting into a fighter's stance, Rein pulled his hands up to cover his face. Then he stood there.

"Come on," she encouraged.

"I can't." Rein dropped his cover.

"I can." Ellyssa stepped forward and punched him in the shoulder.

Woody hooted as Rein stumbled back a step.

Pulling his fists back into position, Rein blocked another jab from Ellyssa, then swiped his hand down in a circular motion to stop a sidekick. They circled each other for a minute, her punching, him blocking or ducking her attacks, but he never took a jab of his own. Finally, Ellyssa swung her arms down.

"It doesn't do any good if you don't attack me."

"I don't want to hit you."

"If you don't let me practice, someone else is going to hit me," Ellyssa lied. Besides her brothers or sister, no one was a match for her.

Rein tossed her a skeptical look, calling her bluff. "I don't even buy that."

"Please, Rein. Practice is good for both of us." Ellyssa brought her hands back up and started to bounce on her feet.

"I'll take a crack at her."

Ellyssa turned her head to Ann's voice; Loreley, in all her dark exotic beauty, stood next to her, at the exact time Rein had finally come to terms with his machismo and let his fist snap forward. He hit Ellyssa right in the sternum. The punch wasn't hard but caught Ellyssa off guard, violating the first lesson she'd ever learned from any of her dojo instructors—*never take your eyes off the enemy*. Stepping back, more from astonishment than impact, Ellyssa's head whipped around, her gaze landing on Rein. He dropped his jaw and widened his eyes.

"I'm so sorry," Rein said, reaching for her.

Ellyssa backed away, her chin dipping down. Blood pounded anger through her veins; she felt it feeding her. She wasn't angry at Rein; she was angry for being complacent even when the fight didn't involve an actual enemy. Something she wouldn't let happen again...ever. There were some lessons The Center had taught that should never be forgotten.

Rein let his hand fall to his side. "I really am sorry."

"No, my fault," Ellyssa said after taking a deep, calming breath. She didn't want to hurt Rein. "Come for me." She beckoned him.

Shaking his head, Rein held his hands up in surrender. "No. I can't and I won't." He turned away and went to stand by Woody.

Ann strolled to the middle of the floor, her red hair twisted into a braid. She gave a subtle glance in Woody's direction before placing her green eyes on Ellyssa. "I was watching you," she said. "I hope you're better than that, or you won't be much of a challenge for me after all."

Taking in a deep breath, Ellyssa became aware of everything. The intensity with which Rein and Woody watched her. Loreley making her way over to them. The way Ann sized her up, the sprinkle of freckles across her nose, the flare of her nostrils, the challenging smile crossing her lips. Slipping into the comfortable skin of her training, Ellyssa drank it all in. This was more like it.

Narrowing her eyes, Ellyssa said, "I do not think you need to worry about that."

The two squared off, then bowed. They dropped into fighting stances. Less than a second later, Ann struck. Ellyssa easily dodged. Dipping down, the redhead tried to sweep Ellyssa's feet. Ellyssa hopped over. Ann came at her again and again, and Ellyssa blocked every move, never striking back.

Fury started to flick in Ann's eyes. "You're looking," she accused. She propped her hands on her hips.

For a brief moment, Ellyssa was confused by the statement. Then, she understood that Dr. Loki had talked about them. And why wouldn't he? Secrecy in this small population could lead to mistrust.

Ellyssa shook her head. "I am sorry, but I am not," she argued, her tone stilted as it always was when her soldiering side came out to play.

"It's the only thing that makes sense. Besides Dr. Ito, and I give him a challenge, no one can beat me."

A grin popped onto Ellyssa's face. "I hate to inform you of this, but you have just met the one person who will beat you without the aid of my...gift. To rely on a specific talent weakens your ability to respond. You never know when a certain capability might be rendered useless," she said, thinking about her brother Xaver, or even Dr. Loki, for that matter. Although Ellyssa's gift was unique, it wasn't infallible.

Peering at Ellyssa through narrowed lids, Ann seemed to consider what Ellyssa had said. Finally, she removed her hands from the perch on her hips. "That makes sense." A slight twitch curled the corner of her mouth. "Let's see what you can teach me, then."

With a renewed vigor, Ann brought what she had, and Ellyssa countered, practicing her blocks. She had to give the redhead credit; Ann was good, her strikes unrelenting and executed well. When Ann started to show signs of weariness, Ellyssa ended the training. Ann ended up on the ground with Ellyssa's foot pressed against her throat.

Trista, who'd entered earlier with Dyllon, clapped. "That was awesome," she commended. "You still have to teach me, like you promised."

Smiling down at her opponent, Ellyssa removed the threat and reached down to help Ann to her feet. "You're good," she complimented.

"You're not too bad yourself," Ann said with an eye roll. Returning Ellyssa's grin, she straightened out her top. "There is a lot you can teach all of us."

Ellyssa laughed as they went to the side of the room where Rein, Woody and the others stood. She liked the redhead.

Maybe she'd made a new friend. Although she still didn't care for the way Ann looked at Woody.

# 40

Commandant Baer shivered in the corner of the room, the furnace standing like an ominous presence in the center, serving as a constant reminder of all the dead people he'd fed through the metal mouth. Freezing wind whipped around the outside of the building, crawling beneath the crack of the door and penetrating through the grey bricks. Vapory breath escaped in puffs from between Hans' lips. Another tremor rocked his body and clacked his teeth together.

Like a common Renegade, Hans' hands were cuffed together behind his back, where a chain led to another set of cuffs tightened around his ankles. His usually pristine *Waffenrock* was crumpled and dirt, his medals stripped from his breast.

The pain of the girl's infernal fire and ice through his veins still raged unrelentingly within his memories. He'd thought, during his career, that he had known how to torture. He had no clue.

Aalexis was a master.

He had also had no clue what true pain felt like, and how there was no way to escape it. He'd tried. God, how he had tried. But he'd failed. At the time, he couldn't think of anything but how much he hurt. It dominated his thoughts in a perpetual loop. Even now, he still couldn't escape the phantom pain.

Hans hadn't talked, though. Somehow through all the misery, he'd kept his mouth shut, refusing to answer any of the questions the little bitch and her bastard brother had bombarded him with. Not that he could have, anyway. Their words had meant nothing to him; he couldn't grasp onto a single syllable, much less comprehend what they were saying. The intensity of the torment dominated his thoughts.

Maybe that was something Aalexis had never considered.

Hans had a new respect for the people he'd thought inferior. Their resolve was beyond commendable.

Taking in a deep breath that felt like ice picks nicking his lungs, Hans tried to concentrate on how to stop Aalexis and Xaver. How was it that the colonel and general, and all any of the other superiors, did not see that everyone would become extinct to make way for the new world order?

How could they be so stupid?

But Hans knew. The possibility of uncontested power beyond the scope of what was known blinded them with temptation. They were too thick to realize that they wouldn't be able to control the young girl. No one could. Despite Aalexis' own outward appearance, Hans doubted that even *she* had full control over herself.

Fruitlessly, he struggled against the cuffs, trying to yank his hands through the cinched metal. All he accomplished was pinching his skin. If he could somehow slip his hands through the connecting chain and under his feet, he could at least have them in front, where his movements wouldn't be as restricted.

The chain limited his ability to bend forward, which would be much easier for a man his age to do. Instead, Hans fell to his side and tried bending his back in an awkward position. The chains clinked together, a tinny ring, as he struggled against his bindings.

Hans was getting nowhere fast. Frustrated, he thrashed about, bending back and forth until exhaustion grabbed hold and left him on the cold floor, panting.

What would happen if he got free, anyway? Burst through the door and end up with a significant hole through his chest?

Resigned, Hans settled on the cold floor, feeling the heat slowly seep from his body, like it was draining through a sieve.

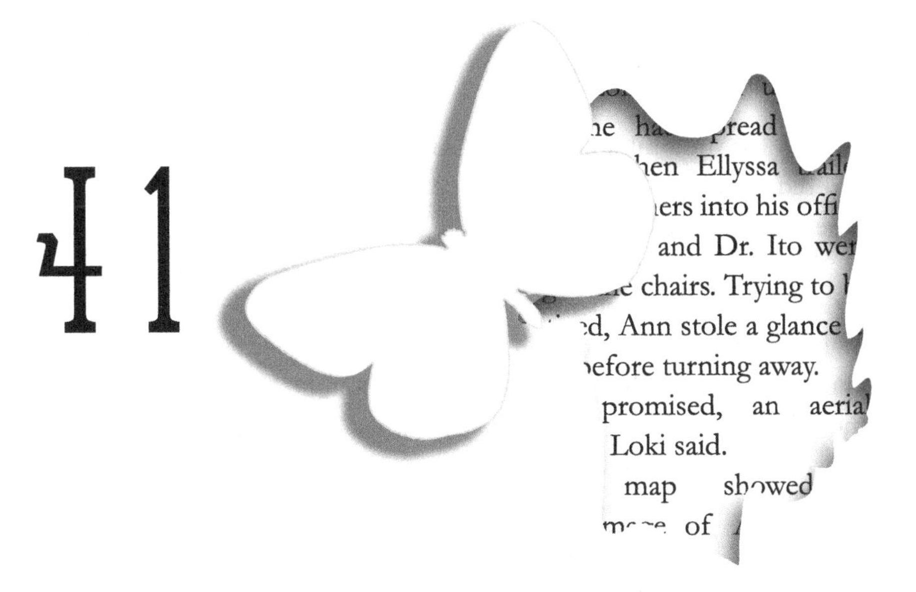

# 41

Dr. Loki looked up from a map he had spread across the table when Ellyssa trailed behind the others into his office. Ann, Loreley and Dr. Ito were sitting in the chairs. Trying to be unnoticed, Ann stole a glance at Woody before turning away.

"As promised, an aerial view," Dr. Loki said.

The map showed a detailed image of Amarufoss' compound. Digital whites and dark browns showed the layout of the land, while greys and reds showed buildings.

"How'd you get that?" Woody asked.

"We pinged a satellite and downloaded it."

Nestled within the crook of Dyllon's arm, worry crinkled Trista's brow. "Is that safe? What if they traced you?"

"They didn't."

"But how do you know?"

"We have our safeguards. If anyone noticed, all they read was cyber-dust. Don't worry. We've been doing this for years. Our computer whiz kid is good at his job." Dr. Loki turned the image around so that everyone could see. "I wouldn't jeopardize our establishment. Not for you. Not for anyone.

"To continue. On this side," the doctor said, pointing toward the right side of the map, "are the male prisoners. Over here are the females. A brick wall separates the two. The perimeter exterior consists of a chain-link fence, and the interior is a four-meter wall. The main gate"—his finger slid across the map to another break in the perimeter—"and the delivery gate.

"As for the buildings"—Dr. Loki started to point at the various grey and red buildings—"the main office of the Commandant, the garage, and here is a new addition, but I don't have the slightest clue what its use is."

Ellyssa memorized the details as Dr. Loki continued showing the prisoner barracks, soldier barracks, another office and the building believed to be used for the extermination of what society considered dregs. A knot formed in Ellyssa's throat as she thought about Mathew, about all the others, wondering who had survived and who hadn't. The rest of her Missouri family must have shared her sentiment, because they all looked away. Trista covered her face with a hand.

Dr. Loki paused, apparently sensing the dark cloud that had settled over the room. After a few seconds had passed, he cleared his throat. "We haven't gone anywhere near the base since they doubled the patrols. It was safer to keep away, for obvious reasons." He opened a folder. "Based on collected data, perimeter patrols are conducted every ten to twenty minutes. Both gates are always manned.

"There is a port between the fences filled with razor wire, and both fences have it strung on top. The bad thing about razor wire is, if you get caught by it, it will slice you to ribbons. The good thing is, when cut, the two ends will lie over, leaving a small opening."

Studying the map, Woody ran a hand through his hair. He looked at Rein and Ellyssa with grey eyes filled with hopelessness. "How are we going to breach that?"

Dr. Loki said, "My advice is to go in at night. As I've already stated, we can't help you, but we can give you the tools needed to cut the wires, clothing that will conceal you in the dark, and quieter weapons."

Ann frowned. "What do you mean, we aren't going to help them?"

"Ann, you know we can't. We can't jeopardize this institution."

"And you speak for all of us?"

Leaning over the table, Dr. Ito said, "Our time will come."

Ann flashed the *sensei* an irritated glare. "When? When exactly is that? You've been telling us that for years. Loreley and myself, and everyone else for that matter, have trained for something like this since we were little children. Right now is the perfect time to test our skills."

"I'm with Ann," Loreley said, pushing her chocolate-brown hair behind her ear. As soon as she moved her hand, the piece fell forward again.

Dr. Loki shook his head. "Now is not the time."

Leaning back in her chair, anger carved in her face, Ann crossed her arms. "I'm going."

"Me, too," Loreley added.

"No, you're not," the doctor said, an exasperated note in his tone.

"Are you the dictator now, too?"

Fury chiseled deep lines between Dr. Loki's eyebrows, his eyes narrowing into thin slits, his jaw working the tendons in his neck. "How dare you?" he sputtered, his words seething between thinned lips.

"How dare I?" Ann said, standing, her fists clenched at her side. "How dare you decide what we are going to do without ever putting anything up for a vote?"

"You know we can't risk the possibility of you being captured. That's not a secret. Think of all the lives you're endangering for a few outsiders." His eyes moved to Ellyssa's group as if sorry for the way he said the words, although, judging by his look, he'd meant what he said.

"Which is exactly what we are supposed to do, isn't it? Aren't we supposed to change things? Isn't that the whole purpose?"

"Yes, but not now."

"Then, when?"

The doctor's harsh stance deflated, like someone had let all the air out of his anger. Rubbing the bridge of his nose, he said, "I don't know."

Loreley said, "Then how do you know now is not the time?"

Sitting back down, Ann nodded her agreement. "Look, we understand the risk, and we appreciate everything you have accomplished. Without the knowledge you brought from the outside world, from your work at The Center, we wouldn't be in the position we are now. You, of all people, know what it's like above ground. You lived it. Before you veto the whole idea, please give me a chance to explain how we can help without risking The Pit."

Dr. Loki glanced at Dr. Ito, who just shrugged. "Hear her out," he advised.

He took in a deep, slow breath and let it out. "Okay, the floor is yours."

"They need help getting over the fence, right? So what if Loreley..." Ann stopped, looking at her caramel-skinned friend before continuing.

Approving, Loreley lifted her chin. "...and I help them over the fence and give two extra sets of eyes. No one else has to come. We won't go into the compound at all."

"And what if you're caught?"

Leveling her gaze at the doctor, Ann said, "We know the consequences."

"I don't like this. Not at all. You and Loreley are the best Dr. Ito has produced. It would be a hard blow if we lost either of you."

Knowing she had won, Ann smiled. "If you are so sure of Dr. Ito's success with us, then you have nothing to worry about. With all the chaos going on at the camp, we'll return without anyone the wiser."

Leaning back, Dr. Loki stared at the overhead light, his hands propped under his chin. Silence settled in the room as he thought. Ellyssa watched all the different scenarios playing out in his head, one after another, and almost all of them ended with the facility being raided, everyone being killed, and all the intelligence they'd gathered throughout the years ending up in the hands of the State. A mental shrug later, Dr. Loki came to a surprising conclusion.

"If I'm risking two of my best soldiers, I guess I might as well extend the invitation for you all to return here—we really could use your expertise, Ellyssa—but only if you are successful. If you are discovered—" he gave Loreley and Ann a hard look for emphasis—"none of you can come back here."

Slowly, blinking in disbelief, Ellyssa said, "Thank you." Her group had discussed somewhat where they would go with their rescued family, but nothing concrete had been decided, besides going west, where the population wasn't as dense. The invitation Dr. Loki extended was a blessing.

The doctor sat up and gestured for them to all move closer. "I suggest two groups," he said, his words infused with uncertainty as he struggled with the possibility of all the things that could go wrong. "One for the females and the other for the males. From past surveillances, there have always been more males than females."

Huddled around the table, the small group made plans. Once again, Ellyssa would find herself as well as the people she loved on the move and risking their lives. Only this time, two more had gotten dragged into their mission, and if the doctor's fears proved true, two hundred and fifty at risk.

# 42

The moonlight glinted over the snow, like a scattering of diamonds. A strong wind captured the icy dust and tossed it in the air. Floodlights swept back and forth, cutting a bright line through the inky black.

Aalexis stared out the window of her newly acquired office. Xaver stood at her side. His hand drew patterns on the small of her back, out of sight where no one could see.

"Soon," she whispered, as if the sound of her voice would shatter the peaceful setting.

Xaver nodded.

"Can you feel it?"

"Yes," Xaver answered, his voice soft.

Quickly, he brushed his nose against Aalexis' hair and inhaled, then withdrew. If any of the imperfections happened to be looking through the window, they would've seen the loving gesture. That would usually anger Aalexis, but she didn't care right now. Everything was going to plan, and soon, Ellyssa would return home without a fight. Her sister's wrongly placed love would betray her as Aalexis had planned it would.

"I wonder what her face will look like when she sees us—ghosts from her past."

"I do not know," Xaver answered, pulling her away from the window. When they were safely out of view, he placed his hand on her cheek and traced the curvature of her bone with his thumb. "I have never said these words before, but I am now. You are beautiful."

As confusion played tug-of-war between what had been instilled in her and what she'd opened her heart to feel, Aalexis leaned into his hand. The warmth from Xaver's touch was pleasing and too seductive to ignore.

"I want all of our creations to look just like you."

Aalexis smiled. The emotion displayed so freely on her face felt so foreign, but Xaver's words made her feel...happy. She closed her eyes. "They will be a combination of both of us."

For a long moment, Xaver didn't say anything. Then she felt his soft breath wash over her skin. She opened her eyes to find him close, leaning over her, the pupils of his eyes dilated to the point of almost covering his sky-blue irises, and his lips pressed in...indecision. Before she knew what was happening, her brother closed the gap and brushed his lips against hers. Pulling away, a smile played with his lips and lit his face.

Aalexis' mouth tingled, pleasantly, and a warmth she'd never experienced before clenched in her stomach. Disbelieving, confused, shocked, Aalexis shoved him away. Hurt replaced the happiness Xaver had just held on his face.

Her hand covering her mouth, Aalexis backed away. "You kissed me," she stated. A mix between anger and desire twisted in her muscles. She fought between the desire to fling herself into his arms and flinging herself with a knife-strike to his throat. "Why?"

"I had to know," he simply answered.

The familiar feed of anger decided the war going inside her. Aalexis' hand dropped from her mouth at the same time Xaver dropped to the floor, his face scrunched in torture. Less than a second later, he pushed himself to his feet, his shield in place. She'd never used her gift against her brother, and a finger of guilt tapped in her chest. She brushed it away as easily as she'd brushed annoying flies away.

Expecting him to come at her, Aalexis braced herself, but Xaver didn't make a move. He just stared at her, his hands nonthreatening at his side, and instead of anger cutting across his chiseled features, he looked...sad.

"Did you not like it?" Xaver asked.

Aalexis didn't know what to say. The truth was she did like it. Liked it a lot. Even now, the faint trace of tingles pricked her lips. But the act seemed wrong. A lingering lesson her father had taught? She clinched her fists in defiance. "It is not allowed."

"By whom?"

"*Der Vater* taught us that physical outlets of intimacy weaken the mind. Is it not enough that we touch without taking it further?"

"He also said bonds weaken. I do not feel weak. Every time I feel your warmth, your touch, strength fills my whole being. Do you feel weak?"

"Of course not."

Xaver stepped toward her and didn't stop until they were close once again. The anger Aalexis had felt sizzled out as the warmth from his body that she was all too aware of caressed her. Tentatively, as Xaver studied her, his hand moved back to her cheek, and Aalexis let him touch her.

"Although *der Vater* was a genius in his own right, created us as a step toward the ultimate goal, he had his faults. Many things he was wrong about. He was inferior."

Drowning in the intensity of his eyes and in the confusion of his words, Aalexis stood still. Despite his intellectual visions her father had contributed toward a perfect world, he really had been inferior. He'd been mistaken about so much.

"The bond we share is not wrong. Ellyssa has proven that, though her insight is misguided. The touching we alone share strengthens us." Xavier bent his head closer. "We can do what we want, Aalexis. We are gods."

Dr. Loki led the group to the site right under the spot where the former American people had built bombs, Pantex. The area they passed through was a lot darker than the rest of the facility, and colder. If the temperature served as a gauge of what awaited them in the night, Ellyssa was glad that she, like the rest of them, had dressed in their snowsuits. She adjusted the straps of her backpack, then shifted the rifle snugly against her back. From behind, hollow steps echoed from Ann and Loreley, who had visited the artillery room to gather a few more supplies.

"The builders were originally going to put the elevator here. It's a good thing they didn't. It definitely would've been found when the State tore down the building," the doctor said, as he moved through and down a narrow passage way. "The builders built this hall so that, if they were invaded, only one soldier could come through at a time. Easier to pick off until ammunition was depleted. You have to remember, at one time, this was the only way to enter and exit. When they descended into the Pit, they barricaded the door. No one opened it for years."

The doctor stepped through an entrance and off to the side. Ellyssa, Rein, Trista, Woody and Dyllon spilled from the tight passageway behind him into a cramped room. Right in the center, taking up the majority of space, was what was essentially an elevator without walls resting on a hydraulic system of cogs and gears. The top part covered the opening in the ceiling. A motor connected to a generator sat against the wall on the right, and right above it was a panel with a green button, a yellow button and a red button.

Woody examined the simple mechanism. "Are you sure it still works?" he said doubtfully. His snowsuit was unzipped to his waist.

"It hasn't been opened for a while, but we keep it maintained. The real problem is the snow and ice that is covering it."

Tapping his finger against his lips, Woody looked up toward the opening. "What I would do is break the ice by moving it up and down, like jiggling it."

"Sounds good," Dr. Loki agreed.

As Woody and the doctor checked over the mechanics, Loreley and Ann came in, carrying two large duffle bags that clinked and jingled. Ann dropped her load onto the ground and unzipped it.

"Come and look," Ann said, yanking out a crossbow.

"Oh," Trista said, kneeling next to Ann.

"Do you know how to shoot one of these?" When Trista shook her head, Ann said, "It's relatively easy."

"More importantly, it's quiet. May I?" Dyllon held his hand out, and Ann slipped the weapon into his grip. "I haven't used one of these for years," he said, weighing it in his hands. He brought the bow up and looked through the power scope. "How far? Seventy meters?"

"At least," Ann answered.

"We're bringing four crossbows. One for me, one for Ann, and one for each group," Loreley said. Binoculars swung from her neck as she reached into her bag and withdrew a smoke bomb. "And a couple of these."

Interest piqued Rein's expression as he took the cylinder-shaped container from Loreley. "These are great."

"Never hurts to have a little chaos," Ellyssa said. "They won't be expecting us with all of this."

"Nope." Ann pulled out a magazine with bolts preloaded in the slots. She took the bow away from Dyllon to show Trista. "All you do is slide this here, lock the string behind this point, aim, and pull the trigger," she said, as she demonstrated the procedure. "After the initial loading, it will load itself. Just like a rifle."

Just as Ann finished unloading the weapons, the generator cranked to life. Woody flipped on the motor. It chugged with age.

"Looks like we're in business," Woody said, with a satisfied smile.

Woody pushed the green button. The hydraulics moaned and a crack sounded. He released and pushed the yellow, repeating the process until Mother Nature's elements loosened. Freezing air fell into the room along with a dusting of snow.

"That's it," Woody said. He turned and met Ellyssa's gaze. Worry mixed with fear settled along the grey of his eyes. But there was a lot more there, too. All the things he had told her or hadn't. Ellyssa could read it on his face without intruding into his thoughts. He grasped her hand and gave it a gentle squeeze. "You ready?"

Ever since they had discovered the macabre scene back at the cavern, Ellyssa had been ready, and the prospect of finally going to free their family fed excitement into her veins. Beneath the excitement, anger slithered, lying in wait for her to release it. With a small, reassuring smile, Ellyssa nodded.

Dr. Loki went over to Ann and Loreley, and hugged them both. "Come back," he said.

Ann gave him a kiss on the cheek. "No worries there," she said. "After all, you trained us."

"Okay," Dr. Loki said, rubbing his hands together as if trying to rub away his fear, "hop on board."

Armed with their weapons, backpacks, and binoculars, and clad in white snowsuits, the team of seven stepped onto the platform. Holding hands, Ellyssa stood between Rein and Woody. Both she loved desperately, although differently. The thought of losing either of them struck a chord in her heart, and an undertone of apprehension coiled around the excitement she'd felt earlier. With all that was at stake, Ellyssa couldn't afford for the opposing emotion to take root and interfere with her judgment. She smothered it.

Dr. Loki pushed the button, and the lift jerked. "Good luck."

As the platform rose toward the dark sky, and icy air and snow whipped down through the opening, Ellyssa looked down at the retreating doctor. His teal eyes moved with the ascent, and his thin lips tightened behind the trepidation his expression held. Slowly, he disappeared from view, and the elevator clanked to a stop.

A moonless sky greeted Ellyssa as she stepped off the platform; stars flickered against the black backdrop. Wind gripped hold of Ellyssa, pushing and pulling, trying to claw its way inside her snowsuit. Leftover snow from the blizzard swirled in the moving air and pecked at her exposed face. Cold was an understatement. Ellyssa finally grasped the full meaning of the phrase "When Hell freezes over".

Ellyssa moved against the blustery weather that seemed to be determined to make the trek as hard as possible. At least the doctor wouldn't have to worry about prints leading back to The Pit that evening.

# 43

The sun had started to dip in the western horizon over what Ellyssa had started to think of as the Small Squad. Rein had laughed when she'd mentioned it, and countered that they were the Small Squad of Doom. Woody had agreed, and shortened the term to Squad Doom. Then everyone laughed. Tension's death grip on them had loosened, but only a little.

"Have a look," Rein said, handing her the binoculars.

Lying on her stomach, her suit keeping her warm against the elements, Ellyssa took the binoculars and gazed through them. Through the snow, barely visible, she could make out the black dots moving around the perimeter.

"Every fifteen minutes," Rein confirmed. "From what I can tell, there are three sets of patrols. Maybe four."

Woody took the binoculars from Ellyssa as she moved to her knees. "That's not going to leave us much time."

"I still don't like the plan," Trista said.

"We have to. One group needs to free the women, the other the men," Woody said.

"It will work out fine," Dyllon said as he wrapped his arm around Trista. "You and I will do the women's side. Okay?"

Biting on her lower lip, Trista considered the options. Her eyes darted away, a sure sign of fear taking hold.

Shuffling over to Trista, Ellyssa placed her hand on her shoulder. As Ellyssa thought about calming images, like the feel of Rein's arms around her when they'd lain in bed, her own mind quieted. She wanted to transfer that feeling to Trista. "It really will be fine. I promise. We need you."

Inhaling deeply, Trista said in a gush, "I guess." Then, under her breath, she continued with, "Don't think I don't know what you did." She paused for a moment. "Thank you. It helped."

"Ellyssa's right. It will be fine," Dyllon reassured, casting a knowing look over at Ellyssa. "All we're going to do is go through the fence, get your family, and hightail it out of there."

Trista gave Dyllon a dubious look. "Do you really think it will be that easy?"

"Hey. Since everything that has happened since...you know"—Dyllon referenced the massacre in the cave—"you've been through so much. If it wasn't for your persistence, your strength, we would've never found Woody, Rein or Ellyssa." Dyllon cupped Trista's cheek. "We are going to get your family back. It might not be that easy, but we're going to do it."

"Always hope for the best and be prepared for the worst," Woody said. "We have everything we need, and they aren't expecting us. Here. Take a look." He handed Trista the binoculars, and she used them. "Their security is a lot lighter than I thought it would be. Thanks to Ann and Loreley, we have extra help and extra supplies. We have things that we didn't have before. All we have to do is wait for night."

A halfhearted grin appeared on Trista's face as she nodded. "Okay. We can do this," she said. "We really can."

Dyllon reached over and pulled Trista into his arms, placing a kiss on her temple. "Of course we can."

"So, to go over the plans again," Ann said, as she started to draw a picture of the compound in the snow. "Loreley and I will set up here and here." She drew Xs. "We will cut a hole in the fence here on the female's side, and here," she continued, looking over at Ellyssa. "We'll help you over the wall, but that is as far as Loreley and I go." She stopped and looked up to make sure that was understood. When everyone nodded, she continued. "The male barracks is on the left. Take out the guards posted there. And for you, Trista, the female barracks is also on the left. Same thing, take out the guards. Get your friends and get the hell out."

The unfurling of excitement fueled Ellyssa's drive as they went over the rest of the plans.

# 44

Aalexis' reflection looked back at her in the darkened windowpane as she absentmindedly touched her bottom lip. Xaver's kisses lingered there from the night before, and the swollen flesh served as a constant reminder. Still, she couldn't believe she had taken the step into the taboo land. Even more, she didn't really care. The fire Xaver had elicited in her had burned through her veins in a relentless desire of wanting more of him. Of wanting him closer. Aalexis remembered how she'd clung to him as he pressed his mouth against hers. In a way, it had almost been magical, if she believed in such illusions.

She didn't.

Bringing her hand down, Aalexis glanced at her brother over her shoulder. He must have felt her eyes on him, because he looked up, a grin on his face.

"It will be tonight," she said. "I can...feel it."

"I agree."

"The conditions are perfect."

"Are you ready?"

"I have waited a long time for this."

"As have I."

"Things should go smoothly. Ellyssa has already proven that she will risk her life for the inferior beings."

"As I would for you." Xaver moved behind her. Aalexis could feel his breath brushing against her hair.

"I still will not for you."

"I know, my beloved sister."

Aalexis closed her eyes at the term of endearment. She did love her brother, there was no doubt. Her heart inflated whenever she thought about him; she assumed the physiological reaction was due to love, but her life was still more important.

She knew it, as did Xaver.

"Are the guards ready?" she asked.

"The sergeant-at-arms has been informed. I have no doubt he will be efficient. His love for power is equal to that of the colonel and the general. The delusions of substandard humans."

"Yes. His willingness to subject himself to our experiment proves that. He will make a good soldier for the facility until our work is complete. Then we dispose of him."

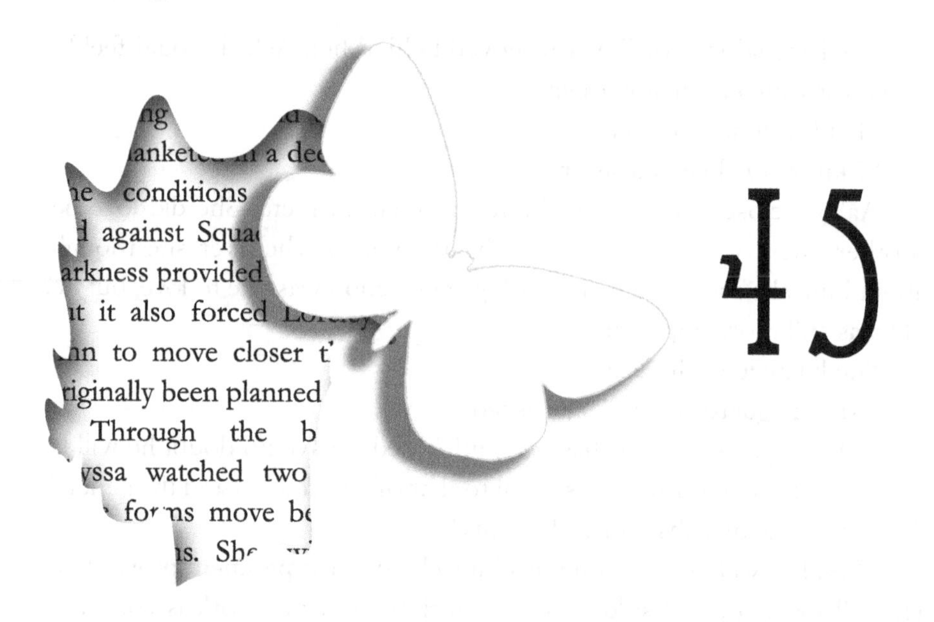

# 45

Clouds blew in with the unyielding wind, and the plains were blanketed in a deep ebony night. The conditions worked for and against Squad Doom. The darkness provided a great cover, but it also forced Loreley and Ann to move closer than had originally been planned.

Through the binoculars, Ellyssa watched two hunched white forms move behind two black forms. She swiveled the view over to where Trista and Dyllon had gone. It took her a while to distinguish their white lumps through the wintery camouflage.

"We got to get closer," Woody whispered, as if afraid his words would be heard over the bluster of the wind.

"Let's do it," Rein said, pushing up on his hands and knees.

After the sweep of the spotlight passed, he scrambled off. Ellyssa and Woody followed. They moved in a few meters, until Loreley and Ann could be somewhat seen without the aid of the binoculars.

Ellyssa's excitement mounted as Ann made some sort of waving gesture to Loreley. The two black forms had moved to where the wall divided the two camps. The time for action had arrived, and Ellyssa blanked, letting loose the training that had taught her to move swiftly...deadly.

Ann and Loreley brought up the crossbows at one moment, and within the next, the two black forms staggered then dropped. Their skill was just as cold and efficient as Ellyssa's, and she couldn't help but be a little impressed. Dr. Loki's program had trained them well.

"Let's go," Rein said, excitement and a tinge of fear coating his voice. He twitched in anticipation.

Clear of the revolving light, they took off before the other patrol rounded the corner. Ellyssa glanced to the side, hoping Dyllon and Trista were on the move, too. She couldn't see anything except Loreley bolting toward where her two friends were supposed to be, over at the female side.

Ann's white form was at the designated spot. She already had most of the links clipped by the time they arrived. After making a few more snips, Ann pulled part of the fence back and slipped inside where she cut through the three rows of razor wire. As expected, the coils sprang back, leaving the way clear.

"You have to move quick," the redhead said. "If worst comes to worst, we can probably take out the next patrol, buying a little more time, but I wouldn't count on it." She handed the wire cutters to Ellyssa. "Go."

With the help of Rein and Woody, Ellyssa climbed onto their shoulders. Reaching up with the cutters, she snipped through the razor wire, then dropped the tool on the ground, careful to avoid everyone beneath her. Positioning her hands, Ellyssa easily hefted herself up and over the wall and landed on the other side with barely a sound.

While she waited for Rein and Woody, Ellyssa squatted. The whole area was eerily quiet. No movement, no nothing. She couldn't even see guards posted at the barracks. They were there, though, a conglomeration of voices, too many to single out anything decipherable.

Rein dropped down next to her, and a little bit later, she heard the crunch of Woody's feet hitting the snow.

"Where is everyone?" Rein asked, his voice low.

"I do not know," Ellyssa answered, the robotic tone unsurprising.

"I don't like this," Rein said.

"Neither do I."

Woody shuffled between them. "Can you get a read on anyone?"

"I can get a read on everyone. One second." Ellyssa swiveled her mental wall around and pegged a soldier standing on one side of the doorway leading to the prisoners' barracks.

The soldier was bored and very cold, and more than just a little annoyed. He looked over at the male he'd been assigned with, who was wearing a black snowsuit. Besides his eyes, his face was hidden behind a thick scarf.

"No one is coming. The sergeant is a dumbass." An image of a man with cropped hair, hard dark-blue eyes and a stone face appeared in Ellyssa's mind. "Who in the hell would go out in this type of weather?" the soldier Ellyssa was reading said.

The other soldier shrugged. "I just do what I'm told."

"They are expecting us," Ellyssa said, breaking the link.

Rein's eyes narrowed. "If they are expecting us, then why isn't this place crawling with soldiers?"

"I do not know," she responded.

"Can you get a read on Trista and Dyllon?" Woody asked, looking worried.

Ellyssa latched onto their signals. Trista and Dyllon had made it over to the other side of the fence and were going over the plans again. "They are fine."

Rein shifted his weight over onto his other leg. "Anything else?"

Ellyssa scanned several soldiers, filing through them quickly. Just the same thing over and over—cold, annoyed, waiting for their shift to be over. In a dark building, a male's brain patterns spiked weakly, as if on the brink of death. He was freezing and in pain. They would have to check out the building that housed the incinerator, too.

Continuing her search, a brief signal flared as she passed, a familiar one. Ellyssa reached out with her cerebral feelers, trying to grasp onto the pattern, but there was nothing there, just dead space. Ill at ease, Ellyssa finally let it go, hoping it was nothing, regardless of the warning her subconscious was shouting at her. Time was ticking, and they had to get moving. Loreley and Ann would encounter the next patrol soon.

Ellyssa shook her head. "Nothing."

"Maybe they are still a bit wary. Dr. Loki said they were expecting a possible rescue." Rein's hand swept in a semicircle. "This isn't the type of security they would have if they really thought we were coming."

"True," Ellyssa said, but not really believing it. Whatever it was, the soldiers didn't know exactly what was going on, and she hadn't found anyone in charge. Maybe Commandant Baer was asleep.

Woody huffed out a breath that formed a puff a smoke in the air. "Let's just get this over with."

Glancing at Ellyssa, Rein kissed her, hard, his lips fighting to convey all he felt for her. Pulling away, he said, "I love you. Don't forget it."

"Never."

He touched her temple. "Keep me in your mind."

"I will know if something happens."

Without another word, Rein left as planned. Someone needed to keep watch on the main building and front gate, and Rein had volunteered.

Ellyssa looked at Woody, his grey eyes holding love that she couldn't reciprocate. He reached up and wiped snow away from her cheek, his hand lingering longer than necessary. She didn't mind; she never would.

"You know?" Woody said.

"I do," Ellyssa responded, as she remembered his confession back in the barn before Tim and Sarah had died so violently. She also remembered the way he'd made her feel, and the guilt that had followed.

Woody dropped his hand. "Ready?" he said, with a sad grin.

After a brief glance into Trista and Dyllon's minds—they were moving within the shadows toward what they believed to be the female barracks—Ellyssa formed a mental link with Rein. He stood behind a lone, unaware soldier, easily eliminated. Rein raised the butt of his rifle.

"Ready," Ellyssa said.

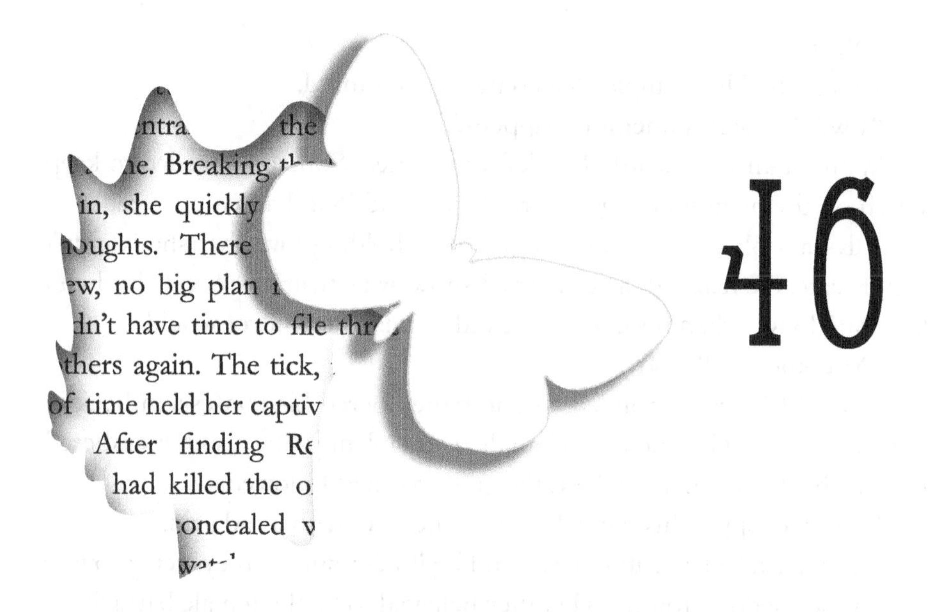

# 46

The two soldiers still stood at the entrance of the barracks, all alone. Breaking the link with Rein, she quickly invaded their thoughts. There was nothing new, no big plan revealed. She didn't have time to file through others again. The tick, tick, tick of time held her captive.

After finding Rein again, who had killed the one soldier and was concealed within the shadows watching the main office, Ellyssa slid the crossbow off her shoulder and took aim. Just in case, Woody had his rifle out too, and was looking through the crosshairs. He wasn't going to fire unless forced to. Hopefully, the need wouldn't arise. They all wanted to get in and get out quickly and quietly, before anyone was the wiser.

A bolt to the neck took one soldier down. The other one watched his friend drop. It took less than a second for the live soldier to register what had happened. At the same time as he swung his rifle around, Ellyssa released another bolt, and he ended up joining his dead comrade on the ground.

"Nice," whispered Woody.

"I am efficient."

Together, they crept through snow, the blowing wind covering their tracks as they moved and stopped when they reached the doorway. Ellyssa pivoted her back toward one side of the frame, Woody the other.

"Anyone inside?"

Not wanting to, Ellyssa released Rein and scanned the inside of the barracks. Fuzzy, unspecific images flickered in sleeping minds. Regardless of her unemotional state, a huge sense of relief filled her when she locked onto Mathew. She rejoined Woody; he still stood safely in the shadows.

"Forty-one people," Ellyssa said, working to keep her voice low while containing her excitement. "One of them is Mathew."

Reaching across the width of the door, Woody grasped her hand with a smile. "Let's get him."

A soft *click* later, the door swung open to the sounds of soft snores and even breaths. Ellyssa and Woody tiptoed inside. A dome-shaped light hung in the corner and cast shadows over sleeping lumps. Woody stayed by the door to keep a lookout while she made her way over to Mathew.

The first person to teach her about friendship, about trust, slept on an old cot, a thin blanket draped over his too-thin frame. His face was smooth in the throes of slumber, and his skin was pulled tight over his cheekbones. More grey flecked his hair than Ellyssa remembered. As she watched him, happiness engulfed her heart and pushed away her stoic persona. She couldn't help but smile.

"Mathew," she said, shaking his shoulder.

Mathews eyes snapped open, revealing sand-colored eyes, and he bolted upright. Confused, he looked around until he focused on Ellyssa.

"Ellyssa?" He rubbed his eyes as if he thought his mind was playing tricks on him. He brought his hands down and blinked several times.

"It is me," she said, her face going blank once again. The happy reunion would have to wait. "Woody and Rein and Trista are here, too. We have come to get you out of here."

"What?"

"We have to leave. Get all the clothes on you can. It is cold. And take your blanket. We have a long hike."

"I can't believe it."

"Believe it. We have to go."

Without another word, Mathew popped out of bed and started to pull on clothing. "What about the others?" he asked, shoving his foot into a boot.

"Everyone is coming, including the females. Trista is helping them now." She gestured to the sleeping forms. "Help me wake them."

Fully dressed, Mathew went one bed over. "Marcus," he whispered, then clamped his hand over the mouth of a male about the same age as Ellyssa,

His brown eyes, rounded in confused sleep, were old and told a story of a hard life.

"Shh. Get up and get dressed," Mathew whispered.

Marcus' stare moved from Mathew to Ellyssa. His eyebrows dipped over the bridge of his nose. "What's going on?"

"We're breaking out of this hellhole. Now get dressed."

Surprisingly, Marcus didn't question any further. He got up quietly and moved fast for someone who looked so malnourished. Other people had started to stir, and Mathew delivered the news before they started to panic.

While everyone scurried around like mice, tossing on layers of clothes and wrapping up in the sorry blankets they slept under, Ellyssa stood at Woody's side. He was peering through the small crack he'd left ajar. Wind struggled against the door, trying to push it open.

"Check Trista and Dyllon."

"They are already moving toward the fence."

"How many?"

"Fifteen."

"Only fifteen?" Mathew said, coming up from behind. "Are you sure?"

Ellyssa turned toward her friend. Behind him stood rest of the prisoners, padded with clothing and blankets, their expressions showing varying degrees of fear, excitement and disbelief. "I am positive," she answered.

"Oh," he stated, a dark cloud hovering in his expression.

Ellyssa squeezed his hand. "Are you ready?"

Glancing over his shoulder at all the expectant faces, he said, "Looks that way."

Woody swung the door open and stepped out into the empty compound. The others filed past Ellyssa and Mathew into the waiting cold.

"There's one more person," Ellyssa said, "closed up somewhere. A small room, the death room. He is almost dead."

"That must be the Commandant," Mathew mumbled.

"The Commandant? Of this camp?" That didn't even make sense.

In a second, a collage of emotions passed over Mathew's face—a frown, followed by understanding, then something Ellyssa couldn't quite identify—a cross between dread and alarm. "You don't know?" Mathew said. "Ellyssa, there's something I have to tell you. I think..."

That was as far as Mathew got. The line she held with Rein thinned. "Rein!" she said, alarmed, groping for Rein's signature and interrupting whatever Mathew was going to say. She started to push him toward the door. "Go," she ordered. "Follow Woody."

"Wait." Mathew held out his hand, but she easily sidestepped out of his reach and dashed outside. "Your si..." His voice drowned in the wind as she ran toward Woody.

"Rein," she said to him, hearing the panic in her own voice.

Woody's face paled. "Wh—"

"There's something wrong. Whatever you do, get them to safety."

Before Woody could respond, Ellyssa spun around and left. She saw Mathew coming toward her, muffled words drowned by the airy howl. She didn't stop.

She couldn't.

The already-thin connection winked out, like someone had flipped a switch. Like Rein was dead. Her mind kept reaching for him and snapping back empty-handed. Not a glimmer, nothing.

Her heart thundering in her ears, with a mixture of anxiety, anger and fear, Ellyssa stretched her legs faster. She didn't care if she could be heard. No one was going to stop her. Through the swirling snow and whipping blustery weather, Ellyssa zigzagged haphazardly around the buildings. Around her, the searchlights kept sweeping the snowy plains.

A soldier stood at the corner of the soldiers' barracks, his back toward Ellyssa. He turned as she raced toward him, the snow crunching under her feet. His eyes widened as she pounced, then he was on the ground, lifeless. Ellyssa kept running.

Another soldier ahead didn't even have time to turn around before a bolt was sticking out of the back of his neck. He went to his knees, then his face. Some other unsuspecting soldier received the butt of the crossbow across his jaw, making a satisfying cracking noise.

As Ellyssa approached the building that Dr. Loki had said was the new addition, Rein's light flickered. She faltered for a moment, hoping to assess the situation.

Confusion mounted the top of Rein's thoughts, followed closely by disbelief. His head hurt, he was looking at snow and people's boots, and he was cold.

Rage clawed its way through Ellyssa's fear, snuffing out the ineffectual emotion. She let it. As her heart slowed, she allowed everything she'd been bred to be storm to the front.

Whoever was responsible would pay...with their life. Squad Doom's original plan to sneak in and out as quickly and quietly as possible had been carried off on the wind when the perpetrator had captured Rein.

Orienting herself on Rein, like a lifeline connected them, Ellyssa rounded the corner of the unidentified building and started down the length of the exterior wall. No one was in sight, which rang a warning bell, but she couldn't worry about that now. She dropped the crossbow and swung the rifle around into her hands, pushing the safety to open fire.

Take out as many as possible in the shortest amount of time.

Ellyssa popped out from the cover of the building and...skidded to a stop, her fingers loosening around the cold metal. As her brain tried to swallow what her eyes were feeding her, the weapon fell from her grip and dangled from its strap. Surprise pasted on her face as her brain jammed on, *How?*

"Ellyssa," Aalexis said, standing on the porch of the Commandant's office, like the Greek goddess Nemesis. Like Ellyssa's nightmare. Light streamed through Aalexis' pale hair, fanning around her head. Her sister was much taller than the last time Ellyssa had seen her, close to Ellyssa's height now, and Aalexis' body was more womanly in appearance. Puberty had kicked in, releasing raging hormones and starting to erase the childlike roundness of Aalexis' face and body, just like Father had programmed it to.

Next to her younger sister, head hanging, was Rein. A sergeant, the one from the soldier's thoughts earlier, had his arm wrapped around the upper part of Rein's chest, holding him like a child would a doll. He aimed a 9mm at Rein's temple.

As soon as Aalexis had spoken, Rein's head had snapped up. Fear and memories of his torture thrummed and muddled in his brain, then jammed in incredulity.

Slowly, the wheels in Ellyssa's head began to grind, and as much as she hated to let go of Rein, she closed her mental wall before Aalexis had a chance to incapacitate her. The few seconds of debilitation could mean the difference between life and death, and Ellyssa couldn't chance it. She had to think. She had to focus. But with Rein in danger, the rolling waves of fear and anger and desperation were making it almost impossible.

*If her sister lived, did the others, too?* She knew her father was dead—Ellyssa had killed him herself—and so was Micah, by the hand of Detective Petersen. But Ahron and Xaver? If Aalexis had lived through the explosion, what were the possibilities for Ellyssa's two brothers? Ellyssa scanned the area, but the only people present were Aalexis and the soldier.

"I have been waiting for you, Ellyssa. Night after night." Aalexis reached toward Rein, who tried to shrink away from her touch to no avail, snapping Ellyssa to the here-and-now. Her sister tapped the side of Rein's head. "You remember. I can see the memory living in your eyes. So inferior." Her head followed her gaze as she faced Ellyssa again.

"Let him go, Aalexis."

Aalexis just stared at her. "If you do not want him to feel the pain, you will come with me."

Stepping forward, Ellyssa said with no inflection, "I thought you were dead." Ellyssa took another step forward; the rifle tapped her side, a gentle reminder. "Where is Xaver? Ahron? Did any of the others live?"

Much to Ellyssa's surprise, Aalexis answered the questions with a smile, cold and predatory. The emotional display almost faltered Ellyssa's approach. Forcing her stride steady, Ellyssa took another step; her hand fell to the dangling rifle.

Aalexis' smile faded and was replaced with a stone-faced expression as she watched Ellyssa's movement. "I do not need to read your mind to see what you plan."

From behind, soldiers stepped forward. Ellyssa heard their boots crunch in the snow. Whoever was manning the searchlight had abandoned his duty. It had taken Ellyssa a moment to notice, but the searchlight wasn't sweeping the area any more. She chastised herself at letting her sister's unexpected appearance lower her defenses.

Ellyssa repositioned her hand. She could take out Aalexis and the male holding the 9mm with no problem, but she had to be faster than her sister could issue the kill order to the sergeant. Without the ability to see the command before it was released, Ellyssa had to be careful.

"What do you want, Aalexis?"

"You," her younger sister answered, simply. "You are meant for more, as I am. *Der Vater's* work must be completed."

Ellyssa couldn't believe her ears. "*Der Vater* planned to kill all of us after he created his new idea of perfection."

"Did he?"

"Yes."

"It does not matter. He is dead now. You killed him."

Ellyssa tried a different approach. "If you continue *der Vater's* work, you would go against your natural instincts and kill yourself as an inferior, then?"

"No."

"But you would be inferior."

A slight flicker of anger played across Aalexis' face and disappeared, like a shadow quickly eclipsed by light. Ellyssa had touched a nerve.

"I am not inferior." Fury wove through Aalexis' tone.

"Your conclusion is illogical. If the unborn creation is to be a combination of us all, or even just the two of us, as seems the case, his abilities would far surpass ours. His superior genes. According to *der Vater*, inferiors should not live."

Anger rippled through Aalexis' countenance again, before it slid back under the stoic expression. Her sister defiantly lifted her chin. "Did you think *der Vater* would have killed himself afterward?"

Ellyssa had no answer. She had never really thought about what her father would have done when his new set of Perfections came into being.

"He would not have." Aalexis continued. "Gods do not die."

Ellyssa stilled. Her sister's words were against everything Father had taught. Pride. Conceit. Literally a god complex. Also, such a display of emotion. Aalexis seemed to be confused, struggling like Ellyssa had at one time. Offhandedly, Ellyssa wondered, if things were different, if she could have helped her sister, but it was too late now. Fresh revulsion for her dead father twisted in her gut. "You are not a god, Aalexis."

"I am," Aalexis countered. "And you will be one of lesser value, but still a part of the creation." Aalexis held out her hand. "Come and take your rightful place, Ellyssa."

Ellyssa began to understand. Aalexis was experiencing something more than an emotional breakdown. Against everything Ellyssa had thought possible, her sister was insane. Cold, calculating, deadly and crazy. She had to think...and fast. Her eyes moved from Aalexis to Rein to the sergeant, then repeated. If she just could just take out her sister first, the surprise of the action would distract the soldier, his focus on Rein would waver, then Ellyssa could take him out before he could recover. She had to take the chance.

Ellyssa whipped her hand to the side, glancing the cold metal of the rifle, but the contortion of Rein's body made her stop. His scream echoed through the dark night.

"I told you I did not need to read your mind. Your misplaced emotional bond is your Achilles' heel."

Shrieking, Rein convulsed, like a high-voltage current ripped through his body. Then his cries of pain stopped. Rein's body fell against the hold of the soldier, who stared at Aalexis with awe and worship. Rein's face was still contorted with the throes of agony. Short pants burst from his lips in warm clouds.

Aalexis hadn't released her hold on Rein, just lessened the intensity. With her sister preoccupied, Ellyssa seized the opportunity to peek. Her mind reached and met the manipulation of Rein's neuroreceptors dominating her sister's concentration. Ellyssa tried to dig deeper, but her sister's focus was too concrete.

Aalexis knew. She tweaked the receptors, fresh flames ignited, and Rein's screams followed. The soldier pressed the muzzle of the pistol firmly against Rein's temple.

Ellyssa's hesitation slammed shut the window of opportunity. Desperation had interfered.

Rein screamed again, his body thrashing within the grip of the sergeant.

Unable to stand it, Ellyssa shut the door to her sister's thoughts. "Enough, Aalexis."

Her sister apparently extinguished the fire, because Rein went limp, his head hanging.

"I grow weary of this. You cannot win, Ellyssa," Aalexis said, seemingly irritated. Another emotion that caught Ellyssa by surprise. *Was her sister even aware?* "Did you really think you could get away?"

After shifting an unconscious Rein in his arm, the sergeant retrieved a flashlight from his pocket. Pointing it toward the tower, he flicked it on and off. The searchlight swung into the compound, reflecting a brilliant white against the snow. The sergeant pressed the muzzle of the gun back against Rein's head.

Ellyssa waited, wondering what her sister had planned. A minute passed, then two. Finally, the sound of crunching snow reached Ellyssa's ears; afterward, people filed in. Males and females, thin frames struggling against the wind in their striped pyjamas, their blankets stripped from their backs, shivering. Amidst the captive group, Woody, Dyllon, Trista and Mathew appeared, hands behind their heads. Armed soldiers flanked the sides and followed behind, prodding the group like cattle.

Quickly, Ellyssa glided into Woody's mind and grasped the gist of what had happened. After Woody and the others had escaped with the prisoners, they had run into the camp's soldiers. The trap had been the reason behind the absence of military personnel.

Fault lay at Ellyssa's feet, like an abyss ready to consume her. If she had taken the time to probe deeper instead of shuffling through quickly, she might have seen, might have been able to alter the outcome. Once again, she'd failed.

Ellyssa searched for Loreley and Ann, but didn't find them among the familiar and unfamiliar faces of the crowd. Maybe they had been lucky enough to get away.

"I have waited weeks for this day," Aalexis stated, waving her arm toward the prisoners. "You will put down your weapon and come with me. Or I will begin by taking out one inferior pestilence at a time. Let me demonstrate." She nodded toward a soldier, who grabbed a female prisoner Ellyssa didn't know from the group.

"Please. No," the female cried, struggling to break free.

The soldier threw her to the ground, unholstered a pistol, and without a bit of hesitation, fired. Ichor painted the snow in crimson as the prisoner crumpled.

Flames of fury licked within Ellyssa's veins, but to no purpose. If it were only Aalexis and a few soldiers, the odds would have been in her favor as long as she was able to get the trigger-happy male before he shot Rein. But with everyone at risk and a whole platoon of soldiers, Ellyssa's odds of success plummeted.

Funny how her father had been right after all. Regardless of the strength Rein or her other family members had given Ellyssa, the bonds she'd formed and the emotions she felt had weakened her at a time when she needed to be the monster her father had created.

Tasting defeat and incapable of being responsible for any more deaths, Ellyssa unstrapped the weapon and tossed it into the snow. It sank into the white depths. She raised her hands.

A cocked smile lifted the corner of Aalexis' mouth. "Weak."

Awake now, Rein's green eyes locked on Ellyssa. He shook his head. But what choice did she have?

Ellyssa stepped forward, her hands stretched in front. "Let them go, and I will come willingly. I will not fight."

"I will not let them go, and you will come anyway. You have lost, dear sister."

Mind reeling, trying to find a way out, Ellyssa took another step. Woody and Trista's desperate eyes, and everyone else's, followed her. Rein kept staring at her, willing her to stop, to think of something, that he would be ready. Comforted by his courage, Ellyssa's mind slowed as she latched onto one thing.

Aalexis would die.

Ellyssa wouldn't be able to take them all out, unfortunate people would be sacrificed—herself included, possibly even Rein—but Aalexis could not be allowed to live. The conclusion of her sister's will would end in a world of annihilation.

The monster unleashed. Her muscles hummed with satisfaction. Ellyssa glanced at Woody and Mathew. The others might not understand, but Mathew and Woody knew without reading her mind. She could see the acceptance of death in their faces. Facing forward, Ellyssa moved, taking one step and another, her foot kicking the rifle.

But before Ellyssa could even burst into a sprint toward Aalexis' death, all hell broke loose. Time slowed.

All at once, repetitive fire sounded; red strobes flashed in the darkness; people screamed and ducked as confused military personnel dropped. Blood colored the white, and its warmth melted the snow. More gunfire, and now prisoners fell.

From the side of the buildings, people dressed in white manifested like ghosts. People Ellyssa recognized. At the front of the pack, Dr. Ito charged and struck a soldier's throat with his fingers, a perfectly executed knife-strike. As the soldier went to his knees, gagging and eyes bugging, Dr. Ito brought a rifle slung over his back around and opened fire. More soldiers dropped. Someone else finished the gagging soldier; the back of his head disappeared.

Like a fiery angel, Ann dropped from the roof of the new building. She sighted the enemy in the tower and let off a burst of gunfire. Trista and Dyllon grabbed firearms from a dead soldier, as did some of the other prisoners. Woody and Mathew had disappeared, but Ellyssa didn't have time to search for them.

For less than a nanosecond, as everything unfurled into the future, Ellyssa stood stunned, her muscles seizing in the mayhem. She couldn't believe Dr. Loki had risked The Pit.

Smiling at the turn of events, even though Ellyssa's deadly side was in full command, she turned back toward Aalexis. Her sister watched the chaos, her pale face even paler, anger struggling under the flawless surface. Her lackey had lowered his weapon a fraction, enough to give Ellyssa the upper hand.

While her sister's attention was captivated by the pandemonium, Ellyssa fell to her haunches and groped in the snow. The rifle remained elusively out of reach. Ellyssa swiped her hand in a bigger arc. Finally, her fingers wrapped around the freezing barrel of the rifle. In one swift motion, she yanked it free and stood, the butt already pulled tightly against the hollow of her shoulder.

At the same time Ellyssa's finger tightened against the trigger, Aalexis snapped out of her stupor. She pushed the soldier holding Rein out of danger as the report sounded and the butt kicked into Ellyssa's shoulder. Light streamed through a hole in the door.

Either by accident or purpose, the sergeant's gun fired. Aalexis said something, her words lost in the commotion. A second later, Rein's head drooped. The sergeant let him go.

In slow motion, Rein traveled toward the floor, and Ellyssa's defenses shattered. Her visual cortex refused to process what her eyes were witnessing. She couldn't think. She couldn't move. A rift tore through Ellyssa's heart, ragged edges sharp and biting as she watched Rein hit the floor.

Even as glass shattered from the window next to Aalexis, and unseen people opened fire, Ellyssa stood transfixed. Her life no longer mattered. Nothing mattered. Her world had ceased to exist.

The next thing Ellyssa comprehended was that she was on the ground, snow covering her face, and a rifle poking into her ribs. Someone held her down. Instinctively, she began to struggle.

"Ellyssa!" Woody shouted.

# 47

Ellyssa sat on the bed. Alone. Her thoughts looped around on the image of Rein falling, like her mental processes were stuck on replay. Her eyes were dry now, but they still felt raw and hurt when she blinked. She imagined they were red, but she didn't know; she hadn't looked in a mirror recently.

For the last couple of days, this had been her position. People had come and gone, Trista, Dyllon, Mathew, Woody, all in an effort to console her. How could they be so stupid? Her reason for living, for being, had been severed the moment Rein had died.

An untouched tray of breakfast sat on the table next to the bed, the eggs cold and congealed. A brush she hadn't used recently lay next to it. The small cave pearl, her reminder of the revenge she'd failed to extract, rested against the handle.

She was aware enough to know that she couldn't go on like this. Being aware didn't change the hollow, dead feeling in her chest where her heart beat.

After Woody had tackled her and in effect saved her from whoever had been firing from the office windows, Ellyssa still had the need to see her sister pay, to die. She'd pushed Woody off and rose to her feet. The porch was empty.

What purpose would Rein's dead body serve Aalexis?

*To torment me*, had been the answer.

Fury had unleashed within her with a vengeance, and Ellyssa moved with it, her feet pounding in the snow, passing dozens of dead bodies, most wearing black snowsuits. She'd burst onto the porch where blood tainted the snow and through the office door into a tomb. Woody skidded in after her. Three soldiers lay dead on the floor. Another moaned behind a desk. Ellyssa followed the moan and found a Corporal Kraus, according to his nametag. Blood streamed from his mouth.

Ellyssa lifted the dying male by his collar. "Where is she?"

"Storage room," he'd managed. A blood bubble formed in between the corporal's lips and popped. Corporal Kraus was no more.

Ellyssa had moved quietly toward a door closest to the desk with Woody. She counted to three, then barged in. The room was empty. White sheets of paper rustled in the wind coming from another door leading outside.

Even though she knew Aalexis was gone, Ellyssa had moved toward the back door anyway. Tire tracks that were quickly disappearing under the windy flurry cut across the snow. She'd followed the tracks, though she'd known it was too late. They led to the delivery gate and more dead guards.

Aalexis was gone. Ellyssa shot out the tendrils of her mind, trying to latch onto Rein, to anything, but there was nothing. Just emptiness. Dead emptiness.

Reliving the nightmare she'd lived through before.

Ellyssa was pretty sure that was the exact time she'd lost whatever control she had. She couldn't even remember walking back through the cold to The Pit.

A knock sounded at the door.

"Go away."

Ignoring her, Woody opened the door and came in with Mathew. At least they'd been able to save him and most of the prisoners. A total of eleven lost, ten males and the one female Aalexis had sacrificed. Dr. Loki had lost twenty of his people. They'd had a memorial Ellyssa didn't attend.

Right behind Mathew and Woody, an older male, over fifty, stepped inside. He had silver hair, meticulously parted to the right, blue eyes—of course—and thin lips. His movements were angled and sharp, and Ellyssa knew, without peeking that he was military. Her muscles involuntarily twitched with the prospect of snapping his neck. She stood, and blood rushed to her head, making it spin. She needed to eat. The thought of food nauseated her, so she plopped back down on the mattress instead.

She really just didn't care anymore.

"Ellyssa," said Mathew, coming toward her. He felt her forehead, then took her wrist between his fingers to feel her pulse. After a few seconds, he slid his hand down and wrapped his fingers around hers. His palm felt so warm compared to hers. "You have to stop this."

Mustering up the best incredulous look she could produce, Ellyssa shot it toward Mathew.

Shaking his head, Mathew smiled. "I love you, my dear friend. You have lots of people who love you. What you are doing hurts us as much as it hurts you."

Ellyssa didn't want to hear that. She just wanted to be left alone.

Woody knelt at Ellyssa's knees. Looking at her, sadness swimming in the grey of his eyes, he cupped her cheek, his warmth sinking into her cold flesh. Once again, Woody was there to try and pick up her fragmented pieces. But once in a while, the pieces were too broken and jagged to adhere. Closing her eyes, willing away the tears that threatened to spill out, Ellyssa swallowed the sob that was stuck in her throat.

"Mathew's right. Rein was my best friend, my brother. He wouldn't want this." Woody's voice hitched, and he had to wait a moment before he could continue. "You can't give up. It's not over, Ellyssa."

"I know," she whispered. "I just don't know how."

"With our help," Mathew said, pushing a straggly strand of hair behind her ear.

"I'm sorry for your loss,"said the older male, who still stood by the door. He stepped into the room as he spoke. "I'm Comm..." He paused. "My name is Hans Baer. I was the Commandant of Amarufoss before your sister stripped me of my command."

Ellyssa figured he was military, but she hadn't expected this. That's what she got for not using her gift, but since Rein, she couldn't. The dead emptiness she'd felt when she lost him was just too new, too raw. Part of her still wanted to tear Hans apart, though, just for being what he was. She ignored that part.

"We don't like him," Woody said, referencing Hans.

"I actually despise him," Mathew added.

Woody slowly loosened his grip. "He has something to tell you."

"You compromised The Pit by bringing him here."

"He has no idea where we are. We bagged him," Woody said.

"He isn't leaving, either," Mathew continued. "Before the thing with... Rein." He paused as if expecting her to break down. When she didn't, he patted her hand. "You said someone was in the room with the incinerator. I knew it was him. When it was all over, I saved him." Mathew faced the former commander.

Hans nodded. "It's true."

"Anyway, when you came into the barracks to save us, I tried to tell you something. I've tried since we've come back, too, but the state you were in...you just weren't listening. Besides, the Commandant—I mean Hans—knows more."

Mathew gave Hans a *go ahead* nod to start his story.

With a hesitant step, Hans approached Ellyssa, and stopped at a respectable distance. "Your sister wasn't alone," he stated.

Ellyssa narrowed her eyes. "What do you mean?"

"Your brother, Xaver, is with her."

"Wh—Wh—" The easy word stuck on Ellyssa's tongue. She glanced at Mathew, and he nodded.

"I've seen him myself."

If her brother was still alive, that explained everything. Maybe shuffling through the soldiers had nothing to do with why she didn't at least get a glimpse of the plan. Xaver had to have had those in the know shielded. And maybe he had shielded Rein from her, too.

Which meant Rein might not be dead.

He couldn't be dead.

Closing her eyes, Ellyssa took in a cleansing breath and grabbed hold of the dangling, frayed thread of hope. Her despair lightened a little, giving her a reason to continue.

"Rein might be alive!" She popped up onto her feet, the elation smothering out the weakness. "We have to go save him."

As she whirled around the room, snatching the pearl and shoving it in the pocket of her backpack, grabbing clean clothes and cramming them inside too, she began to notice that no one else was moving. "Don't just stand there. Either help me or get out."

Lifting from his knees, Woody caught Ellyssa's hand. Doubt about Rein's survival covered his expression. "Ellyssa, I saw him fall."

"I did, too," Mathew uttered. He couldn't even look at her. "The blood. There was so much."

Hans just stood silent. He didn't know Rein.

Silence spread across the room, threatening Ellyssa's refreshed optimism. Rein had to be alive. If she failed to keep hold of that hope, the despondency would crash down again like a ton of bricks, squashing whatever remained of her. Ellyssa couldn't let that happen, not if Rein still lived. Not if there was still a chance. "I don't care what any of you think."

Sharing a worried look with Mathew, Woody said in a low, calming voice, "First, listen to what Hans has to say, then we will discuss...other possibilities."

Woody led her back over to the bed. Ellyssa let him, but all the while her brain whirled with plans. Obediently, she sat next to Mathew. He placed his hand on her knee.

"Go ahead," Ellyssa said as she leveled her eyes on Hans.

The former commander broke into a tale of his first meeting with Aalexis and Xaver, to somebody named Colonel Fielder and some general and the greed for power the two males shared, to his removal from command, to his theories of what Aalexis had planned, and working with Mathew.

Ellyssa heard the words of Hans' story, but she wasn't really listening. She was too wrapped up in the resentment toward her siblings, the fury, the loathing, all the things she'd always had been allowed to feel freely. The sensations fueled her as they unfurled, feeding her revenge, her will to live.

Ellyssa would either find Rein alive or find Aalexis and kill her.

If she was lucky, she would do both.

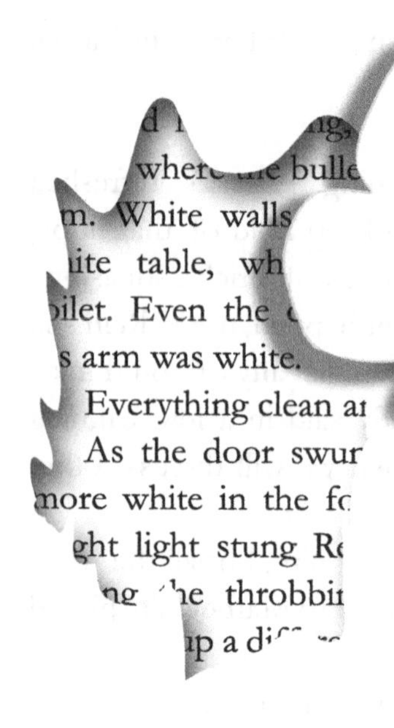

Rein woke in a white room, his head hammering, his arm aching where the bullet had hit him. White walls and ceiling, white table, white sink and toilet. Even the cast covering his arm was white.

Everything clean and pure.

As the door swung open, more white in the form of a bright light stung Rein's eyes, making the throbbing in his head pick up a different tempo. Shielding his eyes from the glare with his good arm, he blinked several times until his vision adjusted and the stinging stopped. Unfortunately the *thump, thump, thump* in his skull kept a constant beat, the remnants of being constantly drugged.

"What do you want?" Rein asked the platinum-haired, blue-eyed demon standing in the doorway. His speech was a little slurred.

Aalexis stepped over the threshold, wearing a white lab coat. She looked much different than the little girl Rein had first met when he was introduced to her by Dr. Hirch. She was taller, her childhood roundness slimmed away, but what had really changed was her subtle display of emotion, which had become more and more frequent as time passed.

"Time for breakfast." Alexis moved aside. "Lukas."

Like an obedient dog, the military thug dressed in, surprisingly, a white tank and stretch pants that rode low on his waist stepped inside, carrying a covered tray. Lukas' face was all lines and angles joined together in anger. He wasn't happy playing Rein's nursemaid.

"That's a good boy," Rein said. If he was smart, he would have kept his mouth shut. Being facetious to the military ass was like poking a lion with a stick. No one had ever accused Rein of being smart, though. For added measure, Rein smirked. "You may set it on the table over there."

Lukas' jaw clenched as he dropped the tray onto the counter. The cover bounced and tipped to the side. He turned and faced Rein, dark-blue eyes like lasers, fists clenching and unclenching, veins pulsing in his forehead. If it wasn't for Aalexis putting what was apparently a calming hand on his bulging bicep, Rein knew the man would've torn him apart, limb by limb.

The size of the lackey's arm bothered Rein. Bulging was an understatement. It was more like a quivering, mountainous muscular mass. All of him, not just the arms. Rein's eyebrows dipped as he studied the man. Lukas' neck was thicker than the width of his head, and powerful tendons stretched under the skin. His tank was pulled tightly over a chest that could crack coconuts and a sculpted stomach that would put most men to shame. Rein was damn sure that Lukas hadn't been that size just a few days ago.

"You have noticed," Aalexis said, pulling Rein's attention away. "He *is* bigger."

Lukas folded his flexed arms over his puffed-out chest. Smugness poured off him.

Rein shrugged, then winced as the muscles pulled around his wound. "So? He's been working out?"

"Yes. But there is more. He has help from a little cocktail Xaver and I have concocted, and a bit of DNA manipulation of stem cells injected into specific muscle groups. Simply put, it floods testosterone into the system, better than the body produces naturally. As you can see." With her finger, she traced one of the many indentations carving his upper arm. "Also, his fighting techniques have improved drastically. The new training Xaver and I have designed is producing the most splendid results."

Judging by the way Lukas watched Aalexis as she talked and touched him, Rein figured there was much more than just hero worship going on, which was more than a little sickening. Although her mature body said differently, Ellyssa's sister was too young for the twenty-something-year-old man. Gross on so many levels.

Pulling her hand away, much to Lukas' visible disappointment, Aalexis continued, "Imagine what a whole army could do."

Much to his growing horror, Rein imagined it.

# THE END

# ACKNOWLEDGEMENTS

There are so many people to thank for helping me through Flawed.

First, I'd like to send a truckload of gratitude and virtual chocolate to all the readers and bloggers and my beta-readers for being absolutely wonderful. If it wasn't for you, I probably wouldn't be writing an acknowledgement.

I have to extend a special thank you to all the people at Spencer Hill Press. To the awesome Kate Kaynak, for seeing what I could see in the Perfection trilogy. To Vikki Ciaffone, editor extraordinaire, who is always there to hold my hand. Both of you just absolutely rock. A jumbo-jet plane full of thanks to Richard Shealy, Owen Dean, Rich Storrs, and Marie Romero, all of whom are so full of awesomeness that words cannot even begin to describe. I hope to make each and every one of you proud.

To my mom for showing me that nothing is impossible.

To my wonderful children and granddaughter. You all make me prouder each and every day.

# ABOUT THE AUTHOR

Photo by Trista Semmel

Judy lives in Texas, where she wanders out in the middle of the night to look at the big and bright stars. Besides knocking imaginary bad guys in the head with a keyboard, she enjoys being swept away between the pages of a book, running amuck inside in her own head, pretending she is into running, and hanging out with her kids, who are way too cool for her.

CPSIA information can be obtained at www.ICGtesting.com
Printed in the USA
LVOW04s0706250814

400666LV00001B/1/P